CATCHING STARS

Evie O'Kane

For Isy.

PROLOGUE

It was a hellish, frosty winter night when seven heavily armed palace guards broke down the door.

My door.

A furious storm drove its fists into the walls, causing the whole place to quake as the clinks of silver chest plates flooded the seemingly empty room.

It was a pathetic sight: two beds which were nothing more than wrinkled old blankets thrown onto blocks of straw, a crate we used as a table, and a handwoven grocery basket.

The line marched inside in the typical 7-man unit formation. The Captain strode in first, gun raised and loaded, and the rest followed in three rows of pairs behind him. Rasor-sharp swords swung from their belts, and pistols were strapped neatly in their place beside them. Each soldier had their fingers clenched tightly around their weapon. Technically, they aren't allowed to draw their guns until there's visible danger, but Frost guards don't care about the law.

They tore through the small, cramped room, stripped the makeshift mattresses bare, and destroyed everything in their path.

"They're not here," one of the guards said quietly.

"She must be," the Captain spat, grinding one of my shirts under his boot.

She. Instantly, I knew that though my friends resided with me, *I* was the target. I was the vermin to be exterminated.

Eyes narrowing, he seized my satchel from under my bed and tipped it carelessly upside down. An apple, a fist-sized rock with a jagged edge that I used as a knife, and a stolen water bottle tumbled onto the floor. I took a sharp, scared breath from my hiding place inside the hollow, grimy walls, and my two friends hunkered down beside me.

The only reason I could distinguish the Captain from the rest of the men was his chest plate, engraved with a sharp, four-pointed symbol that resembled a snowflake: a diamond overlapping a circle, with a spike protruding from each corner, each one representing a different element.

Once, that was the Flai Kingdom's symbol. A sacred crest the Elders wore on strings around their necks, entrusted only to those with the most powerful magic and admirable wisdom. When the King of Frost shunned my kind and turned man against us, he used it to symbolize power beyond human control. A symbol used to instill fear instead of wonder. It's one of many things that were once ours that they took and demonized, like wings.

Professional and hired Flai hunters —Flunters— make up at least half of the Frost Kingdom's armed forces. The strongest, most successful Flunters are blessed with a promotion, a thousand shackles, and the snowflake crest so that people will recognize their authority over ordinary citizens wherever they go.

The Captain spun around, and his crest caught the dim light, flashing into my eyes as if to taunt me.

"Contact troops thirty-four and fifty-two. Tell them to search the W-Quadrant and round up the villagers. You know how these children are. Unpredictable abilities. Like bloomin' bombs. We must find them before dawn, for all our sakes."

One of the other members of the team met his eyes. "And what about their own sakes? We can't disregard the fact that they're only children. What will become of them if we take them into custody? There are fully-grown adults in that prison, Perseus..."

"Did you forget the rules? Did you forget your *place?* Don't call me by my first name. Use your throat properly, and address me as "sir", or I'll slice it open," the Captain said, gritting his teeth, and the other man fell silent.

I watched them tear apart my home through a crack in the wall with my knees drawn up to my chest. My best friend Peter sat beside me, watching me with a pale face and terrified electric-blue eyes. I was the eldest; therefore, I was supposed to protect him and assure him it was alright. But it *wasn't* alright.

My thoughts were knotted and twisted, and I wanted to scream so desperately, but fear ate me up. There seemed to be something slithering behind my eyes, splitting open my head. A part of me that wanted survival and nothing more. *Forget everything. Drop everything. Run.*

"Don't you see the massive hole beside your shoulder!? Get your head down!" I gasped, groping out to my side for Bronwyn, the small, shy girl who lived with us. We called her Wynn for short, the name of an old runic symbol originating in Ra, the Kingdom of Sun, on the other side of the island.

She whispered to herself with her eyes shut, a long, frizzy curl of black hair streaking across her cheek. Perhaps she was wishing, praying, or both. Reflecting on that moment, I realize I never noticed the traditional wooden good-luck charm clutched between her fingers. Ha. We needed far more than luck that night.

Again, the snake lashed out at my thoughts.

Run.

I can't!

Get out.

I have to hide.

Run hide leave get out you aren't safe you'll never be safe never outrun them never-

Peter cried out in distress and clasped a hand over his mouth, eyes glistening with tears. My arms were instinctively shielding him within a second, and my train of thought was smashed into incognizance. As though blocking out a noise that had already been unleashed would help. He whimpered.

We were packed so tightly together that whenever one of us dared to breathe, warm air blew across my face. I squeezed my eyes shut, willing myself to believe we weren't loud enough to reach their ears.

"Raven, I'm so sorry..." Peter began whispering to me. His tiny fingers reached out to intertwine with mine, and I squeezed them tight.

Each tap of a silver-studded boot on the floor was rewarded with a flinch from Peter, Bronwyn, or me.

They found us.

"Raven, what are we going to do now?"

How did they find us?

"Raven?" Peter said again.

"I'm trying my hardest to think of something, Peter. Please just..."

"But Raven—" he interrupted.

"WHAT?" I snapped, whipping around to face him. My voice echoed along the cold, rotting wood, ringing out for the world to hear.

Suddenly, the noise and commotion behind the wall ceased. I rose two shaking hands over my mouth, knowing it was already too late.

"They're in the walls," Perseus growled. The men burst into action, their boots making metallic, heavy clunks as they stalked toward us while my hands grew feverishly hot.

I urgently attempted to calm myself, but fear shot through my body like venom, and the familiar tingling that signaled magic's approach had already invaded my senses. I closed my eyes, trying to push down the lump in my throat. The snake lashed forward into my eyes, piercing them, blinding my vision with adrenaline, except there were a thousand reptiles this time.

Some wound up my legs, and others rocketed up my spine, setting my feet on fire.

Run.

My palms sizzled, hotter and hotter.

Peter stared at me, his gaze desperate. I tried harder, pressing my hands onto the damp, cold wooden wall. No. Stop.

"I want all three, dead or alive. Do what it takes," the Captain spat, drawing his sword and striding backward to bark orders at his men and oversee our struggle. He knew guns wouldn't be effective when they couldn't spot their targets through a blaze.

It was my fault. I couldn't control my magic.

Jade-colored fire shot from my palms, spreading up the wall and slithering along the floor to kill them.

Curses, screams, an onslaught of weapons. They struck the wall until a hole widened enough for three small bodies to squeeze through, and nails dug into flesh as they wrestled us slowly out.

Bronwyn kicked and punched, shrieking. She was small but mighty, lashing out with force and precision. She flicked her wrists, and enormous tree roots shot out of the ground, curling around the guards' ankles. They quickly severed them, cutting themselves free. Bronwyn pressed her hands to the floor, and torrents of grass shot up from between the floorboards, sea-green and littered with ants.

She was an Earth Flai, powerful enough to handle herself. Powerful enough to have kept them at bay. Bronwyn continued to fire these unexpected attacks, but the guards closed in slowly.

Two men came for me next. I wrenched away from one as another seized me from behind. I shot fire into his face, not stopping to see if it hit the target. There was no reward in firing anywhere else; the armor they wore was a combination of silver and gold, and my flames are useless against that.

Peter was helpless and weak from years of malnutrition. He had very few magical abilities and was instantly snatched by guards. Bronwyn's head turned at his cries, and distracted, she was suddenly cornered and cuffed too, unable to remain consistent in attacks that demanded so much of her strength and energy. Her fight extinguished like a flame, and she crumbled, exhausted, into a soldier's waiting arms. It was the same man, I noticed, who'd dared to question the guard captain earlier. He blinked like a confounded sheep, unsure what to do with her limp figure.

The guards then turned their attention to me as I blasted fire everywhere like an idiot and set the room ablaze.

A pipe ran through the wall opposite me, connecting to the roof and serving as our primary water source. The Captain drew his rapier and slashed into the tube so the flow, collected in a bucket below, was redirected right between my feet. It sliced effortlessly through my shield of flames, allowing Perseus to aim his weapon.

"Little girl, do you want to die?" he sneered.

"I... I'll fight you! Don't come closer!" I gasped, tears

threatening to overwhelm me.

"Will you? I don't think so. Look at you. You're so thin you could float away... *fly* away..."

I froze. I couldn't fly; I hadn't matured fully yet. My wings did nothing, and the Captain knew this. He was reciting my weaknesses right before me, spitting his message clearly: *You don't stand a chance.*

Cowardly as it was, I snatched my empty satchel off the floor and ran.

And that's how I ended up sprinting through narrow, frosty alleyways barefoot, with the cold biting at my skin and an evening breeze whipping at the hem of my rags. My palms were still warm, and my breaths came out in short, petrified gasps.

They were coming. Hundreds of them.

Reinforcements had undoubtedly been summoned now that I was loose on the streets.

It was all I could do to keep dashing forward as the tears forming in my eyes were carried away by the wind.

When I somehow reached the gate, it was already groaning shut, trapping me within the walls of the Frost Kingdom.

Leaping as far as I could and throwing my body into a roll, I slid through the gap between iron and tarmac, grazing the tip of my chin on the spikes that hammered into the ground almost instantly after I jerked out of their path. Then I continued to dash, ignoring a splitting headache, until I reached the backfields of the kingdom, just beyond the outer ring of farmland. I stood out in the open, surrounded by crops under a black, swallowing sky.

And I waited.

I just waited for... something. Maybe for a shred of hope, or perhaps for a demon, its claws brandished, to swoop down and tear apart my vocal folds that refused to scream and unleash the bombardment of despair and guilt unloaded on me in less than an hour.

The moon glared down, bathing me in its swollen, oversized glow like a spotlight.

I was an easy target for anyone who wanted me, but at least out of the kingdom, beyond their search parties and far from where they still believed I was hiding.

Scanning the landscape in all directions, trying to make sense of the world, I sucked in air in ragged breaths. The line where the Frost Wilderness began was just a field or so ahead. I would be safe there, presented with many hiding places. Places they wouldn't think to look. I could make it.

Maybe.

Long, wild grass tickled my thighs as I ran with a new flare of something akin to hope in my chest.

Hope, desperation, or perhaps misery? Sorrow? Terror?

Honestly, I couldn't have cared less because whatever it was, it saved me.

Finally, I reached the forest and propped myself up against a tree trunk, exhausted. I felt like a fish out of water, my mouth opening and closing as I tried to inhale more air.

My limbs moved of their own accord in slow, robotic motions, and with the sliver of energy I had left, I clambered to the highest branches of the sturdiest, tallest pine in sight, settling on a thin wooden arm that creaked under my weight.

Soldiers' heavy bodies couldn't reach me there: I was high enough to touch the stars.

I'd never been so tired, caught off guard, or scared as I was that night. All I wanted was to slip away from the world and stop *fighting*.

Yet, I fought for a long time. My ears pricked up at the whispers of even the branches themselves, my heart thumping steadily... However, resisting unconsciousness was not an easy task.

My lip bled from my anxious fingernail's pecks, and my skin was torn and stinging where I grazed my body on thorns and tarmac.

The first thing I thought before I succumbed to sleep was that they'd finally done it. My friends were gone, meaning that my old life had all crumbled into nothing in less than an hour.

And the final thing I thought before I succumbed to sleep was that it was entirely and utterly my fault.

PART 1

CHAPTER 1

When I was six, my name was alien to most girls in the playground. I was a shy, reserved child with only one recallable friend.

Nobody knows my name now, but almost the whole island knows I exist.

The King placed a bounty on my head, calling me a "dangerous creature from hell, with power beyond what is safe to humanity".

Well, good luck with the hunt.

They don't even know what I look like. Just that I am here, and I am alive, and that means the King and his army have failed.

I'm safe, at least until Flood Tide. When that day comes, the Flood Market will move out of this kingdom and, on their way, make as many last-minute sales as they can. If they catch me —which they won't— it'll make them rich beyond their wildest dreams.

Just imagine it— a net pulling tight against my skin, the excited shouts as they reel me in, blood pounding in my ears. And me— hopelessly trying to burn through my restraints. I'd be carted away to a wealthy lord or a cage in a village square.

It is not as though I could hide from the Flood Market, either. They sweep the landscape in a straight line, stretching from border to border, scouring out every nook and cranny. If I were to be sighted even once, somebody'd report me to traders. And then it's easy. Tracked, followed, and sniffed out by vicious wolves.

See, this is why I must leave as quickly as possible. Of course, escaping the island is ideal, but everyone knows *that's* not happening. The island is inescapable, and it acts as its own minature isolated planet.

On Evrilore, every climate on Earth is concentrated onto one tiny landmass, divided up by even smaller kingdoms. It is a place of farming, research, trade, adventure, and danger. But most importantly, it's a place of order. Absolutely everything must be structured into neat systems that run under other, more extensive systems, like a complex capillary network. And we all serve one heart: the Frost Kingdom. Or, more accurately, the Moon King.

His goal is to destroy what thrives in the shadows of Evrilore— unexplained things and unexplained magic.

If people like me escaped into the rest of the planet... *well.* It doesn't matter because nobody has ever set foot on soil that isn't Evrilorian, and nobody ever will. An invisible shield separates us from the Far Lands, preventing signals or communication. We're completely alone, and nobody knows why.

Despite the mystery of our entrapment, there is one thing everyone can be sure of in this sealed-off corner of the globe: the power over us is shifting.

You can feel it rising in the air and the miserable, hunched clouds hanging over us: Tension and conflict. A new age is beginning, where people like me have no place. Efforts to capture Flai are soaring over the treetops.

I learned from my usual round of eavesdropping last week that a new batch of Flunters (Flai hunters) moved into the Frost Kingdom, searching for the rumoured Flai girl, and with Flood Tide tomorrow, it's just too dangerous. I can't take any chances after they took my friends last year.

Gathering my belongings, I take a hasty drink from the fountain in the cobbled square, wipe the wetness off my lips, and set off sustainably through the snow, my feet making a soft crunch as I walk.

My body knows this route better than I do. Down this alleyway, up those stairs, onto the balcony of that house. Both hands on the gutter, legs around the drainpipe.

Now you jump, Raven. And now you crawl, Raven.

I'm silent and invisible as I scuttle along the rooftops on all fours.

The only obstacle I ever face is the guards, who're as incompetent as ever. It's hardly surprising because they only began posting them at the kingdom's exits after my escape last year.

When I reach the ill-kept, run-down houses beside the boundary wall, it's only a matter of hopping into a few overgrown walled gardens and dashing out a few groaning gates, and then I'm out in the open again, flitting down the street in the dark like a glitching shadow.

It is peculiar how the enormous estates in the city centre have electric fences and hundreds of cameras to trace your movements like huge black, beady eyes. Still, here, people have resorted back to medieval methods of defence: iron spike-topped gates and high, unstable, crumbling walls.

What an unpredictable bundle of old and new technology it is that people use, depending on their wealth.

I stick to the places where the moonlight cannot quite reach me, never bothering to glance over my shoulder. The streets of the Frost Kingdom extend out from the centre in maze-like patterns, the houses decreasing in value the further out you go. Here, there is nothing worth stealing. I will be the only one out tonight.

I reach the eastern exit, and it looks the same as it always does: a tall arch carved into a stone wall, with rusty metal bars cutting off the pathway for anyone who wishes to leave, and a small stone building with a window where guards are supposed to stand on their shifts to approve or decline the citizens' requests to exit the kingdom.

My eyes scour out the highest, darkest corners before I proceed. There are enormous cameras here to remind you you're being watched. They stare you down, and if you're identified as Flai, guards spring out of seemingly nowhere and shoot immediately.

However, until trouble's face emerges, this place will be desolate. Soldiers line the exits during the day to prevent escapee criminals, but at the emergence of dusk, bars slam down into the earth with a force that sends shockwaves through the kingdom, sealing off the archways, and suddenly, there is no exit at all.

I smirk.

For most people, anyway.

I touch a single finger to the ground, and a spark erupts into a wall that spreads from my hands to the house on the other side of the street, creating an untouched corridor between the fire and the gate.

The camera footage is monochrome, so thankfully, the green eruption of flames will look normal.

Darting stealthily behind them, silently thanking my powers for working tonight, I squeeze myself through a gap in the bars.

One of the metal joints loosened a few months ago, and they had to remove it, so the slim hole in the gate now serves as my door. I slip through without much fuss by stepping sideways and sucking in my stomach. An average child my age couldn't, but having a stomach that you can't afford to satisfy has its perks.

Leaving behind what's been my home for the past few months isn't sad. I've been moving from place to place, sleeping wherever it seems least likely Flunters will look, for a long time, so I don't call anywhere home.

That word is foreign to me.

I've lived in the Willow District for many years, but I often travel back to Frost for a few months to escape Ice Tide, or the "Holiday Season", as they call it there. All the families invite one another over for turkey and fatten up their children like piglets for slaughter.

I despise Ice Tide because I haven't had the luxury of enjoying it for eight years— I don't have the good fortune of sitting *inside* insulated walls, looking *out* windows at the snow. No, I grit my teeth and lie in it.

Truthfully, escaping festivities is only part of the reason I came here. The real motivation for staying in Frost was the rumours of one of my kind here. By "my kind", I mean other Flai, of course. Maybe I was mad, hoping to find them, but I've spent a whole month searching in Frost and have to suspect that I took a false lead.

It was unlikely from the start. No one like me leaves trails or clues about where we are. The wrong people find and use them. Flunters have even learned to bait us with "top secret" Flai gathering locations, the details of which they leave lying around on paper in the street. And, believe me, some Flai take the bait like mice squealing giddily after cheese. You see and hear it everywhere. In the newspaper, from the mouths of gossiping townspeople. The stories are usually grim, but I force myself to listen.

I must endure it to keep updated on how quickly we're dying out.

I'm headed for the border between the Frost Wilderness and the Willow District. If I can cross it safely, I'll be able to travel south and have another few months of cover in the capital of Ra, the kingdom famous for its vast arid deserts and sweltering heat.

There's no point trying to cross Ra's north or east borders, because I'll dehydrate in a matter of hours at this time of year in its deserted landscape, with at least thirty miles to travel on foot before reaching a settlement with clean water.

So, here I go, hiking again while the weak winter morning grows bleaker. It's the twenty-eighth of February, in the early morning hours of the annual Winter Frost Flood Tide, and this day, one year ago, my best friends were captured by guards.

Honestly, it was too easy. I let myself settle and developed a sense of safety in my home. Was I ever safe there, or was I pretending to be for my own comfort?

Bronwyn and Peter certainly seemed ready for an attack.

Their survival instincts to hide had surfaced quicker than mine, and their hands dragged me into the walls moments before the guards stormed in. Why had I let myself go like that?

Gritting my teeth, I dig my heels into the slippery grass of the backfields surrounding the Frost Kingdom. It won't happen again. It can't. I've decided I must survive for my friends and Flai everywhere. So many of us have died out too many. And the rest of us are hiding, so if I can escape capture and do something to stop my species from going extinct, by all means, I will.

On days like today, I sometimes consider returning to the

Flai Realm, my birthplace, or the Flai "Kingdom", as they call it in the history books. Maybe I could be safe there.

Unfortunately, the Flai Kingdom has been sealed off since the end of the Fall. No one has come in or out since. I believe that ancient defensive enchantments keep the gates locked, or perhaps it's punishment for the men who started the war who must painfully dream of building their precious castles and digging their pointless mines on our land. They attacked first, after all. It only makes sense if they're punished for it.

You know, it's hard to understand what they have against us. As far as I know, they're just afraid of what they can't understand. Our wings. Our magic.

I'm getting off-topic.

The point is, there's no way inside the Flai Kingdom, so it'd be foolish to seek refuge there. Rumoured prophecies exist of a single Flai whose touch will open the gates. A prophecy child, a chosen one, blah, blah, blah. The tale states that they will claim back everything that was once ours, and Flai will be freed from the grasp of Man.

No one knows if the prophecy is real or who foresaw it. It could be Man's idea of a joke.

But even so, I like to stop and think about it every so often for a minute.

Or two.

I've never known my parents. As far as I'm concerned, they're dead as a doornail. I was laid down on a doorstep at birth by a family who wished to give me a war-free life, and I lived on a small farm with a family in the Willow District until I was bordering on seven years old.

When I first fluxed into my Flai form, I was only a tiny girl, short and skinny for my age even then, and yet they were still terrified and handed me over to guards instantly.

The memories are soft and faded in my head, like listening to a row through a wall. I mostly remember sounds and shapes moving around in blobs with me at the centre of it all, like the eye of a hurricane. I remember Maman grabbed my siblings and backed away from me in horror. Papa dashed incoherently downstairs to call the police, and my Tante shouted and swore for a few minutes, then, with a cigarette hanging off her bottom lip, eventually just shook her head and muttered, "bloody hell" over and over again. Somebody bawled— perhaps it was me.

Everyone was afraid of me that day. I can taste the fear just thinking about it. I was scared of myself, of my strange new body and abilities that nobody had taught me or warned me about.

That was the first time I ever used magic— to escape the guards when they came for me. I still remember the mixture of fear and devastation in my Papa's eyes when he discovered what a monster I truly was. A thousand different thoughts had crossed my mind. Was I even his daughter anymore? Did he still love me? I was closer to him than anyone else in that household, maybe even the favourite of his three adopted children. However, I was just a burden when they discovered my true identity.

Humans cannot love Flai, and nor could my Papa. Not only is it forbidden, but it is seen as betrayal beyond the farthest measures. It is unforgivable. Unthinkable. Such things are simply not right— we are weeds in The Moon King's perfect little garden, and the owners of the given allotments are not allowed to like us.

If a human family was found to be hiding a Flai girl, the consequence would be a simple public execution.

Everyone dies, and everyone is punished. And for what? A child. Still, the Flai would be blamed for every death. This is the art of the system, perfected to convince men that we are the problem.

But the system, alas, must be flawed. That's evident, if nothing else— my heart is still beating.

I've been on the run since I left home, trying to find others like me, other Flai who were deemed outlaws before they could even have a childhood.

That's why I was so envious of Bronwyn. She displayed her first signs of being an Earth Flai at nine, a remarkably late age, which means she got at least a few years to be a normal child.

I frown at this thought. "Normal child". I hate the word "normal" because Flai are the first thing that comes to mind when you think of *not* normal. And I can't even help this: for my entire childhood, I was groomed to believe of Flai as strange, dangerous outsiders, just like any other human, and such strongly enforced beliefs are hard to rid yourself of, especially when it seems like an expectation in society to never challenge them.

To humans, we are the invaders, the unwanted, washed-up villains of the world that landed on their shores.

To Flai, it is the inverse. We work with nature. We help, heal, and thrive while Man kills themselves, trapped in an ignorant bubble of pleasure and privilege. They're the impostors in our world.

There will always be the occasional human who sees through the fog, who cannot understand why we deserve this treatment, but what can they do to help us? They become just as undesirable as Flai when they realize the truth. That is why nothing has changed, and nothing ever will.

Even though the Fall happened so long ago, Evrilore is still, in a way, at war with itself. It always will be, as long as they want to keep their awful concrete jungles from us.

Peter is the only other Flai I have ever met aside from Wynn. I ran into a small cave in Ra one day to shelter from a sandstorm, only to find that some hogging, spluttering, coughing git had gotten there first.

That was Peter, of course, huddled into a ball, weak and unable to channel his powers into anything. He was... still learning to be at one with nature.

It hardly mattered, though, because Flai can survive through almost anything. If it makes sense, the world has a way of keeping us here. And, of course, our powers allow us to do many things that help us benefit from natural disasters or harsh weather conditions. For example, being a Fire Flai sometimes lets me stay warm in winter.

Until I am older and have more control over my powers, I will continue to struggle to conjure flames into existence, but it is possible. Typically, fear triggers my magic, not a determination to live or provide for myself.

The only thing about Peter was —the thing that caused me to feel so much closer to him— he was born to a Flai mother who was already in the custody of Floodonora and was captured during late pregnancy. Despite her pleas to be released, they kept her for the whole birth.

Peter was lucky enough to be saved by a hunter who took pity on him and managed to hide him until he was five, but from then on, only Mother Nature allowed him to live. I'm perplexed as to why or how he survived, but sometimes the world does crazy things, and you just have to accept that there is no answer.

After I met Peter and Wynn, we began living together, taking turns stealing food and listening to Frost citizens' conversations about the latest law updates on Flai treatment across the island. We planned our time together carefully, deciding exactly when we would eat, sleep, build our small shack, and eavesdrop.

Originally, our home was just a piece of cloth hung over a fishing line to make a pathetic tent, but then I discovered that an abandoned cart makes a fine den, and... as you can imagine, it only escalated from there.

Until last year on Stone Tide, of course.

That's pretty much the story of my life. It started when I was born, and I don't know when it ends or where it'll take me, but to hell and back seems like a pretty good guess.

CHAPTER 2

It's never hard to notice the ghost of a breath condensing in the freezing air drifting before you when it comes from your own lips. Or the slight sting in your cheeks that accompanies it.

The temperature is dropping fast, signalling the end of Stone Tide, when the sea is pulled far out, revealing the rocky shores beneath. In just a few hours, I'll be confronted with the horrors of the beginning of Flood Tide, when enormous waves come crashing back into shore and conjure a great storm that gradually sweeps the land in a large, ovoidal cloud.

The Flood Market, Floodonora, trades in precious gems and stones that are only accessible during a Stone Tide. However, when the tide comes in the following day, their trade is completely lost to the ocean, swallowed by walls of salt water, and they must hastily exit the kingdom they are in and follow the storm to where Stone Tide will occur next.

I follow a similar pattern. When everyone is drawn into the excitement and festive traditions of the Tides, I can finally spend as long as I wish hunting for food, supplies, and weapons, scouring the empty streets for scraps like a stray dog. Then, on Stone Tide, I have to evacuate and retreat to the cover of the woods as quickly as possible.

I glance, paranoid, over my shoulder, even though I know the travelling market is not yet moving. The city and my small bed of crates and rags are far behind me, isolating me in the early morning.

Usually, sweet, thin silence and loneliness bring me comfort, but today, the foggy air hangs in thick swaths of cobweb over these lands, and the gaping spaces surrounding me only make me terrified that something lurks unseen.

The Frost Kingdom, or "Frost", is the coolest, most perilous kingdom of the four on the island, proposing two reasons for its tendency to be referred to as the "Kingdom of Ice". Its King, laws, and incredibly tight national security are all hard, cruel, and ruthless.

Built on an artificial concrete landmass, the city is surrounded by a raging, ice-cold ocean or flat, well-kept farmland sealed off by towering stone walls, making the borders almost impenetrable.

It's Floodonora's second-favourite trading ground because Stone Tide happens twice yearly in Frost. And more Stone Tide means more valuables. More customers. More Floodonora. Not exactly a tea party.

At this time of year, Ra is my safe place. It's the furthest from Floodonora that I can get. Raes (citizens of Ra) are divided into two categories: those showered in luxuries, exotic foods, jewelry, and fine clothing... and the very, very poor. Nothing partitions first and third-class citizens. You're either surviving on scraps or tossing them to your inferiors.

Ra's towns are labelled as "AD", "HD", or "IN". AD stands for "average development", a name given to towns where clean water and some railway routes are accessible.

"HD" means "highly developed", the label given to the few settlements with electricity and air conditioning. "IN" means "invoke Nadou"— a title for the worst villages. Nadou is the god of peace and joy for the *Nashaaki*, a religious group in Ra and Willows. "IN" means that Nadou ought to be called upon to save the people from starvation and poverty because, ultimately, only an immortal has the strength to overcome the level of suffering in IN towns.

The poorest Raes are similar to Flai in many ways, so they mind their business. Some even throw me scraps sometimes.

The world has a habit of shunning us, pretending we don't exist, and beating and berating us when we dare to try to climb higher on the ladder of quality of life, so we share mutual empathy and understanding. We're ashtrays for our tyrants' cigarettes, and Raes and Flai share that knowledge like a bridge between species. I feel safer in Ra than elsewhere.

Finally, there is the Willow District and the Flai Kingdom, but technically neither are independent countries.

Before the Fall, the Flai Kingdom had "districts" everywhere, enormous clusters of Flai living all over the island. The Willow District was the biggest by far, nearly twice the size of Frost and growing ever more expansive as entire communities decided to relocate, enthralled by rolling hills and beautiful meadows.

Man and Flai lived in one community, and all was peaceful until the Fall.

During the war, the Willow District broke ties with the Flai Kingdom and rid its land of anything magical. All the other districts were colonized.

I suppose the Willowfolk enjoy being told what to do (or maybe they don't like the idea of having a monarchy) because now the Willow District is the equivalent of a kingdom-sized village. Everyone does their part to keep the kingdom alive, and their laws are just copies of Ra and Frost's. Despite trading with the other kingdoms, nobody is in charge. The landlords and the farmers are about as high as it gets. No fuss.

Even though they're a new, revolutionized country, the Willow District has kept its name. Nobody knows why, but historians say they want to preserve a part of their history and remind people that they managed to survive alone against all odds while the other districts fell and are now under the rule of dictators.

The Willow District did fall, however. It shed its values and held public executions for Flai. The people turned on their neighbours, and my kind was exiled. It became no different from the conquered districts that now belong to Ra and Frost.

The reason for that fact is simple: All humans are the same. It sounds unfair, but it's the motto that's kept me alive.

With clenched fists, I enter the forest with the taste of damp, dark earth rushing forward eagerly onto my tongue. This is less of a visit and more of a homecoming. I spend more time deep in the forests of Evrilore than anywhere else.

Sighing comfortably, I let my face elevate into a small, careful smile. Here, peaceful silence is disturbed only by animals lurking in the dark, and the sky is murky and squally but not entirely black. It raises the hairs on my skin and nudges them fondly.

I have, at most, seven hours before Flood Tide. Glancing hopefully up at the sky again, I frown. *Six.* Six hours to cross the border. Six hours to not get caught, which is considerably easier said than done.

Considering the Flood Market travels through Evrilore every year in the same repetitive cycle, it's surprising how much Evrilore revolves entirely around the Tides.

There are three, each spawning unique festivals, travelling businesses, and sporting events. They're called

Stone Tide, Flood Tide, and Ice Tide.

Ice Tide is when the Frigid Sea freezes for at least three days. Ice skating, fishing, and under-ice diving are popular at that time of year.

I've heard that you can walk straight across the sea to the Far Lands. Or you could if it weren't for the shield encasing the island and the unspoken law that forbids us from crossing our borders. To some, it's logical. Evrilore is where we belong. It is our place, and we are its people, and we are not supposed to question what lies in the outside world.

If you want to travel, you save up your money, but the price is always raised at the last moment, the boat provider falls ill, a new type of flu breaks out, and everyone is quarantined. Some unseen force prevents our escape. That's what everyone's brainwashed into believing. Before I ran away, my "parents" told me that the Elders of the Flai Kingdom used to fly for day-long journeys, then never spoke a word upon return. Nobody knew where they ventured, but speculations arose that they were travelling beyond Evrilore.

That was just one of the many reasons The Moon King found to dislike us. We were secretive.

I draw in a tight breath. The thought of the King's face and his horrible punishments encourage me to pick up my pace.

With the hoarse whispering of overgrown grass and the promising scent of wet earth ahead, the first mile or two is easy. I pick blackberries from bushes and easily navigate the winding dirt paths, alternating between running and walking. I carry my thick leather satchel full of supplies, and it is only when I stop to open the flap and draw out the first cold, stale bread roll that I hear it: Something's rustling quietly in the dark. The hairs on the back of my neck rise, sensing… something.

CHAPTER 2

Footsteps.

I glance behind me at the pitch-black gaps between tree trunks, listening... Nothing.

Relax, I tell myself, there's nobody there. Even so, I quicken my pace, weaving in and out of the bent, weathered trees and occasionally glancing over my shoulder.

The Frost Wilderness is a maze of branches and paths leading nowhere. Weeds stick out boldly in patches of grass, and thorns and nettles sprout from the bases of tree trunks. Each plant appears to be attempting to outgrow its neighbour, throttling while being throttled, and this density of the forest is perhaps the only thing stopping helicopters and drones from swooping down and snatching people like me straight off the ground- that is, of course, if aircraft still exist.

Perhaps Frost destroyed them as they did the cars and mobile phones back in 2042. Thankfully, if Flunters and soldiers desire to chase us, they have no choice but to pursue us on foot.

I open my ears for more sounds. A part of me is on edge, trying to separate a world of creeping shadows from reality. At least nothing non-human will harm me in these woods. Nothing that belongs here. Nature isn't through with me yet, and my species is dying. It'll protect me, not harm me.

When I'm starving on cold winter nights, a berry bush blooms. When I'm dangerously close to dehydration, a shallow stream trickles past my feet. Mother Nature has never abandoned me.

I take a sharp left, a sharp right, cross paths... do whatever I can, just to be sure. And then something echoes through the trees again.

This time, it's two separate taps, one after the other, each menacing and purposeful.

Anxiously, I try to calm my breaths, eyes scanning the floor for hidden threads glinting in the moonlight. Snares and tripwires aren't strangers to my stumbling feet. I can use them to my advantage. Fishing wire is useful for self-defence, though I prefer not to get blood on my hands— and I say *that* as though I have a choice.

Tap. Just... quicker.

Tap.

It's a bird, I reassure myself.

Tap.

Just a bird...

Tap.

It's keeping pace, never fading, never dying, just there.

Tap.

It's speeding up now. The rhythm is disrupted as it breaks away from its regular stream to pursue me as I jerk left, diverting from my usual course. A sweat breaks out on my forehead.

That's not a bird, Raven.

Tap.

That's not a bird!

LEFT! Sixth Sense screams. I sense the danger before I see it and throw my body out of his path.

Adrenaline rushes up my spine, my heart slams itself into my ribs as if trying to push me forward, and my feet are on fire as I run a thousand times faster— but I'm not fast enough.

The Flunter's hand slides over my mouth in one smooth motion, and his other snags at my waist before my attacker curls his arm further around my head and pulls me back by my bedraggled hair, seizing my wrists and knotting them together behind me with a short length of rope.

His grip is painfully firm as he pins me against freezing wet bark.

I don't know him, I think, *I don't know what he wants. He could be like me.*

My brain counteracts these thoughts. If he's like me, he should be dead or hiding.

I could scream, but to who? *For* who? I'm alone.

"Hi," he says, panting, which gives me time to take in his appearance and give a startled gasp.

He's young. Incredibly young. The teenager has a dark mop of messy hair and a pair of sharp, chocolate eyes that peer at me with the wit of a hawk. Yet, the boy has the hesitation of a timid deer.

What are you waiting for? He's got me, and he knows it, too. I can see it in the excited flush of his cheeks and the glint in his eyes. Yet, he hesitates, and the hesitation causes my muscles to slacken, my screaming, read-alert instinct to run to cease.

What are you waiting for? I think again, *I'm at your mercy. Look at me! I'm not fighting— I'm pathetic.*

Maybe that's it. Perhaps I'm so weak, pathetic, and dead that his morals urge him to release me. I'm just a kid, after all.

His heart or his head? An hourglass flipped, sand falling fast. One signal to his brain will decide which he chooses. And it will be that quick. Bind me, capture me, sell me. Or... not.

The trees surrounding us shadow his face, and a carefully curated brown mask covers the skin around his eyes, the edges thick with fingers of waxy sculpted feathers. Almost as though they are making to cover his eyes, to conceal the view of an innocent girl and replace it with a Flai, nothing more than a demon, a fallen angel.

You see, Flai are half-angel, half-fairy. And angels aren't meant to live in the mortal world, right? But we do, and no one knows how we even got on this planet. So, surely we were kicked out of where we're supposed to be: heaven.

We momentarily hold one another's gazes, waiting for the other to attack. But then I snap out of my trance, seize my opportunity, muster all my strength, and jam into his side with my knee. He sways where he stands, crying out with pain and shock, but keeps his grip on me firm.

He's trained, Raven. You won't get away that easily, the voice in my mind says almost jeeringly.

The boy draws a knife from his cloak and raises its steel tip to the centre of my throat like a pen. All it would take is a flick of his wrist, and ink would flow in rivers. The metal is shockingly cold against my flesh, and it takes everything in me not to scream.

I don't want to die like this, alone and bloody in the woods, crumpled against a tree under black starless jaws, watching my life drain out of my neck, just waiting to become a part of that darkness above.

And I don't want this boy's hands on me. I don't want to be carted away and sold. Terror overwhelms me, and I try, once more, to hit him.

"Stop!" he finally cries, "Please, calm down!"

"Get away from me!" I choke weakly, somehow managing to say the words with some strength. I transfer all my weight onto my back and lean against the tree, eyes squeezing shut, feeling my fingertips tingle. Come on!

A sickening crack is audible as the bones in his wrist collide with those of my wings as they spring from my back.

His mouth hangs open, but no noise emerges, perhaps

because of the pain and alarm. I strike him in the stomach and bend down to the earth, ripping my arms in opposite directions so forcefully that the rope snaps and my fist scoops up the handle of his knife.

I dash away, feathers retreating into my back, leaving a broken little boy on the ground as the only evidence of my presence. As I run, my stomach twists into a panic.

You idiot, Raven. You idiot! You fluxed in front of him!

As I stumble forward, my feet catch on roots and vines. *Just don't look back, and you'll be fine. Just don't look... Please, please, don't look—*

I look. Of course I do.

He isn't far behind, but I've bought myself a little time. He has suffered no serious injury, meaning my ten-meter distance from him may be ten too little. My palms tingle again with growing urgency, and I press them to the floor, attempting to subdue the flames within.

I can't do this. I can't just start a fire without broadcasting my location to the whole island. Groaning, I sprint on.

Being a Flai child is far much more trouble than it's worth. You can get a random burst of magic at any age between five and eleven, and from that moment, although you're at least aware you've developed powers, you have zero control over them, so it's pointless anyway.

And all those years of trouble, for what? Wings that only work once I'm a certain age?

Frustrated, I curse under my breath as my hands grow hotter. Not now. Not here. They flare up more urgently, growing scalding to the touch. I look behind me to see that the boy is much closer than before. Too close.

Five meters... Four meters...

Breaths growing shaky, I trust my instincts, crouch low, and thrust my palms to the forest floor. Emerald flames burst from my flesh, erupting into magnificent pillars of green as though the grass is rising up into a roaring army. The closest fire licks my ankles, nudging me fondly like its mother, and I sigh with relief at the familiar welcoming tingling because it means that this, at least, cannot hurt me.

Formidably spilling out limbs of searing fire when he dares approach it, the flames don't stop my attacker but slow him down, forcing him to find a way around the wall in the maze of tangled wood. His footsteps, distant but growing nearer, keep pace with mine as I run, maybe thirty meters to my right, and my thighs burn with the effort of the chase. Occasionally, there is nothing I can do to stop myself from falling. The ground is slippery, and the sky, heavy with gloomy storm clouds, makes it seem ever more hazardous. I'm still ahead of him. But... I sneak a glance over my shoulder.

He's broken free of the fire cage and is slowly but surely closing the gap between us. I must switch to a new tactic.

Run, run, run...

The chase seems endless, just one more reminder of my stupid little life. All I ever do is run. Run from guards, run from Flunters, run from enemies, from friends...

I throw myself into a roll and then hastily stumble into a crouch behind a tree hidden by shrubs on the outskirts of a clearing. *Hide.*

My chest rapidly rises and falls as I recover, but I need more air, and I'm fighting to keep my breaths quiet. I feel my heart with my palm. It's racing, screaming with exhaustion. I suck more air in with gritted teeth to calm it. Blood stops rushing through my ears, and finally, I'm silent and still, melting into the forest floor. I listen. Where's the boy? Is he still chasing me? As I lean against the rough bark, I realize I can't hear his footsteps anymore.

"Stop. I don't want to hurt you. That's not what I'm here to do."

My heart nearly stops at the sound of his voice. He cautiously inches towards me. The boy's movements were so calculated and eerily silent in the dark that I didn't realize he was approaching me mere seconds ago.

I gape helplessly, panicking, as my mind forces me to recite the brutal facts: I'm trapped in a clearing with a Hunter. Alone. And yet... He doesn't attack me.

"Listen, I- I'm sorry I frightened you, but it was the only way to get you to listen: I knew you'd run otherwise. Plus, you're as much of a threat to me as I am to you, right? You're tired and famished. We're in a forest all alone. If you scream, no one will come running. If you run, there's nowhere I can't follow. As I said, I'm not here to hurt you, Raven. But you need to let me explain myself, and I can't do that if you're prancing about like a deranged show pony."

His voice is odd and icy, tinged with a commanding tone, yet soft and gentle simultaneously. The combination sends a shiver down my spine. *How does he know my name*, I think?

Squeezing the knife tighter in my palm, I feel a spark of hope flare in my chest. I'm armed. He isn't. I can fight.

"I won't hurt you," he repeats, wary of the knife in my fist. "I-I'm here to help. I'm a homefetch."

Homefetch? "You're lying," I gasp, shredding up leaves with my fingers, silently trying to find a branch I can use to pull myself up.

Never mind how he knows my name. He's probably just the son of a Floodonora merchant who's been watching and following me since I was born, waiting until I was at an age of value. But instantly, I know I'm wrong. I'll be worth far more when I can fly, and at birth, you'd have no guarantee of my species. But then again, Floodonora merchants are greedy. Perhaps they could simply not wait to get their hands on me, put me into a circus tent, and have the money rolling in nice and early when I've got time left to look young, beautiful, and entertaining.

"Roll up, roll up! Come to see the mad bird try and fly out of her cage! Whoops, what's that? Looks like she's trying to say something! Ten shackles from each of you, and we'll give her a microphone!" And then what? When I've done my years of service, they'll hand me over to the Frost guards, and I'll have landed myself a front-row seat for the destruction of my species, locked up in a cell while they slowly kill us off.

My train of thought crashes as he steps toward me, and I shrink back, preparing to launch myself at him. He reaches out to grab me, and I brandish the blade, stumbling to my feet.

"I believe you have something of mine?"

I freeze, blinking at his hand. It is extended out politely, his eyes on the knife in my fist. He does not attempt to seize me; for a moment, he's just a boy wanting his property back. Maybe he didn't even see me use my magic or sprout wings and thinks I'm just a scared schoolgirl from Frost. Is it possible...?

I stiffen. Don't trust the human. Never trust a human, my heart whispers.

"I-If you don't want to hurt me, then why are you chasing me?" I challenge.

"If you don't want me to chase you, then why are you running?" he replies.

I arch a brow. "Smooth. But why are you answering a question with a question? That's awfully suspicious."

"Can I have my knife or not?" he asks coldly.

I slowly rise to my feet. "Who are you?" I ask, furious yet curious.

"I'm Sparrow."

"No. I said: *who* are you? What are you doing here? What do you want?"

"I can't tell you that yet for security reasons, as I don't know for sure that you are who I think you are. That's why I tied you up. Until I confirm you're Raven, you're technically a threat."

"If you can't tell me who you are, then show me your face."

"If I did, I would have to kill you," he says, completely serious.

I clamp my teeth together. "Then at least tell me your name and who you think I am," I say, keeping my voice low and unrevealing. I learned a long time ago that if you act scared, it's not long before you stop acting.

"Sparrow," he repeats, "And I think you're Raven, surname classified. Is your name Raven?"

I say nothing. His eyes run over my face, his fingers twitching. For a moment, I think he might take off the mask or try to grab the knife.

"I could lie. Maybe I'm not Raven. Why would you take my word for it?" I say boldly.

"Because I was given a face, a name, and a location. You match the face. The chance you match the latter is highly likely. Plus, you have powers. So I'll ask again: are you Raven? You know what, don't answer that. You recognized it the first time I addressed you. I saw it in your eyes."

Finally, I manage the most minor nod. "Who else knows I'm here?" I ask carefully. He holds my frosty, untrusting gaze.

"Specifically, right here? Just me. But this area has a whole team of homefetches. We've been trying to reach you for six months, but it's been difficult because tracking you down was almost impossible."

"You're alone?" I ask, surprised. He nods.

I eye him up suspiciously and then hesitantly open my fist. The knife drops onto wet soil.

He's just like me. Just a kid. Young, cautious, and alone. What's the worst he can do? Have your knife, boy.

I hitch my satchel higher up my shoulder, attempting to look fierce. The boy's face remains unfazed. "Listen," I begin, wiping perspiration from my forehead. "I... er. Don't... don't go after me again. I-I know you know my name, and you've obviously been following me, but I've met your kind before, and most of you don't know what I'm capable of, so..."

He stares at me, and I trail off. "My kind?" he repeats.

"You know...Flunters? Floodonora leaves at dawn tomorrow, which is technically today, and they'll be storming these woods looking for everything and anything to sell before they leave. But I'm not for sale, so leave me alone before I..."

"Before you...?" he prompts as if knowing how utterly clueless I am.

"Before I do something I'll regret!" My voice is laced with threat.

I cast him a final wary look before sprinting past him and slipping between two bushes into darkness. I trip clumsily over a root shrouded by fallen leaves, protruding slyly from the earth, and press my hands onto the damp bark as I do so.

The flames spreading through the forest behind me instantly vanish into wisps of green smoke.

"Thanks," Sparrow calls dryly to me, pausing before offering a cheery wave.

I draw in a tight breath, and when I speak, my voice has gone all wobbly, my body exhausted of strength. "Please," I gasp, "Go home. Tell whoever it is that sent you that you couldn't find me. Just pretend I don't exist."

"Right. You don't exist."

"I'm serious. What is this, a game, to you?" My voice cracks as it slices sharply through the air. "My life is on the line! I have hours to get out of here, and if I don't, I'm a goner. Don't you realize that? Maybe you think I'm just some dumb criminal, but I'm F—" I catch myself just in time. "I-I'm not."

He sighs, his playful attitude gone. "I know what you are, Raven. Do you think I saw you strike a match to set me ablaze? Do you think I saw you toss water over that green fire to put it out?"

I freeze. There it is again! "Alright, how do you know my name?" I hiss. "I'm giving you one chance to explain yourself. I-I'm warning you!" I rasp, overwhelmed with anxiety, fear, and curiosity all at once. Wisps of hot air ripple threateningly between my fingers.

"Okay, okay! I know your name because I'm a homefetch, as I already said. And if you don't know what that is, it means that I was sent to bring you—"

"By who—?" I interrupt.

"—Home," he finishes simultaneously.

I almost collapse into his arms as the word escapes from his lips like a demon unleashed from Pandora's box, magic surging wildly through my limbs.

Suddenly, I'm dizzy as memories bleach away the scene my eyes paint for me.

And I'm in an empty carriage, with no Bronwyn, no Peter. A silent cottage, with no Papa, no Mama. A calm sea of sand, undisturbed by vicious sandstorms. A thousand rejected manuscripts of a simple necessity for a child, a million pasts that I've shed, discarding lumps of emotion and personality along the way.

"Home?" I echo, testing the word on my tongue.

Home: the Willow District? The Flai Realm? Does home mean a family? Mean that I'm *wanted*?

A lump rises in my throat, and my legs quiver, barely managing to stay put. Every fibre of my being advises me to run, but I've a million questions.

"Who. *Are* you?" I demand, choking on my own words.

"I'm Sparrow. Sparrow Fenimore," he says simply.

"A-And you come from?"

He grins, shrugs, and stuffs his hands in his pockets. "Who knows?"

"You don't know where you come from?" I repeat in deadpan disbelief.

"That's right. I mean, I *live* in the Flai Realm, but—*Alright!* Alright. Stop glaring at me. I'm sorry, okay? I'll talk, but you might want to sit down."

"I'm a big girl," I say sweetly.

Rolling his eyes, Sparrow leans back against a tree. "I know your mother. She sent me here."

I scoff, already beginning to walk away. "Nice try. In fact, no. Not even a nice try. It's actually a very bad try. *Why* would anyone believe that?"

He swallows, desperation creeping into his tone. "What if I can help you? She's alive. With Flai! They're hiding. I-I can take you there!"

I glare at him. "I'm not interested. And I'm leaving."

"You'll be protected there," he insists.

Decisively, I march away. I'm not letting this boy delay me further. I've lost nearly an hour, and time will show no mercy.

"I can keep you safe!" The boy calls after me, "But walk away if you want. I was ordered not to take you by force. Just know I can help you."

Whipping around to face him with a sour expression, I cry out, "Listen, you self-proclaimed saint! No means no! If someone tells you "no", it means "no the *bloody hell* not", "bogger off", "have a nice life", and "don't ever talk to me again"! People like me are hunted by worse than you will ever understand! No one can protect us but ourselves. So just leave me alone and quit it with your crap about my Mother. Don't even try to empathize with me because you don't get it at all, and you aren't my friend! I know what you are. You're a hunter."

He strides forward another two feet, evidently tired of being ranted at. God, how much I want to run. But something's keeping me here. Something about his voice has me tethered to the ground, stopping me from leaving. Maybe it's his smug little face, how everything he says is tinged with sarcasm, or perhaps the awful calm expression on his face, as though he just knows he's hit the jackpot.

"I'm trying to help you. I'm trying to *save* you. There's another side, another life waiting for you, and you look at me like I'm something on the bottom of your shoe. I get it: you don't believe me. But you're making a mistake. At least let me explain myself," he says.

"I have no reason to trust you," I snap bitterly.

"I'll give you a reason. What if I can get you across?"

My jaw sets, and I freeze. Okay, now I'm interested. "You can get me there? Across the border?" I ask slowly.

"If we move quickly, we'll arrive before sunrise, and I've smuggled others like you. I know how to get you through undetected. I have devices to conceal your wings. After that, feel free to leave me in the Willow District. Run all you like. But that's the only thing I can do to prove to you that I'm not lying," he sighs.

"How do I know you aren't leading me into a trap?"

"You don't," he answers pointedly.

"Then why should I—"

"If you want to cross that border, you're just going to have to trust me," he says sharply, cutting me off, "Your travels are delayed by at least an hour, you set off later than you should've, and Floodonora isn't travelling on foot. You'll be dead by dawn at this rate, and there's nowhere to hide from that travelling market… or at least, nowhere you know. But I know places. People. I know ways to disguise you, get you into the Willow District, get you shelter and supplies."

I shift from foot to foot, uncertain.

"Consider your situation, Raven," he pleads, "The worst scenario is that I'm a Flunter. I lead you into a false sense of security and then take you to my evil base, where we cut off your wings and dump you on your knees before a troop of Frost guards. Best scenario… You get out. You exit this state of just existing, just surviving, and move on to something bigger. You live, Raven. You're free. What I'm offering you is a chance. And even if that's still not enough to convince you, and everything in your body is pleading with you to run right now, let me at least ask you this: if you run from me, what will change?"

What will change?

Still running and hiding with a fragile heart that thrums every day only to serve a body constantly fleeing the demons of its nightmares. Plodding through every day alone and defeated, questioning my existence and pondering why the jaws of death haven't snapped shut on me. Hopelessly wondering why the door of fate is still inexplicably ajar. Is this boy— is my "mother" and my "home" a chance to open that door? To finally exit the loop? Even if Sparrow's a Flunter after all, perhaps I'll be freer in his chains than anywhere else.

I bite down hard on my tongue, weighing up my chances.

"So?" he asks.

I stare into his dark, dark eyes and draw in a single tight breath. A memory surfaces in my mind.

Freezing gold chains press into my face, searing my skin, and I try not to move too much despite the agony. Excited shouts and jeers ring through my ears, and my cloudy memory recalls the low grumbles of warning from yesterday as the Flunters told one another not to get too close to me. The bound wrists that I writhed together in desperate attempts to free myself last night have accessorized me with raw rope burns, and my arms are crusted over with blood. The sight makes my head spin, and I'm dizzy, disorientated, and motionless. I must be dying. Maybe I'm already dead.

Maybe I always was.

Trembling, I push away my haunting nightmares, a warning of what is to come if I entrust this boy with my life.

But that wasn't real. It wasn't. It can't have been real because I'm alive.

If I'm dead and simply drifting through this existence without meaning, then something should've swept me up by now and taken me to whatever's after this world. I wouldn't just be here forever.

Cyclical. Completed. Done. There has to be something else...

Hasn't there?

I raise my head to meet Sparrow's eyes.
What will change?

"You don't know me and you don't know what I've lost. If you try anything, I- I *swear* I'll... You can't hurt me, Sparrow," I say, my voice thick. "You *won't*."

He pauses, staring rather intensely at me as though to blaze his signature into my vow's contract. "So you mean to say that you're coming?" Sparrow finally says, raising his eyebrows.

"Obviously."

CHAPTER 3

I watch the boy get to work, pulling up his hood, examining the ground, and kicking a log out of the shrubs to sit on. "We should try not to touch anything. I'm afraid your little campfire may have broadcasted our location to Floodonora and the Guard. Frost track people like there's no tomorrow."

"I know that. I've been on the run since I was *six*," I snap at him before gathering myself. The more I tell him, the more dangerous he is to me. Sparrow pulls the bulging sack off his back. "Hemp," I notice, arching a brow. "Good stuff."

If I can maintain a casual conversation, I can trick him into thinking I won't desert him at the first opportunity. He shrugs modestly, murmuring something about a "cheap discount" and "marketplace", and draws out a crinkled, grey blanket.

"Here," he says, pushing it into my hands.

"What's this for?" I frown, unfolding the material.

"Covering up your wings."

"But I'm not in my Flai form," I protest.

"They have special devices at the border. And wolves. They'll sniff you out in ten seconds flat. We'll both be dead. But that's specially designed to throw off your scent," he explains. "And that round bit —like a hood— absorbs light to help cover your eyes. They're a dead giveaway."

I frown. "My... eyes?"

He nods. "They're... Really bright. It doesn't look human. Trust me, only Flai have eyes like that."

"And you know this how?" he hesitates before responding, encouraging me to leap onto his case again.

"You say you know my mother," I remark, "But you haven't spoken of her since we made our deal, and you're claiming to know a ton of facts about Flai that even I've never heard of." The accusation in my voice is explicit, and I don't attempt to hide it.

"I *do* know your mother," Sparrow insists, "Or, at least, I know she has black hair and bright emerald eyes like you, and I know she gave birth almost sixteen years ago, and I know she had a child with a man whose surname was Asgard. I know my story is weak, and I have no evidence, but I'm being truthful."

Our eyes lock, his wide with desperation and mine frosty and hateful. "How did... how did you know I was here?" I ask slowly, selecting my words with caution.

Sparrow grins. "I admit you were very, very good. We almost gave up, y'know? But when reports of guards discovering Flai hiding in Frost surfaced last year in the newspapers, we knew we had you. You had to be our ghost girl. Our invisible Flai. Then, when the Willows Guard plastered wanted posters with your description onto every lamppost in the Willow District, we knew it had to be you. You perfectly matched your mother's physical features, were the right age, and were a fire Flai. So, we began searching for you," he shrugs, "And a month ago, in frost, you were sighted. After that, we posted men disguised as guards at the exits to Frost. No one saw you leave, so we knew you planned to leave after Stone Tide. Today. It made sense, after all. And, yes, maybe I could be a liar. Maybe I'm a hunter. But have I hurt you and threatened to make you come? Attempted to contact a troop of guards? I swore that I would keep you safe until you were home. I'm not a danger to you, Raven. I swear it."

When he finishes his sentence, he seems older somehow. I sense an unnerving loneliness and responsibility about him, a shadow behind his eyes that I can't quite understand yet but am familiar with. He's human, alright, but he doesn't act like it.

"Do you have weapons?" I finally ask.

He nods as he shifts around the fallen leaves and brambles on the forest floor with his foot and then returns his full attention to me, studying my body in such a way that it makes me feel like a specimen in a science lab.

As he analyses my strengths and weaknesses, I cross my arms across my chest, half convinced he is purposefully taking his time.

"You're malnourished but strong. You're fast but can't outrun a fit adult across a long distance, and your stamina is low. As for as close combat, you might be decent with a dagger —your reflexes are brilliant— but I'm not too sure about aim; you'd panic when in a tough situation and stop thinking logically about where to stab your attacker. I think long-distance attack is your best bet. Do you know how to use throwing stars?" he finally asks, retrieving eleven steel cut-outs from the sack.

I take one from him. It's the size of my hand and brandishes four deadly sharp points. "Well?" Sparrow prompts.

"I'm a Flai, the most hunted creature in existence. And to defend myself, you give me a measly old bit of metal?"

He pushes my fist closed around the throwing star. "This is all I've got for you. Take it or leave it. And call them what you like, but if you can throw, you can kill, which might keep us both alive."

I glare at him, feeling almost cheated. "We had a deal. You

said you could protect me."

He throws the sack of weapons at my stomach and continues to shift the earth. I catch it just in time to stop myself from getting winded.

"If you learn to throw, I'll consider teaching you how to shoot a gun. I just don't believe in killing, okay? It's a personal thing."

I give a sigh and grudgingly nod, extending my hand. "Fine. Look, I'm Raven. Yes, I know that you know already. I just want to introduce myself properly and not get off on the wrong foot."

He shakes my hand and offers me something close to a smile. "You know, it's pretty cool to be in a job like mine. I'm lucky. Some people would give their lives to see someone like you. Probably in a cage or something, sure, but still."

I fiddle with the stars, shooting him a look, but he only chuckles, shaking his head.

"Not to be rude, but have you ever actually encountered a human before, aside from strangers on the street? Or talked to one?" he asks.

"Besides you? Not since I was about six." I grumble.

"I can see that from the way you talk. So… You've never had a real friend?"

"Not a human one. What's up with you and interrogating people?" I mutter, stopping playing with my weapons to glare into his eyes, carving the words out of my buried anger at him.

He talks too much and does far too little. I understand needing to stop and sort through your pack, but you don't do it here. Not out in the open, so vulnerable to attack. The boy's an idiot and possibly a liar.

"Just trying to break the ice. Jeez. Were you really alone until now?" Sparrow continues.

"I'm too busy staying alive to make friends, Sparrow!" It comes out sharper than I intend, and he arches a brow.

"Well... aren't we friends?"

I almost choke on my saliva. "I don't think a human and a Flai can be friends. Plus, we just met, and I, quite frankly, don't like you."

Amused, he smirks as I shift around in the sack he gave me, and I pull out a long, shining rapier. Its hilt has a strip of leather that instantly feels warm in my palm and a long, sharp blade. "This, I like," I muse. "More my size."

Horrified, Sparrow snatches it from my hands, a noise like a strangled cat's mewl escaping his lips. "Raven! Get back! That's the same model Frost soldiers carry! It contains gold!"

I step back sharpish.

"Yeah," he says darkly, "Very nice, isn't it?" Waving it at me, he shakes his head.

I leap back, flames dancing under the skin of my hands. "Get that away from me," I hiss. "What are you trying to *do*!?"

Everyone knows gold is a death sentence for Flai. It symbolizes greed, power, and wealth, and its production in mass quantities is toxic to nature, the very source of our magic. Men have dug, destroyed, and mined to reach the most miniature pieces of it. It opposes everything we stand for, weakens us, and drains our powers. It makes us human.

A decade ago, the Sun Queen and the Moon King declared it as the official punishment for Flai. That's the worst thing— They don't kill us. They just make us normal. They make us "safe". They take away everything that makes us who we are.

It's what they do at the Berg.

Even the slightest trace of gold in anything disgusts and terrifies me and sends a shiver up my spine. "God, bird boy, how do you *sleep* at night," I choke, digging the corner of the throwing star into my flesh just to bring myself back to reality.

Ashamed, he sees my expression and hastily slides the sword back into the sack. Just like that, it's gone, but that doesn't change the fact that he just brandished it at me. That's the problem with humans— they take something away and expect no consequences. They take land, animals, and Flai. They just take everything.

"I- sorry. I shouldn't have... I didn't mean to... I... Just stick with the throwing stars for now. They're relatively Flai-proof," Sparrow says, changing the subject.

I nod, saying nothing, knowing it's better to push my lips together in silent fury than to voice my thoughts and endanger myself. It is frustrating to be so at his mercy. One wrong move, and he could call guards.

"Floodonora will be right behind us soon. We need to go," I mumble. "Time to take us to your secret hiding place."

"Okay, but let me just finish—"

Abruptly, a soft hiss slices through the air as the surrounding sea of bushes is disturbed. I whip around, eyes scanning the undergrowth.

Sparrow looks at me. I look at Sparrow.

"Don't. Move," he mouths, withdrawing his knife. "Don't...make...a sound."

The breeze sends a ripple through his hair, and his face is stone as he moves silently into a battle stance. Watching him pose like that might have been mildly amusing if not for the situation.

I observe him, a lump in my throat. Is he trained to fight? He looks as though he's done this a thousand times, which just inspires another unnerving question of his past that he'll surely refuse to answer. But if he can fight... Could he fight *me*?

I clutch my throwing star tightly, wishing I'd taken the other ten instead of putting them back in the sack, but shake away my thoughts with a nervous lick of my dry lips. Now isn't the time for remembering how unprepared I am for combat. It's the time for running and running fast.

Sparrow advances cautiously forward, using his back foot to push dirt over the footprint he made, and a spark of gratitude flares up in my chest. So *that's* what he's been doing: covering our tracks.

I catch my reflection in the blade of his glinting knife. I'm afraid, pale, and vulnerable in the weak pooling moonlight above the trees. The sweeping curtain of swelling fog obscures the forest behind us, masking hidden enemies, and the nets of tangled branches embracing one another above prevent us from climbing any higher than five meters. The branches at that height are easily accessible for Flunters and undoubtedly sturdy enough to bear their weight. Our routes of escape are fatally limited.

"Holy crap. We're actually gonna die. I'm *actually* gonna die beside an imbecile," I whisper in disbelief.

"What?"

I shake my head, pressing a finger to my lips. Slowly, silently, Sparrow tiptoes back into the center of the clearing and lowers his lips to the height of my head so that his breath grazes my ear.

"When I make the call, run," he whispers. "Do you hear me? Run, and absolutely do not stop for any reason. You're the priority, understand?"

I nod, my eyes frozen on the shrubs. I can't see it, but I can still hear it. Something slowly, softly padding along the floor... someone crawling or crouched, maybe. Rustles... Footsteps...

"Now!" Sparrow yells.

I break into a sprint, my hair flying out behind me, and I race out of the clearing. Branches and brambles snag at my clothes, and thorns shred my knees through my trousers. Yet, on and on, I run, my chest rising and falling rapidly. Sparrow was right about my stamina.

Grunts and yells of surprise echo from behind me. Some are young and smooth, like Sparrow's voice, and the others... *others?*

I halt abruptly, my voice feeble as I whisper into thin air. "There's more than one."

A scream tears through the air, and suddenly, I'm stumbling over my feet, my brain and heart sending me in two different directions. *Help him!*

"Sparrow!" I gasp, turning back, "Sparrow, are you—?"

"RUN!" His voice comes back in a strangled cry.

Left, right? Forward, back!? The world is a blur.

I risk taking a second to glance through the trees, my heart pounding against my ribs. Sparrow staggers after me, and behind him, I can make out a second figure, fleeting through the trees with a slight limp... whoever it is, I don't want to stick around and face his fury.

Maybe he'll realize that Sparrow is a diversion, that the real target is getting away. I'm who he's after, of course.

Sparrow joins my side, and we dash together, calves aching, past the trees, over fallen branches, through thick, thorny shrubs—

I'm too slow. He seizes my hand, and I jerk away in panic. We both skid to a clumsy halt.

The boy's eyes are manic, his breaths quick and full of terror. "Please. Trust me, Raven. Trust me."

I reluctantly offer my wrist. He instantly grabs it and

steers us away from the path-like area we've been running along.

I struggle to stay on my feet, propelled by his legs, twice the size of mine. Sparrow stops suddenly and turns, gasping, "It's a dead end."

I shove past him, scanning our surroundings in every direction. Beyond, I can see no more forest. There's only sloping ground and a pebbled lake beach. At this time of year, the water is freezing. Maybe deadly.

A towering, vertical cliff face surrounds it, looming over the glassy, mirror-like surface. It wraps around the entire length of the lake like a shawl, leaving us with nowhere to swim.

A tiny stretch of wood sits on the other side of the lake, but only stone is behind it. We could never climb. And behind us, all around us, are possibly even more Flunters.

Flustered, I spin back to Sparrow, tearing off my muddy shirt. "We'll swim for it," I say decisively, "And we'll just have to stay underwater until they leave. Most Flunters that work for Floodonora can't swim, anyway. I saw their coats, and they were in the Willowfolk style. I doubt they're Frost professionals."

"But you don't know, Raven. What if they're working with the Guard?"

"They aren't."

"*IF* they *ARE*?" he roars. "Just think about what you're saying!"

"I'm not some ditzy teenager, Sparrow! I can think logically for myself!"

"I know that. I'm SORRY! Damn it, is that what you want to hear? I never meant to insult you, alright?" Sparrow gasps. "I'm just trying to do my job. I'm just trying to save you."

"Save. Your. Self." I reply through gritted teeth.

"Raven—"

"You were sent to help me, right? To take me home? *This* is the way home. So help me."

"JUST LISTEN! It's the middle of winter, and if we don't die from drowning, we'll surely get hypothermia. Raven, I can't let you go in. I can't. You'll die in there."

I stare at him. "Hypothermia isn't my main concern when the men chasing us have golden bullets designed to tear through my wings and inject poison into my bloodstream that'll knock me out for a week."

"I know that, but- but this is delusional," he splutters.

"If you have a better idea, say it now!" I cry, glancing desperately over my shoulder, "We're running out of time."

Grinning, the hunter wades through bushes towards us, crushing everything with his enormous hiking boots.

Shadowing him, a second menacing figure pursues us. Terrified, I wrench the shoes off my feet.

"What are you doing!?" Sparrow gasps as I stuff them into the shrubs.

"Getting rid of some weight. We won't be able to swim dressed like this," I explain, snatching his sack and stashing it in the shrubs.

"Raven, this is mad. We are not going in there. You are not going…" he begins sternly, then gives up. "Raven!" he yells, exasperated, "You're out of your goddamn…" he trails off, and I follow his gaze, trembling.

There are three of them. They're giants, tearing and stomping through the woodland in fur coats rippling like manes in the wind, assisted by wolves snarling and snapping at their sides. The panic is red. Loud. It's a scream, roaring at Sparrow, at my naïve choices, and at the absolute idiocy I've demonstrated.

"You... you..." I splutter.

Sparrow's jaw sets, and he grips my shoulders, pivoting to lock eyes with me. "Raven, listen, I didn't send for anyone! I have nothing to do with this, I swear it!"

"I never should have trusted you... you liar! You *lied*!"

"Raven, snap out of it! We have to do something right now, or we're both dead meat! If we try to swim and they see us dive in, they'll only follow us! The odds that they just *happen* not to be able to swim are too low to make that kind of gamble!" Sparrow begs.

My knees are locked together, and my feet nailed to the ground. "So, when did you send for them?" I ask quietly, calm washing over me in a deadly wave.

"RAVEN!" He slaps me, striking me hard across the face so that tears sting in my eyes.

Only then do I finally raise my head and greet the petrified little boy swimming in his eyes, a reflection of a younger self, and somehow understand.

I'm thirteen once more, sprinting through the Frost Kingdom with my insides clenched together, my ribs knotted, and my tongue too heavy with apologies to make a sound. No scream can escape me, and no tear can trickle down my face before the wind whips it away.

My chest rises, falls, fails.

I've failed.

My lungs cannot function, and my eyes cannot focus on one thing, whipping from side to side, alive with paranoia. Daggers, my fingernails dig into the flesh of my palms, the sharp stabs of pain bringing me comfort because that pain, at least, means I'm alive. It means that the crushing, clawing terror has not throttled me yet. I just need to know I'm alive.

I'm seven, curled up in an alleyway on the outskirts of the Willow District, icy rain crashing down on my cheeks and merging with my tears. My calves wail with agony, and no part of me isn't aching with fatigue from running miles from home. I don't know what to do or where to go. Maman and Papa are a maze of cobbled death traps away, police officers patrol the central village squares, and yellow-toothed men lurk in alleyways, their eyes glinting with the type of greed my Papa once warned me of— hunter's greed. *Trader's* greed.

The scene shifts, and I'm in an empty room without doors and windows, locked eternally inside myself and unable to escape the anxiety and alarm that no child should experience. Ever. Running a hand along the faded wallpaper, I recall that this spot where I stand is the same place I discovered my magic. These are the same floorboards that supported my thin, quaking seven-year-old body as my family pointed and screamed.

I curl up, drawing my knees to my chin, and do the only thing I can.

I sob.

And then the memories fade, and I'm a fifteen-year-old boy standing opposite Raven Asgard, overwhelmed with identical terror, panic, and hopelessness, lost somewhere in between the will to survive and surrender.

And I understand.

A kind of electricity is threaded through Sparrow and me. The darkness in his eyes mirrors mine. And now that trauma, that miserable creature living inside his heart, is facing me, begging for trust. I blink several times and shake my head as though to rid myself of a blindfold. Trying to ignore my trembling fingers, I skid down the slope to the water's edge, grazing my hand on jagged pebbles.

Just to my left, the land elevates into a tiny hill overhanging the water's edge. I stride up it, testing the earth to ensure it'll bear my weight. "Sparrow, I believe you. Let's go."

"This is crazy," he repeats sharply, drawing his knife and pulling away from me. "You're crazy."

"How many escapes do you think I've made in my lifetime? I know what I'm doing, Sparrow. You have your talents, and I have mine."

"There's no time to be messing around. We have to find another *way*!" he yells, finally losing his patience.

Our eyes lock, but nothing in his distressed pupils can change my mind. I've made my decision. I know there's only one option left.

"You're just going to have to trust me, Sparrow." I take his wrist and dive into the freezing water before he can utter another word, taking him with me.

The cold engulfs us like a roaring inferno, the two of us crashing onto the lake's floor. Blankets of icy waves drift past my shoulders, draping from my fingers, pouring and swirling as the discombobulated dust and pebbles attempt to rearrange themselves.

Where I expect pain, there's only a kind of beautiful numbness. I'm not in the water. I'm drifting through time and space and stars... Then Sparrow shakes me back to life and kicks up for the surface, dragging me towards the sky, towards the light.

Our heads emerge simultaneously, and he coughs, spewing saltwater from his mouth. "Take a deep breath. You'll need it," I croak shakily before taking in a single mouthful of air and pulling us both back under the surface.

It's numbingly cold, pitch black, and disorientating. I still tightly grasp Sparrow's wrist, but my fingers are white.

Piercing the water are heated yells of confusion, irritation, and rage, but they are distant and milky.

After maybe thirty seconds, gunfire zips through the water, and my limbs jerk with alarm, propelling me away from the danger. A bullet skims my leg, grazing the flesh and causing me to cry out with shock. But I force myself to stay underwater.

Following the bullets, everything is just tranquil and murky. Minutes pass, both of us waiting for the commotion caused by the Flunters to disappear. It is so peaceful I almost enjoy it...

Until I feel Sparrow kicking up for the surface again beside me and suddenly realize how tight my chest is, as though someone has stretched out my lungs and twisted them into a knot.

There is no peace here. Nothing lies for me in these waters, and nothing will be awoken by my presence. There's no bright end of a tunnel waiting, not here, where it's icy and dark and cold and... and I'm scared. There is nothing for me in death. Not yet.

There is no glory in this.

The voices above the surface become louder, and my heartbeat pounds in my eardrums. The cold is no longer numbing. It's stabbing me from every direction like a thousand needles.

I reach out and tug at Sparrow's cloak. My vision is blurry, but the voices are still there. I shake my head and pull him back down as best I can, his body snaking and twisting into the kelp. What? Where am I? Where's Sparrow?

Never mind about him, we just met. I don't care about him.

And if I do, I'm a dead girl walking.

But now I, too, need breath, and the promise of air is painfully teasing.

No. I have to stay down.

Air... I need air...

But if I can just hold on... Just a few more seconds...

Disorientated, I attempt to listen. Are the Flunters still there? Is it safe? It's impossible to tell. Now, I want to resurface, but where are my legs? Am I lost in kelp? I can't see anything.

I've forgotten how to swim.

Panic sets in, and I find myself flailing. "Help!" I gurgle desperately, bubbles spewing from my mouth. "Sparrow... Sparrow, help me—!"

My heels brush the pebbled floor again, and suddenly, logic is driving me, and I know exactly what to do. I push off the bottom of the lake with every last inch of strength I have, reaching up a hand. My fingertips break the surface—

And then I don't know what's happening.

Emerging from the deep is an indescribable force, a soft vibration that morphs into a static charge, running through my body, raising the hairs on my arms, and surging to my fingertips.

As it does, I notice that my skin is paling rapidly. As though a paintbrush is sweeping me, I'm becoming lighter until I am white all over, my veins bright blue like gushing rivers in hard, cold marble. My hands pulsate with bright, cyan light, and my vision is lost in a whirl of dizziness. Black clouds are slowly blinding me...

And then the world around me freezes into a million sheets of solid, icy waves, and I black out.

✻ ✻ ✻

My eyes snap open to a haze of green. Dark green, light green, fern green, lime green. Firstly, I can recognize only circles and blotches, fuzzy shapes that I absent-mindedly trace with my fingers. They sharpen into squares of color, overlapping in complex patterns, weaving together like bits of yarn.

And then it strikes me that I'm meant to be dead at the bottom of a lake. Dumbfounded, I hastily sit up. I'm on a bed of moss and damp forest floor, looking up at a ceiling of branches. My back is warm, but my front is freezing.

I wince and lie back down to roll over because I don't think I have the strength to climb to my feet yet.

Maybe I can crawl.

As I turn onto my front, soft feathers whisper past my arm. My wings are folded back against my shoulder blades, trapping warm air between the feathers and my skin.

Wait. *My wings!*

"Oh, for crying out—," I begin, but stop myself abruptly as I realize the earlier dangers of Flunters and guards are not yet guaranteed to be gone, and I need to stay silent. Then again, wouldn't they have found me by now? Maybe they already have.

After all, how did you get here? My mind whispers.

I look around hastily and exhale before rising unsteadily to my feet and fluxing back into my human form.

Every inch of my body hurts as though a stampede has trampled on me. Small, melting ice crystals fall from under my fingernails when I move my fingers. My hair is straw, but the underside of my head is hot and wet. I speculate I've been lying here for a while.

Thick, dense growth surrounds me in every direction. Surely, I'm still in the Frost wilderness? I recognize these pines. But I have my safe zones on this island, the places I always resort to living in when I'm traveling, and there are still forests I haven't entered, trees that I haven't climbed. Theoretically, I could be anywhere.

It's unnervingly quiet, and the only sign that I'm not alone is a bundle of abandoned clothes and shoes under a bush. Puzzled, I look down to find that my feet are bare.

Where are my shoes? Why did I remove them? I crawl over to the shrubs, pick up one of the boots, and pull it on. I can about manage to move for this, but I hate being so low. If I were to be attacked now, I would never be able to get up fast enough to react. I'd be a goner.

Moving as fast as I can bear, I begin to work the strength back into my muscles. To begin, the progress is good, and I must be about thirty from the clearing with the bushes when something makes a sharp dig into my stomach as I crawl, stopped from falling onto the dirt only by my shirt. I reach down to my waist and feel under my top before withdrawing a throwing star, its edges hooked into the material of my cloak. I frown. Where did *this* come from?

My palms flare up with heat as if in answer to my bewilderment. Bright green flames shoot up through my fingers and rise above my head.

For a moment, they hover there before dispersing in all directions until only a tiny wisp of smoke remains, one that forms a single shape: a sparrow in flight.

And then a boy in a bird mask steps through the trees, shouting something that I make out to be, "I found you! Thank God!" and my memory rears its head from the depths of my mind like a lion, causing everything to rush eagerly back all at once.

CHAPTER 4

We hobble through the woods as he finishes bandaging his raw, bloody knuckles. Glancing down at my own clammy palms, smooth and unharmed, if not a little stiff from frostbite, there are no words to thank him with.

Shrivelled and filthy from the lake, his bird mask is falling to pieces, yet he doesn't remove it, and I don't dare ask him to, for the air already hums with a million questions. The leather has curled at the edges, revealing more of his warm honey-brown skin, but half of his face is still covered. In short, he remains a masked stranger, not to be trusted.

We trek through the wilderness for a while, me supported by his arms. I hate that I'm so helpless without him to lean on, but what other choice do I have? Scuttling through the undergrowth on all fours like a dog?

Sparrow explains that I froze the lake to ice, and I'd been trapped under the surface, while he managed to free his legs from the water just before it solidified. He smashed through the ice and dragged my limp body onto shore, but when he returned, I was gone. I was frozen in Flai form, unconscious and unable to change into a human.

"I was so worried, Raven. I thought they'd found you and crammed you in the back of a wagon."

"Nice to know you care so much," I say hollowly, too exhausted to show genuine emotion.

"Of course I do. If anything happened under my supervision, your mum'd be *so* mad at me."

I jab my elbow into his side, laughing weakly.

We take refuge on a small, sheltered stone ledge halfway up the cliff face, where he's already built a fire. It leans directly over the ice lake, where there's no trace left of the presence of Flai except the mysterious sheet of ice that could easily be courtesy of the weather and the small hole in its centre owed to Sparrow's fist.

To access the ledge, you have to press yourself against the stone and creep carefully along a tiny path that would crumble under the weight of an adult, and it's barely a foot's length wide. The trail wraps around the inner face of the cliff in a rickety ramp, climbing sickeningly high, and several times, we both lose our footing, clinging onto each other's wrists for dear life.

It would've been easy to desert the Boy in the Bird Mask in those moments. I could've let him plummet and run, but I didn't. *Why?*

With my head aching and my eyes fixated on the floor, I mull over today's events, occasionally glancing at Sparrow when he's turned away from me.

"If you keep looking at me like I'm going to attack you, I might just do it," he says, finally breaking the silence.

I blink. Once. Twice. A third time to see if he's joking. Do I really still look scared and tense? After the Flunters came after us, I'm especially paranoid, but I didn't realize that the expression of fear was still carved into my features.

Suck it up. You're showing him weakness. "Sorry," I say quickly. And I genuinely am, but that doesn't stop me from staring at Sparrow, wondering... No.

He punched through the lake's surface to save me from

suffocating. To save a girl he just met. And a Flai, of all creatures. Surely, absolutely, he had nothing to do with the attack.

That doesn't mean you can trust him. Maybe he only saved you because you'll sell better when you're alive, my mind whispers.

I gaze at the stone beneath my knees, prying moss up from the cracks in the floor. The ledge slopes inwards so that it's scarcely visible from below, cutting into the cliff face to form a miniature cave. I have a million things to say, but my mind is racing. Why's he helping me? Why, when I'm worth thousands of shackles?

He glances up at me, then at the fire. "I'm going to get more wood."

Then he makes to stand, but I stand too, blocking his path. If he leaves, he could contact someone. Send out a signal and return with Flunters. "Those men are still out there," I warn, disguising my distrust as concern, "Now they've seen us, they know we're here somewhere. They'll be after you, too, on their way back with more Flunters to search the area. We have enough kindling for now," I add.

Our setting betrays my words: a beautiful, silent valley of ice, earth, and fog.

"We're alone," he says. "Any noises from below would echo, and we'd know someone was here. It's safe."

I step sharply forward, my palms tingling and my wings unfurling threateningly without warning. A violent whip of wind lashes at my white feathers. "No," I say, so sharply it surprises me. "We were spotted, Sparrow. People could be hiding below us right now with guns. And... and..."

And I don't want you to die, I add silently.

It's annoyingly true. I have too many questions and too much curiosity. If he's dead, I'll never get my answers. Never know if his motives are as sinister as I presume or if... my heart sings with hope. *If.*

Oh, *If*! If Mother is truly alive and waiting for me.

Sparrow's eyes run over my glowing emerald hands, my unnaturally bright eyes, and the hundreds of grey-white feathers framing my body. Sighing, he sits down again. I shrink to my human size, slump beside him on the cliff ledge, embarrassed by my outburst, and stare down miserably at the lake.

"I don't know why you're helping me, but I sure hope you know what you've got yourself into," I mumble, face in hands. "I've been alone for a good portion of my life. I don't know what to say. I'm not used to this sort of thing," I admit reluctantly.

He meets my eyes, his own full of buried resentment, and I already know he hates me because, next, he snaps, "Well, join the freaking club. Me neither. You think I feel any more comfortable around you than you do around me?"

I shift my eyes to the sky, not because I'm bothered about the time or the storm, but because I'd rather look at anything other than him. Traces of light appear as minutes pass, like shreds of paper camouflaged in a deep, inky black, signalling the approach of a new day. The clouds hiss tiny curls of rain at us, bulging with rumbling thunder.

I close my eyes, feeling the hairs on my arms rise as the cool air descends, and cup my hands, reaching out. When I open them, a small, silver stone shines in my hand, emitting a pleasant, tingling warmth.

"Here," I say wearily, placing the glowing diamond in the boy's palm.

Sparrow stares at it. "What's this?"

"It's a star. Worth hundreds of shackles— more than

enough to get your knuckles checked out by a professional doctor when this is over."

"A star?" he repeats in bewilderment, and I nod, pondering if his tone masks disappointment. "But...stars are...you know... Big. And hot. And this isn't... how did you...?" His mouth opens and closes, unsure of what to say. Then he shakes his head and pockets it. "Well... thanks."

I nod, absent-mindedly flicking moss into the fire. "You use it to make a wish," I explain, "Just one. Anything you want, as long as it isn't too ridiculous. It's almost like a lucky charm. No matter how low the odds are, if it can potentially happen in another time, place, or universe... this thing will make sure it does. They used to use them in the Fall to heal wounded warriors," I say, staring thoughtfully into the shrinking, dying flames and adding quietly, "But now we just use them for staying alive. Getting out of sticky situations."

Something invasive flashes across Sparrow's calm expression. Something close to sadness. "They don't tell me things like that in the Realm. They don't tell me a lot of things, actually."

"Don't they trust you?"

"I was raised alongside Flai, *by* Flai, and I work for you, now. But that doesn't change what I am. What reason have they to trust me?"

His eyes meet mine, and I swallow my pity. "Sorry," I mumble.

"It's not your fault. Some things can't be wished away." At that, he turns away and leaves me with my thoughts.

I'm not sure why I did it— catch him a star.

My mind is so foggy with thoughts and fatigue that logic and common sense have drained from my head. I wish I could look into my mind and understand myself.

Perhaps it's simply a thank-you— an attempt to repay the debt between us. The debt that is my life. Or maybe... maybe it's just another defence mechanism. A way to turn the tables and empower myself.

I know that by giving him that tiny star, a gift he will never really understand or know how to use, I'm also giving him a weakness. For all I know, he's taking me to a Flunters' camp. He's blackmailed me here, in a way, hasn't he? He left me with no choice but to go with him and told me that if I do not, he'll let the guards find me and leave me to die.

But say they caught up with us, after all, and they demanded to take me into custody? He'd never make a shackle off me, and in a confrontation with the Frost Guard, that star could be his only escape left. An escape only I know how to trigger, only I know how to use. And there I have it- leverage. I've always told myself I'm too quick to trust others, and that's probably true. Alliances get you help, power, and sometimes safety. But all alliances eventually break unless they aren't formed for survival but for companionship or even romance.

It's the difference between like, love, and *in* love. This alliance is none of those things.

So that's why I'm trying to give myself an upper hand. To keep Sparrow here long enough to escape him. Perhaps Flai are as manipulative and calculating as the King says.

Why I don't trust Sparrow, I don't know. I depend on him, so I should try to have faith. On the other hand, his species, his words, and his actions all tell me otherwise. They're stained with the mark of humanity.

Yet, despite all this, I still give the star to him. So there must be a reason. There must be... With the fire's sighing flames go the answers to all my questions. The smoke stumbling higher and higher signals the departure of my train of thought.

I suddenly shudder at a prickly feeling climbing up the back of my neck and sneak a glance over my shoulder to see Sparrow watching me carefully. Why?

Because he doesn't trust you, either, my mind answers.

I narrow my eyes, stiffening. Two can play the game of deceit, trust, and betrayal. I take a breath, plaster a kind, gullible, trusting smile on my face, and turn back around.

"You okay?" he asks, his brows drawn together.

I nod, waiting for him to talk. My throat's as dry as sandpaper.

Sparrow holds my gaze. "You know... your mother and the other Flai... they've never done magic in front of me. They trust me, but not like that. I stay in the homefetch training centre almost always. Probably because I'm not... you know... like you. I thought maybe you didn't actually do magic. Maybe it was just a myth."

It takes my brain a moment to register that this is supposed to be funny and force a laugh. "I have angel wings, Sparrow. I just froze a lake in front of your bare eyes, and *that* wasn't even on purpose. What do you want me to do, pull a bunny out of a hat?" I joke.

He regards me with a searching look. "Why are you suddenly so perky?"

"Because..." I stop, pretending to listen to a bird's call momentarily to give myself time to think. "Well, because..." The silence stretches on, and eventually, I stand up. "Listen, there's something I meant to mention about the throwing stars. I've never actually used a proper weapon before," I admit, changing the subject.

He raises an eyebrow, leeching onto the bait. "Maybe I could teach you? Do you still have the eleventh star, or did you put it back in the sack?"

I give him a hopeless smile and shrug, reaching for the weapon sack and retrieving the throwing stars from within. "I think I put the last one back while we were walking. Yeah, it's here. You reckon you can teach me, then?"

"Is that supposed to be some sort of challenge?" Sparrow asks.

"'Course it is. I'm a bad listener, and my parents always called me a stubborn child."

"Alright then. Er. Aim it. Throw it," he shrugs, shuffling back to watch me.

I nod and aim for a spot on the opposite curve of the cliff's face, only to discover that my feeble throw barely carries it six feet. As it plummets towards the water and then skids across the ice, Sparrow sighs.

"Okay, now we have *ten* stars."

Determined to get this skill right, I turn on him, demanding a more precise set of instructions, but he eyes me as though I'm going to explode. "Uhh... baby steps. Try holding the star the right way around to start."

"There's a right way to hold a symmetrical star?" I repeat incredulously.

"Yes," he insists. "When you said you're hard to teach, I didn't realize you'd be this bad. Put your index finger on top and your thumb underneath. Traditionally, you hold it vertically, but these are a little different. Don't grip it too tightly."

As he fusses, I glance down at the floor and catch sight of my strange silhouette as he rises to his feet to assist me further.

My shoulder blades protrude out uglily where my wings sprout, and my ribs are more defined than ever by clouds that cast shadows on my nimble frame. Sparrow frowns as the wind blows the cocoa-coloured bangs out of his eyes, and I realize I've been standing here, staring at myself like an alien, for several seconds.

"What is it?"

I shake my head and raise the star. "Nothing. Is this right?"

He moves behind me and gently tilts my elbow up. "Relax your shoulder. Lower your arm a bit. Pull back— no! *Gently*!"

I adjust my position, flinching slightly at his touch. By now, I know he's not going to attack me, but the fear that he could, if he wanted to, remains. He places his hand on my back and pushes me slightly, straightening my spine.

"Perfect. Now move your wrist left... and release."

The blade sails through the air smoothly, and lands in the centre of the cliff face opposite us.

"How was that?"

His wide eyes flick from me to the target, a stunned expression on his face. "Brilliant."

My face flushes with pride. "I-I've never seen anything like them. What kingdom are they from?

"None. A place in the Far Lands called Japan."

"The Far Lands?" I repeat, stunned.

"Mm-hm. There are bits of history scattered all over Evrilore. Clues as to what's out there. People just aren't willing to look. Anyone would think the citizens of Evrilore are preoccupied with the genocide of literal fallen angels."

I laugh away the spots of colour on my cheeks.

"Anyway, that's probably enough for today," Sparrow says.

"Am I really that brilliant? No more training needed?"

"Get back to me about training when you're as good at magic."

I glare at him. "I'm still a fledgling. My powers aren't fully developed. It's not my fault if I freeze a lake or too." I argue, "And, in my defence, I'm a fire Flai, so I'm not ever going to be good at the hydraulic arts, because my abilities are usually all —"

"Fire-related? Who'd have guessed?"

"Oh, shut up."

He plucks the rest of the stars from my hands and stuffs them back in his sack of weapons. "Whatever. But for the safety of us both, just try to lay off the magic for now. Your wonky powers might not be your fault, but they'll definitely be mine if they kill you. And I'm not sure your mother wants her daughter returned in a block of ice."

I crack up, but Sparrow remains serious as ever, turning his attention to the sky. "Okay, we have... five hours to sleep before dawn, maybe four and a half. Take it or leave it."

I look at him, puzzled. "Aren't we supposed to be travelling?"

"Flunters'll storm these woods for the rest of the night after what happened. They'll surround us in an hour. In three, the news will spread to Ra, and more will come. But most will have arrived and set up camp in the woods by tomorrow. It'll be safer to travel because there won't be merchants racing across the country."

"And 'Nora?" I prompt.

"She won't catch us just yet. They're probably only just clearing out in preparation for Flood Tide, and at dawn, they still have to drag their carriages through the Frost Wilderness. But we'll be long gone before they get here, and then I have a plan for after that, so I know they won't catch up with us. We'll stop and refuel properly at my hiding place."

"What about the traders and Flunters who set up camp?"

"We can't do anything about them," he says. "Your cosy

little fire summoned half of Evrilore. We'll be careful when we leave and pray they don't see us," he says, settling down on his back to gaze thoughtfully up into the stars.

I do likewise, staring at the thousands of tiny little lights that ought to guide me but only illuminate endless empty highways of space, a million worlds out of my reach.

I wonder for a moment, as a shooting star whizzes past us, if I should catch one and make a wish, but it feels immature, like something a child might do.

If I made a wish, what would I wish for, anyway? I roll onto my side, thinking.

And I think for a long time, but there are too many options, and it becomes increasingly difficult to keep my eyes open.

I slowly sink into a deep sleep, still without an answer.

For anyone else, it might be an easy question. "What do I want that I don't already have?"

I wouldn't wish for equality, that's for sure. For peace, happiness, and love like the Sun Queen pretends to in her speeches.

Hidden in the crowds, I witnessed one of those public addresses when I was eleven, searching for the hope others are inspired to find within themselves upon laying their eyes on Her Majesty.

She posed on her balcony, mouth wide open to display a set of glinting teeth under eyelashes painted heavy and black and so very, very beautiful to highlight her warm and lovable eyes, for all of those things apparently made her trustworthy. Glossy lips, hair twisted into art, accessorized with flowers. She stood, talked, and with her lips, she birthed a million promises that are now forgotten and lost.

She will never be held accountable, nor will those dreams come true. There will never be peace on this island, and anyone who contradicts that statement contradicts the nature of all living creatures.

So, instead of wishing for the impossible, I'd make a wish for myself, plain and simple. Something selfish.

Surely, I deserve at least that?

The actual reason I don't know what to wish for is that I can't just want something. I'm a girl who has nothing in a world that has everything I dream of, so if I could have anything, where would I even start? To simply want is an understatement.

I suppose I've made my decision, then.

If I could wish for anything, I'd wish for the world.

CHAPTER 5

"Raven."

"Mm?"

"Raven."

"*What?*"

"Raven."

"Shut *up*, Peter," I groan, pulling the bag of weapons over my head like a pillow.

Usually, I would never be so lazy, especially in these circumstances, but how long has it been since I slept with someone watching my back? The need to protect myself has slipped away slightly.

But only slightly, and now that I'm regaining consciousness, urgency and paranoia hits me like a tidal wave. I order myself to sit up, take a breath, and recall the facts: Peter isn't here, I'm still alone and exhausted, and a human boy named Sparrow is yanking my blanket away and stuffing it into a sack.

He throws the heaped bag onto my stomach, the edge of one of the weapons poking through the hemp and digging into my side. "Ow."

"Sorry to interrupt, but it's half past six in the morning, and we have to be long gone by seven o'clock. Sleep well?" Sparrow asks sarcastically.

"No. I lay on a stone floor for four and a half hours, and

you snore."

"You talk in your sleep."

"You lie diagonally in small spaces."

"I do *not*," he says, offended, as he shoves a bread roll into my mouth, and I stare at him, plucking it angrily from between my lips.

"What?" he says, "It's not poisoned. It's out of *your* satchel. Eat."

I grudgingly agree to settle my stomach's growls.

"I'll tell you my plan while you finish breakfast. Since the minor inconvenience of the Flunters, I've had to rethink a few things. But it'll work in our favour. The Flunters from last night have summoned their friends, but their search was fruitless— we're too well hidden. They stayed overnight, and they'll search here for at least another month. It's a decoy, see? When Floodonora passes through the Frost Wilderness, they'll be halted by the promise of potentially capturing a Flai. Or, at least, slowed down enough for us to get to my next hiding place without being spotted, as all the Flunters and traders will be distracted searching here. All we have to do..." he says, grinning as he breaks into another roll, "Is not get caught leaving this lake."

"Probably easier said than done," I mutter dryly, peering over the edge of the ledge.

My Sixth Sense flares up before it happens. *BEHIND YOU!*

My heaps whips around just as Sparrow yanks me back sharply by the collar of my cloak, pulling the material tight against my throat. I reach up with desperate hands, my fingers grappling for my collar as it presses against my windpipe.

"Get- off- me!" I wheeze.

He releases me instantly as I gasp for breath, and I realize he's not attacking me, only warning me. Maybe even saving me.

"What are you doing?" he hisses.

"Looking," I reply, as though nothing could be more obvious.

"You're going to get us killed!" he exclaims.

Composing myself, I frown at him, dusting crumbs off my still-trembling hands. Don't show fear. "What's so terrible down there that I'm not allowed to see?"

"It doesn't matter what you see. It only matters that they don't see you."

I raise an eyebrow. "Who's "They"?"

"Let's just say that if they're a bloodthirsty tiger, we're dangling above its mouth," Sparrow states grimly.

I slap him across the face with the heavy sack of weapons, all my rage, confusion, and frustration finally erupting. It hits his cheek with a satisfying amount of force. Not hard, but hard enough to make a point and send him doubling over. Which is bloody hard enough for me.

"What," I growl, hitting him again, "Kind of metaphor," I cry, delivering another blow, "Is that!?"

He snatches the sack before I can reach for it again and slings it over his shoulder. "You're exhausting," he scowls, rubbing his face.

"You're the most irritating person I've ever met!" I hiss, "No, there isn't a camp of armed Flunters down there who probably have massive Fluns. There's a *bloodthirsty tiger*!"

He casts me his dirtiest look, and I cross my arms, feeling my palms tingling with annoyance. How little force it would take to burn him to a crisp right now…

He climbs to his feet, groaning. "Will you just put a sock in it? You're gonna get us caught."

"No," I say with a snort, "I won't."

He glares at me. "It isn't a question. I'm telling you to shut up, or..."

"Or what?" I challenge, narrowing my eyes.

He sighs and mutters under his breath, "*Else*."

I regard him with a tight inhale.

"I should've known you'd be this difficult since the moment you kneed me in the woods," he mumbles, shaking his head with a half-smile, "But if I have to drag you home to keep you safe, I will."

"Oh yeah? You and whose army?"

"The King's. I could hand you in and split the reward money with our lovely hunter friends anytime," he jokes.

"You wouldn't hand me in if your life depended on it," I scorn.

"Yeah? And what makes you think that?"

Our eyes meet for a second, and I swear that something darker and more sinister flickers across his eyes for a moment.

There is no reason. Sparrow could hand me over to those Flunters, and he'd have every right to, the way I treat him... I twist around and pull out the remaining nine throwing stars, tearing my gaze away from his bright, inquisitive brown eyes and stuffing them into the pockets of my cloak. His face is almost daring me and daring me to give him a reason why he should be helping me. But I can't.

"Nothing. Forget it."

We hastily gather up our things and finish breakfast. Sparrow hangs over the ledge on his stomach, proclaiming to be almost invisible despite looking like a suicidal slug, and observes the sight below.

"It's worse down there than I thought," he finally concludes, wriggling back into a sitting position.

"How do you mean worse?"

He runs a hand through his hair, sighing. "Worse, worse. Raven, there are thousands of them. Three hundred tents, maybe. They're mostly asleep, even the Flunters posted on watch, but they'll wake up at the smallest noise. If we were to drop something or slip and fall through the ice... We have no choice. Going down the way we came isn't an option. Maybe I could slip past them, but I look like a hunter. They'll notice a teenage girl, for sure. We have to go up. Can you climb?"

"If we climb, we'll be spotted for sure," I protest.

"We happen not to be 50-year-old men who live on raw meat and beans, Raven. This ledge can handle our weight, but they'd take a few hours to scale this cliff. It's a risky bet, but climbing down is a death wish," he says, looking up and producing a rope from the sack of weapons.

He lassoes it expertly over a jagged, outstretched limb of rock thirty meters above his head, looping it around three times, then turns back to me, "So I ask you again: can you climb?"

I roll up my sleeves, shrugging. "Trees, yes. Rocks, yes. Fifty-metre cliffs? No, but I can try."

He moves over to me, wraps two thick loops of rope around my waist, and then ties a firm knot. I stiffen up.

"What? Why are you looking at me like that? Like I'm patronizing you or something?"

"Because you are! Teaching me this, teaching me that. Hand me that rope. I can do some things, you know."

"Well, what do you want me to do? Lie? Sorry, your majesty."

I raise my eyebrows as he secures the rope around his torso. "Excuse me? I'm not a queen or anything, and I couldn't be if I wanted to. Flai don't have monarchs. We have chiefs and Elders, and even they have limited power over the people. Which you would already know if my mother sent you."

He sighs. "I meant you're acting like a queen, ordering me about and acting as though I ought to beg your forgiveness. I get enough crap back home for existing, and I really don't need it from you, Asgard. And a lot has changed in the Flai Kingdom since the Fall. Now, you live in castles and cottages, not cucumbers, and you have royalty. Besides, it's a cute nickname, and it suits you."

I stare at him. "Call me cute again and I'll set your hair on fire."

"Be my guest. 'S your grave when the hunters see it."

I cross my arms, face like thunder.

"Oh, cheer up, your royal angry-ness. Come here, and I'll give you a boost up to that foothold. From there, I can tell you where to go. Oh, and one more thing: try not to die."

"Some teacher you are," I mutter, following his instructions.

He offers his knee to me, and I push my boot on his thigh, scanning the rock for a foothold. Catching sight of a slight hollow in the rock, I shove my foot into it, reaching up and grabbing onto the lip of a tiny ledge. "What now?" I call back down.

"Alright. Lesson one. Don't look down."

I look down, and my stomach drops like a stone. Then, and only then, do I suddenly realize just how dizzyingly high up we are. The large expanse of the frozen lake stretches out below like a gaping set of jaws, surrounded by densely packed pine and oak trees on either side. There is nothing but forest for miles beyond that, and on the horizon, the city I left behind. It's funny how, from a distance, the threatening reputation of the Frost Kingdom fades away, leaving behind only a sparkling line of glistening snow-covered rooftops.

"You okay?" Sparrow asks, brow creasing.

"No. I looked down." I gulp, my arms trembling with the effort of holding on. "We're so high. I-I think I'll fall," I admit.

"My first time, I cried. You're doing very well. Take a deep breath, reach up to your left, and grab that bit of rock. It'll lessen the burden on your right arm."

I feel about above my head, grappling for the handhold. "Where?" I ask, a bead of perspiration trickling down my forehead. It's challenging to keep a solid grip without my hands slipping.

"Hold on," he grumbles, pulling himself up beside me and climbing calmly to the top. He turns and leans over the edge. "Throw up the loose end of your rope."

I do. He disappears out of sight, and the rope suddenly pulls tight around my waist. I yelp and scowl angrily at him. He gives an apologetic glance downwards at me. "I've tied it to a tree. You won't fall. Give me your hand, and I'll pull you up."

I mutter under my breath and reach one arm up, leaning into the cliff face so my weight won't be thrown backwards. He grabs my wrist tightly and heaves me towards him. I dig my foot into small chips in the rock, scrambling up with his assistance.

Finally, I reach the top and flop onto my back to catch my breath, gazing up at the cotton clouds overhead that shadow the weak sun. Raising my head, I take in my surroundings. Ahead of us is woodland, and beyond that, I can see only flat plains.

"For a fairy girl, you aren't that light," he gasps.

"I'm not a fairy. I'm half."

He rolls his eyes. "Tomato, tomato."

I tug at the rope around my waist, ignoring him. "Can you get this thing off me? I can hardly breathe."

He moves over to the measly rotting tree stump my leash is attached to, unties the knot, and yanks the rope away. I rub my sore stomach. "Thanks. So where are we headed, then?"

"We're going to head east towards the Willow District and then northeast towards one of the entrances to the Flai Kingdom, where the village is."

I look at him, stunned. "Wait. Hold on. There's a village? Of Flai? When you said my mother had sent for me, I didn't realize you meant there'd be a whole- But no one's been in the Flai Kingdom for centuries. It locked itself, right? After the Fall, it..." I trail off as he walks ahead, waiting for me to finish, and jog to catch up.

"Yes and no. It's complicated. You see, there are weak spots in the shield that covers the Flai Kingdom. The kingdom's centre, near the Jade Palace, is still heavily protected by the spell, but the outskirts aren't that hard to cross through if you know where to go. 'Course, I'm hardly allowed to know anything about it. They don't trust me, despite what they say. But, anyway, I do know this," he lowers his voice, his tone serious. "When a Flai dies, the shield's magic loses some power. And holes are opening up in the shield, holes that keep widening until they become entrances we can fit through. That's why the Queen wants everyone rounded up- to protect the shield. Without it, you're basically screwed. We don't know how many more deaths the shield can take."

I struggle to take it all in. "So, all these Flai... they're alive. And safe. And I never knew!?" I splutter incredulously. "I mean, for crying out loud, we have a queen!"

Sparrow laughs at my dumbfounded expression. "You really have no idea, Raven. There's still hundreds of Flai in this world, and one way or another, they all find themselves washed up on the same shore— with a little assistance from homefetches, of course," he adds, winking and giving a little bow. "They're all there, hiding. Didn't you ever wonder why you never met one of your own kind?"

"I did meet others of my kind," I say before I can stop myself.

"Well, where are they?" he asks, which turns my tongue to dust.

A sharp, painful memory of a small, skinny boy with terrified, piercing blue eyes struggling for his life against guards stabs at my heart. I still remember the look he gave me. It stalks my mind like a ghost does a graveyard. Help me; his eyes had pleaded, don't let them get me. Don't let me die! My heart sinks.

And Wynn. She had fought like a true Flai until the end. Like the warrior she always was at heart. And yet, it hadn't been enough. The faces of the guards who came for us that night still swim silkily through my memory like indestructible eels. The way they had been rough and merciless with us, even though we were only children. The way the captain's barrel had pointed directly at my forehead.

"Raven?" Sparrow touches my arm lightly, and I snap back to reality, jerking away from his hand.

"I- What?" I blurt.

He studies me, eyes narrowed. "It doesn't matter. But... are you okay? You looked different for a second."

"What? Is it my eyes? Oh no, I haven't—?" I feel behind me, running my hands over my shoulder blades, and exhale in relief. "—*Fluxed*," I sigh.

He laughs. "Wouldn't you know if you had? Don't you feel it? Surely, those things are heavy. And boiling. Gosh, how do you *breathe* under there!?"

I stare at him. "My mouth isn't on my spine, Sparrow. I can breathe perfectly fine. And yes, I can usually feel it. But when I'm scared, worried, or furious, sometimes I change without realizing it. It's a survival instinct."

"Hold on... Are you scared now? I scare you?" he asks, hurt.

"Why would you scare me? It's not like you're human, is it?" I say bitterly, "Anyway, I'm the one with magic— you saw what I did to the lake. You should be the one cowering in fear."

"Blimey, 'course I should. You're genuinely scary, you know. Completely mental. Last night, I thought you might kill me in my sleep."

"Trust me, *I've considered.*"

"Shocking," he mutters, rolling his eyes, and I chuckle, then compose myself.

Now isn't the time for jokes and bonding. I remember a quote they taught me in school when we were learning about Flai. It was a mass of misinformation, a jumble of random facts thrown together that didn't even make sense. But the quote was good. "Know thy enemy".

And indeed, I decided I should. I should know every part of his mind. The way he thinks, reacts, and feels. What he's afraid of and what he holds dear. And I know exactly where to start.

"Alright, but seriously." I say, locking my eyes with his, "Are you? Scared of me?"

He swallows, a haze of thoughtfulness glazing over his eyes as he seeks a suitable answer. "Why should I be?" he finally says. "Your magic? I know it's powerful, but I also know that it's there for a reason, and blasting orphaned teenage boys off the face of the planet isn't it."

I raise an eyebrow. "Orphaned?" I repeat. He goes silent, stuffing something into the bag of weapons. "Sparrow...?" He won't look at me. "You're an orphan?" I press.

"I don't like talking about myself," he snaps. I open and

close my mouth, sensing I should change the subject, but I can't deny it— A wicked part of me is pleased. I've found a weak spot and touched a nerve. "But science can't explain our powers. You don't know what we could do. Or when we might do it." I remind him.

"Just because I don't understand it doesn't mean I should fear it," he shrugs.

"That's nice to hear, and I wish everyone thought that way, but it's unrealistic. It's in your nature to fear the unknown. Evil is fear's accomplice, and while the people of Evrilore are under the influence of terrorization, my kind will be persecuted. The interesting thing is, we're the opposite of you. We think of you as the bad guys. So who those bad people are, who your fear influences you to hate... well, that depends on which side you're on," I point out.

"Side?" he repeats.

"You know. You and us. Us and them. Flai and Man."

Sparrow stops walking to stare at me, his expression full of wonder and puzzlement, "What if there's more to it than that?"

I tear away my eyes. "If there ever was, Peter and Wynn wouldn't be rotting in the Iceberg. And if there ever is, we can talk about it when it happens," I snap.

Ah. My weak spot. My turn to be exposed and show unwilling vulnerability.

Clever boy.

He slings the sack of weapons over his shoulder, finally satisfied that all his things are back in place, and we continue walking. Neither of us speaks for a torturously long time. We head east, with him glancing continuously at me and me graciously ignoring him.

I can't help but dwell on the fact that every second I'm not gaining knowledge of how the hell I'm going to get out of this situation, I'm getting closer and closer to a potential threat.

As we trek further, it becomes evident that Sparrow's itching to say something. "Spit it out," I mutter.

His face lights up. "Who's Peter!"

It's impossible not to smirk at how desperate his tone is. "I don't like talking about myself," I reply, using his own words against him.

Play along. Make him believe you're his friend. Joke. Tease.

"Oh, come on!" Sparrow begs.

"No."

"Was he one of the people who got arrested the night you escaped? Did you know the other Flai they discovered hiding in Frost? Were you all living together? I thought that the guard found three Flai separately, not together. Raven, the newspapers are barely allowed to say a few words. Please tell me. I'm dying here."

"Don't pressure me," I tut.

"You brought it up by mentioning him in the first place!" he gasps, exasperated.

I chuckle. "Alright, I'll talk. But you only get three questions, deal?"

"And here I thought it'd be a sensitive subject."

"It is," I say stiffly.

"So what kind of questions can I...?"

"I'm going to count to ten."

"What! No, I—"

"Ten," I yawn.

"Is he your boyfriend?" Sparrow blurts.

I stare at him. "That's your question?"

"Is he?" Sparrow presses.

I cross my arms. "No."

"You're telling me he doesn't fancy you a bit?"

"Nine."

"*Was* he your boyfriend?"

"He's eleven years old!" I cry.

"Is he dead?"

"Eigh— What!? No! He- he's…"

My shoulders drop as I realize I honestly don't know. I struggle for words. "Missing."

Sparrow pauses. "So why is he in the Berg?" he asks slowly.

The Iceberg is Frost's prison. It's located in the middle of the Frigid Sea, equidistant to all the kingdoms, and —what'd you know— it's a hollowed-out Iceberg. The prison's official name is "The Frigid Sea Penitentiary for Those Charged with Criminal Acts", or "the FSPCCA", but who can be bothered to say that? No, instead, it's just "The Berg".

The thing is, once you're in, you don't come out. It doesn't matter what you're found guilty of. If you commit a crime, you're chucked in there, forever awaiting a nonexistent trial. The worst part is, if you die in there, they just toss your body into the sea like you're nothing. Nobody.

Unless you're a Flai, of course. They'll drain us of magic, then leave us to swim for it. They don't care about keeping us there. As long as we lose our powers, we're safe. "Cured", as they say. Out of their way and none of their business. *Monsters*, I think, before turning back to Sparrow.

"We… we were hiding together in Frost with another Flai girl— Bronwyn. When the guards came, we were… we…" I fight back the wave of emotion threatening to turn my words into sobs. "We fought, but it wasn't enough. I got away. They didn't. They took Peter and Bronwyn, and I never saw them again." My voice is oddly flat, drained of emotion. It feels strange to recount what happened that night, like retelling a dream. It seems so far away. So long ago. Almost unreal.

"When did it happen?" Sparrow asks softly.

"A year ago yesterday. That's why I wanted to get out of Frost so badly. I thought if I escaped 'Nora this year, it would be like I was doing it for all of us," I say, "Like a rematch, and this time I swore I would win. But then, well, you came along and complicated things."

He picks up on the blame in my tone and averts his eyes. "Sorry."

I smile, but it's a strained one. "It's okay. You're a pain in the neck, acting like my mentor and whatnot, but it's kind of nice to know I have a different future, someplace else where I won't spend the rest of my life in hiding, wondering if I could still be with my friends. If I was too much of a coward. If things could have been... different."

A mournful silence floods the air between us, and I stare straight ahead at the woodland. Little bluebells sprout near the base of some of the trees, clusters huddling together with their petals closed to battle out the chill.

Peter used to love flowers because they bloom every year. He believed that if tiny flowers like bluebells could survive the winter, then we could, too.

Sparrow coughs awkwardly. "It's seven-thirty. She's been on the move for half an hour."

"Who?"

"'Nora. Keep up, your royal disengaged-ness. As I was saying, the Frost Wilderness will slow them down, but they'll catch up quickly if they follow their typical route. The one we would've if not for the Flunters. My first safe place for us is about ten miles from here. Is that alright?"

I'm absolutely icy after talking about my friends, but I

flash him a very nice, friendly smile. "Definitely."

We set off travelling again through the plains, the trees thinning out even more as the warm Willow District air blows in from the East. The sky bulges sluggishly with rolling grey storm clouds that threaten to burst and shower us with rain but always seem to manage not to.

Sparrow swaps the sack from hand to hand to stop his palms from blistering as we trudge on to stop his blistering palms. I offer to carry it, but he waves me away dismissively.

If we're lucky to find one, we rest under the low, thick branches of oak trees to catch our breath, nibbling half-heartedly on bread rolls.

I feel as though I'm walking in invisible chains to my own death, and I can't stop imagining his gang's hideout. I can't stop picturing my grave. A dilapidated shed in the middle of nowhere? A dug-out pit full of grown men and gold with wooden boards hammered over the top?

My mind conjures up every possibility, each one so real I can taste blood on my tongue. Just as my nerves are bordering on being unbearable, smoke and rooftops appear on the horizon. *Fire! Civilisation*! Miles and miles away, but at least there are multiple buildings and perhaps someone who'd take pity on me inside.

Frost-filled air nips at my arms, the sun now dipping out of sight between clouds overhead. We don't falter or stop, even as a thick fog tower rises all around us. Eventually, the trees disappear, depriving us of shelter. Now, the ground slopes, and the landscape gradually changes.

Sparrow glances in my direction and notices me shivering. I try to look stronger, drawing myself up to my full height to prevent myself from appearing weak or vulnerable. Normally, the thick feathers of my wings would keep me warm, but I can't risk fluxing even here in a desolate meadow.

Soon, the fog is so thick that it's impossible to see five meters in any direction.

"D'you want my cloak?" Sparrow offers reluctantly.

"N-no, thanks," I mumble, rubbing the standing hairs on my arms back down. "This whole mission is useless if we've both got frostbite and dropped dead by the time we arrive. B-better me than you, s-since you're the one who has t-to get me home, and you can't do that if you're swollen and black."

"Well, the temperature's about three degrees and dropping. We're not staying out all afternoon. It'll be night before we know," he says decisively. "Snow is on its way. We've got to hurry up and get to the shelter."

"Oh, n-no! Let's just k-keep moving at this pace." I try to mask the panic in my voice. This is it. This is the part where he takes me to a hunter's wagon, isn't it?

"Raven, that's ridiculous. We should..." he trails off and dashes forward suddenly, not finishing his sentence as he disappears into the wall of swirling white uncertainty.

I step cautiously forward. "Sparrow...?"

"Raven! Look!" he calls. I jog toward his voice. "What is it? Sparrow?"

"Over here!" he says, grinning. I spin around to see him standing under the bare skeleton of a birch tree, holding thick leather reins in his hands. He walks towards me, and a beautiful white stallion with a long mane and wide, blue eyes emerges from behind the trunk. A coat of snow covers its back. "Raven, he's a cremello! Do you know how rare he is? Oh, he's stunning, isn't he?"

Sparrow beams. He handles the horse with ease in a practised, caring manner. I sense it isn't his first time. Perhaps he's some kind of stable boy back in the Flai Kingdom— if that's even where he comes from at all.

His soft, loving expression makes me feel inclined to like

him to believe that he is genuine. And when he offers me a seat on Casper's back, I truly consider his offer, then freeze. "Uh... we can't just take him," I say slowly, "He's not ours."

Sparrow's face falls as he strokes a hand down the horse's mane. "But we can't leave Casper out here all by himself to freeze!"

"Ohhhh, you gave it a *name*?" I moan.

"*Him*," Sparrow says defensively, "I gave *him* a name!"

"Well, we can't steal someone's horse!"

"How do you know he isn't a wild horse?" Sparrow argues, "Casper here isn't wearing horseshoes or a coat. Someone probably left him here to die!"

I cross my arms. "He obviously isn't wild; he has reins, for goodness sake. And looks fine to me."

"Oh, no, no, no. Don't you dare? Casp here has had a tough time! He's faced abandonment! He needs to heal from his psychological wounds!"

"Wounds, Shmounds. We can't keep it."

He looks up at me with big, pleading eyes, but I turn away.

In the end, we keep it.

I'll give Sparrow some credit. A snowstorm soon arrives as Flood Tide begins its tantrum, and riding through it is much easier than walking. Casper, as the horse has been officially named, gallops easily through the wet, slippery grass. The snow is watery and melts quickly, but we'd still be soaked on foot as the water sept into our shoes.

Sparrow shows me how to sit so that it's comfortable, and I won't lie, I grow fond of the horse.

Soon, the village comes into view, a little cluster of cottages packed closely together with winding, cobbled streets and no lampposts. Good. I want as few people to see us as possible.

This hamlet is only fifteen miles or so from the border between Frost and Willows, a comforting thought because it means my goal isn't far ahead.

The storms Flood Tide brings annually are pounding down on us worse than ever, but once I'm past that last stretch of plains beyond these houses, I'll have crossed into the warmer regions of the island, where it's not freezing like Frost, or scorching like Ra, but pleasantly neutral. The thought warms me internally, and when Sparrow glances back at me, I notice an identical smile to mine is plastered across his face.

Somehow, it's such a genuine, kind smile that I want to leap off the horse and run for my life.

CHAPTER 6

"Welcome to Boots 'n' Shackles. Quality rooms for all, whether you're headin' somewhere, leavin' somewhere, or jus' need a decent place to lie low for a while. You're in room 17, fellas. It's a twin, but the bathroom's communal. I'm the landlady, Spok, and I'll run yez over the rules 'round here. Rule number one: no vandalism. Don't want you muddyin' up the damn walls. Rule number two: your keys are your responsibility. I ain't replacing lost ones, alright? Rule number three: We ain't nosy 'round here. We don't want no personal information. Just first names, fifteen shackles for the both of you per night, and nobody has to know you were ever 'ere. Final rule: all —well, most— Willow District and Frost rules apply here. That's no stealin', no killin', and absolutely no Flai. Any Flai found to be with you or under your protection will be arrested an' *you will be charged,*" she says, narrowing her eyes at us from behind the chipped wooden counter in the dingy lobby. "Say, neither of you are Flai, are you?"

My eyes meet Sparrow's in the small, chilly room. He gives a barely visible shake of his head.

"No," We both chorus to her. Sparrow slams the money on the counter before snatching the keys and dashing for the stairs.

❖ ❖ ❖

I stare furiously at Sparrow and throw the sack down on my bed with as much force as I can muster. "*This* is your big idea?" I cry, "A hotel?"

"Do you have a better one?" he argues.

I pound my fist down onto the thick quilt of my bed with annoyance. "Well, we could have slept outside instead of coming here and leaving a trail!" I yell heatedly, "How do you even know that woman? You said you knew places to hide! You said you could protect me!"

"I *can* protect you! *This* is the hiding place. And don't you dare act as though you didn't think this was a trap. You think I don't see how you look at me?" he snaps.

I'm speechless, thrown off-guard by the sudden confrontational shift in his voice.

"We'd die outside in that storm; you know it as much as I do! Sure, this place is questionable, but I've been coming here for years, and not once has she let traders lay a finger on me. We're safe. That woman saved my life once. I trust her."

""*Boots and shackles*", Sparrow! Her name is *Spok*!" I protest.

"You can't judge a person by their name!" he fires back.

"Maybe not, but I bet it wouldn't take much persuasion to make the old sack of onions talk, either!" I reply heatedly.

He glares at me. "Look, I know it seems like we're just paving your path to The Berg, but I know what I'm doing. This place isn't heaven, but it's not what you think, either. Spok is an old friend. She's kind and strong-willed, and she's never, ever denied me a room. She wants to help kids like us."

"And if she knew what I was?"

"She doesn't."

"*If* she *did*."

He exhales sharply. "Flai or not, this place isn't like the

rest of Evrilore. This inn is her territory; if anyone dared to come stomping in here to kill us, she would have her way with them. We may not be secure. We may not be guaranteed security. But we are safe. Under the slates of this roof, no one'll touch you. Besides, we'll look more suspicious if we're seen sneaking around and then ominously disappear. Instead, we have to blend in. The last thing people will expect us to do is go out in public, so we need to be unpredictable."

I cross my arms, scowling. "What if they predict we'll be unpredictable?"

"Then we'll switch tactics and be predictable."

"And if they predict we'll be predictable because being unpredictable is too predictable?" I demand.

He throws me a dirty look. "Just *trust me*."

I fold my arms, turning to examine the cramped room, and I find my face softening.

The walls are wooden and bare, and there's little furniture aside from the beds and a dresser, but a large overhead light casts a warm, inviting glow on the back of my neck, and my toes relish in the soft fur rug.

Our beds are sturdy, with firm mattresses and roughly sewn bedcovers. There is a used, faded atmosphere to this place. It's... Nice.

I sit awkwardly down, trying to remember precisely how one should act in their homely space. Sparrow has gone quiet, and I don't know how to start a conversation after our row, so I wait uncomfortably for him to speak.

"One night?" he finally asks. "Just while the storm passes, and then we'll leave, I promise."

I hesitate. "Fine. But you'd better stay true to that, or I'll get my mother on you," I say, and he gulps before nodding reluctantly.

Somewhat satisfied with this agreement, I wander over

to the sill and gaze out the window at the raging storm outside. Well, there's nothing outside— just a constant, unbroken sheet of white. One step out there would send a slash of freezing wind cutting across my face, a colossal mass of hail into my head, and icy rainfall onto my clothes. And it doesn't end there. The chill bites into your skin for hours until Flood Tide finally passes, hollowing out your bones and chilling you to the core.

"Maybe this wasn't the worst idea after all," I murmur, shuddering.

"Imagine trying to fly out there," Sparrow says from behind me as he fusses with his bedsheets, "When you're older, I mean, and you can use your wings."

I straighten up, puzzled. "What?"

He raises an eyebrow as though it's obvious. "Flai can't fly in the rain."

"Where did you hear that?"

"It's a commonly known fact!"

"Like not being able to get our wings wet?" I mock, "Yeah, if you're enough of an idiot to believe those stories." Then I pause, frowning. "Where's the bathroom, by the way?"

"Communal."

"I have to share a toilet with you?" I ask, horrified. He nods. "I can hold it," I mutter.

"Speaking of holding things, I'm tired of lugging that sack everywhere. Say we lessen the load, remove some clothes, and change into something more comfortable?" Sparrow suggests.

"Say we do," I nod, pulling off my rain-soaked jacket. "You can go first if you like. I'll wait outside or go inspect the toilet or someth—" I'm interrupted by a stampede of footsteps outside our door. "What in the world—?" I begin, bewildered. Then I notice it.

The best aroma I've ever smelled is creeping under our door, slithering up my nostrils— hundreds of different scents, each more mouth-watering than the last. My stomach growls, and I realize just how hungry I am. I bash open the door, sprint along the hallway, and rocket down the stairs. Sparrow chases after me.

"Wait! It's just dinner, Raven. Calm down! RAVEN! Blimey, we had bread rolls earlier!"

"YEAH, BUT THIS IS REAL FOOD!" I call back to him gleefully. I round the corner, dashing for the source of the smell like a dog, and skid past the reception desk into a brightly lit dining room.

Every inn guest is here, alongside its innkeeper, sitting down to eat at a long wooden table bearing nothing short of a feast fit for a queen.

There are golden-brown roasted potatoes, steaming vegetables, mountains of Yorkshire puddings, and freshly baked bread laid out on boards beside platters of cheese and crackers. Soup of every kind has been brewed and potted, and now it patiently awaits the inn guests, curls of steam snaking up from the liquid like serpents of scent. There are plates of fish and chips, pasta, nachos, fruit, jelly, macaroons, cake, chicken, noodles, broth, spring rolls, curries, samosas, rice, roasted vegetables, and even caviar, which is rare and specially reserved for Frost residents and Floodonora traders.

I race up to the nearest empty place setting, beside Spok, and eagerly pile up my plate. A goblet of light, sweet liquid is next to it. I sniff it, then take a sip. It's fizzy and cool, if not a little bitter, and I savour the flavour.

"Well, you've brightened up. If I gave you this, you'd be testing it for arsenic," Sparrow mutters, dragging back the chair beside me and taking a sip of his drink. I grin and burst into laughter when he places the cup back down. A line of froth covers his top lip.

"Everything looks so good that I don't even care about poison anymore," I grin, already piling up my plate and spearing a steak.

It's funny how a decent meal can always make it all go away, no matter how bad things get. Just for a second, bliss can be found in food.

I look around at all the different men and women sitting at the table and find the atmosphere somewhat calming but also slightly shocking. There are wealthy, clean-shaven men, bedraggled older women bent double with age, stocky, young traders, and even gipsies. Yet, they all sit together, the ladies and the hags, the sophisticated men and the travellers, conversing like old friends.

Can diversity and peace be this easy to accomplish simultaneously? If I transform right here, will they accept me as their equal?

I catch my reflection in one of the utensils laid out beside my plate, and slowly, the hope in my chest deflates.

No.

No, because no matter how different these people are, they are all still human, and I'm not. And that is where diversity draws its line.

I push away my now glum thoughts and attempt to tune in to some of the conversations floating around me. Any information on Floodonora is useful. Are they still frozen at the lake in the Frost Wilderness? Have they moved on? Do they already sweep efficiently across the landscape in a parade of terror that only my species must flee from?

"Yes, I did, mate. Cooked it all myself!" Spok is boasting proudly to a bearded man, "Don' you go doubtin' my cookin' skills! Best of the best, 'ere!"

"But you can't have prepared all this in just a few hours!" the man argues.

"You wanna bet!?"

"I'll pay double my rent if you can prove it!" the man challenges.

"Tha's not a good deal, man. Sure you don' wanna back down while ye can?" Spok asks teasingly.

"Back down, shmack down!" The man bursts, and everyone sitting around him slaps his back, cheering.

Nothing of use there.

I turn away and listen to the conversation at the lower end of the table.

"...Three wishes! Only three!" a cloaked woman exclaims to a hushed crowd, "Anything you desire, my friends. I shall grant them for three nights under your roof and a bottle of liquor... and, of course, a reasonable price," she grins, golden-toothed, "Watch all your fortunes come true."

I scoff and withdraw from my eavesdropping. Nothing of interest. I glance at Sparrow and whisper, "Heard anything good?"

He doesn't respond; his eyes are fixed on two men confiding excitedly across the table.

"...but they had to raise the price 'cause nobody wants to risk their necks to capture her," one says to the other.

"You know, if *I* were a Flunter, I'd personally leave it to the others. Let 'em have the catch and their fifteen minutes o' fame. There are still Flai out there, enough to go around. But the powerful ones— I wouldn't go near 'em," the tallest replies.

The other man nods in agreement. "You're right, Jun. Except I wouldn't step near a Flai, full stop. Jus' nasty business, tha' is." His face softens slightly. "But, I mean, the girl is jus' a kid, out there all alone with tha' boy..."

"Better to get 'em while they're young," Jun interrupts

grimly, "Saves everyone a lotta trouble. An' don' you go feeling sorry for 'em, Rupert. They're monsters, the lot of 'em. Christ, what if they came here after they escaped? They could be sitting at this table an' we wouldn't even know it."

"Crikey, Jun! Don' go 'round sayin' that. You'll get the wrong sort of attention. Of course, they ain't. As if they'd go out in public. Nah, I reckon they're hidin' in a tree or something somewhere," Rupert replies.

Sparrow casts me a smug look as if to say "*I told you no one would suspect us coming here!*"

"Well, the warrant'll jus' keep goin' up, so someone has to find her eventually," Jun says.

"Yeh. Eventually. But for now, I 'eard the Moon King is focusing on the Sun Queen. He wants her out of Ra. Dead 'n' gone. Apparently, he thinks she's…" he scratches his head, "What'd tha' paper say? An unfit ruler an' a disgrace to her realm.' Though everyone knows he jus' wants 'is daughter to take over another Kingdom for 'im, so 'is chances in the election are slim."

"Nah. The League is on 'is side, see? And if 'e captures that Flai girl, mark my words— he'll have it in the bag. All he needs to do is get one more Flai to prove he can protect 'is people, an' he's got the vote for sure."

Sparrow and I exchange swift glances. "Did you hear that?" he whispers.

I nod, then pause. "Who are the League?"

He swallows. "I've heard the League is the new government in Ra. Except it's very fishy. I don't know much, but it's supposed to be a discreet club of high-status, wealthy individuals. They don't overrule the King, but they have money, and their votes are worth five hundred regular ones. Each. In short, they're powerful, so if they back you up in the election, you're almost guaranteed to win."

I press my lips thoughtfully together, piling food onto my plate while staring absent-mindedly at Jun and Rupert. I eventually snap out of my trance and look down to discover that the result is soup-covered pasta with sausage, cabbage, gravy, and beef. "And why would they be on the King's side?" I ask Sparrow.

"I don't know, ask Jeremy or Joseph or whatever his name was. The point is that the Moon King has raised the warrant on your head. That's bad."

"It was *Jun*. And I know. But it shouldn't be a problem since we're already out of Frost, right? And there's the election: surely that will help direct attention away from us?"

"Are you mad? If the Moon King wants to win that election so badly —and he does, with so much at stake—then you're his best shot at getting the League on his side. Plus, capturing you aligns with his fierce and mighty image. There'll be a thick line of Flunters at every border in the damn world. Security will be ten times harsher. Everyone wants that bounty, Raven. Crossing legally is completely out of the picture for us." Sparrow rubs his temples. "We'll have to be smuggled."

I lay down my fork. "Alright. That's no problem for me. I've crossed plenty of borders in my time. But with the tightened security, I don't know. Do you have any... connections?"

He sighs. "Of course I do. The only problem is that with all these recent reports of a boy and a girl, one brunette and one ravenette —no pun intended— we'll look far too suspicious since you meet the exact description of the missing Flai girl."

"Can't you communicate with my mother? Send for help?"

"A direct communication device to the leader of a secret village of Flai in a so-called abandoned kingdom? What do you think would happen if that got into the wrong hands?"

I slump in my seat. "Good point."

Sparrow rests his head in his hands, sighing. "This is going to be tricky. Really tricky. I know a guy, but he doesn't work for free. And he'll figure out sharpish who you are. He's smuggled Flai before, but with this kind of warrant... the consequences would be significantly worse if we were caught. He doesn't want to end up in the Iceberg, let alone hanging from a post in a square. There's still a death penalty for helping Flai, Raven. Times are changing. They want every last one of you captured and killed, and punishments will only get harsher. At the moment, it's not safe to be helping any Flai, let alone the wanted ones. Finding a smuggler is trickier than ever before. We're talking more shackles than I can afford."

"A smuggler is a stupid idea anyway. Flood Tide'll make sailing too dangerous," I mumble, trying to think of a solution through my clouded mind.

I chew my roast beef quietly, concentrating hard, trying to think of something. It's suddenly like glue in my mouth. Then I notice Spok staring directly at me, and fear surges through my body. How long has she been listening? How much does she know?

"Sparrow," I say through gritted teeth, swallowing my mouthful. I casually point my fork beside me to where the innkeeper holds her gaze. I can feel her eyes burning into my cheek. But Sparrow only shrugs cluelessly, looking distracted. I glance over my shoulder...

But Spok is gone.

After dinner, we retreat to our room and divide clean, warm clothes between us. Sparrow slung them over the rusty radiator before dinner, so they're only slightly damp from the rain that leaked through his sack.

Awkwardly granting me privacy, he bows out of the room and disappears, returning a few minutes later in a black hoodie. I pull on a knitted brown jumper that's slightly too large and a pair of joggers. He returns just as I finish draping my old wet clothes on the radiator, and after he's in the room, we shove the weapon sack in front of the door and sit down to plot in hushed voices.

"I told you; she was looking right at me. She definitely heard something," I insist.

"She was probably just... just... I don't know. Can we please just focus on one problem at a time?"

"But what if she calls the guards and then—?"

"She won't. Spok's not like that."

"There's no guarantee that—" I begin.

"I've known her for over two years. She won't," Sparrow says again, his tone firm. "Now shut up and let me think."

"About what? Getting across the border? I thought we already figured that out: we're in a box and can't get out."

"Temporarily," he nods.

"Well, what are we going to do about it!?" I cry despairingly.

"We have to find another way out of the Frost Wilderness. We need to cross the border in a place they can't guard or keep track of."

"Like where?"

"I don't know. A boat or something," he mutters.

"Very smart. And where will we get a boat from? How will we get out of Frost Port and into Willows Port? How will we get through the city when an army of Flunters is there? And most importantly, how will we get past the Berg when we sail?" I burst.

"I DON'T *KNOW,* Raven! I'm trying! I'm trying really hard, okay!" he yells.

His words hit me like a whiplash, and I suddenly realize how ungrateful I'm being. Watching him sit on the bed, head in hands, defeated and exhausted, extinguishes any flames of sarcasm or anger have left to burn.

"Sorry," I mumble, "I'm just stressed."

"I hadn't noticed," he says coldly.

I swallow the lump in my throat, watching him rise to his feet and pace the room, pale-faced. He glances at the storm outside through the window, and I see him pause for a second.

"Sparrow? What is it?" I enquire, perking up.

"The storm." He turns to meet my gaze and strides over to me, eyes bright. "That's it. The storm!"

"Elucidate," I say slowly.

He places both hands on my shoulders, alive with excitement and the promise of a chance to complete his mission. "The Storm! Listen, if we travel out there, no one will see us, not even from ten steps away. We can easily get through this town to the nearest forest —there's one in a valley between a few small mountains near the coast— and it'll conceal us right until we reach the sea, where we can sail across the border, loop around to the Willow District, staying close to shore to avoid the Berg. Everyone will think we came from Frost Port, where security would've searched us already, giving them no reason to suspect us. After all, what kind of Flai could slip through Frost's fingers!? What's more, Floodonora can't travel in this! No one will bat an eyelid, Raven! No one will suspect a thing! We'll have to sneak out, though… if someone sees which direction we go in and tells traders…"

I gaze thoughtfully at him, and it's impossible not to see

how this is quite a good plan. That is, until my eyes stray back to the window. I suddenly remember the perilous blizzard that rages beyond it. "But it'll be dangerous?"

"Very," he nods.

"We could freeze to death."

"Most likely."

"And what about Casper?" I prompt.

"We can leave him at the stables here."

I shrug. "Or, you know, we could get rid of some dead weight and eat him or something. Keep our energy up on the way. It's the circle of life."

He stares at me, horrified. "Oh yeah? You're a bird. You're meat. How about I eat you?"

I step back, alarmed. "I was joking, Sparrow. I'd never harm an innocent creature."

"Well, you shouldn't joke. It's animal cruelty," he snaps.

"Says the boy in a chicken mask!"

He flushes and turns away from me to stare out the window again. "It is not a Chicken," he mutters, "And it was made from the feathers of a bird found dead. Cruelty-free."

"That's nice. Rotting corpse mask. Real classy."

"Take a hike," he scowls.

✳ ✳ ✳

After our discussion, I go back downstairs and wander around until I navigate my way back to the cosy sitting room. The chamber's layout is relatively simple: several deep, cushioned leather armchairs arranged around a coffee table, with a loveseat facing the ancient stone fireplace and a crimson rug to lower the harshness of the stone floor.

No one notices my presence (Or, more likely, they don't care that I'm there), so I sit silently in the corner.

The men complain about the storm while playing cards, and cigarette smoke wafts through the air, causing my nose to wrinkle.

Gradually, they leave one by one to retire for the night until I'm left alone to watch the dancing orange flames of the fireplace. I hardly notice Sparrow wandering into the room until he's beside me.

"Are we... going?" I ask, not turning away from the warmth of the fire to look at him.

"Ten minutes," he replies shortly.

"I'll meet you upstairs in five," I mutter.

Sparrow disappears with a nod, and just as his figure melts into the shadows of the stairwell, something prickles the back of my neck— a fixated, burning pair of eyes.

"Is someone standing behind me?" I ask, attempting to keep my voice casual.

"No," Spok replies from opposite me. She's surveying me with interest, a half-full glass in her hand and her sleeves rolled up just past the elbow. A jacket is slung comfortably over the arm of her chair, and she's poised as though she's been sitting there forever. Her half-unbuttoned brown shirt, blatantly unironed, camouflages her with the wall. "You should get to bed before the singin' starts. People get roudy when it gets late."

"How did you... do that?" I ask slowly, unnerved. "You were right behind me."

"I was."

"But—"

"It's Raven, isn't it?" She rises to her feet and strolls over to me, hand in pocket, to shake my hand. "I'm Spok."

"I know who you are."

"No, you don'," Spok says.

I lean uncomfortably back, assuming a position of relaxation. It comes off as a stiff retreat.

The landlady tips her glass in my direction and brushes a thick mop of brown hair from her face. "I know you, though. You're unsociable, like me."

"You come across as rather extroverted," I comment. "Or at least, you did at dinner."

Spok shakes her head, swallowing a gulp of her drink with a sour expression. "Tha's business, chick."

"What're you selling? Conversation?" I laugh.

"Maybe. What am I worth?" Her eyes lock with mine, and she smiles, her glistening pupils penetrating through the clockwork of my mind as I scan her, calculating my response. "Can't read me, can you?" She cocks her head to one side.

I steer the conversation back to safe waters. "Why... do you drink that stuff? If you don't like it?" I enquire, nodding to her glass.

She rolls her eyes. "Tha's what you ask me? I could 'ave the origins of the universe in this 'ead, and you ask me somethin' so pointless? *Borin'*. Why do I drink? Why does anyone do anythin'?"

"Enlighten me. What am I supposed to say?" I ask crossly.

She raises her eyebrows, takes another sip, and returns to her seat, sinking comfortably into the material.

"I thought that might be why you're here," I mumble. "Because you know I have questions."

Spok nods slowly. "Well, not just tha'. I know Sparrow's a traveller or an independent trader. I've deduced tha' just from 'is mannerisms and fairly predictable movements— back 'n' forth across the landscape, chaperonin', protectin', and almost certainly doin' illegal deeds. I mean, 'e wouldn't be 'ere if 'e wasn't. But 'is companions almost never surprise me, 'n' you..." She blows air out of her cheeks, enjoying herself now. "I want to talk to you. You intrigue me. You're different."

"And you're drunk," I snap, harsher than intended. I don't like the way she looks at me, picking apart my body language.

Spok yawns and stretches, unfazed. She's heard the insult a million times.

I close my eyes, pleading myself not to let the question slip past my lips. But Sparrow's "old friend" is irresistible, and she knows it, too. I can see her counting down the seconds before I snap.

"Who is he?" I finally gasp.

"A valued customer," she grins.

"He's been coming to your inn for refuge for over two years, even though his... *occupation* must remain a secret, especially from eyewitnesses, and you've noticed not a thing about him beyond the fact that he pays you?" I ask, disbelieving.

"Oh, I've noticed things. Like I said— 'e's a valued customer."

I narrow my eyes. "Are you... *protecting* him?"

"I don't know. Do I need to?" Spok asks coolly.

I bite back my response and compose myself, steadying my fluttering heart. "He told me he trusted you. Why?" I ask quickly.

Spok laughs. "He doesn't trust me; 'e trusts what I built. This inn, the people... everythin'. Sparrow didn' choose to be 'ere, but after 'e was forced to seek shelter, 'e began to turn up of his own accord, enthralled by the fact that I never reported 'im nor recorded 'is presence. Tracked, traced, sold, gambled, whispered, traded? Not ever, not to anyone, because despite his —and your— initial assumptions, I'm not like 'Nora, who'd've passed on his coordinates for a bowl o' soup. I'm *better*." She gestures to the room surrounding us, to the old, groaning wooden walls and the tattered rug. "This place is a border, a meeting point of both worlds, see? Respect'll get you far, but a shackle too many and a frost enblem'll have you chased by a mob brandishing pitchforks. People like Sparrow sit on moral fences, and Evrilore? We don' like that much at all. Here, he's probably freer and safer than whatever den of psychos he was raised in."

"Psychos?" I repeat.

Spok's eyes glaze over with thoughtfulness, the fire's reflection flickering in her pupils. "The first time Sparrow knocked on my door, 'e was absolutely forced to. 'E would've died out there in tha' storm, you see? But, naturally, I saw through 'im just as I see through you, and I knew that, alone, Sparrow would've gladly laid face-down in the snow before 'e appealed to a stranger for refuge. Or, perhaps, marched on to find an' save 'is next travelling partner. Sad, really. Self-hatred, I mean. Anyway, the reason Sparrow risked everything by comin' to my inn —includin' discovery and the summonin' of the Frost Guard— is that 'e had something to protect. Someone 'e had to keep alive, even if in chains. He didn't care what happened to 'im so long as his partner survived— and there was Sparrow Fenimore on a slab. He's a selfless, hollow tool sharpened by someone or somethin', an' 'e forces any kind of rationality, compassion or self-preservation onto 'is surroundings for fear of liking 'imself. That left two options: a hunter's gang or a tightly-knit traders' community. AKA, a cult."

I stare at her. "How could you possibly know that from him walking through the door?"

Spok chuckles softly. "The same way I know you're very, very illegal: fear. It reeks." Setting her glass down with a sense of finality, she rises to her feet and gestures to the staircase.

"The singing hasn't started yet," I eventually whisper.

"There's a boy in a bird mask waiting for you."

"I hate that stupid mask," I mutter, procrastinating for time and answers. Then I raise my head to meet her eyes. "Why would you tell me all of this? You said you were protecting him. Protecting his information. Now you spew it all onto me as though I've any right to him or his heart."

"Because you're different," Spok states.

"Different *how*? I haven't done anything."

"Yet you've done so much— you're the first to ask. The first to care."

"About *Sparrow*?" I frown.

"About why Sparrow functions the way he does," Spok nods. "All his previous partners either didn't care to ask or didn't notice his overly selfless tendencies. That's the trouble with people these days. They don't notice things. You're slightly better than average, of course —that'll be paranoia with a dash of childhood trauma— but you don't set out to understand things. That's what bothers me. Everyone's so busy hiding things that when knowledge descends on them like an angel's blessing, they hurry back into the darkness of their secrets like rats scurrying into holes. They think that if they're too distracted by others, they'll be cuffed and marched to death."

"Some people don't exactly have a choice," I say through gritted teeth. "Some people have to live glancing over their shoulders just to see tomorrow."

"Tomorrow's a fools' concern," Spok sighs. "It was mine once, and then life was pulled from my closest friend like a rug from under our unsuspecting feet. Easily, too. If you live in fear, what do you live for, if not even the glory of escaping your enemies? Most outlaws can focus on nothing but their next meal, next chase, next *blah blah blah*. All whilst outwitting armies and 'Nora herself. They never realize just how impressive they are. Never stop for a drink, either. It's silly," she finishes.

"How would you possibly know what it's like to live in terror, with your nightmares indistinguishable from your waking hours?" I ask, furious.

"How would *you*?" she responds, challenging me. Daring me.

But, no, I think as I bite my tongue, *she can't know I'm Flai*.

Spok swigs the last of her drink and gestures to the doorway. "Right, then. Goodnight. And remember what I said — use your senses, Raven. Don't look— *see*."

"I *see* plenty. For example, your accent's gone," I point out, my tone cold and accusing, laced with suspicion.

"Too much to drink," Spok says airily. "It happens."

"Oh? I've never seen alcohol change someone's pronunciation before."

"You've also probably never seen a "drunk" downing apple juice," she grins.

CHAPTER 7

Spok sends me upstairs with extra blankets to compensate for the unreliable heating. I attempt to keep my face neutral as I walk upstairs despite my racing heart. I've certainly stolen from strangers before, but this feels different. Spok feels different, especially now.

There's no response when I quietly knock on our room door, so I push it open and discover Sparrow isn't there. Perhaps there's another stairwell at the back of the house, and he went to swipe more food or something. Or maybe...

Maybe he's doing just as I feared— calling for Flunters. Perhaps I'm already in his cage.

I sigh, annoyed at myself for questioning his intentions again, and push the door closed, taking a mental note of the fact that there's no lock. No lock, no privacy. No secrets, not here. Chewing on the inside of my lip, I sit down on the bed and stare at my ghost-like presence in the wall mirror.

My hair's still knotted in its inky-black waves, and my cheeks look sunken as ever. I certainly *look* like a criminal. And Sparrow? He's warm and kind and human. It's easy for him; he gets to play the role of the hero rescuing me. Me? I'm the barbaric fallen angel invading places of human hospitality. Or so the mirror says, anyway.

My roommate returns a few minutes later carrying a thermal flask of piping hot tea, some swiped pastries, and fruit from the dining room. Technically, this is more stealing, but I suppose I can add it to the long list of things we've yet to be arrested for.

Finally, Sparrow packs all our things into his weapon sack, and I take one last, almost melancholy look around the room. My eyes drink up the rough bedcovers, the thin walls, and the rusty doorknob.

As much as I'd like to, I won't forget this place. It almost felt like home for a few hours, and I can thank Sparrow for that. He's acted as my roommate and my family, and even if it was just for a short time, it has made this place feel different from my past lonely hideouts, where I spent my days longing for Peter and Wynn.

For the first time in a year, I realize I'm not lonely.

Sparrow undoes the latch on the window and pushes it open, sending an icy gust of wind rushing through the room, then offers me his hand. I feel glued to the floor.

"Raven?" he says gently. "We need to go."

"I like it here," I murmur longingly.

Confused, he frowns. "Yeah, but..."

"But we can't stay. I know," I nod. Then I turn to him, readying myself for the cold outside. Just before I take his hand, I pause, looking for the right words. Finally, I settle on "Thank you."

Sparrow blinks, puzzled. "Whatever for?"

I don't answer him, and instead, I step out of the window and dangle my legs over the drop, turning around and lodging my foot into the brick.

"Careful," Sparrow warns.

I latch one hand onto the drainpipe with his arms outstretched above to catch me if I should fall. I feel around for another foothold, testing the brick with my shoe. It's near impossible to climb down, though. There's a skip below our window that rises to just a few feet below me.

Saying a silent prayer, I release the drainpipe and fall into it back first.

The crash nearly masks the unmistakable stride of footsteps outside the door of our room. Panic surges through my chest. Have we been spotted trying to escape? Does someone know my secret? Is it guards?

"Sparrow!" I hiss, "Someone's coming!"

"Climb back in! Hurry! We can't have anyone notice you're missing!" he urges me, reaching out his other hand to pull me back up into the room. With a clumsy jump, I manage to reach him, but I lose my grip and topple out of the window, landing on my back at the foot of the skip.

"Ow," I moan. "I think I twisted my ankle—"

"Be right back," Sparrow interrupts, quickly slamming the window shut and turning around.

I wait as minutes pass, beginning to think that I'm alone with the howling wind and he's shut me out—

Then the Boy in the Bird Mask drops onto the cold, hard snow beside me. "It was Spok. I told her you went to the bathroom, and I don't think she suspects anything, but we need to move fast. Are you ready? Alright, let's go," he whispers, taking my wrist and leading me through the cobbled streets.

As I walk, my breath rises in clouds of steam before me. The snow is already beginning to soak through my boots, halfway up my shins and continuously rising.

A thin sheet of ice covers the ground that's not snowed over, and at times, we both fall and have to double back on ourselves to pull one another up hastily.

It's treacherous business, and we're moving at an agonizingly slow pace.

Finally, we reach the village's local stables, where Sparrow paid a few shackles for Casper to stay the night. They're not much, just two small buildings side-by-side that offer what appears to be very rough shelter. The crumbling walls have no real insulation, and I hate to imagine what it must be like sleeping inside. It's locked up tight to protect the animals— as if the owner expects visitors tonight!

"How're we going to get in?" I ask Sparrow.

In response, he pulls the gold rapier from his sack, takes a swing, and slices the rusty padlock off. It cuts through the wet, old metal easily.

"This is trespassing," I point out.

"Arrest me," Sparrow says.

He steps inside, his hair sprinkled with white, and I wait under the shelter of the overhanging roof while he retrieves Casper.

"Wanna hop on?" he offers, leading the stallion out of the building. He's draped a thick blanket over the horse and strokes him fondly with one hand.

"No, I'm okay. I'll walk. I need to get some blood circulating anyway— I can't feel my legs and it's been five minutes."

We set off travelling away from the inn, heading north towards the Frigid Sea. It takes two whole hours for the rooftops to shrink entirely out of sight, but I have to remind myself that the small "settlement" we just left is barely a settlement at all, and if it were a real town, we would only be on the outskirts by now. I should be thankful we've made it this far unnoticed.

Sparrow and I don't converse much as we head for the coast. The blizzards are taking their toll on both of us, only worsening my miserable mood. With the spitting sky beating down on us worse than ever and the snow-polluted air overcome by fog, its easy to feel trapped, especially alongside my partner. The roar of the wind would muffle my screams, ans my footsteps'd be buried...

"Stay close to me, will you?" I mutter to Sparrow, hurrying to his side. "I don't... I don't like this."

If 'Nora's approaching or the hunters from the lake are on our tails, they'll be masked until a grand total of ten metres from us. I wouldn't even attempt to run at that point.

"We're slow," Sparrow observes. "We need to be moving faster."

"The st-storm'll slow 'Nora down, too," I reason.

"N-Not enough," he says shortly, taking me by the hand and striding onwards twice as fast as before. He stumbles through the snow like a drunken man, barreling madly onwards with a bitternes that has an origin I can't quite place. Maybe it's annoyance at the fact that this plan *must* work, or we die— by which I mean what's at stake. Or maybe it's panic at the fact that we couldn't retrace our steps at this point. Whatever the source, he glowers out into the darkness with cold, cold eyes.

After around three hours, Sparrow suggests a break, and I gratefully accept.

We sit down in the snow, letting it soak through our clothes, and he opens the flask of tea and brings out a bag of baked goods.

"H-how're you holding up?" he shivers, taking a long sip.

"Well... I'm c-cold," I reply, "But I'll live. C-can I—?"

He nods and passes me the tea. I take a hearty swig, then return it to him, not wanting to drain our supply more than we already have just by taking a few swallows. We have so much ground to cover, and we need to ration our resources strictly.

As the night advances on us, then falls through into the early hours of dawn, the temperature drops what I guess to be another six degrees. It must be far below freezing.

The fight against the brutal, constant cold becomes almost unbearable, and a stinging sensation creeps up my throat every time I breathe. Sparrow and I communicate mostly with our bodies, retreating into the hoods of our cloaks. It's all I can do to stay upright, never mind speak.

And besides, even if we do decide to talk, I'm sure the sheer power of the wind would muffle our voices. It's ear-splitting, howling all around as it dances in its mad frenzy. Sparrow is quickly battered into a hunch, ducking his face away from the storm.

He glances in my direction and notices me shivering. I try to look stronger, drawing myself up to my full height to prevent myself from appearing weak or vulnerable.

Usually, the thick feathers of my wings would keep me warm, but I can't risk fluxing even here in a desolate meadow during a Flood Tide. Not with Sparrow.

My companion's skin is beginning to look more like ancient porcelain than flesh, ready to crack and break at any moment. I don't want to admit it, but at this rate, we'll be dead by dawn.

I've felt the power of Flood Tide before, and it's far stronger than anything I can compare it to. Stronger than a hundred men, stronger than Frost's army. Perhaps it's even a worse way to die than the latter because it's not quick and clean, not done by the hand of man. You can feel it slowly happening to your body as your organs fail you. And indeed, I can feel it happening.

First, my speech disappears, becoming slurred when my teeth stop chattering enough for me to open my mouth and mutter something to Sparrow. My palms emit a weak light, but no fire appears, no matter how hard I try.

I also notice the pace of my breathing decreasing quickly. Occasionally, I stop for a few minutes to rest. Still, soon, this develops into a few minutes more, then more, then more, until I can only manage to travel short distances before my legs are completely numb again. We must stop while I recover and eat in small bites, battling the storm with the little energy I have left.

When Sparrow rather sluggishly asks me if I want to seek shelter, all I feel is confusion, and when I try to process what he has just said to formulate a reply, my mind is blank. We sit under a large evergreen, backs pressed against the trunk as we crack circulation back into our fingers.

Perhaps the worst part of the journey is when I stop shivering entirely. When I notice it, I don't feel like hugging or eating, and I don't respond or understand when Sparrow says little things I should be able to process easily.

Numbness overtakes me, starting as a hunched-up ball in the pit of my stomach and spreading outward, growing limbs inside my own. Suddenly, I know that I'm very, very close to dying.

Sparrow attempts to trick me into thinking otherwise, but I know that death is coming, cloak and all.

Gradually, my negative thoughts melt away, and cold, brutal survival instincts are underneath. Without a second thought, we set off moving faster than before, almost jogging.

Though it's worsening my condition, I'm determined to get to the coast. If I'm going to die, Sparrow isn't coming with me. I won't drag him down too. I'll haul him to the beach and into a cave even if I die trying.

I'll force him to cling to life if it's the last thing I ever do.

One of us will make it. One of us has to, or what will become of me? Will I fade into the background like everyone else? Will I join the thousands of Flai with no grave or story to be told? Will I ever know the truth about Sparrow and my mother? Who will know my name?

Suddenly, I'm terrified of ending up in that cold, dark place at the bottom of the lake.

We cross into a large section of wood that could have offered shelter in the summer, but now the trees are bare and dead, of no use to us. As I pass one, I study my white finger and press the numb tip onto the rough bark, then to my purple lips. I feel nothing at all, and when Sparrow takes my hand, gripping me tightly, I don't even notice.

That is, until I feel his weight pulling me to the ground as he collapses into the snow.

"Sparrow! Get up!" I cry, linking my arms under his and heaving him to his feet. I place my hands on his cheeks, drawing close and locking eyes with him. "You're not dying, alright? I'm not just your mission anymore. This is *our* mission, and we *will* get home to the Flai Kingdom. I have every faith."

"That's the kindest thing you've ever said to me," he murmurs.

"*Up.*"

He sighs, managing to smile weakly through the pain of the cold. "It's alright. I'm fine, see? Back to normal, see?"

Finally, the mountains appear on the horizon. A distant screech confirms my suspicions of deep caves, most likely an owl's call echoing from cavern to cavern.

We trek through the knee-deep snow and stumble a little up one of the mountain faces.

They are less like mountains and more like oversized hills

with deep valleys between them, but everything appears large and intimidating in weather like this, especially when you feel so fragile in comparison.

On the way up the slope, I struggle to keep my eyes fixated ahead of me. Darkness swims in and out of my eyesight. Sparrow heaves me up every time I collapse, despite becoming increasingly weak himself, and at last, we reach a tiny nook, a hollow in the hillside, most likely once a home to a family of rabbits that erosion widened over time. It's not much, but it's enough.

Sparrow uses his stiff, fumbling fingers to tie Casper up outside the cave under an evergreen tree with a generous net of branches to shelter him, and then we find the largest hole that leads into the hillside and enter the hollow once more.

The second I crawl inside, the wind that previously whipped at my cheeks disappears, and the feeling of having my legs falling off reduces slightly. The walls and floor are all plain, insulating soil, with ice covering the earth in a large sheet where the entrance lets snow and rain through the hole. I decide we can create a makeshift roof later, and instead of further inspecting my surroundings, I simply sit there and swirl my fingers around the cool, icy soil, running my palm up the wall and letting my shoulders relax at the feeling of finally being sheltered.

This space is cramped and small, but it is just about large enough for the two of us lying down and our things if we bend our knees and squash together a little.

Sparrow slides in beside me, looking something like the abominable snowman, and a burst of laughter escapes my cracked, blue lips, but then I realize I must look just as ridiculous and stop.

The simple act of laughing also causes my exhaustion to grow, and suddenly, with no new destination to reach, I find myself falling back into sleep.

"No... Raven," Sparrow gasps, breaking my train of thought, pushing my shoulders back up against the wall. I drowsily lift my head to meet his sharp eyes. "Raven, I need you to say something. Can you tell me who you are and where we are?"

"I'm me. You're Sparrow. We're going... home," I grunt.

He hangs his head back in relief. "Oh, God. You're okay."

After ensuring I can keep myself awake just a little while longer, we bring out the flask again, and I'm relieved to feel its warmth even from the exterior of the container. In my condition, I can't hold it properly, so Sparrow has to trickle the drink into my mouth as though I'm a sick baby.

It ought to be embarrassing, being fed like an infant, but it's so wonderfully hot I don't care.

Whatever trader supplied Spock's equipment, they certainly sold good quality stuff. *Floodonora does have its benefits*, I think.

It's one of the reasons they say, "may the flood bring you good fortune", though the original tale of how that phrase originated is quite awful.

There is a system with Floodonora. Wherever they are, certain areas of a town, wood, or beach always attract the most customers. New traders start at the outskirts of these areas and, as the demand for their trade increases, are generally accepted into the heart of the Flood Market, rising in the ranks of respect.

So the story goes, there was a single trader at Floodonora, a shell collector and jewellery maker, who was just too eager to make their final sale and was caught in the enormous rolling waves of Flood Tide before they could even register the shock of seeing the tsunami swell on the horizon.

Their stall was swept out to sea with all their equipment and money, and their reputation as a top trader was lost.

They became a figure of ridicule, and the Flood Market community exiled the trader. This allowed new merchants to enter the open spot amongst all the other Floodonora stalls on Stone Tide the following year.

It significantly increased the new merchants' sales as new businesses gradually wormed their way into the heart of the market.

So, I suppose the phrase is kind of demented. It's wishing you luck through another's misfortune.

God, what a twisted world we live in.

After a few minutes, I feel a little less stiff, but moving any part of me is still difficult, for the shivering has returned. This is likely a sign my condition is less severe, and hope sparks in my chest. Maybe it's not the end after all. Maybe death took the day off.

Sparrow takes the flask, and I watch his face relax as the tea trails down his throat. I wonder if he has it worse than I do, with fewer layers of clothing and far less of an appetite. After a second round of food, we've already eaten more than half the bag of goods, so he just shakes his head and suggests we eat the remains.

Now fed and watered, I feel much like a flower, ready to curl up my petals and pretend I'm lifeless until the sun next shines after Flood Tide has passed, but we don't have time for that.

We need to cross the border before Floodonora does, or we'll be swept up by traders no matter where we hide. Every cave, burrow, rock, and stalactite will be thoroughly inspected, possibly collected, and returned to the traders.

Yet, the outside world is so... tiring. Returning after finding refuge here in this tiny burrow feels ludicrous. Why leave?

We take turns collecting damp firewood but cannot strike a spark up between the soggy twigs. The roof of our den is beginning to pile up with snow, the ice is cracking, and the temperature still feels like it's dropping. Symptoms of frostbite settle in after another ten minutes, but we both know we aren't headed for death, so we just pull all the clothes and blankets out of the weapon sack and lie with our backs to earth, buried in soft materials, with no willpower to crawl to our feet.

My eyelids grow heavy, but at least one ounce of resistance must remain in me because I don't want to let down my guard and sleep next to Sparrow— only heaven knows what he could do.

I glance at him, expecting a rigid, accusing look to mirror my own, but he just looks utterly deflated. After everything he's done for this trip —and for me— I realize how harsh I'm being. How unfair. I have never considered myself cruel, but how I treat Sparrow is far beyond reasonable.

I give in to guilt and curl up beside him, shivering in my damp cloak. I draw into his embrace even more as minutes bleed into hours, and he doesn't object. If anything, he seems relieved to have earned my trust at last.

With the wind howling and the blizzard furiously hammering its fists into the roof of our den, it's impossible to sleep. Not just because of the noise but because weather like this brings back painful memories.

As Flai, we can't get healthcare anywhere, but in the winter, we still get sick like anyone else.

Some days, it's just a cough and a cold, and others... On other nights, I would sit against the wall of our shack in Frost with Peter's head in my lap, trying desperately not to cry.

A coat of sweat covered his forehead, and yet he shivered uncontrollably. Sometimes, when he coughed, he would cough for minutes at a time, and every breath was fragile and thick with mucus.

Bronwyn sat curled up in the corner, face pressed into her knees. Medicine wasn't something we could steal, nothing that people tossed into skips or sold on the street. It was locked up on the highest shelves of the most secure shops— the kind with square ceiling lights that never stop humming and little machines by the door that detect when you haven't paid for something.

And so, all we could do was hope with every ounce of our hearts that he would pull through.

On the eighth night of his sickness in 2052, when things looked utterly hopeless, he reached out for my hand with a bony wrist, his eyes wide, and looked up at me. It was barely a whisper, but I heard it as it floated from his lips.

"Sing."

And now, slumped beside Sparrow, the strangest thing happens— I do, the words slipping through my lips in slurred, indistinguishable chains.

Gradually, my throat warms, a friend to familiarality.

It's a song I've always known. I don't know where it comes from or who taught it to me, but it's been there in my head for as long as I can remember. My voice is rough at first, but then I slowly recall how to sing. Or, at least, how Peter liked me to sing every night after that one. Soft and gentle. Sad but kind.

I never had the heart to explain to him what the song meant, but I think a part of him must have known, deep down, that it was a goodbye— a goodbye in case there was no tomorrow.

The lullaby comes easily to me, and every word holds a thousand whispers, a million things I want to say to the boy sitting beside me. When I finish, I realize I'm smiling because I've regained a part of myself that's been slowly shed away in tiny pieces over the last year. I remember who I am. Not just an outlaw but a sister. A friend. Someone's family.

I close my eyes and imagine Peter is here beside me now. He would've loved to hear that. To know I haven't forgotten him and that I still think about him every day.

My eyes flutter open to see Sparrow staring at me with great interest. "I didn't know you could sing," he says thoughtfully.

"I- yeah," I say awkwardly. "Sometimes."

"You're a beautiful singer. How come... how come you've never done that before?"

I shrug. "It's kind of a personal thing. I don't have people to tell, so I don't tell people."

He stares at me for a long time, eyes searching. Finally, he shrugs and nestles down to sleep beside me.

"You should."

Beaming uncontrollably, I attempt to hide my flushed face.

Sparrow thinks my voice is beautiful. And another thing—

Suddenly, I don't feel so cold anymore.

CHAPTER 8

I'm awoken by Sparrow's soft murmurs, which soon became annoyingly repetitive, and roll over to find him in a deep slumber.

For a moment, I consider simply going back to sleep, but there's too much bright daylight shining in through the entrance to the hollow, and no matter how much I toss and turn and curl up with my knees to my chest, it eats its way into my vision.

At last, I sit up fully and make quiet work of slowly shifting around our supplies to access each one easily. I begin counting our things just because it's something to do.

We have roughly twenty weapons in the sack, including eight throwing stars, a rapier, and several guns. Additionally, carried between Sparrow and me is an inventory of supplies: a nearly empty flask of tea, which I drain onto the snow and replace with rainwater, all the extra clothes, and more food swiped from Boots 'n' Shackles.

While I wait for Sparrow to awaken, his breaths become louder and more irritating. I consider muffling him for a second, but then I might accidentally suffocate him, too, so I think better of it.

Then I lay down and gaze at the ceiling, and all at once, he stops snoring, and the world goes silent.

It's the kind of silence that's so peaceful, so unscathed, that you simply wish to stay in it forever. It's the first moment of true calm I've experienced in days. No wind roars at my ears, no icy droplets pound at my skull, and no Sparrow terrorizes and excites me all at once, twisting my emotions into knots as I battle with distrust.

I know Sparrow isn't awake, just that he's slipped into a more peaceful slumber that consumes his mind entirely. Still, the childish thought that he could have been awake and watching me raises the hairs on my arms.

I tell myself I'm being silly, that I'm just paranoid. Yet, the more I mull over my strange, random bout of unease, twiddling the throwing stars between my fingers, the more it deepens.

Did I not wake up in his arms? Chest rising and falling slowly, no weapon in hand, at complete vulnerability? At complete contentedness and comfort?

Panic flares in my chest, and I push myself up again, my eyes fleeting to Sparrow's face. The face of a stranger. A stranger who, despite helping me all this way, trying to protect me, and taking an interest in my past, is still nothing but.

All my thoughts from last night about being too harsh were surely just the cold messing with my brain because now I wonder how I ever grew to briefly believe him. Now, it no longer makes sense. I can practically hear him preaching. "Oh, look at me! I'm an orphan. I'm rejected for my species! I've been sent on this long, tiring journey to come and bring you back to your mother despite having no home, family, or friends!"

I curse myself. I should have seen right through it.

Overall, I have no real reason to trust him. For all I know, he's a hunter's son, yet I gave myself to him completely last night. I trusted him like—

Like I trust *Peter.*

This thought hits me so brutally that I'm completely paralyzed, rigid with terror.

Raven, what have you done? A tiny voice whispers.

I turn and seize the sack of weapons, pulling the strings tight to close its mouth, and then scoop up our remaining clothes, quickly dressing myself in the extra layers.

My heart pounds against my ribs as I swing the sack over my shoulder. Guilt's already brewing in my stomach, but I can't focus on that. I have to leave before it's too late.

And where will you go? The voice in my head sneers.

I'll go somewhere, he can't find me. Somewhere no one like him will ever find me again.

Uh-huh. And where are you really going?

I swallow, pausing for a millisecond to reconsider my decision. Behind me, lying on his side with bangs strewn across his face, is a boy. Simply a boy asking for my trust. Can I really do this? Leave him to die?

"I'll tell you where I'm going," I whisper softly, hoping that, somehow, he can hear me. Maybe even forgive me for what I'm about to do. "I'm going somewhere where I know you can't hurt me."

Because that's just it. Now that Sparrow's gained my trust, he has the power to hurt me.

And of all things, even a thousand armies, a hundred Icebergs, that is what scares me most.

When I emerge from the hollow, I stop dead in my tracks.

Directly in front of me, with his back turned, is a Floodonora trader cooking breakfast on a portable stove. An early departure from Frost Beach before Flood Tide, I assume. He must be. Otherwise, he'd have been delayed with the others.

The scent of sausages wafts towards me as the hunter's big, meaty hands poke them about. He curses as his fingers linger on the meat for a moment too long, and he bends down to scoop up snow to lather over the burn.

My mouth is sand, and my heartbeat rapid. I duck back into the hollow, taking quick, clumsy breaths as the facts lay themselves out before my eyes.

Sparrow called Floodonora.

Somehow, when I was asleep, he snook out and hiked to the Flood Market. Some of them gave up searching for us at the lake and were impatiently on the move again after they visited Boots and Shackles, and Sparrow gave our location away for fistfuls of shackles. Either that, or he made a fire to signal our location and arranged this meeting before he found me in the woods.

It all makes sense.

It's perfect.

We're surrounded by Floodonora, and I have no option. I must stay here with Sparrow.

A bead of sweat trickles down my forehead. I can't! I *can't* stay here. I'm physically incapable of the act. My body convulses with terror at the thought.

He'd kill me, sell me, rope my hands together, and take my wings. Tears are brewing in my eyes, and Sparrow's stirring. Time is slipping through my fingers as quickly as water.

So, I make my decision and rip my shoes off, transfer them into the sack, and place a foot on the sturdy earth. I'll be quieter this way. I have a chance this way.

I place my hands over the lip of the entrance and heave myself up and out into the open. It's like becoming a bullseye.

Dropping down onto the earth and raising my shaking

legs into a crawl, I curry along, kick rapidly up into a sprint, and dash away from the hollow. Do I turn the hunter's head? Am I seen? Was that a gunshot or a falling log?

Creeping through the snow as quickly as I can, I round the corner of the hill, loop around to the back... and here, not a single human in sight. My heart's still pounding, but I don't dare stop. I keep walking until I find a cluster of evergreens, their thick needles closing around me like fingers as nature becomes my armour.

Magic fizzes at my fingers, delighted to be surrounded by greenery, and it's only here that I allow myself to rest.

The icy, chilly wind still bites at my skin, but not as brutally, harshly, or as painfully as it did yesterday. I'm far less likely to freeze to death in the morning. The sun, weak and pale like a sick child, barely manages to groan through the sky as it births light to the world, and the cold has retreated significantly.

However, the same awful conditions I faced last night will return when dusk falls. Perhaps less extreme, but less is still only less. It's time to get out of here.

I find myself wondering what time it is. Definitely early, but the sky is still bright, and it's the middle of winter, too, which suggests that I'm just crossing the boundary between morning and midday.

The thick, grey storm clouds that were previously hunched together are beginning to thin out, breaking off into small wispy trails that are blown towards the coast. This is where I'm headed, so at least the weather's one thing I don't have to worry about now.

I sigh and lean back against a tree, panting heavily. I'm sure it was around here somewhere that Sparrow tied up the- I halt. A neigh rings through the trees, clear and bored.

I push myself up and venture deeper into the maze of

pines until I find the one Casper's tethered to.

I run my hand along his neck, and his large, sad eyes meet mine. I consider hopping onto his back, knowing he'll make me travel much further, much faster, but then I'd also have to feed him and care for him. I can't carry the extra burden. Besides, someone might find him. Someone could stumble upon him and take him in and—

And ship him away to a circus. Take him to the army to be whipped and abused. To shoot him dead if he can't run fast enough.

"I'm sorry, buddy," I whisper regretfully, stroking his neck a few times and entangling my fingers in his mane. "I'm so sorry."

And I am. Really. I wish I could bring him because it's one less life my distrust will cost today, but it's impossible.

Plus, I'm quite possibly giving the stallion a more peaceful way to go. I'm a danger to him as much as to anyone else.

With the weight of two lives on my shoulders and knowing I will be responsible for this horse's starvation, I almost miss my old life for a moment, back when I was simply running without worrying about any friends.

But then I remember my daily unhappiness, the loneliness that consumed me at night, keeping me awake, and I remember that I'm done with running. No more running. Ever.

Then, something tugs at my thoughts. Am I not running right now, though? Running from my problem instead of confronting it, as usual?

I shake away these thoughts. My safety is more important than my choices. My heart yearns to return to Sparrow, but my head tells me otherwise, and I know which I trust more. My heart keeps me happy, but my mind keeps me alive.

For a second, I pause. But then again, which is more important, happiness or life? I mean... what's the point in life if you have no joy? Is that really living?

I stand for several long seconds, weighing up my decision, swaying from one foot to the other, my body still deciding which way to walk. Then I turn and plod away, trekking miserably but determinedly through the snow.

But I wipe a single tear from my cheek as I do so.

It takes around an hour to reach the landscape which tells me I'm near the coast. The hills on either side of me flatten into a vast expanse of evergreens, and seagulls soar overhead, squawking noisily.

Every step in my freezing boots makes me feel smaller, like I'm just a mite trapped in the snow, a small child caught up in what's supposed to be a winter wonderland. I'll just have to grit my teeth, pull up my hood, and bear the awful weather.

My stomach seems to twist and writhe inside me as I travel further and further away from Sparrow. At this point, there's no way I can navigate my way back to him and no chance he can make it to civilization before the jaws of starvation will clamp down. Returning to Boots and Shackles in this snow is impossible, especially without food.

I know I left him to save myself, but somehow, the prospect that I have killed him in the process makes me far more uneasy than it did this morning.

Running away from the little hollow in the hillside is tough work. The snow built up at least six inches during the night, so now I'm wading through snow almost up to my waist.

Rushing through layer after layer of it grows tiresome, and I find that I'm still exhausted despite having slept for a good few hours last night. It becomes clear that I'll never get far at my current rate, and Sparrow will probably be able to follow me. This thought unnerves me as much as it excites me. I'm embarrassed to admit it, but a part of me almost hopes that he's perhaps watching me right now.

Maybe he'll run out from behind a tree, and I will stand there in shock before running forward and embracing him. Maybe he's been following me since the moment I left.

Or maybe not. Maybe you left him, and that's that. He's not coming back for you this time.

When I occasionally stop to rest, I climb up the trees and survey my surroundings from the uppermost branches. My stomach growls with hunger, so I dig around in the weapon sack for Sparrow's dagger and carve out the outer layer of the bark to reveal the soft, chewy, edible stuff underneath. This takes some hacking, but I eventually find a tree to satisfy my needs, open up a hole big enough to scrape out a snack-worthy pile, and nibble half-heartedly until I finally reach the beach.

It's not much— just a long stretch of damp sand and wave-cut platforms littered with pebbles everywhere. When I finally set down all my things at the water's edge and raise my head, I swallow hard and let myself look at the Berg for the first time in real life.

From a distance, it looks like the sea has risen into an enormous wave, only one that has frozen instead of collapsing into seafoam. Rising out of the Iceberg itself is the top of the Penitentiary. Made of stone and as large and ugly as its reputation, it looks at least two hundred feet tall. Waves that are easily visible even from such a distance crash against the base of the fortress, spraying a foam of saltwater over its bricks before the building is wiped clean of the stuff by what I suspect to be some kind of forcefield.

Seeing the Berg is an unexpectedly harsh shock, as I hadn't even thought about the giant fortress since Boots and Shackles. Somewhere inside, cries for freedom reverberate through giant underground chambers. And in one of them... are Peter and Bronwyn.

I can hardly bear knowing they're in there while I stand outside, free and alive. Who knows what torture they've been subjected to?

Part of me wants to rise to my feet and bolt from the beach. I can't look at the misshapen lump on the horizon again. The action alone feels deadly enough to kill me.

But it isn't as though that matters now. The prison always lingers at the edge of my subconscious, always awaiting my rare moments of peace like a devil at my door so it can ensure I spend every spare moment crushed by guilt. Even in my dreams, I can see my friends begging me to rescue them, and I just know I will have to live with these nightmares.

Unless...

Well.

Unless I choose a different ending for my friends.

I move past the beach onto the base of a cluster of boulders, listening to the waves lap, swell, and then break at the edges in a tedious cycle. My body still feels compelled to turn back, but I must ignore the urge. The only problem is that I'm alone now, with nothing to distract me from my thoughts and no other goal to reach.

I chose the coast because it's a source of water and food, but now, where do I turn?

The thoughts come easily as I look out at the waves, feeling rather exhausted and considerably guilty. *What if you're doing everything wrong? What if you shouldn't have left? What if you weren't a coward last year and stayed with your friends? What if you had all escaped together?*

On and on, and I cannot shut them out. First Sparrow, then Peter, then Bronwyn. Each of their faces flashes through my mind, and I find a single tear trickling silently down my cheek for everything that could have been.

I let it fall, the salt reminding me of the ocean bowed down before me.

Maybe it would have been better if I'd never betrayed them and come quietly. Sure, we'd still have been locked up, shipped away, and sealed off in the world's darkest corner... But at least we'd have been together. *You were my friends...* I think, my eyes stinging, *and now you're gone.*

Suddenly, I stop crying. What am I *doing?* Sitting here, crying like a baby!? I don't care what the odds are! I don't care that it's too late. I have to save him. I have to go back. I can't lose him, too!

Just as I'm about to climb to my feet and set off running, a small brown piece of fabric slaps the uneven, gritty floor beside me.

Confused, I crouch to pick it up, carefully turning it over in my hands.

"What will it take for you to trust me?"

I freeze, not daring to blink at his words. That voice. I know that voice.

"*Sparrow!?*" I choke, looking wildly around.

"So NOW you're happy to see me!?" he cries, snatching up his mask when I'm facing the opposite direction and slamming it back onto his face.

I whirl around. "Oh my god, Sparrow..." I don't quite

believe it. "How... when...?"

"When you left me for dead, and I came after you, that's when!"

I open and close my mouth but can't find a response.

"I came after you, Raven," he says again, quieter this time. "I came after you because I didn't want you to get hurt. I came after you, even though you abandoned me. I came back because I'm your friend. Clearly, the feeling isn't mutual."

"I... Sparrow, I am your—" I begin, my tone weak. "I... I panicked! I'm so sorry. I was scared, Sparrow. There were traders everywhere, and I was about to come back, I really was, because I felt terrible, and..." But my sputtering is useless, my tongue sandpaper.

"Then say it, Raven. Say that with every fibre of your being, you would have absolutely, certainly come back for me!"

I cast my eyes onto the floor, shaking my head. "I-I don't even know you, Sparrow. Floodonora is hot on our trail. At least try and understand that it looked like you called that trader! I mean, what do you expect from me?"

"What do I expect? *Faith*!" he gasps, "Just a little. Just a molecule of it! D'you know how much I've risked to do this? To take you home?"

"I never asked you to do anything!" I cut across him sharply.

"*YOU DIDN'T HAVE TO!*"

I throw my arms up in annoyance. "Okay. Fine! I'm sorry, Sparrow, for not trusting you. For not being your best friend five minutes after we first met. But you have no idea who I am. If today has made anything clear, it's that we could not be more different. We do not understand one another, and you were given the wrong girl to rescue because I don't want to be saved. Saving me is not what this is."

Sparrow gapes at me. "*Given* the wrong girl? I *asked* for you. I asked to be the one hunted, arrested, and murdered. I asked to be here. I requested to take you home," Sparrow interrupts bitterly, and his voice is so disappointed and hurt that I physically flinch. "I was willing to risk everything to get you home to your mother, and you know why? Because I've only ever rescued groups before. Siblings, families. And I wanted you because I know what it feels like to be alone. I have no family, Raven, so I wanted to bring you to one! And you can't even... you won't even let me—" His voice breaks away into inaudible crumbles. He just sits, composing himself for a moment, lost somewhere between tears and fury.

I move forward to comfort him, but he shakes me away. So I do the only thing I can.

"The food is in the sack. Take it and go home, Sparrow. Just go. Clearly, I'm not ready for this. I'm not ready for a mother, a family... not even a friend," I say, miserable.

"Oh, for God's sake, Raven. I didn't come for the food. Only had you kneeled in the snow, I'd have left! Only had not a snowflake cooled you, not a noise stirred you!"

"Why?" I breathe, utterly baffled. Utterly astonished by the complexity of this boy's compassion for a girl unknown to him.

"Because I want to give you what I'll never have. Because I care."

"But you *don't*," I whisper miserably. "You- You *can't*. No, Sparrow. *No!* Just... listen to me for a second. You don't come close. You're nowhere near me. I am so, so far away from you. You don't care about me because you haven't even brushed the surface— and trust me when I say you really, really don't want to know me. And if you did, you wouldn't care at all. You'd find me repulsive in every way."

He holds my gaze. "Then throw that sack in the ocean. I'm

not here to survive or fulfil a mission anymore. I came back for *you.* And I may not know who you are... but I want to."

I tear away my eyes, disconsolate. "What, because I'm your stupid mission?"

"I may be a homefetch, but I'm also a person," he reasons, sitting down beside me. "A person who cares about you very much. You don't have to understand why, but you must understand that you've really upset me. You left me to die today. You did something unjustifiable."

"I said sorry. I'm *sorry*!"

"Oh, for God's sake! Look a bit deeper, will you?" he says harshly, rising to his feet and striding away down the beach.

He doesn't wait for me.

I stare after him, crestfallen and numb with shock.

The worst part is that I can't understand my pain any more than his. I'm just incapable and immature. It's agony.

So, look at that. In the end, he hurt me.

And it was all my own fault.

CHAPTER 9

Sea water kisses my feet, carrying away dirt and grime, and slips between my toes, sending a chill up my body like a thousand daggers scraping into me all at once. Each lap of waves carries a million tiny grains of sand and pebbles, mini razors.

It's uncomfortable.

But maybe that feeling's just courtesy of the permanent pain carved into Sparrow's expression.

The Boy in the Bird Mask stands beside me with his foot kicking the sand aside to gradually reveal a rope: The key to finding our boat.

Before now, I might have questioned Sparrow, thinking he was setting up a trap, but I must allow myself to trust him now more than ever. If I don't, today's events will only repeat, and I'm unwilling to let that happen.

The tension between us is almost too great to bear, so thick that I could slice it with a knife. We're absolutely unmistakably worlds apart, and I've no idea how to bridge the gap that I've so cruelly widened. Perhaps a partnership is all this is now. Maybe I'm just a mission, and he's just a homefetch, and pursuing any kind of friendship is a fantasy.

I watch him as he works, wishing he could hear my thoughts and see how much I regret everything. My mind is conjuring up all sorts of cruel scenarios as punishment for my actions. The worst of them all, perhaps, is a scene in which he spreads a pair of remarkable brown wings, like a true sparrow, and soars away, leaving me standing alone on the shore, tears streaming down my face as I call his name out to the empty starless skies that crush me.

I attempt to stifle my silent tears, locked in the surreal but frightening world of my mind's stories. Still, eventually, they overcome me, and I become a part of the ocean itself, my tears merging with the salty, open arms of the water's embrace.

Without his concerned glances and calming, reassuring, slightly mad optimism, I feel... lonely, I suppose. I miss his voice, constantly making stupid jokes.

Sometimes, I try to start a conversation, but it's evident that he's not in the mood, not to mention my mountainous guilt constantly getting in the way.

Any words passed between us are short, simple, and emotionless.

When he finishes uncovering the rope, I notice that it snakes up the entirety of the beach and disappears into the thicket of trees. He wipes his forehead and turns to me. "Can you give me a hand pulling this thing out?"

I nod, hastily wiping my eyes, and shake back my sleeves, bending down to pick up the rope. As I wrap both palms around the material, I notice it's incredibly stiff, as though it's been buried under layers of sand for hundreds of years.

"How did you know this thing existed?" I pant as we pull back a few meters of rope together.

"Spok was telling tales of her ancestors at dinner. They're a mixture of sea merchants and outlaws, which hardly surprises me. During one of her tales, when she was blabbering about five of them who supposedly escaped the Berg but had their boats sunk by Frost soldiers, she mentioned that the small batch of rowing boats they used had been dragged up by currents and hidden on an "Icy wasteland of desolate beach, between two great kingdoms, where only the washed-up villains of the world could discover it"." Sparrow gestures to our surroundings. "Sound familiar?"

Honestly, it's a terrible description that could have led us anywhere, but I refrain from mentioning this. The icy wind is bitter enough already without my comments.

After labouring in silence at the rope, the boat finally comes into view with one last defiant tug. It's small, and the wood's a little rotted and sandy, but usable for the short journey we must make to cross the border and appear as though arriving from Frost Port.

A small silver plaque is nailed to the side, bearing the carved word "Valerie".

"Right, now we just have to get her on the water. I've crafted my best attempt at a makeshift anchor from rocks so she won't float away. I think," he adds.

"You think?" I repeat, arching a brow.

"I hope."

He sets down the sack, the last item, and looks me directly in the eyes. "If you want to, erm, sit down... I guess we need to talk."

I exhale a sigh of relief. At least he wants to get this over with as much as I do. We lower ourselves onto the sand, and I wait for him to speak. He doesn't.

"Sparrow, listen, I—"

"I've been meaning to tell you something," he interrupts, "About the plan to get you home."

I nod slowly, spirits drooping as I realize this talk won't be what I hoped.

"I've told you the truth," he says, then pauses, "Just not... all of it. I was still figuring everything out, but I finally decided last night that... well..." he struggles for words as if trying to decide how to phrase them, but then just blurts it out. "Raven, we aren't going straight to The Willow District."

"What... what do you mean?" I ask slowly. He smiles just a little, but it doesn't hold the same warmth that it used to.

I'm not forgiven. This isn't over. So why can't we just talk about it and get it out of the way? For the first time in a year, I'm actually *with* someone. I might even have a friend. And yet, I've never felt more isolated in my life.

"Raven...? Are you listening?"

"Sorry, what?"

He clears his throat awkwardly. "What would you say if I told you we're going to pay Peter and Bronwyn a little visit?"

I'm ice in one swift question, delivered easily by Sparrow but intercepted with panic, guilt, and terror.

"Yeah. That's right. I've been thinking that we could rescue them."

"That's impossible." The words fly out of my mouth so quickly that I almost believe that they're true. Almost. But I still have a single spark of hope, enough to light a fire if I allow it to... which I won't. Yet. "How?"

He stares thoughtfully at me, then shrugs. "I've been rescuing Flai all my life, sometimes from more than fifty armed guards. It's part of my job as a homefetch. Remember what I said to you in the Frost Wilderness?"

"I'm your priority," I recite.

"Exactly. It's my job to get you home safely no matter what it takes or die trying. 'S why I'm human. Because there's a good chance I will, and they don't want to risk one of their own kind. Anyway, I've rescued Flai surrounded by traders and Flunters. I've picked locks, burned through ropes, coordinated teams, and then reformed plans at the last moment. I don't see why I shouldn't be able to rescue Flai directly from the cell, either."

"Look, I don't care if it's possible. I already tried to kill you once today, and I'm not losing you again. Especially not in there. Plus, we don't even know for sure if they're alive, let alone in that... that *thing*!" I gasp.

"They're Flai, Raven. And they were arrested by the Frost Guard. Why would they be anywhere else?"

"I don't know! Floodonora could've stolen them when they were transported to the fortress, or they could've been humanized and freed!" I exclaim.

"You and I both know you don't seriously believe that. It doesn't matter if you haven't got powers anymore. You think Frost really ever lets anyone out of there?"

"Yes! No... I don't know! I don't care if it's true or not! There's still a chance we'll be taking a pointless risk, and it's not a gamble I'm willing to make!"

"Then wait here, and I'll do it. This is... It's like my thing about killing, okay? I just have certain... beliefs. And I can't take you home knowing that those children will die in there," he explains, "It's why I volunteered to be a homefetch in the first place. Plus, I know you're always thinking about them anyway. I could have run up and stabbed you in the back these past few days when your eyes glazed over, and you wouldn't have even flinched. The closer we get to that place, the harder it's getting for you." His gaze solidifies as he glares at me. "Isn't it?"

I tremble under his cold scare, goosebumps running up my arms. "Excuse me? What are you saying? I-I'm... *weak*?" I splutter.

"You've been running for so long. But eventually, we all have to face what we've done. You abandoned them that night, Raven. Didn't you? You could've tried to save them, couldn't you?" His eyes cut straight into the darkest part of my heart, the place where my secrets lie.

All I can think is, *he knows*. He *knows*. But I can't show it.

"Y-You don't know that. You don't know anything about me," I stammer.

"Yeah, you keep reminding me. But I've seen guilt before, Raven. It's a timeless thing, and it's not specific to you. I saw it the day you told me about your friends," he replies, softening his tone. I know he's trying to get through to me and crack me like an egg.

"I didn't abandon them. I *didn't*," I shoot back, tearing my gaze away, but I can repeat it as much as I wish. The thickest blanket of snow does not hide the stain of blood and betrayal, nor will my lies.

Something stirs inside of me. Something deep, something I tried to forget—

Love.

As though every spotlight in the world is burning brightly onto my skin. The devil looms overhead, smiling upon me as I struggle to push down tears.

Peter, the boy who could be my brother. Bronwyn, the girl who I fell asleep beside in the dark. My friends, my family. The people I loved and still do. I yearn for them.

I raise my head out of the dark and the shame and lock eyes with Sparrow. I know that he's right. Not only do I owe them this. I owe myself this.

I owe myself an opportunity to right my wrong.

How can I possibly sail past that floating fortress knowing they are inside somewhere, chained up, left for dead? The answer is: I can't.

I will break.

I don't want to break, I silently communicate to him.

Then make up for your cowardice, his eyes reply.

The next hour or so is spent preparing for our stakeout. I check over all the equipment at least three times, laying it all out on the beach until our inventory has Sparrow's approval, and then he begins to draw out a complicated plan of action on the sand with a stick.

Even after he teaches me the basics of using every weapon in the sack, I still feel like this is hopeless.

In books and movies, there's always a secret floor plan that's uncovered from an ancient library or a weapon that can be used against the "bad guys". But we have nothing, and the most we can do is hope.

We're walking into a room full of horrors with the lights off! Attempting something that no one has ever tried before - or, well, so we think. According to Spok (who is honestly not very reliable in terms of information), there have been others to try and do this before, except they were breaking out of the Iceberg, not in. And there's a huge difference.

The Moon King doesn't want prisoners escaping because it humiliates him, questions his authority, suggests he cannot protect his people, and destabilizes his throne... but there has to be a reason he doesn't want people getting inside, as well.

Is there something we aren't supposed to see? What are they hiding?

A tingle shoots up my spine, and I turn, eyes scanning the pine trees behind me, but, as always, there's no one there.

This is when I finally remember Casper. "Sparrow, where's the horse?".

"I sent him galloping back to Boots and Shackles."

"But he doesn't know the way. He'll get lost and freeze when the next blizzard hits!" I panic.

"No. He's a clever boy, and the second I untied him, it was like he instantly knew what I wanted him to do. In a few hours, he'll be warm and safe."

"Oh," I reply, relieved. Then guilt floods my stomach. "I really thought..."

"That you'd kill him too," Sparrow nods, and his tone isn't spiteful or nasty, but simply factual.

That is, perhaps, the worst thing. He's right. I *was* going to let them both die.

"Yeah," I answer, remorseful.

"Well, he's not dead. That's all that matters. Now, to get back on topic, I've drawn up a basic action plan. I managed to get a few words out of the guests at the inn. They were mostly fables and useless stories, but an ex-guard mistook me for a fascinated little boy and let a lot of stuff slide. Granted, it took some alcohol, but... now, that's irrelevant. This is the Iceberg, its rough shape, and this is the sea."

He points to two places on the map he's created. It's pretty detailed for something assembled of stones, twigs, and leaves, and it's quite obvious which bits of the Berg he's pointing to.

"This is the port entrance, or "the alcove", as the guard liked to call it. It's surrounded by a load of guards and soldiers and is where all the prisoners who're shipped to the prison enter via boat. And this —see here?— is the southern entrance, where people of great importance arrive. People like the Sun Queen and the League. Of course, they still arrive by boat, except no outlaws and criminals are coming in, just high-status individuals with personal bodyguards that travel with them instead of waiting for them at the Berg— meaning prison security is much less tight as they don't require protection. There's only one other entrance to the fortress: the underwater entrance used for submarines. This is the one we'll be using."

"Okay, and what does it look like inside?" I ask.

He clears his throat. "Well, that's kind of the problem... I don't know. Once I started prodding for details surrounding the inside of the Berg, the man got suspicious and kicked me out of his room. The only thing I can really do is give you a bunch of weapons and tell you to shoot on sight, or perhaps we could pretend to be prisoners? Maybe if you transform into your Flai form... But no, because we'd surely have a guard escort and handcuffs..." He trails off, and I know he has no sensible, safe plan, so I plaster a smile across my face.

"Sounds like a piece of cake," I reply, brushing a strand of hair back from my face, "We'll be in and out."

Unfortunately, my reassurance is a pane of glass, and he sees right through it.

"You don't think this is going to work at all, do you?" he sighs glumly.

"Well... how bad can it be in there?"

"Oh, please, Raven," he mutters. "You're Flai. You've seen the most heavily funded, tactical parts of Frost's defence system. And you know exactly what kind of tech they use. So how can you possibly think that we can beat them?"

I stand, uncertain, searching for an answer... and then I find it, snatching it easily out of the air as though it was a leaf in the dancing breeze. I know precisely what to say. "Because you're doing this for someone else. Because you know you have to, or I won't make it across that border, and my friends won't get a childhood. And anything you do for others, you put your entire heart and soul into it. I didn't trust you before, but I do now. If it's for me, I know you'll find a way. You always do because that's just the selfless person you are."

He processes my words, then smiles. "Thanks, Raven. But honestly, I was relying on you for a sarcastic comment."

"Sorry, I'm out of those today." I shrug.

"No kidding. It's like you were just cleansed or something. Are you sure you're only half angel?"

I snort. "Oh, shove off. I was just trying to be delusionally positive for once like you are."

He blinks. "Oh. For a second, I thought maybe you were just being nice."

And then he walks away.

I move away, swearing under my breath. Just when things were getting better, I slipped up, and now his walls are back, guarding his feelings and his friendship. Great.

Sparrow leaves me alone with the voices of the mountain singing somewhere in the distance. It reminds me of church choirs singing in Ra and Willows, where religion overrules most people's lives. The churches are astonishingly beautiful, carved by many delicate hands over centuries to form the most incredible architecture on the island.

The choir sings as the wind moves from cavern to cavern, and the sunlight beats down on my face.

Except now, as I fall into a nap on the soft dunes of the waterline, I don't rise out of the water, and their voices turn repetitive and evil.

Instead, I look up with two terrified eyes as someone shoves me under the salty waves and holds me firmly there.

The real sand and sea around me warp into a baptism pool. Golden curls catch the fractured rays streaming through the church's stained-glass windows, lighting up one familiar, merciless face.

"Peter!?" I blub, inhaling a mouthful of water.

His hands press me to the very bottom of the pool as I

thrash, lungs burning, gasping for air. "Help!" I gurgle, "Help!"

But the church is empty. No one hears my screams. The choir is somewhere far away, and they won't see him or save me!

Suddenly, the water and the tiled stone walls that contain it disappear. My wings unfurl, and I attempt to fly away from my friend's grip, but it's useless. He pushes me harder and harder against the church's marble floor, causing my chest to scream with agony as I'm squashed.

Without warning, the tiles beneath me crack under my weight, splitting apart to reveal nothing beyond, and I plummet into the void with them. I try to flap my wings, but —I forgot— I can't fly yet!

Instead, I plunge down through the darkness, the light above shrinking until it is nothing. My stomach seems to fly into my throat, and I find that as I fall, the walls are slowly closing in on me. The fall seems never-ending before I finally smash face-first into the bottom, blood spurting from my nose, my skull cracking, my bones fracturing—

And then I'm in a grave, bloody and pale, as my solemn-faced friends stand around me in black robes and shovel dirt into my mouth.

Slowly, rhythmically, their spades clatter about. The earth is slippery and impossible to climb, but I desperately thrust my chin up to the sky, out of the soil, and fill my lungs with air. I have to breathe. I have to try and get help.

"Wait! I'm alive! Don't bury me! I'm *ALIVE!*" I cry before Sparrow appears above and delivers the final forkful of dirt that piles into my throat and cuts off my vision, filling my nose with the stench of earth.

As he does it, our eyes lock, and I know instantly that he has no intention of saving me. I can hear someone crying above, but I cannot determine who.

There's no hope of crawling out of the grave now. The earth presses down on me, and the wails get louder.

It occurs to me that I could shove aside the dirt and use it to climb. There's still time, still hope— But I don't move. Instead, I just lie there and wait to die.

That's the most awful thing.

I lie there and wait to die.

Gasping, screaming, and scrambling up the beach, I bolt away from a grave that never existed.

"Afternoon," Sparrow says coldly from beside the boat. He must have carried it down the beach while I was sleeping because now the waves lap at the hull.

Either that or the tide has come in. I stare around wildly, feel the back of my perfectly intact skull, tenderly press two fingertips to the tip of my nose, and touch my soaking wet hair for signs of earth.

"Sparrow... what time is it?" I ask faintly.

"The sun is going to set soon, so about four o'clock. You only fell asleep about two hours ago, but I figured I'd let you rest before I pulled any more of my dark and evil tricks. And then you started screaming. Tell me, what horror awaited you?"

"You're still mad at me," I observe. He says nothing, and I sigh. "I was in a church, and Peter tried to drown me."

Despite asking, he seems hardly interested, and I know he's only making conversation because he wants to dangle the fact I dozed off and left him to finish prepping the boat in front of me like a shiny gold medal in front of a cat.

Another reason I'm in debt to him. Again.

"Also, you buried me," I add matter-of-factly, though I

still feel shaky inside.

"Sorry," he shrugs. "Now hop in the boat, your royal sleepiness. We don't have forever."

I swallow and bite back a feisty response, walking over to where he stands and wading a few meters into the water to swing both legs over the rim of the *Valerie*.

He comes up behind me and tugs the anchor out of the wet sand, causing the boat to drift a few meters out. I dangle one leg over the side to drag it to a halt with the top of my boot.

"Get in, quickly!" I call back to him, "I can't hold this thing in place forever!"

"Coming," he replies, splashing water everywhere as he runs into the sea. His cloak billows outward like an expansive black storm in the water around his ankles, causing him to trip and stumble, but he manages to get to the rim of the *Valerie* and scramble over the side just in time.

I exhale and collapse with relief, removing my foot from the water and flopping onto my back, and Valerie is instantly grasped by the wind, drifting forward and away from shore.

Rolling over onto my back to look up at the white and grey blotchy sky, I feel a sort of triumph.

We're on our way and moving, with no more delays and no more distractions. My vision wanders to the fortress on the brink of the horizon as I climb to my feet and sit in the boat, feeling a tingling warmth in my palms that has nothing to do with my powers.

Peter, Wynn... My jaw sets.
I'm coming.

CHAPTER 10

"Alright," I say breathlessly, dropping the anchor over the side of the boat. "What now?"

He watches as the length of the rope descends toward the ocean floor. "We wait until dusk."

"And then?" I prompt.

"We swim," he says.

The rope stretches out like an uncoiling snake as the anchor burrows itself into the ocean floor, and the boat shudders to a halt.

The waves gradually turn black as the sky paints its reflection, the swift brush of dusk working efficiently to conceal us in its canvas of oily, star-filled ink.

The wind is monstrous and ugly, whipping at us, and storm clouds roll sluggishly overhead. But the blizzards and rain are headed for the Willow District as the island resets, preparing for another Flood Tide three months from now. The storm is subdued, like a nest of angry hornets caught in smoke, and gradually, the winds die, leaving the waves to still into a glassy mirror until absolutely everything is silent, and I've returned to that dark place at the lake's bottom.

The place where heaven and hell could join hands and strangers' unrecognizable faces could converse like old friends. The place where you can't differentiate between blood and water or Ravens and Sparrows.

My eyes wander to the horizon, where, in the distance, the Berg sits patiently and silently, its lights all shut off like a predator awaiting its prey in the dark. Within, its underground laboratories still hum with electricity. Its corridors are still patrolled by guards carrying enormous guns.

I can already hear the stampede of guards' footsteps pouring into my ears, all coming for us in a tidal wave down those long, disorientating corridors, each equipped with high-tech weaponry. Each blade, each pistol, is specially designed to kill.

Whoosh. Ping.

And just like that, I'll drop dead, bleed out on the floor, and die.

I look back down at my knotted hands to find they are shaking. No, Raven, I tell myself, that's not going to happen.

But it might, my mind whispers cruelly.

But it won't.

But it might.

The temporary unnerving darkness of the Berg's exterior is nothing but a large, deceitful cloak. Who knows what trickery awaits us within if it can be this easily disguised on the outside?

Sparrow and I sit in silence as we wait, both of us slumping. I attempt to catch his eye, but he's gazing into the distance, lost in thought.

I wish I could open up his head and view the careful clockwork of his feelings so I could at least know where we stand. But, as always, his calm, logical expression remains unrevealing, offering me no insight into his large, icy eyes.

I've noticed that Sparrow's two major frustrating

personalities never seem to mix. Either his eyes narrow as he calculates logical escapes to seemingly inescapable situations, or he's beaming and unreasonably delighted. It's like watching a clash between normal, joyful Willowfolk and the grim-faced Flunters that stride through their towns on patrols— and it's utterly inhuman.

When we met, it was immediately apparent that he'd been trained like a hunter, but his mood drops to a thoughtful, collected calm when he's not being delusionally optimistic. It makes me wonder what feelings and thoughts are locked tightly away from me, the rude Flai girl he just met.

Makes me wonder who —or even what— Sparrow Fenimore is.

Though I suppose I'm mirroring his behaviour because perhaps I've guarded myself, too. Certainly, strips of me have peeked through in our conversations like clouds parting for the most minuscule slivers of sunlight to reach the Earth, but the sister and best friend I am to Peter has remained sealed tightly away. What would he think if he knew the compassionate, selfless person I can be? What would I think of myself if I dared to show her to him?

No.

That person is not for him to hear, not for him to see.

She was cuffed and marched away to a prison of ice with her family in 2053.

After an hour that feels like a thousand years, I've collected a fairly small handful of stars in my palm, and the night has completely concealed us.

Now, from a distance away, we're invisible.

Sparrow is the first of us to take action when the time

comes, turning around and handing me a short, shiny blade from the weapon sack.

He also retrieves a shocking number of pistols and tucks them into his cloak before passing me one for my own use, as well as the throwing stars, and then finally, he pushes all our other belongings under his seat.

"Okay. We're ready. You have your weapon. I have mine. If anything goes wrong, shoot first and talk later. These people won't reason with us. They *will* kill you, and you must walk into this with the same brutal mindset. You *must*, Rave. That being said, we're better people than they are... or less brainwashed, anyhow. Aim for their feet and try not to fatally injure anyone. These men don't deserve death— they're just taking orders. One last thing— if we get separated, and you get in trouble, get the hell out of there and don't look back once." He says that last part with a ferocity that I've never seen before, gripping my arm. "I mean it, Raven. Promise me you'll get out."

"I promise," I pledge.

Sparrow's face relaxes as he peers over the rim of the boat. "It looks clear down there, but you never know. There's likely underwater protection surrounding the fortress, so stick close to me and watch the seafloor."

I nod, my stomach swimming with nerves. "But how will we see?"

Sparrow points to his lap, where a headband rests, a torch attached to its front. "Stole it from Boots and Shackles," he explains, "Works underwater. Figured we'd need it, and it turns out..." he pauses to fasten it in place around his head, "...I wasn't wrong. It's pitch black, so we'd never be able to stay close."

The thought that he was already planning all this for me back at the inn causes my guilt to rebound so intensely I can barely contain myself. He's always thinking about me and never about himself. What did I ever do to deserve that?

Sparrow's selflessness no longer spikes distrust in me, just curiosity. Was he conditioned to be this way? Are his actions a disguise for a lack of self-value? How does one care so little for their own well-being?

Who is Sparrow Fenimore?

I genuinely don't have the faintest clue.

Just as he swings his legs over the side of the boat, preparing to dive in, my hand comes down on his shoulder.

"Wait," I gasp.

Sparrow turns, looking slightly impatient. "What is it? If you're feeling too nervous, I can do this alone. If you need to go back, we can—"

"Look, Sparrow, I... I just... I'm sorry, alright!" I rush. "Just- please! I can't do this without you."

"Raven, I'm right here. I'm coming with you. What do you mean?"

Our eyes meet. *You know damn well what I mean.*

"Raven, do you really think now is the time?" he finally asks.

"It might be the only time left I have," I reply.

The silence stretches between us, wider than the Frigid Sea, as more precious seconds tick by. "Alright then. I forgive you. And you're *not* without me— it'd be stupid to try and pretend anything but."

"You really aren't mad?"

"I'm just... frustrated. But I know it's not easy for you, and —"

"I am trying, though. I know I don't get it right

sometimes, but I want to trust you. I do. I'm just scared, I guess."

"Scared? Of... me?" he asks, surprised.

"Of you and me. Of this unjustifiable attempt at a one-sided friendship... I'm scared that if I let you... If I let anybody..." I bury my head in my hands, "You wouldn't *like* me, Sparrow. You don't even like me now. None of what you're doing is for me. It's just what you do. And I'm not this. I'm not anything. Not sarcastic or cold and secretly soft. Not a sister, a singer, or caring. There's nothing beyond what you think is a frontier. There's nothing to like. Not in me." I lower my gaze, shameful. "That's why I'm scared I'll only end up alone like I did after I lost my friends," I finish.

Sparrow nods, sits back, and sighs heavily.

"Sparrow?" I ask in a small voice.

"Yeah?"

"I don't want to be alone anymore," I whisper miserably.

He takes my hands in his, gripping me tightly as if to remind me I'm in the presence of another living, breathing person. "You aren't alone. And you don't have to pretend you're somebody just to be anybody. We're all "anybody". Do you understand what I'm trying to say? Nobody has to *be* anything. You can just exist. And Raven Asgard existing is always going to be alright with me, no matter what kind of a person you are. No one will hate you for your true self unless you're an absolute son of a gun, and I don't think you are. Is me being alright with you alright with you, too?" he asks, stumbling slightly on his jumble of words.

"Yeah, that's alright with me," I whisper with a soft chuckle.

"Also, if it's any comfort, I found your sarcastic persona almost likeable."

"Almost?"

"Almost. I could've liked her, but I'm finding talking to this one much better."

I laugh. "I haven't changed anything yet!"

"Nothing you can see," he says softly.

I blink and adjust my gaze to stare at the bottom of the boat, feeling slightly deflated and pleased simultaneously. All my anger, hatred, and annoyance for Sparrow that I've kept balled up messily inside my chest has just completely and utterly fizzled away into nothing. Acid is water, rendered unable to sting and hiss.

I swallow the heart thumping in my throat back into my chest. Sparrow's looking at me again, his eyes ticking away the seconds until—

"It's time," Sparrow says. "Ready?"

I give a strained, nervous smile, pressing a handful of stars into his palm. He catches sight of them, then the smaller quantity in my own hand, and opens his mouth to protest, but I speak first. "I'd rather at least one of us made it out. Here's how they work: you think of what you want and do it fast and clearly, then whisper into it thrice and kiss it. It sounds weird, but trust me. And please. Do use them. Be safe."

I close his fist around them and push his hand close to his chest. He tries to argue again, but I cut him off. "Just take them, Sparrow. And don't die," I whisper, joining him at the side of the boat.

For a second, he says nothing, and I wonder if he's still considering refusing the good luck charms.

"Likewise," he replies at last, securing the light around his head. We exchange one last glance at one another, swinging our legs over the side of the boat.

Then we just sort of stare at one another.

"Are you going to, um, you know?" I ask, nodding to the water.

"Ladies first? No?" he offers.

I don't reply and instead cautiously dip my foot into the sea. Shivers shoot like rapidly falling dominos from my toes up to my neck. The water ripples as the tip of my boots brushes the surface delicately. It's waiting.

"Peter and Bronwyn mean so much to me," I say, turning to look at Sparrow.

"I know they do."

"We'll not fail," I say. It's a command, almost. A desperate promise to myself because I'm so scared. But the terror in my voice is masked with steely determination. The words emerge harsh and unforgiving, carving the declaration into a gravestone.

"We'll not," he says firmly, and then, before I can realize just how much of a death wish this entire mission is, I'm jumping into the ocean with my eyes squeezed tightly shut, leaving the safety and comfort of the *Valerie* behind.

Before the water rises to meet me, one of my last thoughts is that I'm so glad I collected the gleaming diamonds tucked tightly in my pocket.

I know somehow that I'll need them. And if I don't... well, then at least I can still protect Sparrow and ensure his safety just in case it should ever be necessary.

My limbs jolt as my legs pierce the water like needles, and the ocean swallows me up whole. My scream is muffled and emerges in a stream of bubbles as the cold slaps me. Hard.

My scrambling, chalk-white fingers grip the edge of the boat, and I cling on for dear life as the pain slowly numbs me, water replacing my organs.

"Raven, it's alright. Breathe. C'mon, I have to jump in, too. You're scaring *me*, now..." Sparrow mutters.

My scrambling fingers grip his arms tightly, my slippery palms desperate to hold on.

"You're okay," Sparrow says. I raise my head, gasping with pain, and he glares directly into my eyes, unblinking. "You're okay," he repeats.

The first few minutes of swimming are tough as I adjust to the freezing water, but soon, I grow used to it, and the pain becomes bearable.

The water temperature cuts right down to my bones until the cold has seemingly hollowed out every part of me, making my head spin and my limbs ache, and yet the Berg doesn't seem to be drawing any closer. We both persevere, though, with my friends' faces etched into my mind.

We'll not fail.

Sparrow leads us, and I swim blindly after him. The rush of water hitting my body as his arms scoop it out of the way in a breaststroke comforts me. It reminds me that someone else is finally plunging into another terrible idea with me.

As all the warmth gradually seeps from my body, I focus on the fortress ahead, finally stopping when I finally realize that we've been swimming far too long. "We aren't moving," I gasp, "What's going on?"

He stops swimming and manoeuvres to face me with flushed cheeks. "I noticed, too. At first, I thought we were just swimming against the wind direction or a current, but now I think it's more than that. I think there's some kind of defence system— two giant magnets with the same poles facing one another, or a jet stream or something— that's pushing us back so that we can't even swim close to the fortress."

"Okay, so what do we do about it?"

"We'll have to dive deep to where the magnetic field doesn't extend," he answers.

"Well, how do we know the defences won't cover the ocean floor?"

Sparrow shrugs. "This entire sea is designed for boats. Frost expects the attempted attacks on the Berg to be made by boat, so they haven't considered going deeper than what's necessary to stop a ship. It's the Moon King's weakness, really. He assumes the whole world thinks like him and works to his standards."

I nod. "I get that. Often, when Flai run into trouble with 'Nora, the traders have mounds of gold to stop Flai from using magic and attacking them. But most Flai don't even try to use their powers because they already know it's too late. They just assume we're violent, too."

"To be fair, you aren't the friendliest people. It's easy to find angels intimidating."

"Not an angel," I grunt, bluntly ending the conversation's topic. "So, we dive?"

"It's our best option. Either that or hypothermia. We need to get to land soon," Sparrow nods.

I gesture to the Berg. "Land?"

He grimaces. "Ice."

I frown, looking down at the black water. "What happens if we swim too deep? What if there are things in here? We could die."

"Quite frankly, Raven, I think that's kind of the idea."

We both take deep breaths and dive under the surface. I propel myself easily for a second or two, shooting neatly down through the dark, dark depths of the water.

Then it happens. The pain explodes from my forehead and I clutch my skull, exclaiming in shock as the world warps and disorientates. Water floods my gaping mouth, and my lungs and my chest are burning with the need for oxygen, but I cannot resurface yet. First, we must glide forward.

Sparrow taps my shoulder, pointing desperately up. I understand, nod, and block out the pain to continue forward. After a moment, I swim straight up, feeling the resistance of an enormous push trying to force me back.

But I've still advanced towards the Berg.

I take a series of rushed, frenzied breaths, trying to calm myself despite the cold and the agony. There. Easy!

I'm not dead.

Not yet.

Almost instantly, however, I'm back under, diving down deep into the safe zone where the Berg's defences cannot reach me. It's an odd transition, feeling the amount of pressure on my body versus the quiet underwater world beneath the magnetic field.

It's impossible, I think to myself, *physics doesn't allow for this.* Whoever created this defence mechanism is diabolically brilliant, yet the people of Evrilore are without electricity in most places. Cars, phones, entire planes... everything was confiscated. All for this? For impossible technology that only dictators can access?

With my head being the only part of my body constantly rising above the water, the frosty air seems to slash away at my cheeks in a way that the water does not.

Sparrow's huffing just a few feet ahead of me, his headlight carving out a passage of light in the water as we kick deeper and deeper, leaving the ocean's shallow waters behind to collect dust like a forgotten antique while we continue into the deep zone.

When you go under the surface, your entire being and everything you know and understand is fractured. You are beyond mortal lands, straying into uncharted territories. And you have to strain and fight against your body's pleas to resurface until you've covered enough ground to emerge and gasp in a mouthful of air for the next dive, which is never more than a moment away.

A part of me suspects this will be the only stage of the Berg's defence, apart from the hundreds and hundreds of guards.

But I'm terribly wrong, and it's evident because the pressure suddenly disappears, and a sharp drop in the water temperature occurs shortly after.

We've passed into a new zone.

Sparrow's still slightly ahead of me, as he made it through the magnetic field first, so he suffers the first blow.

I don't see anything out of the ordinary until I notice something small and white zip past me through the water, and then it's gone just as quickly as it appeared. My eyes widen, and I yell as loud as I can.

"Sparrow, there's—" But *what* is there? "STOP!" I scream, which is substantial enough.

His head whips from side to side as he looks around. My warning is too strong to ignore. But then he sees nothing, so we continue, the feeling of unease rotting, unaddressed, in my stomach. The knowledge that something sinister swims unseen beside us sticks to my insides like tar.

A few moments later, I spot another one. And then another. They aren't all where I'm swimming, but mostly ahead, where Sparrow is.

My position is where a boundary partitions the second strip of defence from the first, and the creature I saw earlier was straying from its herd.

I want to run to Sparrow and call out to him, but what kind of warning can I give that will help? He's already in too deep, both literally and metaphorically.

"SPARROW!" I yell.

"YEAH?" he calls back, oblivious to the ambush-to-be surrounding him.

I pause, deciding what to say, but there's nothing reasonable to settle on except— "*RUN!*"

You can't run in water, Raven, a sinister voice whispers, slithering around the crown of my head.

"Shut up and do what you're here for," I snap out loud. Sixth Sense falls silent, but I can still feel its presence, hand-in-hand with my adrenaline.

I reach out my hand to pull Sparrow back into the safe waters, but a wall of white things smashes into his side just as my fingers grasp his collar. He screams, twitches, and then falls unconscious as they shock him, his head smashing through the water with a violent splash.

They know who an imposter is. They know who to kill.

Betraying every instinct I have, I lurch forward into the danger zone, charging madly into the White Army.

LEFT! Sixth Sense yells. I clumsily manoeuvre to the right, but then—

RIGHT! I feel one, then two, sting my leg. There's an army of them, burning, bright, and white. My calves scream with pain, but before I know it, I'm already diving deep down for Sparrow's limp figure. He's sinking faster and faster to the bottom of the ocean with every second. I must get him now, or he'll drown.

Maybe he already has, Sixth sense cackles.

Get out of my head, I shoot back.

My fingers hook the collar of Sparrow's shirt, and the thought dissolves into nothing. Nothing except: You aren't dead, Sparrow. Don't be dead, Sparrow. You aren't dead.

Let's find out, Sixth Sense grins.

The White Army surges for me, and with the help of Sixth Sense, I navigate my way to safe water through a series of clumsy dives.

White hot and fizzing with excitement, they are coming from all directions now, and I know I have to go deeper. But what will happen to Sparrow if I do!?

Panic claws at my chest. I have to do something. I have to escape.

My legs are screaming where the things caught me with their electrical stingers, but Sparrow looks far worse, his entire body motionless and floppy. Minuscule red blisters cover his limbs. I struggle to move forward with the weight of his body, but I finally seem to pass into a ring of safety.

It takes a lot of struggling to find a good position, but I eventually decide to heave him over my shoulder and swim so that he has full access to air while he's out cold. I don't know if he's dead —I certainly *hope* not— but I must make sure he can breathe.

At last, I feel my feet brush a hard surface as the seafloor curves steeply upwards. I wade the rest of the way to shore and set Sparrow down on the rocks, my breaths lost somewhere between pants, coughs, and gasps of pain that spew seawater everywhere.

Only now do I confront the truth: this was stupid, and we were naive. We're no match for this fortress or what lies beyond its defences. Sparrow almost died, and we aren't even inside yet.

But at least I can be sure of one thing as I survey the innocent swaths of waves, silent and still like a hibernating predator:

There's no turning back now.

CHAPTER 11

"Sparrow," I whisper hoarsely, shaking him. "*Sparrow!*" I lean over his chest, my fingers roaming for a heartbeat.

He begins to mumble as I finally find it, slow and regular. "Raven, I... no, don't..." Small segments of conversation slip from his lips, but nothing is distinguishable. At least he can speak.

The sound of footsteps on the other side of the wall beside me tells me at least two guards, most likely armed, are patrolling the area. How they didn't hear us thrashing around in the water is a miracle.

We must be beside the southern entrance, which is a stroke of miraculous luck because it means fewer guards to deal with.

I hitch Sparrow further up the steep, rocky slope that encloses the Iceberg. It appears they've turned the Berg into an artificial island, not unlike Frost, surrounding it with stone to keep its icy walls in place. I can only stay here for a while until I find a way to get past the guards. My brain tells me to create a diversion, and my hands just want to reach for a weapon, but I ignore them both, too concerned and weak to make a proper decision.

With the recent weather, I doubt there'll be any royal visitors anytime soon, so we're relatively safe from boat spotters here. The guards are, however, bound to do a perimeter check.

Luckily, Sparrow returns to consciousness within fifteen minutes or so. He's still drowsy and cannot form proper sentences, but he can move and certainly doesn't seem to have suffered any fatal injuries.

When we're both strong enough to stand, I help Sparrow to his feet, quickly informing him of our current situation. For a moment, he just stands there, running a hand through his brown mop of hair and thinking long and hard about what to do.

"We've really gotten ourselves into a bad situation, haven't we? Or, at least, a stupid one," I find myself whispering. "We never should've come here. The boat's oceans away, and we can't go in the water. We're basically doomed."

"No, no, it's okay. We'll find another way, we really will. This isn't your fault— it's mine, for underestimating them," he mutters.

I shake my head. "Don't, Sparrow. It's my friends we're rescuing, isn't it?"

He dismisses me with a wave of his hand and then sighs, leaning against the wall. "You do know we're going to have to change the entire plan?" he asks quietly, "Now, there's no way we can just go down there and swim to the underground entrance. After seeing that swarm of... *things,* we never know what could be in the water. We have to be more careful. And, I suppose... We have to do what they expect us to do now."

"What d'you expect, a welcome mat that says "be our guest" by the front doors? They kill us," I argue.

"That's the point. It's their way or no way. We either play the game by their rules or not at all. This isn't about strength or power... it never was. We have to outsmart them."

"How are we supposed to beat them at their own game?" I press.

"I..." he looks genuinely stumped. "I guess we just have to figure it out as we go."

I arch a brow. "Figure out what? The game or the enemy?"

He laughs. "Both. The enemy is the game, and the game is the enemy."

"Did I not already establish my passionate detest for metaphors?" I mutter.

He pulls a devastated face. "Must thy annoyance be a most lethal dagger to my soul?"

"Shut up, Sparrow," I scowl.

"Alas, the radiant angel speaks only Satan's tongue."

I throw him a dirty look, and he shuts up.

We begin edging along the boulder we're stranded on to take turns spying on the guards and determine their different routes.

They're patrolling the area by walking around a platform surrounding the main doors in organized shifts. The entrance we're beside is partly ice, partly stone, leaning into the Iceberg in an inverted "U" shape, with connected, railed-off balconies protruding from each wall.

There are three guards to cover the three walls, and they march back and forth. When the guard pacing the wall closest to us turns his back to face the wall bearing the threshold, that's our best window of opportunity to dash for the doors without being noticed.

Just as he turns, the two other guards cross paths, momentarily blocking out each others' view. However, we'll have to time our movements carefully... a second too late, and— *Bang*, Sixth Sense finishes cheerily.

"Raven, you're shaking."

I turn back to Sparrow, leaning against the wall, and look

down at my trembling fingers. "Sorry," I mumble, "I'm fine. Just nerves, okay?"

Shoulders relaxing a little, he reaches over and squeezes my hand. I gratefully squeeze back, flashing him a smile.

We decide that I'll go first because I'm smaller than Sparrow and harder to spot when I'm fleeting between shadows. Sparrow will follow closely behind to defend me from a potential oncoming spray of bullets.

It's all so hazardous, and there's not one thing that couldn't go wrong, but to move positions, we'd be forced to swim again, and not only did Sparrow nearly die the first time, but we were both robbed of strength and confidence.

Honestly, robbing us of confidence is probably the primary objective of the whole defence mechanism- not to kill the enemy but to weaken them. After all, the White Army didn't kill Sparrow.

This is odd because you would think the Moon King wanted his rivals disposed of quickly and carefully, but I suppose he only wants to take away our pride. That's why he humanizes Flai instead of just killing us. Humanization means we've nothing left. Anything that was ever special to us is gone.

He doesn't need to destroy people, just their spirits. It's a way of seizing power that is horrific, brutal, and sick... but very, very effective.

I double-check I have all the weapons I need and then pull out a particularly cruel-looking pistol from my damp cloak.

We wait until, as practised, the guard turns around, and that's my cue. I nod at Sparrow and then drop into a crawl, quickly turning around the corner and moving along the ground until I reach the double doors.

Carved into the stone above them are the words:

I shudder to imagine what this means and who it addresses. Then I realize how long I've been standing still, and I sprint for the doors, my heart racing.

I think the other guard has seen me for a second, but then he turns around and walks in the opposite direction. But if he's changing direction, that means... I look up to see the other guard looking right down at me. I wasn't fast enough!

Cursing, I cover my face with my cloak, and a "Hey!" barely escapes his mouth before I'm through the doors. I look back, panting, and he's looking around, scratching his head, bewildered. He's sure he saw something but cannot report it because nothing is there. Or at least, nothing is there anymore.

Sparrow follows shortly after me but calculates his movements better so that he sets off a little earlier than I did and makes it to the door without being spotted. We quickly congratulate each other in hushed tones and then stand up to examine our bleak surroundings.

To my surprise, there's no one here. The walls are made of the same hard, hollowed-out, compacted ice I saw from the exterior of the building, and they curve steeply upwards to form a tunnel-like ceiling. There's only one place you can go from this room: a claustrophobic passage with a lower ceiling that leads straight on.

I tug Sparrow's arm and point to it. "Down there?"

"Yeah. I've come up with a bit of a strategy to search as many rooms as possible before dawn, and I'm guessing that actual prison cells are in one of the lower levels of the prison, so we should start down there and work our way upwards."

I frown. "Not that I don't trust your judgment, but why would they be there?"

He shrugs. "Oh, you know. In most buildings, the prisoners are always on the bottom floor. Have you never noticed that in books?"

"I don't read."

He cocks one head thoughtfully to the side. "Sorry- I didn't know you couldn't read. I didn't mean to hurt your feelings."

I can't tell if he's being sarcastic or not. "I can read, idiot. And you didn't hurt my feelings. Did you forget what I told you the day we met?"

He arches his brow. "Yes. You said I can't hurt you. But if that were true, you wouldn't have left the hollow earlier."

My eyes widen, and then I turn to him. "You...you didn't...?"

He sighs and nods. "I heard everything you said before you left. I was only pretending to be asleep. How else d'you think I would've known which direction you went in?"

"I- everything?" I repeat.

"Yeah, and I'm not going to lie, it was kind of refreshing to see a different side of you," Sparrow shrugs. "You even looked guilty."

I'm unsure whether I should be angry or happy that he heard what I said, but I can't think about that right now. We have to get this job done and get out of the fortress before anyone sees us.

I want to change the subject, but I have no clue how.

"Let's just... let's just go," I say weakly.

"C'mon, Raven. I'm sorry. I just didn't want to chase you and creep you out and..."

"We're getting distracted." I snap.

We split to take one side of the room each, signalling to one another that it's safe and continuing down the tunnel, our guns poised to shoot. We constantly check our backs to ensure no one is chasing us, but the halls remain empty. After five minutes of what seems like peace, I grow suspicious of the blanketing silence. I feel deafened and vulnerable. It's like someone's covering my ears on purpose.

"Sparrow, where is everyone? This doesn't seem right. I don't know what it is, but something is off. It's a prison. Why's it so quiet? We should stop and re-consider what we're doing!"

"It's nighttime, and they don't expect anyone to get past their defences. I'm sure everyone's slacking off, or the main defences are concentrated in other parts of the Iceberg."

I'm still unconvinced, but we continue deeper into the fortress. The hallways are long and winding but simple to navigate. We walk silently, our arms brushing lightly together.

When the end of the tunnel grows nearer, and the corner marks the threshold of a new passage, I flatten myself against the wall, slowing my pace and treading more cautiously than before. "See anything?" I whisper to Sparrow.

He shakes his head, but I hang back anyway, uncertain. "The longer we wait, the more likely we are to get caught." Sparrow reminds me. "Just— here. Take my hand," he says firmly, guiding me out of the passage.

The ceiling rises into a much larger, brighter corridor. The walls here are not made of ice but of metal.

Straight ahead, the hall continues with narrow, claustrophobic doorways lining the walls, and to the left, it branches off into another tunnel even more minuscule than the previous ones.

Here, where the cold air is trapped and building up, it's much colder. I pull my cloak tighter around my shoulders.

"It's only going to get worse as we descend," Sparrow mutters.

I stare at the passages ahead of us. "Which way?"

"Your choice is as good as mine. Either," he shrugs.

I analyze each exit for a second, then settle upon the tunnel. "Something tells me there are more guards that way," I explain.

He arches a brow. "Then why are we going there?"

"Well, because they're guards. They guard something, and it might be exactly what we're looking for," I explain.

He shrugs. "You're the boss."

As we enter the tunnel, I begin to hear the first signs of other human beings. The occasional muffled cry from under our feet, the clinks of what I can only imagine are metal cell doors banging against ice, and the occasional scream.

I picture myself in an even colder room than the one we're in, miles below the surface, cramped and squashed up here for the rest of my life. Eventually, I give up because the horrors of my imagination will never equate to those happening within this fortress.

The entire place disgusts me. How have I lived knowing that my two best friends are here?

Glancing at Sparrow, I suddenly realize exactly what he meant, back at the beach. Sailing past this place, seeing it for myself, and knowing they were locked up inside... it would have killed me. And killed him, too, because that's just the kind of person Sparrow is.

I'm too wrapped up in my thoughts to notice the ground disappearing beneath my feet.

"Steady, Raven!" Sparrow exclaims, catching me by my waist and reeling me back in to the top of the stairwell. "You alright?"

"I'm fine," I say quickly, though my heart's knocking at my ribs.

I peer out over the bannister, anxious. From below, footsteps and murmurs reverberate up the walls. I turn to Sparrow, wondering if he's thinking the same as me, and slip my hand between the folds of my cloak to withdraw the gun and raise it before me. Then, I loop my fingertip around the trigger.

"Hey, hey!" Sparrow whispers. "What are you doing?"

"Just preparing, in case—"

"You could accidentally shoot someone, holding it like that. No one's attacking anybody yet. Remember what I said back on the *Valerie*? Don't go shooting anybody unless you absolutely must. I know you're scared, Raven... but think of your guilt just from abandoning your friends. Taking somebody's life? That guilt will be *worse*."

I bite down hard on my tongue, tasting blood, and it brings me back to the present, to the grimy walls, steep stairwell, and to the air infused with chill and malice. I realize, all of a sudden, how desperately I want to turn and flee without ration or reason. Top bolt from this terrible, terrible place. "I know. I'm just paranoid. I won't shoot anyone if I can help it, I promise."

"It's okay. It really is. It's just... well, are you *alright*, Raven?"

"I'm good," I reply, making for the stairs again.

"No, you aren't," he argues, jogging to catch up with me. "Just talk to me. Please."

I shake my head. "I can't. This isn't the time, Sparrow! You're going to get us killed—!"

"Raven," he says, sharper this time, and his tone is so despairingly pleading that I cannot help but meet his gaze. The moment I do so, his voice softens. "Stop being brave," he whispers.

Guilt. Fear. Confusion. Hope. Despair. I'm numbed by too

many emotions to count, and a single tear slips down my cheek.

"Please, can we do this later? Let's just get through this first and then... Sparrow, I can't let anything else happen. I thought you were dead," I breathe. My voice comes out hollow and empty. "I thought those things in the water killed you. I thought you were dead, and I'd never see your eyes open again. Never hear your stupid jokes again. I thought you were... I thought..." I trail off, wiping away more tears.

He says nothing, and I cannot hold myself together this time. I slide down the wall, bury my face into my knees, and burst. "I'm just so scared. I don't know why we're here. I don't know why we thought we could do this. And I didn't want to admit it, and I never have, because you had this great plan, and you've always been so optimistic, and I wanted to be brave and strong and everything you are. But you really scared me, Sparrow. This place scares me. These people scare me, and what might have happened to my friends scares me. That's it, and that's only it! I'm *scared!* I don't want to die, and I don't want you to die. I like you. It surprised me, but I really do. I don't want to be responsible for anybody else's suffering, especially not yours."

He gazes at me for a moment, unsure what to say. I offer him my arms, and he sinks into my embrace. It's the kind of hug that's not a gesture of comfort but the kind where somebody wraps their arms around you so tightly, so desperately, that you know they are doing it simply because they need to.

I blink back more tears and look up, my vision blurry, to see that his head is hung, his hands are no longer strong or steady, and I almost go limp with shock.

Sparrow is *crying.* Sobbing.

Sobbing like a little boy.

Sparrow, whose intellect has a solution to every

situation. Sparrow who is reliable, dependable, and quick-witted. Sparrow, who is always comforting me, but in return, is never comforted.

Overwhelmed, I return his hug, salty tears rolling into my mouth.

"But I'm not," he whispers, "I'm not brave, and I'm not strong. I've been trying so hard to be everything you want me to be because I'm your homefetch and I'm human, and I don't have to deal with half of what you do... but in the end, I'm just a kid, and I'm terrified that if I can't get this right, and if I can't get us out of here..." he goes silent.

I don't know how long we stay there, guns in hands, crouching side by side in the corner of the stairwell.

"I'm sorry," I whisper repeatedly, wiping my eyes. "I'm really sorry..."

"I'm sorry I got us into this mess," he replies.

"No. You did this to save my friends. To make me happy," I say glumly. "It's my fault."

He glances at me, and his mouth opens and closes as if it cannot decide what to say. "And what if I can't save them?" he finally gets out. "What if I can't save you?"

A brief smile tugs at my lips, and at last, I climb to my feet, my voice still shaky but full of newfound determination. "You already have."

CHAPTER 12

Don't speak too much. Don't move too much. Don't fear too much.

That's all I force myself to do, though the latter requires tremendous effort. The panic, doom, and horror of this place are enough to send me doubling over, so it's all I can do to stifle my urge to flee, to suppress the terror. They can smell it, I fear. Like the wolves that make up a tenth of their army.

So far, we've survived the journey three floors down into the death maze undetected, but I'm wary of traps and security cameras. Then Sparrow reminds me that the chambers of the Berg below ground level are built entirely inside ice. Any cable or wire systems would simply freeze unless they were installed in places where the temperature was monitored to contain them, and this is unlikely because the construction of the Berg dates back to when electricity wasn't available to anyone but royalty —and even then, it was poor with a weak current.

We steadily creep down flight after flight of stairs, the voices from below growing more distinctive and the temperature colder. The steps are carved out of ice, with metal ridges to stop you from sliding off the edges of the stairs. They descend steeply in a square pattern, reaching down at least five floors. I halt at the order of Sixth Sense.

Too close, now, it whispers, and for a moment, the voice's warning is so strong that it could be standing behind me. It raises every hair on my neck, and despite being confined to the chambers of my mind and my senses, the caution reverberates down the shaft in the centre of the stairwell.

Sparrow turns to me, and we lock eyes. I give him a small nod, and he silently raises his pistol, then signals to me that he's ready. We creep down to the final floor of the prison, past where humans were ever supposed to reach, beyond where light can reach you underwater.

I take a breath and turn the corner, gun raised and ready to shoot—

And there, the stairs lead into a wide, open room. Gatekeeping the only exit from the room are three men, flashing shiny black guns, gaping stupidly at me as though they have no orders for what to do in the event of an intruder — and who can blame them?

The White Army should've already shocked us both to death.

Each guard models the same cheap armour and short, neat haircut. The first is tall, slim, and pale, and the second is dark-skinned and broad-shouldered. Both look manageable — it's the third I'm worried about. Formidable, tall, and pumped with muscle. His eyes are sharper and far more intelligent than his coworkers'. Large, beefy hands swing at his side, curling into fists ready to punch, and in one hand, his gun is held with practised efficient fingers.

Dragging my eyes away from him, I clear my throat awkwardly and slide my hands behind my back, concealing my gun. "Erm... hello. Don't s'pose you know where the bathroom is? We're a bit lost," I lie, sheepish.

"What are you doing?" Sparrow hisses from behind me.

"I'm improvising! Do you want to fight these guys?"

At Sparrow's presence, Guard One and Two take an alarmed step back.

"There's two of them," One whispers.

"What do we do?" Two asks.

"Level four, cyan alert," Guard Three replies.

I prepare to block the exits with a wall of flames to prevent them from calling for reinforcements, curling my nails into my palms and trying to call upon the familiar tingling of magic.

The men back away from me, inching to the right slightly, and Sparrow meets my eyes as if asking what I'm going to do.

I ignore him and return to watching the men— and it's a good thing I do, because a moment later, they sprint for the doorway.

Desperate, I throw out my palms in front of me and prepare for the worst, most uncontrolled attack I have ever given, knowing the adrenaline charging through my body will maximize my abilities—

Only a feeble little wisp of emerald steam trails from my hand. "Oh, come on," I moan. "You want to do this *now*?"

As if in reply, a large burst of scalding steam erupts from my skin, shooting forward in thin, cruel tendrils to encircle the group. Guard One catches the worst of it, howling in agony as it sends a snake of angry red blisters hissing up his leg. He hops backwards, collapsing into Two's arms. Three hauls them both back, his eyes narrowed as they scan the room. Then they settle on me, and his face shifts.

"You're... Flai," he gasps, eyes widening in realization, and suddenly, all traces of eerie calmness disappear from his face. "You're *FLAI!*" he yells again, picking up his gun and pointing it at my face while stumbling backwards toward the doorway.

Panicking, I shoot a blast of flames at the arch, blocking his path, and raise my gun. But it won't fire anything, and only a hollow-sounding click echoes across the chamber.

Guard Three cries out in panic and hops to the side, all his logic and common sense gone, wildly waving his pistol at my head. "D-don't move!"

I silently prepare a new gun behind my back, my fingers fumbling. My old pistol, with a jammed barrel, clatters to the floor.

"What are you doing?" the guard asks sharply, catching sight of it. "Stop! Let me see your hands!"

"Sparrow," I hiss urgently, "Buy me some time!"

"What do you want me to do? Shoot him?"

"I said, STOP THAT!" Guard Three cries, and I flinch in horror as he pulls the trigger—

"Raven, look out!" Sparrow screams.

Then, before I know it, his arms are wrapped around my torso and wrenching me to the side just as the bullet zips past my ear. He raises his gun and shoots a —dart?— into the guard's foot, causing the man to reach down and pluck it out of his skin with a curse.

Before he can even straighten up, his eyes narrowing to inspect the dart, the heavy knockout drug —already in his blood— sends him crashing to the floor.

Two more darts fly past me, landing neatly in the necks of Guard One and Guard Two, and their knees buckle in a matter of seconds. Quickly tucking away his gun, Sparrow rushes forward, and I follow suit, clearing the flames and unblocking our path with a dismissive wave of my hand. Before we continue, I turn to Sparrow.

"What was that!?"

He grins. "A little something I prepared. Bullets are just unnecessary in some situations."

"So… so, just drugging them is better!? What are we gonna do about the bodies?"

"Nothing," he answers. "There's no time. Someone will have heard that thin man scream for sure. Even if we did hide them, someone'll radio in and realize something's off when they get no reply. We have to move quickly and avoid any more confrontations. That really was far too close, Raven. He almost shot you."

"I know, I know..." My eyes trail back to the pile of unconscious bodies. "They won't die, will they?" I ask stupidly.

"They'll live," Sparrow replies. He crouches down and rifles through the guards' pockets.

"But they'll be okay?"

He shrugs. "They'll *live*."

I'm unsure how to respond to this, so I just shake my head and point to the tunnel ahead carved deep into the ice. "Down?"

"Do we have another option?"

We enter the tunnel branching off from the large room, the low ceiling scraping my scalp. Wrinkles of ice stroke through my hair.

With utmost caution, we venture into a complex network of capillary-like passages, tiny corridors barely wide enough for two children to stand beside one another.

An infestation of sentries lurks around every corner. Upon first sight, the majority are impossible to differentiate between, and we think we see the same man several times. But nobody's following us. They've all been down here, their swords spinning the ghostly silk of blood into webs, for so long that darkness has sucked the colour from their cheeks and hollowed out their eyes, leaving an army of same-faced men.

Sparrow and I wrench one another into alcoves and cupboards, waiting in pitch-black places with pitch-black faces drowned in shadow, only a breath between us, for the guards to pass.

It's not long before, after successfully sneaking down another three floors, my breath begins to exit my lips in a cloud.

"God, why is it so c-c-cold?"

"We're in an Iceberg under the sea," Sparrow points out.

"W-Well, how much colder is it going to g-get?" I ask, frustrated.

"Only heaven knows," Sparrow answers darkly.

"Maybe we should go and ask it, then," I say bitterly, and he gulps.

"Let's just hope it won't come to that."

When we head over to the west side of the building, I've pieced together a rough mental map of the Berg. The floors are all square, and corridors run through them in grid-like patterns. The symmetrical nature of the floor plan makes everything look identical, but the room doors are sloppily hand-painted with labels ranging from A to M with a number beside it, giving us at least some indication of what floor we are on.

As we pan out across the level, the noises I've been anticipating greet my ears. Occasional clinks of metal, heavy footsteps. When the noises grow louder, it's obvious we're drawing nearer and nearer to where the prisoners must be— to the fortress' core.

Guards appear almost everywhere now, causing us to change direction several times— hiding isn't enough. Now I know why the other floors were so deserted, why we rarely saw any soldiers. This floor's absolutely crawling with them.

Sparrow must have noticed this, too, because his eyes

sharpen, and his fingers curl a little tighter around his gun.

I keep hearing footsteps spotting shadows dancing on the walls, but we don't cross paths with any more sentries. We're careful.

Following intense minutes of creeping along the lengths of halls consumed by darkness, Sparrow suddenly jerks to the side, pulling me into another crammed alcove, and draws a finger to his lips. Without warning, a shadow swoops across my vision. I refuse to breathe for a few seconds. Sparrow's body is pressed against mine in the tight space— I could count every hair follicle on his eyebrows. A bead of sweat trickles down my forehead. Time fades to nothing, and then...

The sentry passes.

"Come on, let's go. It's safe." Sparrow beckons for me to emerge.

I hang back, uncertain.

"Raven?" he prompts, gently pulling me by the hand.

Finally, I exhale, then creep forward.

Down a few more corridors, in and out of storage rooms containing packaged food and clothes in metal crates- nothing significant.

Then the real Berg comes into sight, the school beyond the playground. The corridor collapses into a clumsily dug passage that winds into the deep, dark depths of the ice in a way that makes every muscle in my body tense. And this is not the clean, bright blue ice from upstairs, but dirty, foul-smelling ice.

We've reached the slums of the glacial city, where electricity's frail gasps are drowned by the prison's depth. This is where the dead sink. This is the bottom of the lake in the Frost Wilderness.

"It's so awful here, Sparrow. So awful," I whisper.

"We go in. We find your friends. We get out," Sparrow says firmly. "Piece of cake."

"Yeah..." I echo, as unenthusiastically as possible. "Piece of cake."

And then, with the demons of my thoughts dancing in a mad frenzy, we enter the mouth of the beast, surrendering to the jaws of swallowing darkness.

The passage leads us much deeper into the ice than I had initially assumed it would, but we follow it nonetheless. I rap on the icy wall with the barrel of my gun every so often, testing for sturdiness. Smoke seems to be drifting in from somewhere, but its origin is unknown.

Soon, the tunnel opens up into a larger chamber, and I look up to see that we're in a small room made entirely of ice, with a tiny desk rammed into the corner and dishevelled drawers and filing cabinets scattered throughout the room.

It resembles an office— a reception of sorts, where new prisoners are registered as officially residing in the building and undergo final background checks before being forced into a cell.

The room has two doorways on the far wall, branching in different directions: left and right.

I guess that there's one for boys and one for girls, a little bit like the boarding school dormitories you read about in books.

There's no sign of guards, so we explore the room.

I creep over to the desk and begin rifling through the drawers for anything useful. I doubt it'll be easy to spot Bronwyn and Peter among mounds of sleeping prisoners, so any documented placement of them will significantly assist our search.

In the first drawer, there's nothing but a rotten apple core. I have to wiggle and pull at the handle to open the second drawer—this one is practically ancient, and it seems as though the drawer and the desk have been somehow merged by decades of mould. A large pile of papers secured together in a black binder sits inside the drawer, with some torn, dishevelled ones sticking out at the edges.

Everything in the room is incredibly moist, so I'm not surprised to find that when my fingertips finally brush the edges of the paper, it's thin and slightly damp.

"Got anything over there?" Sparrow asks as he roots in the pockets of several moth-eaten coats that hang on a grimy little hook attached to the wall.

"Just a few documents. It looks like some kind of diary. Let me read them," I reply, flattening out the pages on the desk. "Hang on..." I peer at the minuscule print on the paper. "It's in a different language. Here."

I pass him the documents, and he traces each line with his finger. "No, this is code."

"Code?" I frown. "What kind of code?"

He shrugs. "Well, if you squint your eyes a bit, all the smaller lines and dots disappear, and then it's just letters. A bit blurry, but still readable."

"Huh. Frost aren't sweet, but they're clever," I sigh, following his instructions.

Flicking to the very first page, I read aloud. It's from last year.

"April 24th, 2053. Savina Merivez, 24, The Willow District. Crime: Accused of food theft. Brook: Nether yellow. Tony Aricheste, 17, the Willow District. Crime: Caught stealing expensive medicine with a sister from a local apothecary. Brook: Nother blue. Lyla Aricheste —what the heck?— *8 years old*, the Willow District. Crime: Caught stealing medicine with her brother from a local apothecary. Brook: Nother yellow." Sighing, I shut the book. "It just goes on like that for a hundred more pages. Nothing useful. Even if we find my friends in here, it doesn't tell us where to look."

"Actually, you might be wrong. See how they've noted down "Nether", "Nother", or "Nather"? If you look at the crimes, the less serious ones like food theft all have Nether written beside them, and the more serious Nother, but the awful ones —like murder— are Nathers."

"So, these are tier systems based on severity?"

"Exactly, but not just that. The yellow and blue could be male and female. Since being a Flai is about the worst crime in existence —no offence— then I'm guessing the boy is in Nather blue, and the girl's in Nather yellow."

"So that's how we find Wynn and Peter!" I gasp, grinning. "Sparrow, you're brilliant!"

"Hold the horses. Just because we've categorized them doesn't mean we have a map or anything. We still have to find out exactly where these different prisoners' sections are located. I found some keys in those guards' pockets— see if you can find anything else in these coats."

I nod and get to work again, pausing whenever I notice something new, only to discover it's just a cloth, a loose coin, or a paperclip.

The excitement followed by our discovery is short-lived. Soon, the dread and uneasiness I've carried with me all day return to the pit of my stomach.

Every second we aren't finding Wynn and Peter, they could be suffering. Torture, starvation, abuse. Who knows what sickening evil Frost hides within these walls?

I just need to see them, to finally put everything in the past back in its rightful place— behind me.

Finally, I turn back to Sparrow and suggest we simply take a chance and advance into the forks ahead. "It's not like there's any point in waiting," I mutter.

He seems relieved to finally hear the suggestion and is happy to offer to take the left doorway.

I agree to take the right, and then we split the keys between us, bid each other good luck, and go our separate ways with raised weapons.

A sense of realization suddenly washes over me. It strikes me that this could be the final occasion I lay eyes on the boy in the bird mask. This could be my last opportunity to hear Sparrow Fenimore's stupid jokes, to question his motives, to run, to cower, to cry, to sing, and to sit on the brink of death in a snowstorm with him.

And despite his valiant efforts to lead me to this point, this may very well mark the end of our friendship.

I turn to call his name and my gut wrenches.

He's already gone.

CHAPTER 13

Inhuman voices are the first of many despicable sounds to welcome my ears into the prisoners' quarters. The laughter unfurling wickedly along the passage before me conveys no happiness, no joy, and mumbles of gibberish words tumble clumsily through the air like the drunken men who birth them. The reek of cider and cigarettes grows unbearably overpowering as I walk closer to the cells. Laws and illegal sedatives refuse to acknowledge one another's existence in the Berg. If the prisoners are quiet, who cares what they smoke?

The stench is sickening, and I must force myself to take deep breaths.

Do this, I tell myself, raising my gun and sidling up close to the wall.

I raise my head to see this tunnel's exit, marked by a framed doorway with the word "Nether" carved into the ice.

My eyes run over the rough stone walls and the rusty metal bars of the cells, and my throat goes dry at the disgusting condition of the men and children before me. Four or five prisoners are crammed into every cell to share three grubby beds without duvet covers or dividers.

The bedsheets are stained with blood and dirt, and even the cells are not separated— the only privacy offered here is bars. When I realize there's no toilet, I peer into the cell nearest me to see a bucket squatting in the corner.

My heart pounds against my ribs, and I clutch my head, struggling to breathe. This is not real. Surely it's not. Humans and Flai, reduced to animals and savages?

What does this teach? Who does it deter if the Berg is hidden from Evrilore's keen eyes?

Justice has never set foot here, never once rapped a fist upon the door of this building.

Helpless, I proceed to search.

It takes the first pair of eyes mere seconds to land on me. The prisoner has a tangled mane of ginger hair, and his swollen lips drizzle fresh blood onto filthy clothes.

At first, he ignores me and closes his eyes weakly, looking almost too exhausted to care. But his inmate has seen me now, and his eyes slowly move up and down my body, searching for... something.

Then he shakily climbs to his feet and addresses me. "Where's your frost emblem?"

I swallow hard. "I don't... I'm not..."

Bursting into a terrifying mass of screaming, begging, and sobbing, he throws himself at the bars, reaching through. I back away, eyes wide, but another set of hands finds my ankles, and I swivel to see a frail man on his knees before me. Gradually, the whole room becomes alive, murmuring and whispering. But as I look at them all, they're sort of... not.

Something inside of them died long ago. There's a void where the energy and life should be in their eyes, a void that has turned them into zombie-like creatures. All of them are locked in a world of fear and agony, haunted by memories of their days in this place. What if the horrors within these walls have driven my friends to madness, too?

Your friends, Raven. *Remember why you're here.*

As I walk away, the sea of soft pleads grows, and hands grasp for me everywhere I look. Soon, they are shouting, snarling, and scratching. They're wild animals, a pack of wolves that will stop at nothing to get to me.

"Help me!" a boy screams. He's a teenager at most, with cocoa-coloured shaggy hair down to his shoulders and narrow, hooded eyes that are soullessly black and devoid of sanity.

He's found me, smelt his prey, and got my attention. But now that I'm here, he can only plead like everyone else. It is me who must free him. The power is in my hands.

For a moment, it is as though I'm seeing the world through the eyes of the Moon King. This feeling of possessing such mesmerizing, paralyzingly strong power... it brings guilt, nausea, and sorrow. But in a world where everything is out of my control and it seems all the forces of hell are constantly on my trail, being in this position is somehow... comforting. For once, I'm not the caged one. For once, I'm almost... happy. I can relax because these men are restrained, limited behind bars only I can remove. It's so safe. So secure.

So awful. Horrified, I take a deep breath and shake the thoughts away. Power is a drug, I remind myself, and those who abuse it are nothing more than enslaved addicts.

"Don't go! Please!"

The teenager calls after me, but I must leave. And... and say I did set him free? Would he even know what to do? Where would he go? Does he have anyone to go to? Or has he faded from this world and been forgotten like the rest of us outlaws? I, myself, have no one to mourn for me except Sparrow, and we barely know one another.

"Missy! Oi!"

Another boy hisses from behind me. His cheeks are sunken, his voice snake-like. "Come closer. I want to tell you something. It's a secret."

The rest of the pack watches his tactic, examines the hesitation in my face, and leeches onto it.

"Come here, girl! I have a gift!"

"I have a present!"

"Want to see something, girly?" an old man asks from beside me, flashing a gold tooth.

They're closing in, all of them. The noise is unbearable and overwhelming.

The teenage boy lets out a twisted laugh and starts chatting casually with the wall on which he leans.

"Y-you're mad! All of you! Mad!" I scream, backing away.

"We're all just as sane as each other on this bloody island," the old man grins toothily.

I sprint from them, shoving their hands away from me, kicking back the pursuing pack of animals. But the enemy is right on my heel. It's north, west, east, and south. These people will never stop as long as there's a chance I might free them.

They're mad, they're dead, they're-

Only you, Sixth Sense finishes.

The words ring through my head. *"We're all just as sane as each other on this damn island."*

He's right. These prisoners are only me. Only as mad as I am. They, too, have fallen victim to those who abuse power, and as a result, they've been reduced to insane, hopeless shells of human beings. But still human. Still only as good as me. As good as us all.

And now, running from them, I am just as bad as Frost. I reach the last cell and lean against the wall to take a few deep breaths. My eyes are watering from the stench of the place, but what will these people think of me crying? Already, the majority assume me to be their rescuer.

Dreading the Nother chambers, I close my eyes and silently slip out of this world for a few minutes. I envision myself with Sparrow, Peter, and Wynn, crossing the Frigid Sea and becoming the first citizens of Evrilore to touch new soil. The Far Lands, the ones beyond the borders of our island. It's safe there. Together, we can all lie on a bed of flowers, with no one perusing us, no Frost to fear at all. I'll live with Peter in a little meadow somewhere, and we'll make a small den out of branches to stay warm.

Every single day, we'll go exploring and discover new wonderful places. Maybe Japan. Sparrow and I can help Wynn and Peter with their powers, too. Perhaps we will even have mobile phones or television. If there're any in the Far Lands. As far as I know, Frost was the only place to ever produce them, and they were all destroyed after the Fall. But maybe…

Raven! Sixth sense snaps. I compose myself and fumble with my keys until I find one that fits the lock. With an exhale of relief, I give the door a little shove, and it groans open to reveal another long, dimly lit corridor.

Hurriedly, desperately, I step through the next doorway and slam the door behind me, the calls of a hundred desperate prisoners falling unheard at my heels.

Upon crossing the threshold, deafening silence cloaks my ears. Candlelight flickers, illuminating filthy ice. Faces sweep through the shadows, and glares burn into the back of my head, but I have learned my lesson. Don't engage. Act like a guard. Move quickly and get out fast.

"Isn't she the Flai girl in the papers?"

"Hey, I've heard about her!"

"That's the one with a ten thousand shackle bounty!"

CHAPTER 13

Whispers fly and rumours cloud until the prisoners' voices hang around me constantly, and the air is thick with curiosity and caution. It's just like the last block of prisoners, except these people are not quite as dead. They're more dangerous criminals who have committed more daring crimes, and they're intelligent.

Instead of yelling or screaming, they melt into the dark like a parting sea, shrinking into the walls as I pass them. Watching. Waiting. Analyzing me, studying me. Trying to understand exactly who I am and what brought me here.

As I walk, I suddenly notice my fingertips have been subconsciously pressing against the barrel of my gun for comfort.

So this is why men shoot before they think: when your heart pounds louder than a hurricane on Flood Tide, you're already preparing to kill at the slightest touch. It is the darkest, most savage part of Human and Flai nature. Fight, then flee. Survive.

Making it through the Nother hall with my thoughts to distract me and little more than a few whispers, I now come to the door that promises to hold my best friend.

This is no ordinary metal door like the others. This is a huge iron vault entrance with numerous locks.

"You cannot get through," an old woman beside me sighs from behind her cage bars. "You do not have a key."

I turn to see her crouching in the corner of her cell, watching me interestedly like a science experiment. She's filthy, with torn, tattered clothes and a grimy face shrouded in warts and liver spots, but I get the impression that she could be pretty if dragged from this hellhole. She's also the only female prisoner I've seen so far. Covering her hair is a simple brown hijab, the only part of her clothing that seems relatively unaffected by years of imprisonment. "You cannot get through," she repeats, as though I hadn't heard her the first time.

In response, I hold up my stolen ring of keys. All the colour drains from her face, and her grip on the bars of her cell seems to slacken. "How?" she gasps, her eyes large and dark.

"I've come for my friends, Peter and Bronwyn. Peter… he's blonde with blue eyes, skinny, and he was ten years old when he arrived here. The girl is dark-skinned and has a round face and curly hair. Do you know where they are?" I ask, pushing away any pity I have for the woman.

I cannot liberate everyone here without killing most of them. I'm here for one sole purpose. Sympathy will be my greatest enemy.

"Yes, the boy. I, in the past, see the girl. In the girls. But no today. I go because the girl side is too much," she answers in poor English, "You go for Peter, but he is no… you…" Her nose wrinkles. "You go to… to have him? You are bad men?"

"No. Flai," I mutter, wiggling my keys in the door, only half-listening.

"You… Flai! I say in past you Flai! I say in past!" she shouts triumphantly, then moves to the opposite side of her prison cell to shake a curled-up inmate awake. "I say she is Flai! I say, "She go here,"! And she here! And she Flai!" The woman then scuttles back to me on all fours, giddy with excitement. "You have Peter, you have the girl also!"

"We will."

"And you have take Amela!"

"Who's Amela?" I grumble.

"My name. Amela," she explains proudly, "I am Flai! From Ra— my bad English. I speak Sun tongue. You know Sun Tongue? Fierra, no?" she says, greeting me in Sun Tongue.

CHAPTER 13

This gets my attention. Flai? Looking back at her, meeting her eyes for the first time, I find myself frowning. No, the magical sheen is not there. The odd lumps in her shoulder blades are missing. This woman cannot possibly be one of us. "You're... Flai?" I repeat doubtfully.

"I am! But they do no want... the bad men. They, uh... don't! I remember how I say now. They don't want. So, they... how do I say...? They do the water. The yellow water!"

"Pee?" I blink, not understanding a word of her jumbled English. My Sun Tongue is much too clunky to translate anything more complicated than "hello", never mind a whole conversation, so she continues to attempt to communicate with me outside her native language.

"The yellow. It pshhhh." She makes a motion with her fingers to mime a showerhead. "The water. No?"

I nod hastily. "Yes! Yes, water. What does it do?"

"The bad men," she says again, lowering her voice, "The guards. You don't take with them! They take! With the yellow water! The bad men in white, bad, bad, bad. Yellow water is bad. They take! Don't you them take." She is growing desperate now to try and make me understand. However, I cannot stay there and listen to a mad woman's ravings. Precious time is slipping away.

"I-I have to go. Fierra, suza. La'ra dife! Dife!" I repeat the apology regretfully and finally slide the final key into the last lock and turn it with a satisfying click.

"Remember the bad men, yellow water!"

"Bad men, yellow water," I whisper back.

Her eyes light up with triumph. Joy. Maybe even hope. As much as I cannot understand her, she still believes she is helping me, perhaps even saving me.

"Go," Amela breathes.

And then something unexpected happens. She does

something that makes this place a thousand times less horrible, something I never thought I'd see anyone do in the Berg.

She smiles.

Every line in her cracked, ancient face is illuminated with brilliant rivers of joy that flood the lines connecting eye to cheek, drawing out rivers on a faded map.

Heart aching with the knowledge that I must leave her, I return the smile.

After everything this woman has been through, it's the least I can do.

The moment I enter Nather, everything is silent. Silent in a way that's different from the last cell block because this is eerie, unnatural silence. The voices behind me are instantly cut off, giving way to complete quiet, as though all noise has been sucked into a void.

The atmosphere is subdued, created by the loneliness of the people who are so depressed and defeated that each other's company offers no end to their suffering. A smile will not take me far.

Here, the bars of the cells are thicker and new, and the prisoners are shivering and curled up in heaps on unused beds stained with the bloody remains of ancient injuries.

My boots make hollow-sounding taps on the floor as I walk, calling Peter's name in a hoarse whisper as I creep along the rows of cells.

They're laid out very much like the ones in the Nether and Nother quarters, except there is a larger square of floor right at the end, and the four cells surrounding it are smaller than the others.

If I sat around that corner, I'd be concealed from anyone walking in through the door.

I take a mental note of this... just in case.

Cell by cell, I tick them all off in my mind, keeping a careful record of which ones I have looked in.

When I reach the four cells at the end, I notice a gap in the floor that trails along the walls and ceiling, suggesting something is supposed to seal it off.

Perhaps this is an extra safety precaution should the most dangerous criminals attempt to escape. The figures inside these cells are much harder to categorize into "Peter" or "prisoner", especially since some lay opposite to me, so I must make careful judgments using body shapes and sizes.

Just as I'm turning to the last two cells, I catch sight of a small black box attached to the wall on the other side of the mysterious dividing line.

Crossing back into what I have nicknamed the "safe zone", I inspect this discovery carefully and soon learn that there are three basic functions. One button brings a sheet of metal crashing into the dividing line, sealing off the four cells just as I had predicted.

The second button is imprinted with an image of a closed padlock, and nothing happens when I press it, so I assume it simply secures the panel in place.

The final button reads "Eject". I only have one guess what this does, but it's so horrible that I barely manage to process it.

"I go because the girl side is too much," Amela had said.

What if the girls' side is not the only overcrowded section of this prison? What if, instead of draining more resources and building more cells, it's easier for Frost to just clear out a group of prisoners and make way for new ones?

My hand shakes as it hovers over the "Eject" button. I feel my body go limp and immediately deactivate the metal wall by pressing the first two buttons.

Can I possibly imagine myself sitting behind a desk, luxuries at the snap of my fingers, designing this contraption, designing someone's death? A lever pulled, a wall opened, four conscious beings, each with feelings, with lives yet to be lived, propelled into the ocean, propelled into their deaths, and for the sole purpose of creating room for the next batch to eventually follow suit.

Raven, Sixth sense snaps, Focus. *Someone's coming.*

With newfound determination to act with haste, I slowly lower my gaze to the remaining two cells, my heartbeat dragging to a standstill. I realize I'm holding my breath.

If Peter's not here, was ejection his fate? Was he hurled without mercy into the ocean?

I can't be too late, I realise, *I can't be responsible for my brother's death.* If I am, it'll kill me.

It's difficult to breathe as my eyes run over the men before me, as though my lungs are firmly knotted with my other organs. That knot grows every day and cannot be undone because it tightens every time I review my carefully twisted heartstrings and the memories that twisted them. The day I abandoned my friends weighs heavily on my conscience now.

This moment will determine whether that weight will ever be released. This day will change me forever.

I sit back on my heels, trying once again to inhale gasps of air.

Heaven knows I'm sorry.

Heaven knows that not for a moment did I forget the feeling of my fingers dragging through his golden curls, as he sat in my arms, and how they'd spring back up defiantly when pulled straight, and how that represented Peter so well.

How that spring just cannot be lost because if it is, so am I.

I rise to my feet, hastily wiping my cheeks, and reach down with a trembling hand to tug the closest prisoner towards me. His shirt is damp from lying on the ice, and my hands keep quaking from the effort. I'm sure, for a moment, that I can hear breathing. Rapid, frenzied breaths from a gasping mouth.

But then I remember the drugs, the sedatives trapping the men here in slumbers.

I manage to pull the prisoner close enough to grasp his collar and tilt his lolling head toward me. But it's only an adult, shrunken and starved to the size of a weak boy. I move around the cell, my lip clenched harshly between my teeth as the strong, metallic taste of blood floods my mouth.

"Peter? Peter Licht? Can you hear me? Are you here?"

The frenzied breathing returns like a sheet billowing in the wind. It's ever so soft, yet every breath is heavy with terror.

"I can hear you, Peter. Don't be scared. Please talk. I-I need to know you're okay," I beg.

A small whimper from beside me. I lean closer to the bars, reaching for the person at the back... but he's too far away. "Peter, it's me. If you're in there, say something! Peter!"

I'm only met with silence. "I won't hurt you... please."

I push my face closer and glimpse a pair of eyes squeezed tightly shut. Sitting back on my heels and sighing, I try to think of a solution. If I were Peter, what would I want to hear? What can I say to draw him out of his cell?

Then, suddenly, I know.

"U la'cohon reifrauni ser..." My voice is rough, like

sandpaper. I clear my throat before continuing, "Upeora iuni dah kin do'suk'chai..." Slowly, it warms, my vocal folds relaxing, the song beginning to sound like... like Raven Asgard's old lullaby. It's like pulling an heirloom out of a box in an attic, warming every inch of me as I remember the nights Peter, Bronwyn, and I spent together.

And it saddens me so intensely to remember what I gave up that it's pointless to resist smiling because my affection for my family, I realize, has not withered in the slightest over the past year.

I am still kneeling by Peter's side. I am still so much better than the coward who abandoned my friends. The compass of my existence finally points to someone, to something.

Just like that, I'm a person again.

"Ad wollis'reifrauni, dyno pal, fuhn ja en maskap reifsomo." I wince as the next part arrives. My voice always used to crack. Every time. Peter would burst into fits of giggles, and Bronwyn would smile to herself, dimples lighting up her cheeks. "Rhivo upeorap frust-glist quim, kin lo—"

"Hold close to my heart," a voice whispers out of the darkness.

A waxy face emerges, each muscle beneath the skin appearing to be melting as shadows leap from feature to feature. They sweep under his eyes and his nose and surround his chin.

"Peter," I gasp. He's much bigger than I remember, yet somehow much skinnier and smaller at the same time. "Peter, it... it's me," I whisper.

"How do you know that song?" the figure slurs, hanging back in the corner of the cell.

"Because I sang it to you," I reply, shoulders sinking. "Don't... don't you remember?"

Uncertainty. That's all I see in his dazed, tired expression. Confusion, bewilderment, but there is... something. A memory. A name.

"Raven?" he whispers. He reaches through the bars, and I can't help but notice just how thin his tiny wrist is. "Y-you're here?" he asks, eyes widening. I can see it all rushing back in a flood of memory. All the years we spent together.

"Yeah. I'm here, and I'm taking you home. Bronwyn, too. We're going to the Flai Realm together."

He shakes his head rapidly, eyes wide. "No, this isn't real. The dream always ends here."

"You aren't dreaming," I say softly, "I'm here."

"You're... really here," he repeats, still staring at me in disbelief.

I lower myself to my knees and reach forward to take his hand. It's icy cold, and he flinches at first, hesitant to touch me in case I should simply disappear and become another dream, but then I do not draw away, and I keep my eyes locked with his, and a small smile appears on his face.

"It's all going to be okay, now," I whisper, squeezing his small fingers.

With his spare hand, he reaches up and wipes several tears from his eyes. "Y-you came back," Peter blubbers, his speech a little slurred, "You *came*!"

"Oh, Peter, of course I did! I love you. I love you, you hear me? You're more than just my friend. You're my brother. I could never have lived with myself knowing you were in here. We're family, and family do *not* leave each other behind," I gasp.

"I know... I-I guess I just gave up. And after you ran last year..."

I push down a fresh wave of guilt. "I know what I did last year. I'm sorry, Peter, for forgetting what was important. But

I'd rather rot in here with you and Bronwyn than be alone out there. I admit that I made some terrible choices. But living with you? Adopting you and Bronwyn as my family... that was not a mistake. *You* are not my mistake. Not choosing you, always, is my greatest fault. I love you so much, and you have destroyed me every day with the knowledge that I was a coward. I'll understand if you can't forgive me, but I choose you. I'm here for my brother, if he'll have me. If he'll choose me, too. I loved you so much, and I still do. Oh, Peter..." I can't say anymore, overwhelmed as I pull his hand into my chest and lightly kiss it.

He gazes at me, his eyes sparkling bright blue with tears. And then his lip quivers, and he breaks down crying, his curly head of blonde hair bouncing up and down.

"Raven. Raven. Raven." He whispers my name over and over as I press my lips together in a pathetic attempt at composure. But the gasping and the sobbing won't stop.

"I-I'll never leave you again. I *promise*. You don't know how many times the Captain walked through our door. I replayed it, stuck in that room, tied inside those walls. Tethered to my own brain. I thought about you constantly, inching, crawling, and sluggishly approaching the day those restraints'd morph into my noose. I can't be the person who left you anymore. I want to be your sister again. B-But we can't stay here, okay? We need to get you out. We're here for Wynn, too."

"We?" Peter asks shakily.

"Me and... and a friend. He's gone to the girls' side to get Bronwyn."

Peter's face turns a pale shade of green. "She won't be there. I've been spitting out my sleeping pills. When they found out, they forced me to take them last night, but I threw them up. I haven't been eating, either. They drug the food. Anyway, I hear things sometimes when they think I'm asleep. They took Wynn to the fourth floor— underground, I mean. I don't know if... if... They do things to the people here, Raven. Awful things."

"Well... we'll just have to go and get her," I say with wavering confidence. "We can do it together, yeah?"

He stifles a fresh wave of tears and nods.

In my crouching position, I attempt to clear my head. My breaths are shaky and escaping my lips at odd intervals. I have to get him out of here, but where is the key? It is only now that I realize that I used all of them on the doors, and so far, I have not seen any for the cells.

"Peter, I don't suppose you know what the keys to these doors look like?"

"No, I—" he begins.

A loud crack interrupts us. Stealing a glance down the corridor, I see feet beginning to storm the cell block. Guards roused by the hooting prisoners from their slumbers of incompetence and occupational disinterest.

Think, Raven, Sixth Sense urges.

I'm fast, and they haven't seen me yet; I can stick my head around the wall, take aim, attack them now, and be hidden in a matter of seconds.

My heartbeat quickens as I decide what to do. Shoot? Stay put? Try to run?

Someone's coming, Sixth Sense says.

"Yeah, no *shit*," I fire back. My stomach begins to do summersaults. I feel sick right down to my bones. It's as though the events of last year are repeating themselves.

Get it together, Raven. Defend your family like you failed to do last time.

Closing my eyes and raising my gun, I whip around the wall and pull the trigger three times, then disappear back around the corner. Curses, shouts of alarm. Do I dare look up to see the damage I've caused?

Have I killed someone?

My hands are shaking uncontrollably now as I fumble about with my weapon. Pressing further into the wall, I wait for the verdict, gulping back vomit.

"What the bloody hell happened!?"

"Everyone get down!"

At least two men I failed to shoot. Two enemies left.

"He's dead," someone declares.

So, I have indeed taken a life. This means I've stooped right down to their level. Pulling a trigger and sending a man to the skies. A man who is possibly innocent. A man who was just following orders. What would his friends and family say if they could look into my eyes and see the face of their loved one's killer?

This is the kind of hazardous game Frost likes to play. I have to stick it out here if I want to win— pulling triggers, taking lives, acting with the same brutality that they confront me with.

To defeat Frost, I have no choice but to become them. And The Moon King knows this. He is testing me. Using me to his advantage, getting me to sell out information on my strengths and weaknesses to determine how easily I'll break.

In those few seconds of silence, the guards realized they're no longer under attack and proceeded to march forward. Fast.

DO SOMETHING, I internally scream, but what!?

"Raven," Peter whispers from behind me.

I am about to ignore him, still frantically trying to cough up a plan, but then my mind flashes back to last year, to the night he was arrested when he called my name, and I did not listen. If I had never cried out that day, I wouldn't be in this building at all, risking my life, Sparrow's life, and my only chance at going home.

And so, this time, I listen.

"The helmet!" he gasps.

"What?" I frown.

"SHOOT the HELMET of the main guard!" he mouths.

"Why will homicide help the situation?" I hiss.

"You already just committed homicide!"

"Yeah, to save your ass! More murder won't stop them all."

He gives up whispering now. "Just do it, Raven! I know I'm weak, but I've been here a year, and I'm not stupid. Listen to me."

Swinging my head around to take the shot will give away my position in the blink of an eye, but it's better than my non-existent plan to get out of this, so I do it anyway.

My bullet whizzes forward, slicing through the air, and hits the metal dome that covers the closest guard's head with a ping. I wince, expecting it to continue right into the man's skull, but this is not ordinary armour. It's Frost armour, and so, naturally, its properties are... how can I describe this? Phenomenal, yet horribly effective.

The bullet bounces cleanly off the shiny silver helmet and comes hurtling back in the exact direction it came from. My eyes widen as I realize it's headed straight for me, but Peter's hand grabs my cloak through the bars and pulls me down just in time for it to zip over my head and smash into the lock of his cell door. Conveniently.

Eyes shining, I turn back to him, "Oh, Peter, you genius! How did you know it'd land in exactly the right place?"

He grins back at me. "Not genius, Raven. Turns out, I'm an air Flai. I moved it with my mind!"

"Hey!" a guard calls, spotting me as he strides forward. "Identify yourself!"

I'm speechless as I stare at Peter, trying to understand exactly what he plans to do now. Then I realize, with a gasp of exasperation, that he simply didn't think this through beyond the point of freeing him from his cell.

"I said, identify yoursel—" the guard begins again, but the Captain has already snatched the gun out of his hands and is taking control.

A shiver of familiarity runs down my spine as our eyes lock. For a second, he pauses, grins… and then his eyebrows raise slightly, and his lips part in an expression of mild amusement.

"Asgard?"

A very different Asgard, I remind myself. Not a terrified fourteen-year-old. A Flai with a gun and a companion who can use his talents effectively. An Asgard who stands a chance.

His eyes hammer into me, but I remain unaltered, refusing to duck my head and show the panic squeezing my chest.

"*Perseus*," I respond through gritted teeth.

CHAPTER 14

I know you.

I know your eyes, your scent, your thoughts, and every intricate detail of your sadistic existence. I study you. My eyes penetrate deep into black knights and glaze over on hot days in Ra. I think about you often, desperately striving to understand which cogs turned in your mind on the day you stripped my mattress bare and shook my belongings from their places. The day you stole my friends but paid special attention to me. Teased me, humiliated me, demoralised me, taunted me.

Why?

Because you knew I had a chance, and a chance is something to be crushed under your boots.

I am your failure, and the only thing we share is my friends' presence behind bars. Peter and Bronwyn are your unspoken whisper, your reminder of what fate lies ahead for me. And they are my taunt, my reminder that this is unfinished.

That I can still win.

You're my victory, my glory, and protecting my friends from your swordpoint is my triumph.

And I'm yours. It's why you chase me. Why no mission can amount to the one assigned to you a year ago.

And so we have some kind of understanding of one another. We know the desires that drove us here.

Perseus hasn't been a major part of my life. He's run into me maybe thrice so far. But this connection runs longer, deeper than that. I know instantly that he was there the day I ran away from home as a weak seven-year-old. He was the soldier that came for me. And he's coming for me again.

I find myself smiling bitterly because I should have known all along that his crazed perseverance was born long before the first Flood Tide of 2053.

And so here we both are, finally on levelled ground. Both knowledgeable, armed, and prepared.

It tugs a smile at my lips.

"Perseus," I say.

The corners of his lips sink slightly at the use of his first name. "How peculiar that I should find someone such as yourself in prison of your own accord. I assume you were not arrested, given that there are three unconscious men upstairs?"

"I *would* tell you if some other fools had managed to arrest me, but it'd hurt your ego. Not that that's difficult. Anyway," I reply breezily, "It's good that I'm here. I had unfinished business to attend to."

"Then we have something in common," the Captain says. "It's about time I arrested you."

"You think so?"

His face harderns. "The law thinks so."

"This isn't about the law, Perseus. This is about a seven-year-old who hurt your pride in the Willow District eight years ago. tell me— are you *really* still sore about that?"

"Oh, you've— Why, you've grown up!" he half-laughs, genuinely smiling with intrigue.

"Indeed. Some of us age well," I say coolly.

His lips flatten into a tight, strained smile, thin with impatience. "Alright. Enough chit-chat. Move an inch, and I'll shoot you," he snarls, pointing the barrel of his gun at me.

"Do I look like I'm moving?" I snap before I can help myself.

"Put your hands above your head. Slower!" he barks, turning to his colleagues. "Derek, Avia. Grab her."

Two figures dart forward, and I shrink back, brandishing my pistol. A third guard leaps forward and drags Peter and the other inmate out of their cell and into the centre of the floor, shoving Peter to his knees.

The second inmate is beaten with a gun until he stirs, screaming for them to stop in a jumble of disconnected words. Peter was right about the sleeping pills.

While I'm distracted by the moaning man beside me, the gun is prised from my hands. Derek and Avia drag me before Perseus. I arch a brow as though asking calmly if he'd like me to grovel at his feet, and his jaw sets.

"Talk," Perseus spits.

Peter's face is reflected into my eyes by the blade of his polished rapier. The fury running wild through my veins is seeping away now. Despite my efforts to control it, I'm shaking all over.

I can take a slash of his sword, but not the innocent eleven-year-old who never harmed a soul. Not my brother.

I swallow my thoughts, my eyes darting to Peter, who shrugs hopelessly. Maybe he really did have no plan. Perhaps we're going to die, and there's no point trying to think logically.

Perseus nods, and one soldier cocks his gun, striding towards Peter with a grim expression—

"WAIT! No! I'll talk, I'll talk! I'm sorry!" I gasp.

The Captain raises a hand and the sentry falls back into position, away from peter. "Ah, compliance. About time. You've almost pleased me, but I don't find your apology very genuine. So, let's agree not to lie to one another and do this quickly, okay? What are you doing here, Miss Raven?"

"I-I just got here," I lie, my throat like sandpaper. "As a prisoner. Floodonora... T-they caught me on my way out of Frost this morning. The traders were working with the Frost Guard, so they arrested me. I escaped my cell, and I was planning to free my friends, w-which is why I was upstairs. B-Because Bronwyn's... upstairs... I think I'll just go back to my cell now."

The Captain glares at me, his cold eyes scouring out my face in search of truth, before raising his gun. Without hesitation, without even looking, he shoots Peter's inmate in the neck. "Liar," he says.

The prisoner collapses backwards and slumps onto the ice, his blood splattering everywhere. He's still alive, though, his hands fumbling for his neck. He finds the wound, and he's screaming, screaming, screaming himself into a torrent of red ribbons as we all, quite literally, watch the life drain from him.

The Captain shoots the prisoner a final time, and everyone collectively flinches as the inmate's eyes roll back into silence.

Avia steps forward, her lower lip trembling. "Sir, execution requires a warrant. You can't just—"

"I can't just *what*, Avia?"

"Kill someone," she whispers.

"Avia, that is what you are paid to do. What *we* are paid to do," he says through gritted teeth.

Avia moves back into her position beside me, her fingers trembling around my arm.

I'm staring helplessly, horrified and hyperventilating, as the man dies. I clasp two hands over my mouth, but it doesn't matter at all because no sound could emerge even if I tried to scream.

Perseus steps closer and lowers his face so his eyes are at the same level as mine. Every hair on his prickly chin grazes my skin, and every word he speaks emits a cloud of breath that is so vile I can feel myself recoiling at his menacing tone. "I should make an example out of you, you filthy little rat. I *should*, but I might not."

The guard places a hand on my shoulder and shoves me back into the wall with a force that has no purpose but to remind me of his position of power. This seems to be a pattern about him. About humans. They always want you to know that they're in control. "You see... today I'm feeling kind. I might just feel kind enough to let you go unscathed. Am I going soft?" He eyes me up with a searching look. "Hm. But that doesn't matter, does it? The real question is... How are your fortunes, as of late? Do you have good faith in the turn of the tides?"

The gun's barrel presses harder against my scalp as if to remind me of death's looming presence, ready to swoop down at the bang of a bullet.

At least, at this range, I think, *he cannot see me reach into my pocket, bring a hand up to my face, and slide something into my mouth, pretending to cover it with sheer fear.* I can tell this will amuse him. If he thinks I'm clamping my hands over my mouth to stop myself from screaming, he will surely think he's won.

I catch Peter narrowing his eyes as he carefully watches me, trying to decipher what is happening. I can see in his gaze that he's unsure, his mind still clouded by whatever sleeping drugs he's been forced to take, but one thing he knows for certain is this: skulduggery is afoot.

"W-well, you know what they say, Perseus," I stammer, smiling nervously.

He raises his eyebrows and leans closer. "And what is it that they say?"

"May the flood bring you good fortune."

I spit a handful of stars into his eyes. He howls with pain as I leap to my feet and sprint past him, snatching my weapon from a clueless-looking soldier. I seize Peter's hand, tugging him to his feet on the way. I can see he's white with shock, but that doesn't matter. "C'mon, we have to go!" I gasp.

"B-but that man—" Peter mumbles, his head twisting back to see the guards chasing us and the slumped figure behind them.

"Is dead. And you are not. Now, we need to find Bronwyn quickly—"

"I can barely walk, Raven."

"I know, Peter. I know. But we have to try," I pant, turning and slamming the metal door in Perseus's face just as he reaches us.

We. This isn't going to be like last time because we have each another.

A cry of alarm and pain echoes along the cell block as the door collides with Perseus' nose. Hastily, I find the correct key and slide it into the lock.

There are cheers and looks of disbelief from the cells with every leap of my screaming calves. The prisoners' chant feels like a war cry, but it's also partly just a sound of excitement. This is probably the most thrilling scene that has ever played out in the entire duration of their combined sentences.

"*Fierra!*" Amela encourages.

I flash her a grin, then turn to the prisoners before me, clearing my throat loudly.

As a million heads turn my way, the commotion dies away to anticipatory silence. I swallow, suddenly aware of how much pressure, how many lives, are sitting on my shoulders. "We don't have much time— the door behind me will be forced open in less than a minute. But there is something I need to tell you all. These cell bars are not what you think. They are infused with gold, yes, and your food is drugged with chemicals that strip you of your powers, but these cells are old and weak. I know it's difficult, but if any of you are Flai, you need to try and burn through your doors. Get yourselves out of here, okay? I leave my keys for the rest of you, and I can only pray they'll free you."

A man timidly raises his hand. "There are no Flai here."

"None here that the guards know of. C'mon, speak up. You're telling me all of you are human? Not one Flai was arrested for a different crime?"

A few fearful voices begin to mumble confessions.

I lick my lips nervously. "Look, it doesn't matter if you're human or Flai here. If you want to get out, you need to help one another. And that starts with you." I turn to Amela and take a deep breath before pressing two angry, sizzling palms on her cell door. The pain is almost blinding, but then slowly, it lessens.

Beat the metal, beat the metal. Beat it with magic, I tell myself.

The bars thin until they disappear entirely, forming a hole large enough for a woman to fit through.

"Please," I gasp, "Help one another. Right now, you must stay hidden. But when the guards chase us, when this block is empty... all of you have a chance. Please take it."

As I finish my speech, bullets hammer the door, pelting the metal like raindrops. I seize Peter and continue running, ducking to avoid the oncoming spray of death. Finally, a bullet smashes the lock, and the team of sentries floods the cell block.

To delay them, I sweep out an arm of fire. Concealed by the roaring flames, I slide the jacket from my shoulders and turn to Peter.

"Hold this in the air, facing backwards, at torso height."

He nibbles anxiously on his lip as he raises both arms into the air, catching my coat in a gust and hoisting it up.

"You can't hide behind magic forever!" Perseus roars on the other side of my flames.

He tosses his rapier into the blaze, its gold-infused surface cutting a path through the fire, and seizes the collar of my jacket-

Meanwhile, Peter and I disappear down the corridor, and more chants ensue. I've just outsmarted a head guard. Defied Frost like no one ever dared to. And if there is anything Frost hates, it's humiliation. I'm a legend to these people. I reach the mouth of the passage and pause for a moment to consider finding Sparrow.

It's an extremely hazardous gamble, and my heart warns me against it. Sparrow is wise. He will get out of the girls' side of the prison on his own.

I dash around the corner and enter the tunnel that leads back to the metal hallways, dragging Peter along with me. I desperately want to scold him, but the most I can get out in our current situation is a "What were you thinking!?", which feels hardly effective enough.

"I thought that I could hide you in my cell after the bullet broke the lock!" Peter squeaks as we hurry up the first flight of stairs.

"D'you know what happened instead? I fought seven guards alone, a man died, and you almost got us killed!"

"But I didn't."

"But you almost did!" I pant, furious.

"But I *didn't*," he grins.

"Drugs must be wearing off quickly, huh?"

Unexpectedly, his face falls, and he lets out a moan. "Oh no."

Panting, I pull him away from the next flight and into the nearest cupboard in eyesight.

"What now?"

"I have a stitch," he whispers.

"You have to be *kidding* me!" I cry, thoroughly annoyed by this point. I can't see his annoying little face clearly because the only light illuminating the cramped space comes from the crack between the door and the floor, but I know he's smiling in amusement.

"Oh, hullo, Raven," Sparrow says casually from behind a rail of guards' uniforms.

"*GAAH!*" Peter and I both scream, and I lash out with my fist.

"You gave me a heart attack!" I hiss as the bulb I had not previously noticed above my head flickers to life.

"What a shame you survived it," he mutters. "But listen, I couldn't find Bronwyn anywhere, but I thought I heard your voice, so I came up here, and then a guard came past, and I hid." His nose wrinkles. "What are you doing in my cupboard?"

"*Your* cupboard?" I repeat.

"*I* found it," Sparrow reasons.

"Well, you're not going to keep it, are you!" I gasp.

He stares blankly at me, as if puzzled at the concept of exiting a fortress empty-handed— even one armed to the teeth with soldiers trying to kill us. Which, I've come to realize recently, is quite a Sparrow-ish thing to do, along with tying people up as a form of introduction and taking people with ten-thousand-shackle bounties on their heads to picturesque countryside inns.

"Hello. Are you Raven's friend? We're just casually hiding from certain death. It's nice to meet you," Peter chimes in. He may be weak from the conditions of this place, but he hasn't lost the signature cheeky edge to his voice.

"Sparrow, Peter. Peter, Sparrow," I say matter-of-factly, waving a hand about to gesture back and forth between the two boys. "Listen. All we know is that Bronwyn's upstairs on the third floor," I say, "Peter heard some guards talking about taking her up there. But they know I'm here, so we have to find her and get out of here ASAP."

"Got it." Sparrow shuffles awkwardly around in the dark space to face Peter.

"What's up, bro?" he grins, ruffling Peter's blonde curls. "How're you?"

"I just nearly died," Peter states blankly.

"Excellent," he grins, giving him a first bump. "You know, It'll be great to have another boy around. Raven can be *so*—"

"Can we save this for later?" I interrupt, pressing my face to the wall beside the door. "Oh, no. I can't see anything. We're going to have to make a run for it and hope for the best."

"Okay. Peter, you said you had a stitch. Can you run?" Sparrow enquires.

"I can try, but I've been sitting down, chained up, for months, and I'm all wobbly," he answers uncertainly, testing his body weight on his leg.

Sparrow and I exchange concerned looks, which doesn't go unnoticed by Peter.

I can see the fear building in his eyes, but instead of crying or curling up in a ball, he looks me directly in the eyes.

"I'll stay here," he says, "And buy you some time. I've been watching the guards for months. I can use a gun, and I'll run if I can't hold them off —I promise," he adds, "But I have my powers, now. I can fling them across the room like pebbles. Also, they probably won't shoot a little boy if I'm alone. I could even pretend to be wounded. Like, a hostage or something."

""Probably" isn't good enough. You're coming with us, and that's that," Sparrow says firmly. He's trying to be sure, trying to sound confident. It's not working.

"I'll slow you down," Peter says softly.

"We aren't leaving you, buddy."

"Then, at least let me guard the top of the stairs, where I can always run up to another floor," Peter begs. "Bronwyn needs you. *I* need you to protect her. It's like Raven said— she's not just a friend. She's like family to me— like a sister. I love her."

"But *I* love you," I croak, our eyes locking.

"Then take her. Take her away from here. Please."

It's the first time I've seen him look like this, heard him speak like this. Before, in his cell, he was weak, excited, and still a little boy. But now it's as though he's grown up in a matter of seconds.

"You don't have much time, and there's no way you can search a whole floor with guards running around all over the place," he reasons. "I'm strong now, Raven. Please let me help."

Before I can reply, I feel myself being lifted rapidly into the air, rocketing towards the ceiling. However, just as my head grazes it, I'm lowered gently back to my feet. I stumble back into Sparrow's arms, terrified and bewildered-

Until my eyes lock with Peter's.

"See what I can do?" Peter begs, "I can fight them."

I glance at Sparrow, my heart thumping in symphony with the stampede of footsteps approaching outside. "I think... I think we should let him."

Sparrow hesitates. "Not that you aren't strong, Peter, but... Raven's quite skinny and light. She's not the kind of guards you'd be facing."

"I've lived alongside the guards for a year. I know this prison inside-out. A-And I have a sixth sense, now. I called it Brooke because it talks to me, sometimes," he explains.

"Are you sure that, uh, *Brooke* isn't just... Y'know. Voices? I mean, I didn't get mine until—" I begin.

"Cough," Sparrow says.

I stare at him. "You don't have to actually say the word "cough", you know. If we're getting off-topic, just lightly butt in, and—"

"We can't let him go!" Sparrow interrupts.

"Yes, you can!" Peter retorts, "I'm not a child."

"Let the grown-ups talk, please," I say sweetly, tugging Sparrow rather violently towards me.

"Listen!" I hiss, "He and I can communicate through Sixth Sense. I know it sounds crazy, but we can. If I'm in contact with him, we can report to one another on the locations of guards and help one another navigate paths to safety. If we're split, the guards will be divided, too. Trust me."

He stares at me for a long time, his eyes calculating. Eventually, he rubs his temples and nods.

I turn back to Peter. "If there are reinforcements, or if they get too strong, do whatever you can to stay alive, okay? And tell me where you are and what you're doing using Brooke. You *must* keep me informed," I say sharply, turning back to Peter. "Also... take these."

I hand him my pistols and guns, and Sparrow also

contributes, giving the boy a few daggers and revolvers. Peter takes them, studies each weapon briefly for a moment, and then tucks them into his filthy clothes.

"Do you know how to...?" Sparrow begins.

"The guards shoot people a lot. I've seen them do it. I know how they work."

Silence, now.

A thousand words, a million. It'll never be enough. I approach Peter slowly and affectionately, my fingers wandering to his chest to hover over his heart, where I can feel a strong, steady beat. Then I fling my arms around him. "Stay alive, idiot."

"No promises," he grins, the familiar twinkle in his eye returning.

We all take a second to look at one another, drinking up every facial detail, engraving our faces in one another's memories. It is Peter who finally ends this silent, solemn goodbye. "Thank you, Raven. I was so scared this past year, you know? But you make me strong."

"On three?" Sparrow offers, his hand on the cupboard door. I nod, and we begin counting.

"One..." I mentally note the tiny scar on Sparrow's cheek that I'd never previously noticed, never thought to ask about.

"Two..."

The sea-green flecks in Peter's blue-grey irises.

"*Three.*"

We shove open the door, prepare for combat, and take our positions as the noise swells up in the stairwell. Hundreds of guards, by the sound of it. All aiming for us. All here for us.

"We're screwed, aren't we?" Sparrow says from beside me. But he isn't scared. He's laughing, almost. And there is only one reply I can give.

"You're figuring this out *now*?"

It all happens extremely fast. Suddenly, we're all climbing up to the fourth floor, and the chaos of The Berg has exploded from below into echoes that descend from even the uppermost floors. Peter is just a few strides slower than Sparrow and I, a few strides that make me terrified for his fate.

A blaring siren attacks my ears, screaming at me from every direction. Instinctively, I cover them, barging into the wall as I stumble up more steps. A part of me is attempting to escape the awful noise, but it's not coming from below. It reverberates all around.

"Aargh! What is that!?" Sparrow cries.

"I don't know, some kind of alarm? We have to hurry!" I say, face pale, chest heaving, and we barrel on.

Reaching the negative-third-floor landing, Sparrow kicks the door in. But this is unnecessary because it swings easily open. It was locked since we first descended through the east side of the fortress. "Why is it unlocked?"

Sure, it's convenient, but… too convenient?

"Maybe the guards aren't following us, but they're making for the exits," Sparrow murmurs. "Or maybe it's a different staircase entirely."

In the mad whirl of events, I'd barely considered our route of travel, only working off memory, but somehow, this feels unlikely. My forehead creases. "But why would they—?"

"How will we find out which room Bronwyn's in?" Sparrow calls out, interrupting me. I pull Peter up the final few steps by the collar of his shirt, then drag him through the doorway. "Errr…"

"You didn't think of this already?" he cries.

"We were a bit busy down in the cells, Sparrow! A bit busy trying not to die!"

"What, and we've plenty of time to do it now?"

"Just —aargh!— come on!" I groan, racing down the corridor.

"Where are you going?" Sparrow demands.

"Away from the people trying to kill us, if you don't mind." I halt, suddenly remembering Peter, and turn to him.

The small boy says nothing and only nods, flashing me a brief, anxious smile.

"You must get yourself out, Peter. You *must*."

"I got this. I can distract them, and you need time. Time to find Bronwyn."

"We will."

"You have to," he whispers, and we hug in parting.

And then Sparrow pulls me down the corridor, and I do not look back until we have turned the corner and it's already too late.

"We'll search the rooms individually, just a brief glance inside. There's no point searching too thoroughly. It's not like they'd hide Bronwyn," Sparrow instructs. "I'll take doors on the left, you on the right."

"Right," I nod.

"No, I'm taking the left," he repeats sharply.

"No, I didn't mean— Just start looking," I sigh, reaching out for the first door. "Locked."

"Mine too."

I try the next, carefully push it ajar, and listen. "Empty. Yours?"

"Yeah. But they've got some freaky stuff in here."

"What?"

"Test tubes. Equipment for experiments and stuff. God, what are they *doing* down here?"

"Sparrow, keep moving."

"Right, sorry."

The following two doors are locked. The third is a storeroom. There's no sign that any rooms were recently used, and the only peculiar thing I notice is that all the counters and tables are made of metal and fixed firmly to the ground with steel bolts. Other smaller objects are magnetic.

As Sparrow and I continue our search, I begin to feel a pressure building up in my skull, as though something's forcefully pushing itself to the front of my mind. Peter, I assume.

Faint echoes of his sixth sense leap through my mind. Sharp, precise directions to guide him away from danger as he lures the guards away from our corridor. But no direct communication yet. I'll know if he attempts to speak with me.

Sparrow draws in a shaky breath from the opposite side of the hall and turns to face me. "Raven, I think you need to see this."

I creep over to the doorway that's illuminating the entire hall with its bright glow and peer inside the room. It's a large, square, high-ceilinged chamber, and its walls are tiled with blinding white squares, just like the floor. Unappealing scents of various chemical concoctions snake up my nostrils. A large metal counter stands in the centre of the room, and upon it is the most terrifying machine I've ever seen.

It's a cage of sorts, and inside it sits a small, grubby stool. Chains hang from all four inner corners, and at the end are much larger rings of iron that suggest they should be attached to something. I don't want to imagine what- or who.

Above the cage is a round iron plate that makes a mechanical hum. I can make out hundreds of tiny nozzles screwed to the inside, like a showerhead. Amela whispers in my mind. *The yellow. It sprinkle.* Could this be what she was talking about?

Something about this place is different from all the other rooms. It's clearly an important part of the Iceberg, one kept hidden from prying eyes. So, what on earth is it for?

Suddenly, the pressure in my head is released, and a simple message enters my mind. *Left! Right! Duck!* Not a message for me, but it at least tells me Peter's in good hands with Brian or Betty or whatever he named his sixth sense. Then— *Peter*, Brooke adds, for clarity.

I know who you are, I shoot back. He won't receive the words —they're my thoughts, not my sixth sense's— but he'll know I understand.

A hand closes around my arm mere seconds after his warning. "Raven!" Sparrow hisses, "Move!"

Suddenly, the sound of footsteps floods my ears. Several people are striding down the hall. He yanks me inside the doorway, whispering, "Hide!" before dashing for cover.

Dropping to a crawl and disappearing out of sight, I take off in the same direction as him, behind a row of tables. They don't touch the floor, so my knees are in plain sight. I continue to crawl along the aisle, searching for a nook or a cupboard to hide in.

My heartbeat quickens as the footsteps enter the room. I can differentiate between several heavy ones, boots falling fast and efficiently into a march, and small struggling ones. Will they look in my direction?

A hand seizes my arm, and Sparrow pulls me into a small cupboard under a desk. "Got you," he whispers.

Then he silently points behind me, and I turn to see a pair of boots walking down the very counter row I'd been crawling through. A second later, and I would've gotten us both killed.

"Thanks," I mouth, drawing my knees up to my chest and hoping we aren't visible from this angle. I don't trust myself to leave a limb outstretched, just in case.

Safe. I feel the message leave the back of my mind.

Safe, comes Peter's sense's reply.

From our hiding spot, I can see the top half of the machine and two figures wearing long white lab coats circling it. "Bad men in white"?

Another man and two women stride over to a neat array of laptops that are already blinking on and begin to encode complicated instructions.

The smaller figure I heard earlier is nowhere to be seen. I turn to look at Sparrow, perplexed, and he shrugs.

"No! Let me go!"

I freeze, the hairs on the back of my neck rising. A sudden scream breaks loose, along with footsteps making for the exit. Then more join in as well, turning into a stampede of predator and prey. A chase.

I hear a string of curses from the doctors, and someone screams, "THE LITTLE DEVIL IS USING MAGIC!" My eyes widen as the footsteps rush past our row of cupboards and out of the room.

It can't possibly be… a Flai?

Sparrow and I exchange unsettled glances. Just as I'm about to suggest we take a closer look at the contraption, a sharp cry of pain echoes from the corridor, and the footsteps re-enter the room, along with a dragging sound like a brush sweeping over the tiles.

The tiles.

I narrow my eyes. Are those grooves empty, or are my eyes playing tricks? The tiles are firmly fixed to the floor with no adhesive in sight.

My train of thought derails as the cries of the smaller figure turn into moans of pain.

"Please... no!" she begs as they drag her back into the room. One of them is holding her by the neck, and another is holding her by the wrists. Together, they pull her up a little ramp and order one of the other doctors to press a button on the other side of the machine. Part of the cage's bars slide aside like a door, and they force her inside as she struggles, shoving her down onto the stool and chaining her wrists and ankles to the cage.

Through the commotion, it's impossible to see her face.

The doctors quickly exit as the girl thrashes about, and the cage door is shut and locked, bars sealing her inside. The female doctor hurries over to the doorway and dims the lights so that, at last, the girl's face isn't obscured by the blinding white glare of them.

A pair of bright, terror-infused, sage-green eyes, a mane of thick, curly black hair that frames a dark-skinned face...

"BRONWYN!?" I clasp my hands over my mouth, wishing to tear myself to shreds, for I've made exactly the same mistake as I did a year ago. Back in Frost. Back in the shack. Back when I spoke too loudly, my friends paid the price for it.

The worst thing is that what follows my outburst happens in the same nightmarish pattern. Absolutely everyone in the room stops, including Bronwyn. She recognises my voice.

"Raven?" she breathes. Suddenly, earlier sirens from the stairwell blast across the room in an ear-splitting wave.

"Someone's here!" one of the doctors yells over the noise,

sounding hauntingly similar to Perseus. Then he turns to his co-workers. "Humanise the girl! Quickly, before she uses those blasted powers to escape! You! Don't call for a room search— that siren means a level 7. Everyone's clearing out, so who's gonna search it, imbecile? Unless this is another bloody drill... Hey! What did I just tell you!? Don't call for a search. Move it! NOW!"

"Yes, sir!" comes the chorus of flushed replies.

My eyes are fixed on Wynn's. She knows. She sees me.

I want to leap out of the cupboard and help her, to stop the doctors, to do something, but we're outnumbered by three to four grown adults, and though my powers may just be enough to take them on, my abilities are still uncontrollable.

And yet, I can't just sit here... can I?

Sparrow's hand comes down on mine, and he shakes his head, his eyes burning into mine. "Stay."

"But—"

"If you really want to help her, stay. Raven, if you go out there, they *will* kill you. You're no use to Bronwyn if you're dead."

I shake my head vigorously. "I-I can't! I don't know what they might... Sparrow, they could kill her!"

"I know," he whispers. "But we need to be strong, Rave."

"Rave?" I repeat.

He smiles. "Thought you'd like it better than "Your Highness". Besides, you're less stuck-up now."

"It's... er..."

I'm interrupted by the sound of metal on metal filling the air as Bronwyn struggles against her restraints, shrieking. "Help! Help me! Raven! *RAVEN!*"

Eyes welling up with tears, I turn away, burying myself

into the fabric of my clothes. Maybe I will suffocate in this dark, dark cupboard, on this dark, dark day, on this dark, dark island. Maybe slipping into the final peace, the final silence, is better than staying here. Sparrow clutches my hand tighter, turning my fingers white. I don't dare let go.

"Help..." Bronwyn says again, voice growing weaker, quieter, softer now. She knows that I will not help her. Knows she is running out of time. "Somebody. Anybody. Help me..."

"Keys," one of the doctors interrupts, cutting across her pleads. The female doctor holds up a red key, and one of the males has an identical one. "Insert," the doctor instructs. "And together in... 1, 2... turn!"

"*Procedure... locked... keep... clear,*" an automated voice blares. "*Keep... clear.*"

Bronwyn is growing distressed now, sobbing. "Wait! No! Please! I'll do anything! Please, I'm a Flai, I'm a Flai, I'm a Flai! Don't do this! I don't want to be human! I'm a—"

"Shut up," one of the doctors says, glaring at her. "Or do I need to have you punished again?"

Bronwyn only whimpers.

"Sparrow... oh my god... we can't do this," I whisper, choking on my own words. My hands are shaking now, and my legs are already beginning to move—

Sparrow pulls me back. "Raven!"

"Let go of me!" I shoot back.

"No! Raven... I'm sorry. I can't let you help her. Not until they're gone. Not until you're safe. Don't you see? You can't do anything. You can burn every one of them to the ground, but it won't stop it. It won't save her."

"There's a way! There has to be! I can burn through the cage!"

"No, you can't. It's gold."

"Sparrow, let go. *Let go of me.*"

His grip on my wrist slackens. "Please," he gasps.

That one word and the desperation in his voice stops me.

Please. It's pathetic, almost. And yet it's everything, and he's gazing at me like he'd choose me over not just Bronwyn, but the universe.

And I understand exactly why.

I was cold, ungrateful, distrusting, and cruel a mere day ago. But today, Sparrow's seen the tiniest sliver of compassion in me. He saw how desperately I care for my family and friends, and so, suddenly, in his eyes, I'm so much more understandable because he can finally see what I lost and how it killed me.

And the fact that he knows, now, that the Raven who first greeted him is merely a mask, inexplicably gravitates me towards him, and vice versa. I've loosened my grip on my hatred towards him, and for that, the promise of a potential friendship on both our parts is now at risk alongside everyone —and everything— else. I don't want to lose his company, and Sparrow doesn't want to lose mine. A human and a Flai, both rejected by the opposite species and hated by everyone including ourselves. When we find someone else drowning in the same river, we can't turn away. We're possibly each other's last chance at companionship before I return home to the Realm.

Again, I'm struck with a wave of perplexion. Why doesn't someone like Sparrow have more friends back homr? Why is he so desperate to be close to me and give me what he never had?

I'm not special. I don't *matter* that much.

But somehow, he needs me. He needs someone who understands that he's just like me in every way, even if we're worlds apart.

Because that's what we are, I realize, *worlds apart.*

He's a human who rejects his nature, and I'm a Flai who desires to be anything but. We despise ourselves so deeply that we've come to find and scrutinize the similarities in one another, grappling for two ends of the same rope.

World's apart, and utterly the same.

And Sparrow's not willing to risk that connection, because perhaps there's never been anyone like me before in his life. A mirror. An empathiser. A *human*— even though I'm a Flai through and through.

Leaning against the back of the cupboard, I let the tears fall, curled up with my knees hugged to my chest as I try to make the terrible sight disappear. But now it's all slowly clicking into place.

Yellow water. It's gold. Liquid gold— I can hear the splash of it spilling out onto Wynn's head. Her shrill screams become gurgles.

Make it stop, make it stop, make it stop.

Sparrow's arms will never be warm or comforting enough. Not for this. Nothing can hide me from this. This is the worst kind of evil, a kind of evil sick, sick men must lie awake to dream up. This is despicable. And they'll do it to every last one of us. Drain us and humanise us. Perhaps I'm next.

The gold keeps coming in waves, flecks of it sometimes hitting the edges of the cage and hissing as they connect with the bars, suggesting they're designed to repel the substance. Bronwyn's body twitches uncontrollably as her hands try to bat away the liquid in every direction, scrambling to protect her exposed skin. Her face contorts as the liquid penetrates every part of her, gushing straight into her veins and neutralising the blood. Neutralising the magic. "Cleansing" her. "Fixing" her.

I squeeze my eyes tightly shut. They take our possessions, our families, our homes. They take our freedom, our spirits... Why can't they at least let us have this? At least let us keep our wings.

"Alright, that's enough! She can't cause us any more trouble, so let's get out of here."

I blink my eyes open, shaking.

"It's over," Sparrow tells me softly. "It's over, Raven. You can look."

My throat feels sticky, and trying to push the words up it feels impossible. I swallow, mustering the courage to ask. "Is she...?"

"Dead? No, I don't think so. She passed out, though," Sparrow says grimly, "Her body's in shock."

"And the doctors?"

"They're just watching... Wait! I think they're leaving!"

Voices become audible through the wall as someone strides along the corridor outside.

"Who sent out a distress call? Hello? Is anyone still in there?"

One of the doctors turns on his employee, red in the face. "I told you not to send for a room search!"

"There could be another Flai in the building unrestrained! They could attack us all! Even worse, activate the you-know-what!" the other man says defensively.

"Hello?" the voice calls again from the corridor.

"Over here! There's someone in this room!" the female doctor hollers back.

"An intruder!" the other doctor adds.

"Leave it! Someone took out 3 guards and broke into

Nather. They're still somewhere in the building. The prisoners went mad and are in a full-scale riot. A few got out, and we lost track of them. We're evacuating. This isn't a drill."

"But what about—" the fuming doctor protests.

"They'll be lost with the prisoners! Plan Z was activated. We've lost control. It's better to flush the place. C'mon!" the voice hollers back.

The female doctor glances at her co-workers and then at the door. "We should go, doc. We don't have much time." She turns to the others, who're still busy on the computers. "You all heard me!"

"I'm not getting paid enough for this," the angry doctor grumbles, following the woman into the hallway.

The last doctor surveys the room, staring at the sodden lump that is Bronwyn one final time. I can only imagine what must be rushing through his head— *She's a kid…just a kid.*

Come on, doc. Don't leave her. I know there's good in him. There's good in everyone.

He turns and flees.

CHAPTER 15

"Come on!" Sparrow urges me, hastily crawling out of the nook and dashing over to Wynn's cage.

I pause before following him, afraid to see my friend, to see what they have done to her. Her head hangs limp and lifeless as a doll's, flecks of gold trickling through her parting. In its solid form, it would have killed her, burned right through her skin, and turned her into a powerless, bloody mess.

"Wynn?" I whisper, reaching through the cage bars. I gently push aside a stray wisp of hair from her face. "Wynn, can you hear me?" No response. Nothing. "What do we do?" I call out to Sparrow, having to shout over the deafening sirens.

"You stop it somehow. I'll try and get her out," he answers.

"Stop what?"

In reply, he points to the floor, where the tiles are very, very slowly moving apart. Water seeps through the gaps between them. "We're sinking. Fast," Sparrow says.

Stunned, I stare at the puddle of water at my feet. It grows bigger and bigger, joining hands with its neighbour, doubling in size. "This doesn't make sense; it'll kill everyone on the lower floors. What if they didn't get out in time!?" I splutter.

"Raven, look around. Everything is made of metal, and the cabinets are completely glued to the floor. And listen!

Can't you hear the mechanisms in the walls?"

I open my ears, and indeed, I can hear the slow clunk of something as it rolls over, reeling the tiles apart to make way for the water.

"These tiles... they're opening up on purpose," Sparrow continues, "This whole building is designed to be flooded. I'd bet there are secret exits everywhere for the guards, and... well, you heard them— the prisoners went berserk. Most probably broke out before it flooded down there. I'm sure they're all okay. Frost wouldn't ensure the safety of the guards' lives but not the prisoners'. Frost wouldn't..." he trails off as his words dissolve into a grim silence.

Because Frost *would*.

Frost would kill every prisoner in this building without blinking an eye. I can already imagine it: the steady gush of water. The pleading and the slams of bodies against bars as thousands desperately try to escape. But half of them won't have gotten out, and the ones that did were probably murdered by guards. Children. Flai. Men, women, and humans alike.

Barriers between blood and water, between the human and the not, crossed and smashed until sin cannot recognize the sinner. It all makes sense. The bodies were found, and the alarm was raised.

This flood must be a security defence mechanism created to flush out the building and kill everyone inside. This explains the lack of soft materials throughout the fortress and how the doors to every room always seem open except for rare anomalies. The sirens that pierce the air are not a warning that someone has got *in* the building. They're a warning for the soldiers to get *out*.

"Raven, we have to hurry. Do whatever you can to keep this water down!" Sparrow says quickly, dashing over to the machine where Bronwyn sits and tugging at the door.

I root around my pockets for the ring of keys, but remember I used them all on the doors earlier and gave the rest to the prisoners. But maybe...

Maybe one key still sags the material of my pocket.

"Move!" I exclaim, shoving Sparrow out of my path. I easily find the screws on the cage and use the teeth of the key to twist them away. One by one, I send them to the floor. At last, the door swings off its hinges and clashes noisily with the floor, but that doesn't matter now. Bronwyn stirs slightly at the noise of the collision, murmuring soft but jumbled words.

Sparrow wastes no time on the cuffs that bind her wrists and ankles, firing four bullets at the chains and breaking them instantly. I shove anything I can find over the cracks in the floor, attempting to slow the pace of the flooding, but the water is rising at a steady, undisturbed rate, moving outwards to thrum at the walls, and my efforts won't make a dent in it.

Once I've done all I can, I frantically rush over to the laptops and panels of buttons, thinking perhaps I can find a way to disable the flooding. My fingers run over the complex display of levers and dials, searching for something useful.

"Raven, not that I don't trust you, but I don't think messing around with those is a good idea," Sparrow calls from across the room.

"There's a big red one!" I yell back, "It says, *"in case of emergency"*!"

"Do *not* push it!"

"I'm gonna push it," I reply and slam a fist down on the button.

"*Self-destruct activated. Complete demolition in ten minutes,*" an automated voice drones.

"Everything okay over there?" Sparrow asks.

"Just peachy," I reply, breaking into a nervous sweat. Perhaps the "on" button serves as an "off" button, too, like the contraption in the Nother cell block? Hesitantly, I press the button again to see if it'll disable my previous command.

"*Extreme self-destruct activated. Complete demolition in five minutes.*"

"You've got to be KIDDING ME!" I roar.

"Raven, what did you *do*?" Sparrow shouts.

"Er..."

"RAVEN!"

"Let's just say, if we don't get out of here in approximately four minutes and 57 seconds, it's gonna get a little bit... explosive?"

He gapes at me. "You set off a *BOMB*?"

"I didn't mean to!"

"What, and that makes it okay?" he shoots back, scooping up Wynn in his arms. He carefully studies her face, paying no attention to the rising water, and delivers a brutally hard slap with clammy palms. Nothing— her head lolls. "She's out cold. I'll have to carry her," he sighs.

"I'll help," I nod, reaching for her ankles, but Sparrow grabs my wrist.

"Don't. Just... go. Get Peter."

I nod and dash out of the room, trying to ignore the fact that the water is rising close to my thighs now. It's becoming increasingly difficult to walk, but as I splash along the corridor, I find that within a few seconds, swimming is possible.

When I reach the staircase, I find it completely and utterly flooded. If Peter was still down there battling guards when the floor flooded, unable to get out, he's dead for sure. I can only hope he made it. *Deep breaths, Raven.*

"PETER!" I bellow, "PETER! I'M HERE!" My voice echoes, and water sloshes past me. Circling my waist, gushing down the corridor.

"RAVEN?" Peter's voice replies. He sounds distressed, panicked, and as though he's breathing heavily, but my heart lights up nonetheless. Peter is alive and safe! "RAVEN..." he blurts, "I CAN'T SWIM!"

"PETER..." I struggle to think of a good reply, "JUST... JUST GET TO THE GROUND FLOOR!" I shout, trying to follow his voice, but it seems to be coming from everywhere.

"OKAY. I'LL MEET YOU THERE."

I hear large splashes from somewhere behind me, around the corner, and take a sharp left, navigating my way back to Sparrow. He wades out of the lab with Bronwyn slung over his shoulder.

"Raven, are you with Peter?" he calls out, and I swim up to him, shaking my head. My feet no longer touch the floor. We're rising with the water, and I can already feel my breaths growing longer and shallower as the oxygen supply decreases. "Do you know where he is?" Sparrow enquires.

"No, but we're regrouping on the ground floor. C'mon!" I try to remember which way the stairs are... left or right? Sparrow swims forward with Bronwyn still over his shoulder, and I suddenly have an idea.

"Dunk her!" I exclaim, turning around to face him.

"What?"

"Dunk her head in! It's seawater! It's freezing cold; it might wake her up! Hurry!" I add.

He considers the risks of this for a second before remembering how little time we have left to spare and doing it anyway. The floppy limbs hanging over his back suddenly jolt back to life as she thrashes in the water. "Wha- hello? What's going o- *Raven*?" she shrieks, bewildered, then her gaze moves to the boy holding her. "Who are you?"

"I'm a boy in a chicken mask," he replies, "And we're about to die, so if I were you, I'd shut up and swim."

She takes this news surprisingly well for someone who was just unconscious moments ago, which makes me suspect the young girl has suffered brief memory loss.

"This way to the stairs!" Sparrow instructs. He has to yell now, for the water is everywhere, gushing in ribbons, torrents, swathing over everything in its path, drowning out his words.

My legs and arms are aching with the effort of keeping myself above the water.

"DON'T STOP!" Sparrow shouts, "LOOK, THAT'S OUR EXIT! I SEE THE STAIRS!"

And indeed, there they are! We all rush forward, limbs propelling us, muscles burning from such demanding efforts, and I latch my fingers around the bannister to pull myself up.

The water is up to my breasts and shows no sign of stopping. A pipe bursts above my head, spewing water, and sparks fly. The lights above my head blink out, leaving us in darkness.

"I don't think it's supposed to do that, Sparrow!" I gasp.

"Who cares if a pipe breaks? The building is literally going to explode! Two different mechanisms were triggered simultaneously. This place is tearing itself apart. We don't have much time!"

Every step we take lowers the water around us, but every second, it's still rising, and so we're stuck in the cramped space between water and ceiling, unable to breathe. Finally, my feet reunite with the floor, and I can run past the water onto dry stairs.

I offer my hand to Sparrow, and he scrambles up after me, holding onto Wynn, and then all three of us are finally temporarily ahead of the flood and back under the weak but comforting glare of the lights.

The key word here is "temporarily".

We manage to get right up to the second-to-ground floor before the power shuts off entirely throughout the whole building. Then, the three of us are left, exhausted and freezing, to fight for our lives in utter darkness.

"Sparrow, where are you?" I whisper, feeling around. The only thing I can hear is the drip, drip, drip of water as it runs off the corner of my cloak and splatters onto the floor.

"Hello? Raven?" Bronwyn squeaks in a small voice, making me jump.

"Guys, over here!" Sparrow says, "Follow my voice and don't let go of the railing. Hold hands, too. We can't lose each other."

Stairs, stairs, flight after flight. Then—

"Wait. Where's Peter?" Bronwyn asks. "I thought Raven said we were regrouping on the ground floor. I heard her, I swear I did... but it's all fuzzy now, and my head aches. Where even are we? Shouldn't Peter be going up these very stairs right now?" she asks weakly.

"He must've taken the east staircase," Sparrow answers, "There's a bunch of different ways to get around this place, and we definitely took a wrong turn earlier. Raven, how long did you say we had?"

"Not long enough. A minute at most. Come on. Quickly!"

"What are you talking about!? A minute? What's that supposed to mean!?" Bronwyn asks sharply.

"I... well..."

"*Raven!*" she urges.

"She set off a bomb," Sparrow chimes in.

Bronwyn is too stunned to speak, so I interrupt. "We can't explain right now. Feel around for the door on your left! Down that corridor, take a right, and the exit's right there!"

Sixth Sense guides me now, feeding directions into my mind and interweaving memory with action as I subconsciously recall the path we took when descending through the fortress hours ago.

They follow me, just a meter or two behind, and crash through the glass doors just a moment after I do. Upon realizing that we're out —we're actually *out!*— I collapse onto the slippery, icy ground with relief.

"We're alive! I don't believe it... we're alive!"

"Yeah, but we aren't safe yet," Sparrow gasps, "Come on, let's get out of here before it explodes. Then we'll—"

"Wait! We can't leave! What about Peter?" Bronwyn interjects.

"He'll get out on his own," Sparrow replies, coming up behind me, "For all we know, he's at a completely different exit. There are four."

"What if we get separated?" I argue, "And even if he's on the other side of the iceberg, he doesn't know about the bomb, and he can't swim! We should just wait for him."

"I don't think you understand that in a matter of seconds, we could all be dead!" he retorts, raising his voice. "Look— there are people in the water. Prisoners, holding onto things. Even they know it's not wise to stay here. Peter will, too."

"No. He'll come." I say quietly, eyes fixed on the room before me. He'll come, I reassure myself.

With my hands writhing impatiently, another precious five seconds pass. Why isn't he coming? *Peter, where are you?*

"Can't you communicate with him?" Sparrow asks.

"I'm trying! His sixth sense isn't saying anything," I gasp, straining my ears for any sign of Peter.

There's nothing. My sense hangs heavy and isolated in my mind, as though someone's severed the connection between us.

I strain, reaching out for my brother with my eyes squeezed tightly shut. As I lean closer to the building, my sense flares up. *Not safe bomb get away.*

"RAVEN, WE HAVE TO GO!" Sparrow screams, but I'm lost in a storm of panic, and despite how sharply his words slice through my train of thought, they still feel distant and far away, as though denial is blanketing my ears.

Eyes scanning the interior of the Berg, I feel my anxiety grow. Finally, I can no longer bear it, and my hand closes around the door handle. "I have to go back! I can't leave him! He'll never make it!"

"Raven, wait! Stop!" He pulls me back by the hand, and I fight him, trying to wrestle out of his grip, but then he yells my name. I stop struggling, and our eyes lock.

He gestures to the floor, covered by a faint layer of water that glistens in the moonlight. I immediately snatch a glance back at the prison, where water floods out of the stairwell's mouth and onto the ground floor. The Berg is sinking.

I fumble for the pockets of my cloak, digging for stars. There must be one left... there must. I can wish him to safety.

I can save my friends.

But there's no star in my pocket, and Sparrow's urging me to leave, and Bronwyn's eyes are wide and terrified.

Part of me already knows I'll never see the soft, young face of my best friend again. Part of me already knows it's too late.

"I'm so sorry, Raven," Sparrow chokes, pulling me gently towards the railing that separates the Frigid Sea from the balcony.

"No... no, no, no..." I whisper, tears blossoming at the corners of my eyes. "Please, I can't let him die!"

"And I can't let you die," he says, voice so quiet, so desperate, that as he pulls me into him with both hands, I do not resist, only stare into his painfully determined eyes.

"If you do this... I'll hate you forever. I'll hate you. You can't... you promised to..." I begin, but my voice dies with my fracturing heart.

"Please," he gasps. "Please, Raven."

"We'll not fail. *We'll not fail!*" I roar, "That's what we... you *said* we'll not fail! You made a promise!"

"I'll fail them all, but I'll not fail you," he cries, "'S the least I can do! 'S *all* I can do!" he yells with a cry of rage, throwing up his arms. "Why d'you think I'm here!?"

He jabs a finger into my chest, and I stumble backwards, shaking my head frantically. "I don't care why my mother sent you. Let me go."

"Go where? To kill yourself?" he asks harshly.

"To save my friend!"

He places his hands on both sides of my face, tilting my head to look at him and blocking my vision on all other sides. "*Let me save mine.*"

CHAPTER 16

"Hold onto me."

In one swift motion, Sparrow wraps himself around me like a shield and ducks under the railing, kicking away from the ice into a dive. We plummet forward off the cliff into the ocean and break apart on impact with the icy waves, splitting and spinning away from one another in a tumble of limbs as a sudden silence muffles the chaos above.

My body refuses to be shocked by the cold, instead entering a state of bewilderment as my frozen limbs try to untangle themselves into action. I sink deeper and deeper, slowing as friction rejects my descent, but my body is relentless, keen to bury itself into that cold, dark place at the bottom of the lake where the lucent moon's fingers cannot reach me and scoop me up into the heavens.

Here, it is quiet. Here, it is calm. The consequences of my actions cannot reach me in this underwater world. Yet.

I'm well over ten feet below the surface, with milky silhouettes drifting above, when a colossal impact hits me in the stomach.

My eyelids flutter, and my vision and unconsciousness both duel for dominance. I take in a large mouthful of water as I'm flung backwards and up simultaneously like a ragdoll, the taste of salt flooding my throat, burning my tongue, and spiking my nostrils. As my arms pierce the air, I'm thrown upside-down with a sting as something hot strikes my skin—

"Peter?" I gurgle in confusion, hands grasping all around for my friend who will never come.

For a moment, I'm certain that his gentle, peaceful voice responds, singing words of comfort and spindling up from the depths like ribbons of greeting to encase my floating, bobbing figure, lost between the ocean's heartbeat and my own. Oneirataxia overwhelms my senses. Am I with Peter? Alive? Dead? Dreaming?

"Raven!" Peter gasps, swimming up to me as bubbles stream from his mouth. Tufts of his blonde hair ripple in the water, and his eyes are bright, shining, and kind. He reaches out for my hand with tiny fingers, his mouth stretching into a reassuring smile.

Before he reaches me, I'm swallowed by a wave, knocked backwards and spining uncontrollably up. My arms peirce the surface, reaching up as if in celebration.

And then, the world explodes into a soundless burst of light.

CHAPTER 17

Minor burns coat my arms, angry and pink. I can't recall opening my eyes or awakening. I only know I was unconscious, and now I've snapped back into reality. And I'm still underwater.

Sparrow, my brain instructs, Find Sparrow. I spin around in the murky depths, eyes searching for the boy in the bird mask. Is it safe to resurface? Is Sparrow up there now, calling my name? Perhaps he swam away or was blasted out to shore by the explosion's impact...?

No. Something tells me he wouldn't have left my side. And what of Wynn? I cannot see her or Peter anywhere. *Come on, Raven, remember what happened*, I think, desperately swivelling around in the water.

Flashes and shreds of memory teasingly sprinkle my mind like confetti, my senses painting the scene: Someone's arms wrapped around my torso. My eyes dipping below the surface and back up as my head bobs and my eyelids flutter. Open. Closed. Open. My mouth is moving, counting as water floods inside it and hurries out with the pull of the waves. One, two, three, four... A mouth, breathing heavily as something crunches and rolls beneath my feet.

Then it slaps me brutally hard. *Peter.*

The shuddering gasp weaves its way through my body like an eel. Squeezing my stomach, choking me, pushing the tears through my eyes, and emerging through my open mouth as a scream of agony.

CHAPTER 17

Peter's dead.

I clutch my churning stomach and duck my pounding, roaring head. Red, red, red. Blood, blood, blood. Sheets of it, dancing, twisting, floating through the water. Drapes of it, concealing my eyes until everything is a blur. Blood everywhere I look. Blood flooding my mouth, its metallic taste swathing over my tongue. So much blood. Eternal blood, its platelets beads on a throttling necklace as two ends of string come together, and a circle is completed. I abandoned my brother again. I didn't save him again. I've erased my evolution.

I know it now: this is a death I will carry with me for the rest of my life, heavy as a brick and freezing as ice.

My mind goes hazy again as I struggle to take it in. Nothing quite connects. Nothing makes sense. My thoughts are fractured, and my emotions disperse as easily as they came. How did Peter die? What killed him?

And now I'm thinking of—

Ice... Ice... Ice.

Find the Berg. Swimming around, unsure if I should be returning to the place which is potentially full of angry survivors who want me dead, I cannot see much at all, not even the base of the Iceberg, which is making quite the statement as its icy structure penetrates the sea for miles and miles down. I grimace. Well, that can be forgotten.

Then, another perplexing thought surfaces. Surely, I should be surrounded by the remains of the gigantic prison... but the water is clear of wreckage.

Clear, but murky, as though—

"Raven?"

I sit up, gasping for breath in the enormous bathtub, as his voice rings out clearly through the air. I'm in a body of water at least five times the size of an ordinary tub and as deep as a swimming pool.

"Sparrow?" I whisper hoarsely, turning.

And there he stands.

His hair is a little wild, sticking out in odd places, and bruises are dotted all over his body. He's limping slightly, and an enormous bandage hugs his calf. The battered bird mask from before is nowhere to be seen. But there is one thing unchanged regardless: His smile. The smile meaning that everything's okay. The signature grin meaning that it's all going to be alright now.

"Alright, Rave?" he smiles.

The question is so ludicrous that I almost burst out laughing. "My eyes are stinging from the chlorine..." I look down at my lower half, frowning at a new discovery. "Oh, and there's a bloody cut on my thy. Also, I just woke up in an alien place with no idea how I got here, and I think I was in an explosion. So, overall, only a little banged up. You?"

"Honestly... never better," he says, "I'm glad you're okay."

Relief washes over me like a tidal wave despite my lingering concerns over my condition. Despite his state, there's something so comfortingly Sparrow-ish about his tone that makes me want to leap into his arms and never let go. He's still him. Still Sparrow. And for that, I'll be forever grateful.

He throws me a towel from the poolside, and I clumsily catch it, the tail dipping into the water.

"Sorry you had to go in with most of your clothes on. Personally, I was hoping you might sink to the bottom with all the extra weight— it would've been very funny if you'd woken up squatting on tiles— but Spok said a saltwater bath would wake you up almost immediately, so...." He shrugs, and I know it's an attempt at a joke, but all I can think of is deciphering what has happened to us in the last few hours.

My head feels fuzzy, and my thoughts unusually loud, as though my own mind is shouting. There's a faint ringing in my ears.

"Wait... Spok's here? Where are we? Back at Boots and Shackles?"

"Yeah. No. Sort of," he sighs. "It's... complicated."

Silence. "So did we... I mean... is everyone okay?" I blurt.

"Well, we're here, aren't we?"

"And..." I have to force the words out of my sticky throat. "And Wynn?"

Sparrow hesitates. "She's not doing so good. Not after Peter—"

I hold up a hand. "Please, Sparrow. Don't even say it."

He nods, adverting his gaze, his eyes sparkling with tears.

I know what he's thinking almost instantly. "It wasn't your fault, Sparrow. Don't you dare," I say fiercely.

He only shakes his head, staring at the ground.

"Sparrow, it wasn't. I was stupid. I misjudged them. I thought that if... Honestly, I don't know what I thought. But I marched us in there, and I forced you to take me, and I... I..." Before I can finish, I break down into tears.

"No one forced me to do anything," Sparrow interrupts sharply. "I took you to the Berg because I thought I needed to, for your sake. But I was wrong to even go near that place. I was crazy. I was mad. And now, because of me, Peter—"

"Sparrow—" I begin in tearful protest.

"Because of me, Peter is dead!" he roars, cutting me off.

I stare at him, stunned.

"Peter is dead," he says again, quieter this time. His gaze drops to his palms, open and facing upwards, as though to be inspected. I wonder, momentarily, if he sees it too— the blood.

Silence falls between us like a curtain once again. I can tell he's ashamed of his outburst, but he says nothing for a very long time. When he does speak, his tone is delicate, soft, and heavy with grief. "Just... just dry off and get changed. Clean clothes are in that dresser, and painkillers are on the bedside table. Take them with water. The bathroom's through that door. There should be glasses in the cupboard."

I frown. *Painkillers? Whatever for?*

Sparrow notices my expression and gives a dismissive wave of his hand. "I'll explain everything at dinner. We set an alarm, so don't worry about sleeping. You have this room to yourself until then. I'll give you some privacy."

He exits briskly, and I'm left alone, the silence broken only by the quiet ripples I send out through the pool.

My arms are dotted with red blotches, where I assume I was seared by the explosion. They do not hurt in the slightest until I climb out of the water, and the stinging hits me with all its fierce might.

My knees buckle almost instantly as the agony rips through my body. I must drag myself away from the water, wincing at the slightest contact the floor makes with my arms.

The pain is hot. Hot, as though I'm on fire. Air attacks my skin, tearing my torso apart piece by piece. I double over, pulling my arms tight to my chest. Tears come rapidly, cutting trails into my cheeks.

I crumble under the pain and slide back into the water.

Cold water is the best treatment for burns, as the common phrase says. I guess it's true because soon I can bear small breaks from the bath.

The intensity of the burns has lessened, and I can do simple things. Climb out, fumble around with the tablets on the bedside table, and climb back in. Gradually, I can manage longer breaks. The drug helps, removing the knife-edge from the pain and soon cloaking it entirely.

After very gently applying lotion and towelling myself dry, I set about exploring my mysterious new chambers.

I appear to be in a metal, square room with a round, egg-shaped bed that reminds me of a bird's nest. Beside it sits a bedside table complete with a lamp and a single chest of drawers. A dull picture, nothing but a canvas swabbed with shades of grey, hangs on the wall, but apart from that, a table accompanied by a white rug is the only other piece of furniture in sight.

One of the most noticeable things about the place is that there are no windows, suggesting I'm somewhere deep underground. Then there is the mystery of where Sparrow slunk off to.

Some kind of hidden staircase, I guess, as there is no visible exit except a large archway that appears to only lead into a bland passage with no exit. I feel equally unnerved and secure in the place, trapped in a giant metal box.

My feet make reverberating taps on the cold, hard floor, emphasizing my isolation. I begin to wish that Sparrow hadn't left, and after wandering through the long, unfurnished hallway that wraps around the exterior of the chamber for an hour, I suddenly realize how exhausted, bored, and lonely I am.

My mind is still hazy, causing things to drift in and out of my memory. I'm soon led only by legs and drooping eyelids, which direct me back to the bird's nest bed. The sheets are soft, silky, and cool against my skin as I slip between them, unlike anything I've ever felt before. They soothe my burns and sit comfortably against my body, reeking of expensive, clean, nothing-ness, as though not a soul has slept here before me.

Before I can control myself, my head sinks deep into the pillow.

When my eyes jolt open, I find myself lying in the same position I fell asleep in. A distant bleep tells me an alarm is going off, sending panic shooting down my limbs. I hurriedly bundle up the sheet in my arms, head whipping from side to side.

But I'm not in the Berg.

"I'm fine," I whisper to myself, pushing the hairs on my arm back down, "I... I'm fine."

The fear dissipates, but the chills remain.

I haven't found an exit yet, so surely someone will have to come down here and collect me.

Until they do, I recall Sparrow's words. *Clean clothes are in that dresser.* I walk over to the chest of drawers and rifle through them until I find a beautiful, silky, sage-green dress. Running my fingers lightly over the soft folds of the material, I feel slightly bitter.

I've never worn anything like this in my life, never had this kind of luxury. Yet here it sits, patiently awaiting whoever wants it, so long as they're human. Or... or could this place be different? Maybe this dress was placed here especially for me before I arrived at this strange place. As a gift, a welcome.

I straighten up, clenching the dress hard.

I rummaged through a wealthy family's rubbish once in Ra. Their building was a formidable stone square, a giant sandcastle with lanterns strung between each window and tropical cacti and flowers to bless colour upon every outdoor surface. Wealth radiated from it, and I caught its scent riding on the wind. That day, I found an almost new shirt, crafted by hand from cotton into a cool garnet, perfect for travelling. I took it to the nearest river, dunked it clean, slipped it over my head, and set off into the desert to let it cool in the sun.

Later that month, I passed through an IN-3 town. The villagers sneered at me from within the mouths of their rag-tents and stumbled up close to touch the material- some even begged me for money. I told one lady I had no money, and she beat me away with a tree branch, calling me a liar and a tight-fisted princess.

I was eight, then.

Eight and utterly bewildered— it was *my* searchings, *my* crop of effort, that had harvested the shirt. Surely I was entitled to wear it?

When I turned nine shortly after, I realized I am not entitled to anything. I am not allowed to own things because I'm Flai.

Maybe, here at Boots and Shackles, I'm not only safe, but I'm equal. I get privileges like everyone else. I can have possessions. I can have things that are mine. I can be told how lucky I am and express my gratitude for all I have.

I don't think I've thanked anyone for what I have before, for I always had nothing.

My eyes wander back to the pool, where my reflection shimmers between ripples. Alone and undistracted, moments like these make me sometimes question what it means to be Flai entirely. On earth, it means we are dirt, filth, dangerous, and untamed. But what about a bigger place, a bigger picture? A place beyond this world?

After all, no one knows the origin of Flai. According to man, we fell from the sky, but that does not make much sense at all. That is a child's tale. A fable.

Although maybe there's something beyond the sky? A

home. An origin. An explanation as to why I'm here. A realm where my kind is free, where we're normal.

My face darkens as my heart births a new emotion to replace this wishful thinking: fury.

Because I'm *not* there, in that place past the sky. I'm here, on this wretched island. Hated. Shunned. Silenced because of who I am. Because of *what* I am.

I crumple up the dress in my hands, tears prickling in my eyes.

If only man could understand that I don't want to be this way. Why can't they see that? The choice was never mine to make. How can they judge and hate me for something I can't control?

I angrily toss the dress onto the floor. My species has done nothing to deserve this. I have done nothing to deserve this.

Gradually, my breaths steady. At least now we've liberated all those prisoners and destroyed the Iceberg. I know that the demolition of the fortress will not only broadcast a message of hope to Flai hiding everywhere, but it will also threaten Frost and its king. It will tell him we are fighting back. Peter's death won't be in vain.

A smile plays on my lips.

It's maddening, exhilarating, even, to think that I'm experiencing joy right now.

But I am.

Finally, undoubtedly, times are changing. And I'm alive to witness it.

Maybe I'm even a contributor.

CHAPTER 18

After dressing for dinner, I wander out of the room into the hallway, absent-mindedly tracing the grooves between the metal panels that cover the walls.

I have a severe, piercing headache, as though someone is putting pressure on my temples. It's a dull, gnawing pain due to the juxtaposing rush of this intense, pensive quiet from the constant anxiety of yesterday. I turn my head to stare at the water, still and glassy and unchanged like a polished mirror.

It should be rising, thrashing after me, but not one threat arises from the tranquillity of this prison.

It's difficult to breathe. I need air, sky, and fresh oxygen, not this awful filtered stuff that smells of nothing. I long to be outside again, where I can finally clear my head and reconnect with my magic.

I pause and lean back against the wall, exhaling slowly.

Then, the slow, electrical hum of something under the panels causes me to jerk away. A large square of metal retreats into the wall.

I must have pressed a hidden button because suddenly, the wall panels at the end of the corridor slide aside and reveal the entrance to an elevator.

I've only ever been in one once when I was five and a half.

Papa took me to Frost to show me the castle as an early birthday present in June. I'd fantasized about seeing a magic fairytale castle since I could first pick up a storybook, but the only thing I can remember from that trip is a dim, chilly, and unpleasant building filled with Flunters and guards.

I hang back, unsure, at the entrance to this one, wondering if I ought to step inside. In the end, curiosity defeats me, and I enter. The doors shut swiftly behind me, leaving me in darkness before a large chandelier lights up above my head, illuminating the lift in a bright, welcoming glow. I feel my stomach drop as it begins rising. Up, up, up, into what feels like a never-ending shaft. Then, the speed of the elevator decreases without warning, and I'm met with a cheerful ding as the doors open.

It's as though I've stepped into an entirely different world. The carpet is plush and thick. The moment I set foot on it, it's like grass growing and thickening to form a throne specially designed for me between my toes. The walls are papered with large white and silver roses.

A fireplace emits a warm glow from the opposite side of the room, and plants sit on shelves and in pots in corners, giving it a homely feel, sprinkling life and colour into the atmosphere.

In the very centre of the room is a long glass table, and on it sits a feast spiked with familiarity. My eyes linger on the dishes and cutlery, and I'm struck with deja vu. Around it, three people look up in surprise at my arrival: Spok, Bronwyn, and... my heart leaps. And *Sparrow*.

He's wearing a brand-new mask, the feathers freshly waxed, each one curated to perfection, and the beak gleams with polish. Brown layers of material frame his bright, warm eyes. The previous events of yesterday feel distant and unreal now, like a dream.

CHAPTER 18

Even here, nestled away underground and hidden from prying eyes, he's wearing his mask, tucked behind it like a shield. I can't help but wonder if perhaps he's retreating from me after his emotional confessions at the Berg.

But as my eyes settle on him, sparkling with relief, gratitude, and grief all at once, my doubts melt away. Then I frown. The bruises on his face are less noticeable now. His clothes are different, and he appears cleaner. Bronwyn finally has some skin on her bones, and her hollowed-out cheeks are slightly plump.

Everyone has transformed ever so slightly, like a magnificent oak's leaves blooming too slowly to witness, the changes in pigment and bloom noticeable by fractional amounts. Yet, I have remained the same.

Or perhaps not.

Despite my physical condition being unchanged, it indeed seems there are small parts of me that have shifted, rearranged, shrunk, and grown. Perhaps there is less pressure constantly weighing on my heart than before. Perhaps the sight of three humans doesn't bait my adrenaline with the same ferocity as it did a month ago.

Raven Asgard remains unspared by time's gentle undressings, and layers of me have been peeled away and reformed.

But my lack of physical changes alone does raise a question: How long was I asleep?

I turn back to the lift and notice another corridor branching off from this room. It continues for around 20 meters, then turns a corner and disappears out of sight. Still no windows. Still underground. I blow air out of my cheeks, struggling to take it in. It appears that Boots and Shackles is slightly bigger than Spok likes to make out.

I take a seat beside Sparrow, where a place has been set for me.

For a moment, no one speaks, and the only sound is the awkward clatter of Spok's fork.

"Hi," Sparrow whispers, leaning over to me.

"Hey," I whisper back awkwardly. "How, um... How're you, then?"

"Good."

"That's good." More silence.

"The, er, mashed potatoes are really... mashed. Try some," he says flatly, passing me the tray. I scrape a lump of it onto my plate, feeling completely out of place. "The green beans are great, too. Bronwyn loves them, don't you, Wynn?" he adds.

Bronwyn doesn't answer, nor, apparently, does she like the green beans; a plate piled with untouched food sits in front of her.

"Hi," I mouth sheepishly.

She raises her head sharply to glare at me the moment I address her, her dark eyes never leaving my face. I tear my gaze away, cramming a huge spoonful of potato into my mouth, and make a silent wish to evaporate into thin air. Even staring at the floor, I can feel her pupils knuckling my face in one continuous blow, delivering Peter's revenge.

"Hey, Bron, you need to try my broccoli soup!" Spok suddenly bursts, shoving a spoon into Bronwyn's curled fist.

How wrong the clean, shiny silverware looks in her hand, with her grimy fingernails caked in dirt and her skin bruised and burned. Only now do I begin to notice these tiny details, along with others; her wiry mane of black hair is more dishevelled than usual, her clothes are stained and crinkled, and deep bags swoop across the skin under her eyes.

Sparrow and I are both injured, but we've bathed, slept, and cared for ourselves. But what about Bronwyn? Why's she like this? Sure, she's gained weight, which is good, but every other quality about her skidded to a halt at the Berg and has remained unaltered since.

I exhale slowly, pushing out a million emotions I can't presently process.

We eat in silence, the air thick enough to slice through. I speak to Spok to ask for condiments or Sparrow for salt and pepper, but never to Wynn. My mouth is too dry, my tongue too heavy, and I have no idea where to even begin.

Finally, when Spok disappears into the kitchen to fetch dessert, and Sparrow excuses himself to use the bathroom, we're left alone. Bronwyn seizes the opportunity instantly. "Enjoy your beauty sleep?" she sneers vindictively.

"What?" I blink.

"I said, did you enjoy your beauty sleep?"

"I don't know what you're talking about."

"I'll tell you what I'm talking about. It's been three days, Raven. Three days since the Berg. Three times. Once in Frost, twice at the Berg. And now, here. You keep. Leaving," she says through gritted teeth. "What am I supposed to do, Raven? Huh? Are you tired? Need to sit down? Want me to play grown-ups for a little while?"

I'm speechless.

"You were supposed to protect us. A-and you... you..." Her words crumble away into a numb, silent stare.

I killed Peter.

"You woke up, went to sleep, and now it's been three days. Three days of being human. Three days of rolling over in the night, thinking for a moment that we're back in Frost, cosying up to one another, expecting to hear Pete—" she stops, taking a deep breath. "Expecting to hear *his* voice. And all I hear is..." She shoves her plate away from her and stands up. "*Nothing*," she spits, storming out of the room.

I open and close my mouth helplessly, but no sound emerges. I want to call out, to apologize, but I cannot form the words. Instead, I just sit. Empty, blank, hollow.

Hollow, like the seat at this table where my brother should be.

Spok enters the room and sets a large sponge cake in front of me, dripping with chocolate sauce.

I glare at it, wanting to slam both hands on the table, cry, and wallow in my grief until it blinds me. I want them all, everyone outside of this inn, to die. How can I be sat here? How dare I be sat here? How dare I even exist in a way that is any kind of normal?

Cakes are for celebrations, not monsters. Not death. Not Peter.

I've lost my appetite, but even so, I cram mouthful after mouthful down my throat until all I can smell is the sickeningly sweet stench of my own breath.

Sparrow returns. I barely notice.

Cake, cake, cake.

Soon, the smell changes. It becomes thicker, heavier, far less rich but unbearably suffocating. I don't have to look at my hands to know that it's back.

Blood, blood, blood.

Cake, cake, cake.

Maybe I'll choke.

Maybe it's better if I do.

CHAPTER 19

After dinner, I retreat into a living room that branches off from the kitchen and sink into one of the sofas, looking at my hands to avoid eye contact with anyone.

I don't wish for anyone to see the tears glistening on my cheeks.

The loveseat sags as Sparrow sits down beside me. He reaches for my hand, but as he touches me, I realize, with surprise, that it is not Sparrow's young, smooth hand but Spok's firm, wrinkled one.

She sighs heavily. "I, er, couldn't help but overhear your row with Bronwyn. Are you okay?"

Am I okay? I feel like an abandoned puppet on a forgotten stage, with the landlady's gaze fixed on me like a spotlight. No one's pulling my strings or controlling how I feel. I've nothing to run from, only trauma and grief to cope with. Action and adrenaline are far behind, and now there are only scattered leftovers. The unscripted monologue. How do I feel when I finally can? When I'm not being chased or shot at?

I've never stopped to process emotion— I've never had time to. Now, I'm expected to construct an elaborate dam and carefully control the flow of words from my mouth, to somehow describe and decipher the chaotic mess of my thoughts with no experience?

"It's my fault." That's all I can manage to say. "Isn't it?"

Spok shakes her head. "No. You never could have saved him. He was forced by circumstance and soldiers into the wrong place at the wrong time, a place that no boy —no*body* — should ever experience. And for that, we shall all suffer. But your hands did not reach into the dollhouse of the universe and put him in that place. You did not command the ocean to rise and swallow him. What happened last week was out of your control. If it's any condolence, in some universe, Peter took a correct turn. He found a staircase. He made it."

"But he didn't, Spok," I say harshly.

She nods slowly. "He didn't. But he could have. And you weren't there to force him to. To find a staircase, to take a correct turn. So how is it possibly your fault when you were so out of control?"

"But I should have been there, Spok. I allowed us to separate, and I feel like a monster," I mumble, shaking my head. "He was just a boy. Just a kid, like me," I choke. "And now he's gone... because of *me.* I gave him a gun and left him. He's eleven. H-He *was* eleven."

Spok wraps her arms around me like a shawl, and I finally allow myself to cry without shame, shielded from embarrassment by her comforting embrace. I can't help feeling small and scared, just a kid again. After all, I suppose that's what I am. I glance at Sparrow as he strolls into the room. What we are.

Just a bunch of kids playing grown-ups. Running around, blowing up prisons, fighting guards. But when we meet a shield, a protector, a parental figure like Spok, we are transformed back into children. And at the end of the day, we still need someone to go home to, someone to love us.

Her fingers weave through my hair, teasing out the knots as she speaks. Her voice is rough but laced with kindness. "One day, Raven, I promise you that Peter's story will be heard by the world. And when it is, it will be an example of why this hatred between Man and Flai has to end. He will not be forgotten. People like us will keep his memory alive."

I steady my breaths, a little calmer. Then I realize something that makes my eyes go wide. "Spok, what happened to your voice? Y'know, the accent, an' all tha'?" I ask, attempting to mimic her.

She laughs. "Well, I don't actually talk like that, and I'm not really just a dodgy innkeeper, as you've probably already deciphered from seeing the rest of this place. Tell me— do you like it better than upstairs?"

I give a small smile, sniffling. "It's insane, Spok. But — sorry, I have to ask— how did you afford all this? And why do you need it?"

"Well, long story short, you aren't the first of your kind to be here, and a spare room or two never hurts. Sparrow, why don't you tell her?"

Sparrow nods and turns to face me. "Spok's been helping smuggle Flai across the borders of Frost for years. She bought this place specially to help people like you, and that's why she's never failed me a room all these years. And why, I suppose, I trusted her so much. Because she knew what I was doing, and she's been trying to help us since we arrived."

He motions for me to shuffle aside and sits beside me.

"After we blew up the Iceberg," Sparrow continues gently, "I found you hanging onto a piece of wreckage, barely able to open your eyes, and swam you back to shore, where I found Bronwyn already there, coughing up seawater. Together, we managed to send out a distress signal with my headtorch— you were so badly injured, all I cared about was getting you to a hospital. I didn't care if it meant revealing our location to 'Nora. Luckily, Spok saw it before the Frost guards came, and she drove us all the way here in just a cart. I lost consciousness about halfway through the journey. And, um,

I don't know if you know, but I... well, on the way, a guard caught up with us, and he... he had a gun, and I..."

"You...?" I press.

"You might not have noticed when you first woke up here, but I don't blame you, the state you were in..." He trails off.

"He tried to stay awake as long as possible, to make sure you were okay —held your hand through the whole thing, he did— but eventually, he couldn't take the pain. He was shot," Spok explains, gesturing to Sparrow's mummified ankle suffocated by bandages.

I nod, unsure how to respond to this. Eventually, I find my voice, but it's weak and small. "I did notice. I just forgot. Is it broken?"

"Fractured, actually. I took a nasty hit," Sparrow grimaces. "But Spok patched me up."

"And what of Peter? Did you... is his body...?" My voice disappears again, and I have to put my head between my knees to keep from heaving, breaths racing out of control. I feel sick. Really sick.

I can't seem to grasp onto anything, and everything that should be bolted to this reality floats. The loss of just one person has disorientated my entire world and thrown me into chaos, perhaps because of the normality of everything else. Nothing is right. Nothing at all.

Blood, blood, blood.

Sparrow waits for me to recover before speaking calmly, "We went back yesterday but didn't find anything. I don't think he... the explosion..."

I bite my lip. "It's okay. I know. He's gone. Just tell me what happened."

"Well, Bronwyn came too. She deserved a proper goodbye. We just made him a little grave and left, but I could see it meant a lot to her. I'm so sorry you weren't there. It's just...

Bronwyn didn't want to wait," he explains. Pause. "I think... I mean, she's just a kid. She doesn't quite see things how they are. She thinks she can bury what happened."

"She hides from things. Gets it from me," I nod, my headache returning as I bury my head in my hands.

"It was Spok's idea to go," Sparrow says quietly. "I thought you should know that."

I turn back to Spok, amazed. Once upon a time, she was a grubby little innkeeper, offering remarkably cheap accommodation to Sparrow and me, but now she's a different person entirely. A wave of gratitude washes over me, but also great confusion. There're still so many questions unanswered. "I still don't understand... why? I mean, how did you know I was Flai? And with all the laws becoming tighter, and bounties rising..." I trail off.

Spok sighs. "Did you honestly think I wouldn't notice what you were? Maybe others wouldn't, but unlike them, I've seen plenty of your kind in my lifetime, Raven. Your eyes, the way you talk, the way you jump at the slightest noise... all dead giveaways. And you were with Sparrow, who I'd already deduced was a homefetch years ago. It's why I have provided him accommodation for the past two years without fail. I wanted to help."

"Why... why would you let me stay here, though? Knowing that I'd get you killed with the bounty on my head?" I stammer.

"Sparrow did tell me you like to simplify things. I see that now," she sighs.

"What's that supposed to mean?" I ask defensively.

"It means," Spok begins, "That you can't always understand the inner workings of other people, so you choose not to try. I've been helping Flai all my life, no matter the cost, and I refuse to leave a single one behind. That's because of generosity, sure, but other reasons, too. I'm no saint, of course, but I am risking my life for you. It's difficult to understand, and I'm unwilling to tell you where my kindness stems from, so you dislike and reject the concept. Sparrow, may you give us a moment?"

Sparrow nods and slips out of the room, reassuringly brushing my arm lightly as he leaves.

Spok's eyes tail him until he disappears out of sight, and then she turns back to me. "Listen. I want you to know that I saw something in you, Raven. Something I haven't seen in a long time. You see... usually, people like you —Flai— have never really lived. That's harsh, I know, but there's no other way to phrase it. You've never had the chance to live. Always running, always hiding. You don't know what it's like to feel...well, human. To develop and grow as a person. But you... you're different. Mouldable. I could see it from the moment I first laid eyes on you. You're healing, growing, and learning. Your mind is beginning to fill in gaps and form bridges."

"Learning... to feel?" I ask slowly.

"No, Raven. Learning to love," she corrects, and after that, no more is said.

After dinner, I'm free to explore my new temporary home and take pleasure in discovering plenty of hidden doorways, panels, and stairs throughout the building. It's much larger than I had initially assumed, and though trying to mentally map out each room is surprisingly fun, I'm not playing around. I'm looking for Bronwyn's room. I must reconcile with her— she's what's left of my family.

Or maybe not, as I have Sparrow and my mother. But Mother's not been too bothered about me for the last fifteen years, and Sparrow... whatever it is that was between us, it's gone, shifted, been replaced by something else. Family is too light of a word now, and the muddle that is our relationship is too heavy. I daren't think of it, just because it gives me a headache.

The door is closed when I finally find her room, but I can hear hushed, muffled sobs from within. I know it's been a year and that both Peter and Bronwyn have changed within that time, but it's unlike her to be crying. She's Bronwyn. A fighter at heart, a lioness that roars within a small girl's body. Now, what have I done to her? The lioness is slain.

I pause at the door, hesitant to cross the threshold, thinking maybe I should just leave, but then my fist is already on the wood, and before I know it, I've knocked twice.

The sobs stop abruptly. "Who is it?"

"It's... it's me, Raven," I say weakly.

Silence, then... "Come in," she says in a dark voice that does not sound very welcoming at all.

She looks up, clears her throat, and hastily wipes her cheeks. "Hi."

"I just thought I'd... er... see if you're okay?"

"Spiffing, thanks," she says icily.

The guilt in my stomach erupts so painfully that I'm at a loss for words. Her bedsheets are in an untidy, unmade clump, and her hair's a tangled mess. The lights are off, creating an uneasy loneliness in the darkness.

And then there are the papers. Scattered all over the floor are inky blotches of scrawled notes. Each is a demonstration of madness, regret, and grief. And they're everywhere.

I pick one up, smoothen out the wrinkles, and read.

When we were nine, he fought off two guards after they caught us robbing the market. He was brave, risking himself because we hadn't eaten in weeks. Peter was the reason we didn't starve. He was small enough to steal without vendors noticing, and he could writhe out of the grip of adults. I was too big to do that.

So that's why her hands are covered in blisters and sores. Over the past three days, wrapped in memories of him like a butterfly in a cocoon, Bronwyn has been writing down notes, memories, and diaries. A thousand stories, every one of them for Peter.

"Oh, Wynn..." I whisper.

She closes her eyes, taking a deep breath. "I can't let him be forgotten. I *can't*. So, I'm writing it all down. And one day, they're going to read it. The world is going to know what they did. The world is going to know who they killed."

I look at my feet. "Who *I* killed." Eyes smarting, I sit down on the edge of the bed beside her. "He didn't deserve this," I finally say, reaching for her palm with open fingers.

"No, he didn't," Bronwyn lashes, jerking away, "But he's still dead, isn't he? And one day, his memory is going to waste away, just like these papers, and then who'll tell his story? Who'll tell mine? Does anyone even care?" she bursts.

"Listen, I care. Sparrow cares. I care that he was only young, I care that another Flai is dead, and I care that after everything, I couldn't save him. He may've been your brother, but I was somebody's sister. I lost something precious, too."

She draws her knees up to her chest, tears leaking from her eyes. "I know. It's just... he deserves more. Flai deserve more. And even worse, I was..." She sniffs. "This is going to sound so stupid, but I was getting used to... being loved. He was my best friend. More than that. And now that he's gone, the world without him just feels worthless. Like there's not even a point anymore."

Her expression is one I recognize. It's the face you have when you realize for the first time that things aren't getting better. Flai aren't getting justice, people are still dying, and it's not stopping or changing.

As though the sun has swooped down and scorched every inch of my insides, my throat is on fire with desperation, struggling for words. What am I supposed to say to that? Look at her. Look at what I did.

"Everything reminds me of him," she continues, "I try to block it out, but he's still there. A-And I close my eyes, but I can still feel him. I hear him telling me everything is alright, as he used to." A strand of wispy hair falls in front of her face as she cradles herself miserably. "But that's what everyone says. It doesn't matter who you are or what you've been through. The world thinks that if they tell you, "Don't worry, it's alright!", it'll erase what happened." The small girl raises her voice now, half-shouting. "Can they bring him back? Can you? Can ANYONE!? NO! Because it did happen, and he is dead, no matter what ANYONE SAYS! Nothing will change that!" Her frustration is evident, and her grief is building, so there's nothing I can do but wrap my arms around her as she's overcome by a fresh wave of tears.

You did this. You're the reason this is happening. Now you have to fix it.

Gradually, her sobs slow until she can speak again. "You know, Raven... the only way to stop it is to remind myself that he's *dead*." She repeats it like a twisted nursery rhyme. "He's dead, dead, dead."

I gently take her hand, and she doesn't resist this time. "I know I can't imagine what you must be going through because Peter and I were never as close as you were, but I'll try. I hate myself for not saving him... you know that, don't you? Do you know how much I blame myself? You know that if I could, I would take all of this pain away. I wish you could give it to me, Bronwyn. Give it all to me. Raven can handle it. She always did, and now we're back together, nothing has changed. I still love you so much." Silence. "And I know you'll —*we'll*— get through this," I add.

"No, I won't!" she moans, throwing a pen across the room in frustration. It shatters upon impact with the wall, splattering ink everywhere. "You don't know how I feel. You haven't lost the only person you ever loved."

I frown. "What are you talking about? Peter was my best friend, too."

"Oh, please, Raven!" she snaps bitterly, pulling away from my arms. "I'm not talking about Peter. I'm talking about Sparrow. You haven't lost him! Have you?"

"But I don't... Sparrow's my... I don't *love* him! I've barely known him for two weeks! If you think he comes anywhere close to what Peter was —and still is— to both of us, then—"

"I'm not saying he's like your brother, Rave." For the first time, she smiles. Laughs, even. "If you could look at the two of you through my eyes, maybe you'd understand."

"Understand what?"

"It. Him. Everything he does for you for no good reason. It's like... he unintentionally chose one person in the whole universe to become friends with, no matter how she behaved, what she said, or how she responded to his selflessness."

I stare at her, and she shakes her head, bursting into a shiny-eyed fit of giggles. "You really don't get it, do you?"

"Sparrow's my *friend,* Bron."

"Some friend," she remarks.

"You've cheered up," I mutter, and then I exit the room feeling slightly aggravated but better about my relationship with Bronwyn.

"So, how'd it go?" I glance up from staring at my feet, lost in thought, and recognize Spok's calm tone before I even see her face.

Shrugging, I relax. "So-so." Then, noticing the apron around her waist, I add, "I'm sorry I left after dinner, by the way. Do you want help cleaning up?"

"No thanks, I've done it now," Spok replies, "I'm just looking for Sparrow. He cleared the table, then skulked off somewhere, saying he needed a minute."

"Oh," I say absent-mindedly. She arches a brow, and I do a double take. "OH!" I exclaim and flee the hallway without uttering another word.

I can still hear Spok chuckling good-naturedly when I've rounded the corner and disappeared out of sight.

❀ ❀ ❀

"Knock knock," I call, rapping twice on the door of his room.

"Who's there?" he grunts irritably.

"Who do you *think*?" I say, rolling my eyes and crossing the threshold without waiting for permission to enter. It isn't locked or anything, so I figure that, despite his expression of brief annoyance, he minds about as much as I care.

I take in Sparrow's neatly made four-poster bed, his unlit lamp, and the simple countryside painting above his bedside table. He's sitting on the opposite side of the room to me, at a small wooden desk, his gaze fixed on the wall.

I wander over to him. "So, what's up?"

"Nothing," he says instantly.

"Liar," I yawn, "You might as well have got a wizard hat, a

wand, and a cloak, and then *summoned* me. Something's wrong, and you need to talk to me about it."

He laughs, but it's a strained noise. "Yeah, I guess."

"So, what is it then?" I prompt.

"You, er, might want to sit."

He swallows. Hard. "It's about your mother."

Blinking, puzzled, I move over to his bed and perch on the edge. He's rubbing his temples, evidently tired. "I managed to get to the local allaorum yesterday."

"The local what?" I blurt, feeling quite stupid.

A smile tugs at his lips as he shakes his head. "Oh- sorry. It's basically a post office for homefetches. Established by the Flai Realm during the Fall but used by traders too. Very secretive. Private messengers deliver letters and whatnot. The Moon King tried to cut them off at the root twelve years ago, but you know what black market things are like. It's pretty safe, as nobody pokes their noses into other people's business to protect their own privacy." He gestures to a crinkled piece of paper on the desk. "But as a precaution, it's still written in code. Anyway, I'm getting off-topic. What I mean to say is, I got a letter from the Flai Realm."

I instantly spring to my feet, heart thrumming. "You did!? What did they *say*?"

"Well... they aren't happy," he answers slowly. "One: I said I'd bring you home in 3 days, and it's been far longer than that. Two: they figured out who was behind the Berg's explosion, and me willingly and knowingly putting you in danger without evidence of your consent is considered treason. Three: they know about Bronwyn and are unhappy about our extended party."

"How do they know about Wynn?" I frown.

"You'd be surprised," he says, sighing, "They have eyes and ears everywhere. But that's not all. They say there're going to be "serious consequences" for our actions. There's now raised bounties on each of our heads, ordered by the Moon King himself, and if the Frost Guard doesn't find us, the Willows Guard will get involved. Your Mother's giving me another week to get you home. If I can't, she'll retrieve you herself— that part's a bluff, by the way. But under the current conditions, it's just impossible. Won't stop me getting in trouble back home, though."

"Well, write back and tell them it's my fault. Tell them you didn't do anything and that it was my idea to go to the Berg! I'm the reason any of this happened!"

"As if that will do anything," he scorns. "Raven, I'm human, so I'm to blame. That's just the way it is. Homefetches aren't honoured or admired for what we do. We're the leftovers no one cares about. It's why they send us out here— they don't care if we die. And... things are harsh back home, okay? Your Mother has a Kingdom on her shoulders. She's the self-asserted leader and trying to save your species- and her daughter. She can't have any... inconveniences. That means I'll get punished. It's just the way it is."

"It doesn't have to be," I insist, rising slowly to my feet and beginning to pace. "If she has employees, clearly she has money and power! And as her daughter, I will, too. I can use it to protect you, and I will. I promise. Right now, we just need to figure out how we're possibly crossing that border. Forget all of this."

He raises his head, and for a moment, his mask slips. I catch a glimpse of just how tired he is. Dark circles sweep underneath both of his eyes. "Crossing the border... yeah...." he repeats, "That's the thing... we can get to the Realm. And we will. But not in time. Back in the Flai Kingdom, it's not quite what it used to be. They spent years surviving on the smallest quantity of resources, hiding secret entrances to the kingdom from humans. The rules are extremely tight because they can't risk anyone finding out about them, or it'll all be over. And right now, they have absolutely no guarantee I'm not kidnapping you or taking you to Floodonora. Right now, I can't be trusted. I'm a threat. Do you know what happens to people who threaten the Flai Kingdom?"

I'm silent, knowing the answer.

"They'll kill me," he finishes quietly. "If I can't get you home safely soon, they *will* kill me. I-I can't come with you, Rave. I can only take you to the Realm, where your Mother's escorts will meet you, but our journey ends there. I have no excuse for what happened at the Berg that'll save my life." His voice cracks a little with emotion, but, strangely, it's not directed at himself. Instead he turns to look at me, his eyes on fire with guilt and shame. "I'm really sorry," he whispers. And then he shoves himself backwards so that the chair legs screech against the floorboards. He rises to his feet and turns to leave, but I chase after him.

"No," I say loudly. "No, I won't let them. I...I forbid it! You have to come with me, Sparrow! You didn't do anything! And even now, you're acting like this is somehow your—"

"You can't *forbid* anything, Raven! Have you met your mother? You don't know her. You don't understand what power does to a place. It doesn't matter what you say or who you are. If under your mother's command, they'll never stop. She's... she made herself the queen there. She rules the place, and there was no democracy, no true election. Like I said before: you don't know her, Rave..."

"Then I'm not going!" I snap, whipping around to block his path. "It's as simple as that! If that's the home you're bringing me to, a home that's no different from out here under human regime, then I'm not going! We'll stay here forever, working at Boots and Shackles, earning our keep...or we'll run away!" I declare.

Already, a vision is forming in my head, blooming out of desperation. The two of us wandering through these halls, running through each other's rooms, yelling back and forth as we search for a lost possession that we're each sure the other stole.

Sparrow's hand cradling mine as he wraps bandages around a palm I burned while helping Spok cook. I can even picture myself splashing around, water dripping off the tip of my nose, as we muck about in the shimmering waters of the pool in my room.

We could stay here. We really could.

But the second I see his expression, the harsh weight of reality comes crashing down like a wall, sealing me off from the fantasy forever. No. We couldn't.

Because I don't belong here.

"Eventually, we'd have to leave. And even then, where would we go? There's nowhere to run away to. Don't you get it, Raven? The Flai Kingdom isn't perfect. Not by any means. But it's the best place for you. You can be free there. You can be *happy*."

There's a pause in which his expression falters slightly from calamity and joy, as he beams at me with something close to pride, to a dark, suppressed ache.

"Are you... Flai there?" I ask quietly.

"What do you mean?" Sparrow grunts.

"Is the way I get treated out here the same way they treat you in there?"

"I'm human. I get treated like one," he says bluntly, locking eyes with me. "You slept beside me, walked into a blizzard with me, and scaled a cliff with me. I have killed you over and over with my bare hands in everybody's eyes but yours. I'm dangerous to you."

"Sparrow, none of that matters to me! You're not a threat,

and if my mother wants to punish you because she can't see that, she'll have to go through me first."

"One, nobody is fighting anybody," he says, "Two, you're completely outnumbered. We could never fight them if it came to it."

"I think you're forgetting that I'm *me*," I reply, folding my arms. I'm determined, now. Determined to prove to him what I am. What we are: A team.

"That you're a Flai? And what difference will that make?" he scoffs.

"All I need to be able to do is defend you, should it be necessary. How complicated can it be!? Catch a star, and make a wish. Train a Flai girl, make a weapon."

A thread of hope is weaving its way into his mind. I can see it slowly dawning on his face. I cling to it as though my life depends on it. He slowly turns to face me, uncertain. "What... what are you saying?"

"Come home with me. I will protect you if I have to. I'll fight them all if I have to. I want to live in the Flai Realm that includes Sparrow Fenimore, or no Realm at all."

"How will you fight them, Rave? You froze a bloody lake."

"I have something in mind. There's someone who knows Flai better than either of us. A smuggler who knows better than either of us."

❊ ❊ ❊

"*Train* you?" Spok repeats, her forehead wrinkling. "But I don't know the first thing about you! And I've already been planning several methods of getting you across the border since you arrived! But then you did a runner on me and snook off to the Berg! Now you want to fight? When I've already prepared everything needed to smuggle you? Why?"

"Because, face it, Spok. If there's any hope of us both getting into the Flai Kingdom unharmed, she must be able to use magic at will. She needs to be able to defend herself in case we run into guards. You've worked with Flai for years. Surely you can help Raven with her powers." Sparrow reasons.

It's a half-truth, I suppose. Spok doesn't know about the letter.

I throw Sparrow a look, lowering my voice, "I thought we talked about this. I persuade her, you stay quiet."

"With all due respect, you're about as persuasive as a peanut."

"And you *aren't*?" I hiss.

He hesitates. "I have charm. Charisma."

Oh, I'm sorry, is it not in the room with us?" I ask innocently.

"Girls, girls, please," Spok mutters, hearing every word we're saying.

"We're willing to work at the inn," Sparrow presses, ignoring her, "You've already done so much, and we don't expect you to do this for free, too."

Spok studies us both long and hard then reaches up a bruised and battered hand to rub her temples. "Alright. I'll do it. But don't get your hopes up."

My shoulders drop, and I rush forward to embrace her. "Oh, thank you!"

The old landlady freezes for a moment, then returns to gesture, and something about her stiffness tells me affection is something she's unaccustomed to.

This puzzles me as we draw apart, mainly because generosity is something rarely distributed among the citizens of Evrilore, and a woman with her kindness should not be a lonely innkeeper in the middle of nowhere who's forgotten what a hug is.

I find myself wondering why she has no family. No children. No lover. It is odd, and I can't help but feel there is more to her past than she will ever reveal.

Even so, it is not my place to be nosy. The polite thing to do is to thank her again, turn away, and walk through the winding corridors until I reach my bedroom.

Still, I think, plopping down on my bed and resting my gaze on the wall, *what's the harm in wondering?*

CHAPTER 20

Several mornings later, I awake to the mouth-watering sizzling of breakfast and the clinking of cutlery echoing through the metal halls into my room.

"Oh, look who decided to show up!" Spok calls as I enter the dining room. She's frying what I suspect to be bacon in the kitchen. "Take a seat. We have a big day, and it's half over."

I frown and brush a strand of tangled, dark hair out of my face, pulling back a chair. I've been meaning to cut it short, but outlaws still manage to be self-conscious, and battling the many evil forces of Evrilore with a lousy haircut just doesn't appeal to me. "What time is it?" I ask, rolling up my sleeves and reaching for a slice of toast.

"Eleven-twenty. We should set up you and Sleeping Beauty on a playdate," Sparrow chimes in from the opposite end of the dining table.

I roll my eyes. "Yeah, yeah. At least it's not just me who slept in. Where is Bronwyn?" I add, scanning the room.

"She requested breakfast alone," Spok replies with a shrug. "She said to tell you she's not angry, though."

"She's been avoiding me all week," I grunt.

"Give her time. She was upset and angry immediately after the Berg, but that was short-term. It's all starting to sink in now," Spok explains kindly, scraping a generous portion of waffles and various toppings onto my plate.

My stomach growls, and despite knowing I know I'll

never be able to eat it all, I gratefully dig, savouring every bite. I haven't eaten a breakfast like this in such a long time. Years. The past few days, my stomach has adjusted a little, but not much, so I'm still frozen in the mindset that someone's going to snatch every scrap from my hands. Sparrow doesn't help— he pinches things without asking all the time, slowly collecting his compensation for the emotional turmoil I've put him through in the currency of scrambled eggs on toast.

"If I'm wasting my mornings in bed, why do you always serve breakfast this late? Anyone'd think you're encouraging me," I mutter.

"I always prepare everything for the guests upstairs before my visitors here," Spok explains.

"What do you mean "Always"? You've had other guests before?" I ask, surprised.

"Down here? Only once. A girl called Urs."

"Where's she now?"

"I don't know," Spok replies honestly, "She disappeared after four days— just vanished. The girl showed up, walked through the front door, and collapsed. I'd heaved her halfway upstairs when I noticed the feathers peaking out of her cloak. So I hid her down here."

"What knocked her out?"

"Exhaustion, probably, but I don't know. She never spoke, only nodded and clapped."

"*Nodded and clapped*?" Sparrow repeats.

Spok shrugs. "Nod for yes. Clap for help."

"That's so weird. How'd you get her name, then?" he enquires.

"She could write."

"Then why not communicate through—?"

"She could write three letters," Spok interrupts, signalling the end of the conversation. "Now, eat up, both of you. You'll need your strength, Raven. Today, I'll attempt to train you, and it won't be easy. You've had a few days to recover from the Berg, but that doesn't mean you aren't emotionally fragile."

"Emotionally fragile?" I cry.

She arches a brow. "Either that or you're —dare I say it?— hormonal. But given your brother's recent death, I highly suspect it's the former. So today, remain open with me, okay? Or Sparrow, if you prefer. The last thing you need is to feel frustrated or like a failure because your magic isn't obedient."

"I'm not a failure," I snap sharply.

"I know that," Spok says gently, "All I'm trying to say is that if you need more time, that's alright, and if you need support, you have it. Training will be hard, and you're very obviously still in shock."

"What's that supposed to mean? Am I not showing my feelings to the extremity I should be? Maybe I'm just as distressed and grief-stricken as Wynn! I don't have to cry to you, you know. I don't owe you my feelings."

"Hm. Hormonal, p'raps."

I fold my arms, scowling.

Spok cringes as she speaks. "From woman to woman — though I don't know if I'd call myself that— being angry won't help. There's nothing you can do about being fifteen." She wipes her mouth with a napkin and stands, making to leave. "By the way, bring one of those forks to my room with you."

I arch a brow, but she says no more, smiling mysteriously as she returns to the kitchen, so I turn to Sparrow.

"Don't look at *me*," he says, glaring, as he wipes a sticky glob of syrup off his nose, "She hasn't told me anything. I don't think I'm even *invited*."

"And Wynn?"

"Who knows what she's doing? Been in that room in the dark so long she's practically a vampire."

I lay down my fork. "Okay, no. You don't get to say that when she is a child who had her family seperated and partially lost twice. Peter meant a lot to her. And a lot to me, too," I add defensively.

"I know. I'm sorry," he says quickly. "I've never really had to deal with this stuff. Except once, and I was terrible at it."

"Once?" I repeat.

He shrugs. "There were these brothers— Seb and Loane. We got separated in a confrontation with the Ra Guard. I still took Loane home, but Seb wasn't the same. And I could never really understand that, as much as I tried- I've never lost anyone like that. Never had anyone to lose, either. But I try to understand, Raven. As best as I can." He pauses. "What was he like— Peter, I mean? Before he was arrested and the Berg. Before it all."

"He... I...." I want to answer, to tell his story in the same way that Wynn will one day tell it to the world, but my mouth opens and closes hopelessly. I cannot find words, and tears are welling in my eyes, so I just shake my head. Too many memories, too many stories, and never enough time to tell them. "I... I can't. I'm sorry."

Sparrow gazes patiently at me for a very long time, then nods. "Raven, I know you aren't ready right now. I don't know if you ever will be. But when you are, and when you want to talk about it, I'll be here."

"It?" I repeat.

"Your old life. Peter. Everything. Whether it's a day, a week, a year... You can keep me waiting. I'll stick around. I just want to tell you that if you do need to let it out, to vent, or whatever—"

"You'll support me. I know. What are friends for, right?" I interrupt, laughing.

Friends. It feels strange to say that so easily. Strange because I can't decide if I've said too much too quickly, or far, far too little. I stare at him, hoping he'll give some kind of indication as to whether or not I said the right thing.

But he's silent. So I decide for myself: we're friends. Friends is fine.

I stand up, and he follows suit before hesitantly pulling me into a tight hug. I relax into his arms, resting my head on his shoulder, and for the first time since Peter's death, I am completely at ease.

At last, I pull away from him and run after Spok. I try and fail to hide the fact that I am smiling from ear to ear.

I take the lift down to level negative 3 with a spring in my step. It's by far the smallest room in the building I've seen so far, with only a square, carpeted room that greets me at the lift doors and two other rooms: a bedroom and a bathroom.

"Raven?" Spok's voice calls, "Come in. It's not locked."

I timidly push open the door, and light from the hall floods the room. It's much darker in here— two lamps draped in cloths emit a weak glow, and dust swirls in the pillars of light they create at either side of the old, wooden bed.

Spok's stood waiting for me on a soft, crimson rug.

"Hi," I say awkwardly.

Cupboards line the wall which the headboard faces, and on the opposite side of the room is a great stone fireplace, an armchair on either side of it.

A famed picture of a man with dark, messy hair and an extraordinarily hooked nose sits on the mantelpiece. His eyes are wrinkled into a warm smile, and the paper behind the glass has been stroked and folded so many times that the image has almost entirely faded. I don't dare ask who he is, but there's something incredibly unnervingly familiar about him.

The room immediately floods me with a feeling of great misplacement, as though I'm impeding on a place where I truly do not belong.

This room is the dark cave of one entity: Spok. All her secrets, mysteries, family, and friends drift about like rolling folds of fog through the air, thick with her scent— I can feel it in the atmosphere, making me incredibly uncomfortable. The rest of the building is clean and empty, but this space is hers.

"Um... I like your room."

"Thank you. I hope you're finding yours comfortable?"

"It's perfect, thanks. More than I ever would've asked for. I'm so grateful that you're doing this for us."

"You're welcome," she says flatly.

"I think it's really great that you do this. You're one of the most amazing people I've ever met. And brave," I add pensively.

She chuckles softly. "I'm not brave, Raven."

"You're risking your life to help Flai!" I gasp, disbelieving.

She only shakes her head. "Not Flai."

I cock my head to one side, and she laughs.

"I promise I've ulterior motives."

Disturbed, I avert my gaze and dig into my pocket, withdrawing a fork as she requested I bring one. "What's this for?"

CHAPTER 20

"Ah! Yes. So, Raven," she says, sighing as she sinks into her seat beside the lively, crackling fireplace. The material sags welcomingly under the woman's weight, crinkling up like the many deep lines crisscrossing along her face. She looks like a map when she's deep in thought, marked with rivers and lanes unexplored, older and wiser than ever. "Training."

"Yes," I nod, leaning forward enthusiastically. "What do you have in mind?"

"Nothing specifically, but this place is rich with books and materials. I've read the majority and tested the latter, so I consider myself fairly knowledgeable. The key thing I know is that emotion triggers magic. The chemicals in your brain and blood that trigger your body to react to danger and stress are the same chemicals that draw magic into your skin and amplify its effects on the matter around you. The first thing I need to understand is how strong your abilities are and their nature— by which I mean what makes you powerful. Any patterns in strength or weakness in relation to your emotions. So, when do they feel most extreme?"

I hesitate. "When I'm in danger, I suppose? The strongest I've experienced them is when I froze the lake in the frost wilderness."

Spok looks taken aback. "You purposefully froze a lake?"

"No, I- it was an accident," I say quickly. "I trapped myself under the ice."

"Okay, what about a time when you were in control?" she asks gently, her lips curling up in an effort to hide her laughter.

"The night I fought the guards, when my friends were captured. At the start, my magic came without me willing it to. But after that, once we began to fight together... I was really in control then. Sort of. I felt more in command if that makes sense. And I didn't have to do a lot. It kind of knew what I wanted, as though my consciousness had merged with Sixth Sense."

She nods encouragingly. "Ok, that's a great place to start, then. Try and think of a powerful emotion from that day."

I close my eyes, concentrating intensely and inhaling the scent of burning wood from the fireplace. It reminds me of my emerald flames licking the roots of trees, except this firewood wouldn't stand tall and defiant to my heat. It'd blacken and burn and flake away.

Blacken... black...

The sky's dark enough that it could be a pair of beetle-black eyes. A tangle of clouds throttle a weak moon overhead, and a hazardous maze of thorns and brambles conspire below them.

My hands find bark.

It's wet, cold, and devoured by moss and vines. Weeds surround the base of this tree, joining hands in a wicked dance. My foot discovers a crevice as their thorns claw at my ankles.

Wincing, I reach above my head, grip a sturdy branch, and begin to hoist myself up. The distant, patient silence of a sleeping kingdom can reach my ears even from here.

It's the loudest, most terrifying silence I've ever known.

My heart is hammering in my ears, and the freezing air bites my cheeks. I'm desperate to reach a branch hidden enough by leaves to rest safely on.

Rest... and watch... and wait.

My eyes snap back open to find waves of hot air rippling between my fingers, charged with energy and yearning to be released. Spok's lips curl into a congratulatory smile. "Good. What did you think of?"

I inhale tightly. "After the attack, I was running through the Frost Wilderness, looking for a hiding spot, certain that they were on my tail."

"So you were scared?"

"Very," I nod.

Spok leans forward, and her chair groans. "So, Raven. We need to figure out what frightened you."

I laugh bitterly. "Maybe seven fully grown men hunting me with guns and swords."

"Well, obviously," she says, the warm, intelligent glint returning to her eyes. "But what I mean is the common factor. Something you're still afraid of. Something you can face right here, something you can channel."

"Well, I mean… I don't want to die. I'm afraid of that," I say vaguely.

"You and I both know that's not entirely true."

"Do we? Nobody wants to die, Spok," I reply dryly.

"Nobody wants to, but people often think they deserve to, and that turns fear into despair. And despair isn't what fuels your magic, is it, Raven?" Spok's eyes lock with mine, and my mouth goes dry. She continues casually. "So, what actually made your magic kick in that night? What was the trigger beneath the trigger?"

"The… guilt at betraying my friends. The shame of failure," I mutter.

"Did you fail?"

I frown. Is that a trick question? "Yes. And I failed Peter all over again at the Berg," I say miserably.

"But it was Sparrow who held you back," Spok reasons.

"I let him," I mutter, growing petulant.

"You'd have died if you went back inside that prison, though."

"I'd have *died* either way!" I reply furiously. "Do I look alive to you? Nothing about this is living!" I'm suddenly on my feet before I can register the strength of my reaction, bellowing, and the rage is all over and red hot, like a rash. "And you're kind and caring and hospitable, but the truth is, you still don't understand. I don't *want* you to understand!" I pant into the silence, eyes wide and heart pounding. The anger seeps away like blood leaking through my fingers. "I- I'm sorry," I whisper.

"Are you?" Spok asks calmly.

"No," I answer dully.

She surveys me with great interest. "Set this room on fire."

"W-what?"

"Set this room on fire. Go on."

It happens like a lit matchstick greeting gasoline. I crouch nervously to the floor and press my hands onto the carpet. Instantly, the flames roll out from under my fingers, exploding outwards to engulf everything in their path.

"Now." Spok's eyes meet mine through the blaze, the air that separates us rippling and distorting her confident face. My heart thrums as the fire coiling up the legs of the armchair slithers dangerously close to her exposed thighs. "*Save* me."

And I do. I raise my arms high into the air just as the fire kisses her flesh and throw them down to my sides in one quick motion. The fire recedes into the floor at my command, and the room is restored to tranquillity. Not a single piece of furniture is burned.

I stare in wonder, mesmerised, at my palms, flexing my fingers.

"Loneliness. Deep, cruel, desperate to thrive, and determined to keep you from any meaningful relationship.

That is what fuels your magic. That is your greatest self-destructive trait. It's what caused you to feel so much pain the night your friends were arrested, what caused the powerful outburst of magic inside of you on that day and this one. When the guards arrived, a part of you knew that you were already done for. A part of you knew you could escape... but not them."

"Relief," I whisper. "I would be alone again. Unable to hurt anybody else."

She nods, her tone soft. "That's what made you fight so hard. You weren't fighting to save your friends. You were fighting for your isolation. It was over before it began," she says softly, folding her hands across her lap. "Concentrate on that. Let it be your fuel. Burn it to the ground, Raven, and emerge as a better person. I believe you can. You must believe it, too."

I take in a gulp of air, trying to expand my shrunken lungs, settle my racing heart, and nod, exhaling slowly and carefully.

"What was the point of the fork?" I ask shakily.

"Insurance. It's got the tiniest amount of gold in it. Not enough to humanise you, but enough to temporarily weaken your magic."

"You... didn't believe I'd be able to control it?" I ask, crestfallen.

"I'm afraid I have more important things in this room to protect than your ego— and I'm not talking about myself," Spok replies apologetically, turning her gaze away from me and staring into the fire, distracted. "Now, there's something else I wish to discuss with you."

"What?" I ask rather stiffly.

"It's Bronwyn."

I lean forward in my seat. "What about her? Is something

wrong?"

Spok leans back and sighs. "She's... *you.* No. I'm sorry." She grins hopelessly. "I know that doesn't make much sense, but hear me out. The same trauma that consumes you consumes Bronwyn. She's hurt and damaged and broken in all the same ways you are, except she's younger, and her brain is less developed than yours. Bronwyn is only a very small child, Raven. You're ageing into a young woman, but she... she's very much vulnerable. And I fear that someone is going to take advantage of that."

"But surely you can talk to her in the same way you talk to me?"

"I hate to say it, Raven... but I *can't* help Bronwyn," Spok says heavily, darkness swimming in her eyes. "I'm not qualified to deal with what she has. And I worry that, without proper help, she'll deteriorate into something much darker than anyone realises. There's only so much a spirit can take before it's broken. You must watch her, Raven. Protect her," she commands, her gaze rising to make eye contact with me. "Promise me you will."

"I promise I'll try," I say firmly.

She nods, satisfied, and I sense that the time has come for me to leave. I rise to my feet and duck my head in gratitude before exiting and closing the door quietly behind me, leaving the innkeeper and her mysterious life behind me.

It feels like shutting the door to another universe, and once I'm inside the lift soaring higher up the building, it feels like the inside of a tree trunk carrying me away from the roots.

My questions are footsteps I leave behind.

I go about my day, but my thoughts stay in that room.

CHAPTER 21

Fortunately, Spok allows Sparrow and me to take short visits to the outside world. The air conditioning in the Boots and Shackles is top-quality and probably Frost-manufactured, but after years of living on the run, I never take long to secretly crave fresh air when I've been stuck inside. Additionally, our training sessions grow more intense as we pool over books describing various uses of my magic in elaborate detail, and Spok's eyes scour into every emotional scene in my life. I quickly become desperate for "me time". Which, naturally, involves an insufferable boy in a chicken mask.

Getting us safely in and out of the inn is a simple task. First, we creep up the spiral metal staircase in the dining room that winds up to a trapdoor. In it is a small peephole looking up into the cheap, grimy kitchen of Boots and Shackles. Once we confirm the coast is clear, Spok quickly ushers us into the room above and then out the back door of the kitchen into a small alleyway.

When I go by myself, there's a corner right at the back of the village stables, occupied only by Casper, from which the whistle of the bitter winter winds and the neighs of enquiring horses merge, the cold is blocked out, and the hay is piled into a square which I can curl up beside. This little lonely corner is where I first find true happiness at the inn. Momentary relief, the kind offered by making peace with Bronwyn and waking up alive and safe in the saltwater pool, is not the same.

Because I am outside, and I am wonderfully chilly, yet not too chilly, and I am both safe and where Flai are meant to be — wild.

Sometimes, I fall asleep in my special corner and wake up suddenly the following day. When I return to the inn, I'm showered with all the expected "Where have you been!? I was worried sick!" comments, but it's worth it if it means I can escape for a few hours.

On the run, nothing is mine because I have nothing. At Boots and Shackles, I am still just a guest in someone else's home. But in that little corner of the world, something is finally mine. Or at least, for a week, it is.

Then, I'm prized for information during my training sessions with Spok. After that, the innkeeper demands that Sparrow accompany me on what were my independent journeys to ensure my safety and report back to her afterwards.

At first, I evade the stables, not wanting to give away my little secret, but it soon becomes blatantly obvious that it's the only place in the village we haven't gone to together yet.

On a particularly cold day, the kind you get when winter is just fading into spring after the previous year's Ice Tide, and the weather doesn't quite know what to do with itself, it's Sparrow who first leads us inside. I'm expecting a "So this is where you've been hiding out?" comment, but he just keeps silent, gives me a knowing look, and settles down respectfully in the stable with me, rubbing a hand affectionately along Casper's back.

I gratefully lean back into my pile of straw as hail hurls itself onto the stable roof and rub my hands together. "I wish every day was like Ra."

Sparrow laughs from around the corner, on the other side of the stack. "Ra's too hot. Diseases spread like wildfire over there."

"Well, would you rather burn to death or freeze?"

"I'm presuming old age isn't an option...?" he jokes, and I roll my eyes.

"No, Merlin. But seriously. Which?

"Probably freeze," he says at last, "Because you pass out before you die."

"But you know you're dying, and you know it's happening slowly. Every minute, you'd be thinking, "What if it's my last?"," I reason.

"No, I wouldn't. I'd simply stop thinking," he replies, "Stop wondering and just... go. Go in my own small, quiet way, knowing my family is waiting for me."

I think about this for quite some time. It's strange talking about such a dark subject, but a part of me is so tired that my brain has turned to draining me of my deepest thoughts to make room for more.

Why am I so tired? I'm tired all the time. Tired of Frost, of being Flai, of Evrilore.

"Raven, are you okay?" Sparrow asks abruptly.

"Yeah, of course, I am," I reply automatically.

"No... *really*."

"*Yes*," I say again.

He shakes his head in disbelief. "I just can't... not to be rude or anything, but you're unbelievable. *How*? How are you coping?"

"Coping with what?" I mumble irritably. "Everyone keeps acting like I'm going through something because I'm not reacting normally to what happened. But I am upset— I just don't want to show it. Is that so wrong? You and Spok didn't *know* him. He was never yours to lose. I'm trying to be mature and sensible and handle this privately when nobody's watching... and I don't think asking for some time before everyone offers their condolences on a golden platter is atrocious. This isn't even about me— or at least it shouldn't be. This is about Peter. I'm still here, aren't I?"

"Yes, but you don't seem exactly elated about it, Rave. That's why we're worried. You watched them drain Bronwyn of everything she is, survived while all those prisoners were wiped out clean. You're so *fine*, despite knowing that this world is so... evil. Anyone else'd be screaming and throwing their fists everywhere."

A tiny droplet of rain lands on the curve of my wrist, and I look up to see a leak in the roof. I sigh a little, leaning my head back. "Honestly? I'm *not* coping. Some days, I feel like I'm just going to throw up, and others, I feel nothing at all. Sometimes I want to... I don't know. I find myself thinking that it would be better for everyone if..." I take a deep breath, afraid to voice my thoughts. "If *I* was dead, not Peter. That way, Bronwyn'd have a brother, and you'd have less of a burden."

"Raven," Sparrow says softly. "You're not a burden."

Another long, long silence. His voice is hesitant and quiet, barely audible. "I don't want you to do anything bad to yourself."

Half of me thinks I'm going to cry. The other half has completely shut down, numb. "Do you see it?" I blurt out.

The rain fills in the silence as he hesitates to answer. "See what?" he asks slowly.

I turn my head to look directly into his eyes. A raindrop leaks through the roof and falls into my palm, and I flinch. Instantly, simply from his expression, I know he understands.

"Yeah," he says quietly.

"Do you think it'll ever truly go away?"

He hesitates. "Perhaps. One act of slaughter doesn't

define us, nor should it stay with us forever. Forgive me, for I know I sound like Spok, but the world will continue to grow, turn and change, even if in twisted ways. And it will grow and change without Peter. It will grow and change without you and me someday. We have to move on with the world, I guess."

Tears sting at my eyes, and I wipe them away furiously, cheeks burning red. "I know. I just wish this stupid island and everyone on it weren't so wicked. Because that's what they are, you know? Wicked, wicked people. Sick people."

"Raven, you know it's not all bad—"

"Can you change the world?" I ask, my voice sharper than I intend it to be. "Can you soften the blow or change what's happened? There's no point, Sparrow. Comfort is lies. It doesn't make it go away."

He shrugs. "You'll never know if you don't try."

"Try what? Changing the world?" I exclaim. "You must be out of your mind if you think Flai can ever change this world for the better. Especially being what we are."

"Well, you changed my world, and I think that counts for something, Flai or not."

"Well, that's... that's... nice. Um, thanks," I whisper, unsure how to respond. A piece of straw dances across the floor and lands in my lap, swept into the stables by the breeze. I take it up into my fingers, bending, twirling, tweaking. Is he being honest? I am sure of it. But how can Flai possibly ever do good? We have only caused destruction and grief, pain and suffering. Not just to others but to ourselves. To me.

"So, you come here often, then?" Sparrow says, at last, breaking the silence.

"Couple times this week," I reply, "And where do you sneak off when you go out by yourself?"

He smiles mysteriously. "Secret."

"Oh, come on. You've seen mine. It's only that fair you tell."

"Well, if you insist. But surely you don't want to leave so soon?"

"Actually, I do. I'm intrigued now."

"Then, by all means, let's go." he grins, hopping to his feet, and turns to the haystack. Instead of walking out of the stables, he places a foot firmly onto the square heap.

"What are you doing?"

"Climbing," he replies, pulling himself up the hay.

"Well, yes, but climbing where?"

"*Up*," he says, reaching the top.

"You can't just teleport through the ceiling!" I call to him.

"You sure about that?"

With one hand, he easily reaches up and grabs hold of the roof before manoeuvring himself sideways, pushing up, and disappearing through a dark, shadowed gap between the wall and the ceiling.

I stare in bewilderment at where he was crouching just a few moments ago. "Wait— how did you... where did you—?"

"Come up here, and I'll show you."

Without a second thought, I grip the hay and lock my fingers into the tangle of material. It's surprisingly easy to find a foothold, and I easily make it to the top, with the block sagging only a little under my weight. "Alright, now where did you go?"

"Look to your left," his voice replies.

It's like talking to a ghost. I reach up with my hands and search the wall to my side, trying to find the gap. "Hey, there's a ledge!"

"*No way!*" he exclaims in fake shock

"Shut up and tell me how to get up here!"

"You know what? Just stay there."

His fingers close around my wrist and pull me up, out into fresh air, my body slipping through the tiny gap so quickly and effortlessly that I can barely feel the wood brush against my skin. I'm allowed a millisecond of shelter before the cold hits me. An onslaught of icy rain, piercing howls of winds roaring into my ears, and a wave of sleet.

I shield my face, but Sparrow gently pushes my arms down. "Look. Trust me." He has to shout over the wind.

I turn to see him sitting comfortably beside me, his bangs littered with hail, the icy air beating away at his cheeks. "It's beautiful, isn't it? There."

I follow his gaze up to the sky, squinting through layers of thick snow. "I can't see anything."

"Look harder. Look beyond the sky."

Beyond the sky? There is nothing beyond the sky except space. And stars. And— *Stars!* Thousands of them, millions, a bottomless ocean of them. Some large, some small, some bright, some falling. Space is there. Up there. And I can see it in daylight. "*How*?" I gasp

"Evrilore. The reason no one can leave this place— the invisible boundary, the shield, whatever you want to call it. Whatever it is, it brings us closer to the stars somehow," he shrugs. "If you think about it, it makes no scientific sense. But sometimes, the things that don't make sense are the most beautiful. Why should anything make sense? Why can't everything be meaningless? Why can't things just be?"

I shrug, "Because the world's complex."

"The world is only as complex as we make it," he says, waving me away as though I've said something ridiculous.

I arch a brow and go back to staring at the stars, hugging myself to stay warm. It's bizarre that somewhere out there, there could be another me. Another Raven walking around and doing something completely different right now. "Do you never wonder if, out there, this version of normal is weird? If, you know, they don't have Flai? Or kingdoms? Or purification machines, Flood Tides, or even trade? Flai weren't always here, right? But what if that's because they all came from somewhere else? Or because we were never meant to exist? Maybe that's why they'll never let us leave this island. They don't want Flai spreading because we're a mistake."

"Well, then, you're the best mistake ever made, Raven Asgard."

I grin, and he grins right back, and for a moment, alone on our little rooftop, I don't care for absolutely anything else in the world. I hold out two cupped palms and close my eyes, inviting the small, warm, bright glow of a star. One falls into my hand in just a few seconds, flooding my body with energy.

When I open my eyes, I notice Sparrow staring at me. He shakes his head in disbelief. "Still don't have any idea how you blooming do it."

I laugh, taking hail from my hair as the dark locks ripple. "I theorize that it was given to us, the ability to catch stars, to help us survive Evrilore. Which is stupid because it's not like we were ever really going to survive in this place," I snort. "One by one, we're all going home, all returning to the place where angels come from. That's the price we pay for disrupting the balance of what's mortal and what's not. Earth isn't our place," I finish, shaking my head bitterly.

"Don't say that. You have every right to be here. People just… don't understand that yet. Men don't want to kill Flai, they want to kill the enemy, and the enemy is whoever the rich and powerful tell us it is. That's the way it's always been.

We're stupid like that, you know? We believe whoever is in power, and we believe them like there's no tomorrow," Sparrow says.

"Anyone does if it means they feel secure. 'S why the moon king will get so many votes in the election. He's not glamorous, sexy, goddess-like, or colourful and bright like the Sun Queen, but he does promise the safety of his people. And for that, he stays in control." I sigh heavily. "I know that's the way things are. Even so, I wish things were different. But... they aren't, and we can't just change the whole island's mind."

"Why?" he challenges.

"What?" I yell as the wind doubles in volume.

"*WHY*?" he repeats, shuffling closer to me.

I look up at him and choke out a laugh. Is he serious? Is this a real question? I look for something more profound. A test? It's a ridiculous thing to say— it's impossible to brainwash a nation. And yet, he's still asking.

"Because people don't just believe what you tell them. Because people lie and steal and cheat and manipulate, and they don't trust us. Because life is more complicated than that! We're more complicated than that."

"We?" he repeats

"Yeah. Humans. Flai... intelligent beings."

"What happened to me saying, "What if there's more to it than that?" And you saying, "If there ever is, we can talk about it when it happens"?" he asks quietly.

"I was wrong about that. I was wrong about a lot of things," I mumble thoughtfully, my fingers sifting through snowflakes. They find something warm, something human. Sparrow takes my hand, and I silently turn to gaze at him.

"Were you wrong about me?" he whispers.

"Yes," I admit. "When we first met, I viewed you as a human, and only that. You were just a simple monster, a threat, and something to avoid and escape at all costs. But you're so much more complicated than I ever imagined anyone could be, and I was so wrong. Nothing makes *sense* anymore, thanks to you. You've fractured everything. Destroyed everything... and I can't even fall back on your humanity, can't use it to excuse myself or undermine your personality. I hate you so much for that, y'know? For wrecking me. I was so happy to be a part of the narrative— to hate humans. It made things easy. It made it easy to forget who I really hated."

"And who's that?"

I close my eyes and draw my knees to my chest, wishing to disappear, as a tear rolls down my cheek. But at the same time, I don't. I do want to be here, and I do want to tell him everything I'm feeling and thinking. If only I could put thoughts into words. "Me. I really hate *me*, and I think that's the only thing I'm not alone in. Everyone hates themselves a little bit. I hate me because I'm not loving or forgiving, like you, and you hate yourself because you're human. Don't you see? Hate's why humans killed us, and why I stereotype every one of them, and why I hate you, and you hate me."

"You think I hate you?" Sparrow asks sharply.

"I think you despise me very deeply. And I despise you, too." I turn to him, smiling a little, and push my fingers through his, gripping him tightly.

"Despise," Sparrow repeats slowly. Then his tone softens. "In that case, I despise you to the stars and beyond. To Japan."

I shake my head. "I promise I despise you more."

Sparrow leans closer to me so I can hear him over the wind. "So what are we going to do about it?"

I suck in as much cold, painful air as I can bear, for surely, right now, my lungs are collapsing. "Exist for as long as we can. And then someday we'll die, or something will kill us. And when something does, we'll probably deserve it. People aren't supposed to be ravens and sparrows. If the universe's made anything evident, it's that."

"The universe ought to have better things to do."

"It doesn't, Sparrow. I'm nothing. I'm *nobody*. And you're human. That's just how it is."

Sparrow shuffles closer and wraps his arms around me like a pair of wings. "You aren't nothing, Raven. You're absolutely, certainly something."

"But no one sees me. No one sees I'm a person," I mumble miserably.

"I do."

The storm roars and rages, pummelling the sun, making my cheeks pink and my fingers icicles, but we don't seek shelter. We don't move an inch.

I tell him of Peter, and of my childhood, and how I ran away, and of the thoughts heaven'd reject. I *explain* myself. And he listens. Listens, even as I'm plummeting to the ground and somehow still falling, rocking back and forth, cradled in his hands as the storm freezes my tears to ice, and all of me is thawed.

He holds me, and I sob, and I'm in so much pain that I'm shattering in his arms, each piece of me falling and fracturing like a pair of broken wings. My bloody, feathered fragments spear the hands that hold me, and yet they refuse to flinch away at the grotesque creature who impales them, unlike those that came before.

"We should go," I whisper eventually.

Sparrow laughs, his nose pink. "Where?"

He knows I meant we should return to the inn, but his question strays deeper than that. Where'd we go, on this damned island? Or —if we had the chance— even beyond its borders? Is there a place for us, for a human and a Flai, anywhere?

I shrug, shuddering with every icy breath that steams up in the air before me, and curl up closer beside him. "Far, far away."

"Japan?" he offers.

"Japan," I repeat.

CHAPTER 22

For the next two weeks, Sparrow and I study Flai together in Spok's library, pouring over detailed accounts of the Flai Kingdom as I interrogate him about both the past and present Realm, including my mother, her rise to power, and the homefetch program. While studying my species to prepare for my homecoming, I'm also readying myself for the fight that will quite possibly occur in the event of his arrest.

Sparrow is reluctant to give details about the government there or the villagers, and I have to prize names out of him through careful bribery— mainly involving stars. I hear of Lydia, Tyrone, and a girl called George. I'm given fragments of detail about the army and the Jade Palace, simple seeds which blossom into dreams overnight, sparking a million pictures to race through my head.

Meanwhile, Spok teaches us Flai Latin. I know a few words. "Hello" is "Salviet", but it's pronounced as "salviesh". "Goodbye" is "validanya", but it sounds more like "Valtan". Sparrow, of course, struggles, having grown up in the Flai Realm, where the main language is a mixture of slang Flai Latin, Sun tongue, and English. He's constantly fuming over "new" Flai Latin, proclaiming there was "Nothing wrong with the old Flai Latin!". Spok points out that this *is* the old Flai Latin. The version he's fluent in is a messy sub-variation. He just tells her to get lost.

Sparrow does excel in other things, though, proving

himself to be very useful in food preparation for the guests of Boots and Shackles. He's an amazing cook and even better at art.

But what Sparrow's best at is storytelling. At night, we stay up long after the island goes to sleep, sat together, dangling our legs over the poolside. His eyes drink up every ripple sent out by our swaying ankles and turn each one into a tale so realistic I could be reliving it. The water becomes terrain, tsunamis, and people, transforming as his mind moulds something mundane into something extraordinary.

Just a night ago, I was lying on the tiles while he spoke so softly, then fiercely, then gently, transforming his breaths from ragged gasps to triumphant pants, and I truly did think that I could listen to Sparrow talk forever.

"Sometimes I think you're making these things up," I said to him when he finished.

He sighed. "I make a lot of things up. Just stories. Harmless little tales. It's easy to get… bored."

"D'you want to do something?" I suggested, staring thoughtfully at the water.

"What?"

"Anything."

He considered for a moment. "We could do Ice Tide."

I laughed. "Are you serious? Wynn and I are in mourning, Sparrow. Holiday festivities? Here and now?"

"Yes. You ever had an Ice Tide? A proper one, I mean?"

"No," I said slowly.

Yawning, Sparrow got to his feet. "Well, think about it, then. I'm going to bed."

"Already?"

"It's late."

"There're no windows, and you haven't a watch," I point

out.

"I still have a sense of time, thanks."

I stared at him. "Really? It's easy to lose things down here."

"Yeah?"

"Night," I said sharply.

He paused. "Are you angry with me?"

"No."

Sparrow folded his arms. "What did I do?"

I shrugged. "Nothing. Really! I was only thinking that... doing Ice Tide with you, Wynn, and Spok... that'd make us a bit like a family. And I already had one. And I don't know if I can ever be in one again. Not properly."

Sparrow chose his next words carefully. "It might be good for you and Wynn to form traditions without Peter. To try and just be happy as a two. It could help you move on and learn that there's still a future for both of you together without your brother."

"It might help us to *forget,* then?" I said harshly.

"That's not what I'm telling you to do."

"I know. But that's the trouble. I can't understand you, sometimes, Sparrow. All this grief makes my head feel... full." Frustrated, I flopped back onto the tiles to gaze at the ceiling. "Okay. Maybe we'll do Ice Tide. We have to be careful about it, though. I don't want everything to be too... good," I finally said.

"Good?"

"I don't want things to fit nicely together. I don't want everything to be perfect or to replace the family I had. Fixing Wynn and I's relationship is going to take work. It's gritty, ugly labour, and it doesn't happen because we have a festive holiday party. I need you to understand that you're not like

Peter, Sparrow, and you never will be."

He chuckled softly. "Oh, trust me, I know."

* * *

Sparrow stands back to admire our work, his hand on his hips as he scans the wall. "I think it's good."

"I think it's magnificent," I remark.

He raises his eyebrows. "Oh. We're using big words?"

"They're rather appropriate."

"Save them. We're still not done," he says, disappearing down the hallway. His echo chases him.

"Where're you going?" I call to Sparrow.

"Wherever Spok put the tinsel."

"In her room, maybe? Ask Wynn," I suggest.

"Yeah, because Bronwyn's totally in the habit of swiping tinsel when no one's looking," he hollers back.

As his footsteps fade, I turn back to the beaming, twinkling wall of the living room. Fairy lights hang from corner to corner, and glitter is powdered lightly over every service, coating the room in a delicate gold and green shimmer. Despite my general dislike for Ice Tide, having our own late spring celebration in the warmth and liveliness of Boots and Shackles before the many roaring hearths of Spok's underground labyrinths couldn't be a better way to tackle the very prominent issue of boredom.

It's Thursday, and we've been stuck inside for three days now.

Floodonora reached the inn very shortly after our visit to the Berg, and trade is in full swing with the inn's guests, so leaving our underground haven is a death wish. 'Nora's traders swarmed the village —and Boots and Shackles—

upon arrival, scouring out the distant mountains and village stables for goods. Our entrapment left us all in rather foul moods, partly from the imminent peril looming over our heads and partly because Bronwyn and I had no distractions from Peter's death. Spok's been hurrying away upstairs for hours at a time, unable to supervise us. We dine later at night and earlier in the mornings, and Spok hushes us repeatedly when she graces us with her rare presence. Thanks to her absence, Bronwyn can happily soak in her depression and take it out on me.

Ice Tide seems to have consoled her a little, though. I could've sworn she had a sparkly ribbon tucked neatly amongst her curls this morning, but Sparrow tells me I'm being far too optimistic.

We've erected a grand tree in the living room that bears marvellous baubles, candles, and ribbons, and we've adapted the tradition from Willows of planting unexpected notes in one another's rooms. Poems, mostly, and little drawings, accompanied by baked treats. Even Wynn ventured into my room, once, to place a mince pie on my bed. She never claimed it, but she did flash me a small smile at dinner.

Nobody dares question how Spok acquires a turkey, but she does, and I bake a vegetarian casserole for Bronwyn, who's been experiencing bad indigestion from meat recently. We all gather for dinner in the kitchen, which is proudly swathed in tinsel, and Spok even —rather apologetically, as if to compensate for her vanishing— sets a bottle of something fizzy and bitter on the table. Sparrow spills boiling water everywhere when draining the cabbage and rushes away with Bronwyn for first aid, but finally, we all manage to take our seats.

The clinking of glasses floods the room as Spok pours us all a drink.

"Why did you give me less?" Bronwyn asks rather flatly,

peering at her glass.

"You're welcome," Spok replies.

"I didn't thank you."

"You will."

Sparrow's brows draw together. "Is it normal to toast before we eat?"

"In Ra, with tea, it is," Bronwyn says.

"An in frost, there's a drink that, like, empties your taste buds. It's really expensive, and one bottle is passed through generations," I add.

"This stuff is several generations old?" Bronwyn asks queasily, setting her glass back down.

"This "*stuff*" was my father's, crafted just less than seventy years ago. I can assure you it's quite safe to drink. And in response to your question, Sparrow, I used to be an alcoholic, and I find that the longer I'm eating after I have a drink, the less terrified I feel of reaching for another glass and falling into old habits. So, for my sake, we toast now."

The Innkeeper stands up and brushes a strand of hair from her eyes, clearing her throat. "Ice Tide," she says loudly, "Is a time when people all over the island celebrate family." She surveys us, smiling sadly. "Not one family sits at this table— only two broken wreckages of former families do. So I raise a glass to relationships, not family."

"Relationships," we all chorus, nodding.

Spok continues. "I understand the absurdities of gathering in celebration, light, and joy tonight after such a great loss. I assure you we are not celebrating the absence of someone but the chair on which he would've sat. There is always a place at this table for those who have been and those yet to come and those who never will come. It is important to remember the people we loved and that whilst they may be gone, our compassion and care for them does not cease to exist, just as the cutlery we would've laid out for Peter only sits unused in my drawers, out of sight yet utterly there. The ways in which we interact and impact others cannot be erased as a presence can. Presence, after all, is impact. If there is no one to see us or hear us, who is to say we exist? You mourn for Peter because he was a good, funny, kind, beautiful, empathetic soul, and he has impacted you in ways no one can prepare for. But his effect on the people who shared a home and a family with him only assures me that he was a great human being."

Bronwyn murmurs in agreement, misty-eyed.

Spok smiles warmly at her, with just a tinge of melancholiness in her eyes, and Wynn quickly blinks away her tears. Spok's expression only grows in sadness, but also fondness. She beckons to her side, and Bronwyn moves closer to her.

"A great human being," Spok resumes, putting a arm around the small girl, "And so I toast to that. May we all be like Peter, and may we all raise a glass to every emotion and memory we contribute to one another. The relationships we form here are a repurposing of the love whose receiver has sadly passed on. Our compassion for the lost burns where the flame of life does not. I say in complete honesty that to give my love for the only man I ever loved —and yes, believe it or not, I once had a betrothed— to you children is my greatest honour. It is the stroke of the memories of my loved and my lost being written irreversibly into history, just as someday Peter's legacy will be your mark on somebody else. To love, to relationships, and to Peter."

"*To Peter!*"

We raise our glasses and dive into the feast with lifted spirits as chatter rushes to fill the air. There's commotion over the turkey and five-second-rule instances even I, someone who's eaten days-old food from bins, can't condone

— most of which are committed by Sparrow.

He laughs away the stares and cries of disgust, though, and as the night deepens and blue bleeds into starry black, he edges his chair gradually closer to me until he's crying into my shoulder with laughter at Spok's stories, suddenly relaxed and comfortable with being so obviously physically close to me. And I realize that in the company of the girl whose hands I've held countless times and the innkeeper I've sobbed and screamed to, I don't actually mind. Why should it matter if I'm friends with a human? They don't care, and neither do I.

My gaze drifts to Bronwyn, and her face is absolutely glowing, her hair pinned back to reveal cheeks that can't seem to slump into a frown. She keeps looking at Spok, and she stops constantly adjusting her position in self-conscious anxiety. Her eyes are bright, wide open, and engaged, and for the first time since our arrival at 'Shackles, she properly laughs, her warm voice flooding the room like the chiming of a bell. I observe that she's actually really quite pretty, especially with the chandelier's glow sparkling off of her rosy cheeks.

Perhaps it's not just Wynn, but her surroundings, too. All of us uplift one another, coaxing our peers into relaxation and comfort with tales, laughter, and teasing. The empty chair beside my sister no longer seems to invade the conversation, and the ghost boy of the Berg no longer seems confined to that lonely sea. He's here, floating off my lips as a happy, lively brother and not some cold, dead thing— because that's what people are, after all. Not objects, not lifeless bodies. They're memories and interactions and *feelings*.

Somehow, even before the singing begins, we accomplish the feeling of Ice Tide despite it being months too late for celebrations, and for a moment, I could just be a normal girl in a normal family. But then I realize I prefer this. Me, my friend, my sister, and an innkeeper. A bundle of people who aren't really anybody or anything special but who are everything in the world simultaneously. No, this is better than a family.

Around halfway through the meal, rather loud chanting echos from upstairs, and Spok grumbles disgruntledly about the rowdy customers. Their songs, however, are familiar, and Bronwyn and I, through knowledge gathered through our time in Ra over the years, quickly pick up on the melody. It's an old, heavy drinkers' song about Ice Tide with some rather poor translations of Sun Tongue and the occasional dash of Flai Latin, resulting in a jumbled, mismatched peice of music that somehow represents Evrilore quite well. As we erupt into singing and coordinated swaying from side-to-side, Sparrow nearly chokes on his drink, and Spok does her best to clap along, cheering like a supportive parent who'd rather be anywhere else.

Sparrow quickly drowns us out with "A Willowfolk's carol", a song we all know, and the room accepts the suggestion gleefully, especially Spok. I must admit that with the assistance of Spok and Sparrow's voices, the whole thing is a little more tuneful.

Mid-chorus, the Innkeeper suddenly cries out and swears very loudly upon realizing she left potatoes in the oven. Then Bronwyn announces rather loudly that she has to use the bathroom, looking green, and Sparrow eyes up the casserole I prepared earlier.

"Where's Wy- AHH!" Spok bursts into a string of curses, howling as she re-enters the room without oven gloves and carrying a steaming tray.

"The gloves! What are you *doing*!" Sparrow hisses.

"I can't find the gloves!" Spok protests in defense.

"So you just grabbed it?"

"Evidently, yeah. I was distracted by you two belting at one another. Where's Bronwyn?"

"She ran off. She feels sick," Sparrow explains.

"She better not have that new virus from East Frost," Spok mutters, "It's highly contagious."

"Probably just something in the food," Sparrow says.

"'Snot *my* food," Spok grumbles, offended.

"I'm sure it was something I made," Sparrow reassures her, smiling sweetly. I kick him under the table.

"Ow! What the heck was that f—"

The shattering of glass interrupts him. We turn to see Spok's fist sprung open from around her apple juice, a look of stunned triumph appearing on her face, "I-I don't believe it. I've... I've got it. I've *got it!*" she announces, "And it could genuinely... if we... Both of you start packing tonight. I've just thought of a way to get all three of you into Willows."

Sparrow is midway through a mouthful of food, so I'm the first to speak. "I- what? But how? I thought border security was too tight. That's why we attempted to sail."

"It is," Spok agrees, "But there are ways. Instead of hiding you from their eyes, we're going to go right through them."

"What, like... a disguise?"

She smiles mysteriously. "You'll see. C'mon, eat. And- oh, Bronwyn, there you are! I'll need your help with this. Can you meet me in my room after dinner?"

Bronwyn looks up from re-entering the room, perplexed, and we exchange clueless looks as if expecting the other to understand what groundbreaking revelation Spok has come to, both of us unable to say a word before Spok's disappeared out of sight, murmuring to herself.

I whip around to look at Sparrow, but he's just gaping after Spok, the three of us rather stunned and the atmosphere rather flattened.

After all the planning, after labouring day after day through half-hearted construction of plots to cross the border, I realize that we're all still completely unprepared to leave the inn. There's nothing more terrifying than abandoning my only source of comfort, my only safe place on the whole island.

"Is someone going to say something?" Sparrow finally asks.

"She could've at least let us get to the last chorus," I mutter. "I mean, none of us... We were supposed to have *dinner*," I whine. It's rather childish and rather mortifying, but I can't help myself.

"I can't eat anymore anyway." Bronwyn fixes her eyes on the table, taking a seat reluctantly. "Am I coming, too, then? To the Realm?"

"You don't have to," Sparrow replies, "But you'd be safest there, and you're welcome if you choose it."

"I'm human now. I'm welcome anywhere," she says flatly. She has to force the words out, and they're quiet and stiff with acceptance.

Sparrow tries to maintain the flow of conversation, but the festivities couldn't be more obviously over. "Well... Raven? What do you think?"

I'm speechless. The thought of leaving hasn't truly crossed my mind. I've never fully acknowledged the fact that we ultimately must go. Boots and Shackles has become like a home to me, and not once did I think I'd lose it. Lose Spok's wisdom, lose what has become *my* bedroom, *our* dining room, a home and a future mapped out in my mind.

The journey ahead is uncertain, brutal, and hazardous. The goal is milky, cloudy, and difficult to picture.

And my motivation to reach it has slipped. I wanted to go

to the Flai Kingdom with Peter, Wynn, and Sparrow, who I'd be able to see regularly and spend time with. Now that vision is almost impossible— I won't be able to live peacefully with the Boy in the Bird mask, and Peter is dead, and my "home" feels completely undesirable. As this cognizance slaps me, it shatters my calamity because it occurs to me now that Peter's death, my hypothermia, and the deaths of hundreds of prisoners will amount to nothing.

It was all for an unachievable goal, for something my body rejects. I lean back as though to escape the thoughts, to escape my selfishness, but I'm *not* going home. I *can't* go home. I've got no idea who I am or what "home" means anymore.

What's a home?

I desperately scan the people seated around me. They're all I have left now and so much more potent than walls. These *friends* are my home, but in this building? I'm a guest. In Frost? An infiltrator. What has become my family has no foundations to stand on and nowhere to go.

And at the Berg, one of our bricks crumbled, and cement was liquified. My "home" is dying, just like Peter did.

And so I find myself homeless. I don't have a place anywhere on this island. I'm an outcast no matter what. If I stay with Sparrow, I'm a Flai in Man's world. If I stand by him in the Flai Realm, I'm a traitor to my species.

I catch my reflection in my utensils, and my eyes rake over the empty seat beside Wynn.

We failed our mission at the Berg. Peter wound up dead, his body lost to the sea.

Will I lose another friend this time? Will it go on like this every time we attempt a stunt? And if so, who's next?

Her? Me? Sparrow? Spok?

Blood, blood, blood.

CHAPTER 22

I wipe my clammy palms across my dress, leaving behind invisible smears. Smears only I can see. But it's hot, fresh, and so true it can't be a manifestation of the troubled mind.

It won't go away.

My eyes, manic, land on Sparrow in their frenzy, like catching a snowflake on my tongue during a blizzard.

"Raven, are you alright?" he asks, brow creased.

I shove back from the table and march off, not bearing to be in a room with the two of them. It feels like a game. A horrible, terrible game.

I run.

I run and don't stop until I'm inside my room, and the door is shut and locked behind me. Shutting out the screeching. Shutting out the demons.

The air all around is suffocating despite the size of the chamber. The walls are closing in, and the waters are stirring, coming alive. Everything is choking me.

No one else will die... No one else is going to die.

It is alright telling myself that, slowing my breaths, and crawling over to my bed while I feel my heart thump against my ribs, but the real problem is believing it.

The sheets strewn across my mattress offer no comfort, so instead, I slump hopelessly down at the pool's edge and dangle my legs into the water, swaying my ankles slowly back and forth in an easy, repetitive pattern.

Here, it is quiet and cool. The only noise is the gentle rippling of the water and my breaths. They comfort me, reassuring me that I am alive, I am not hurt, and nor is Sparrow. We'll be fine.

I side my whole body in and push gently away from the poolside, slowly allowing the water to soak through my clothes, and my hair, and stare at my fingers, confounded. At my hands and my wrists, ever so clean with beautiful patterns thrown onto them by the refracted light. So pure, so beautiful.

I turn away from it, from that foul cleanliness, rolling over in the water so that my back is turned to the light.

In the silent underwater world where nothing is quite real, I can almost pretend I'm back in the lake in the Frost wilderness. Right back to when it was just Sparrow and I. To the beginning of this mess... The moment I had thrown the both of us into that lake.

Back then, all I was thinking about was staying alive. No one else to worry about. No large mission to succeed in. Bliss... That dark, cold, numbing place at the bottom of the lake was bliss.

The chlorine stings my eyes, but I allow it to. The water reels me toward the pool's depths, but I allow it to. My mouth opens of its own accord, perhaps to scream or perhaps to swallow water. Maybe both.

I just keep swimming until I swim past the tiled bottom.

When Sparrow enters my chambers, I'm completely submerged in the pool, watching the folds of my dress spread out all around me like the petals of a blooming flower.

"What the bloody hell are you doing!?" Sparrow exclaims, heaving me out of the water. I gasp for breath, coughing and spitting up water. "You're soaked! Look at your dress!" Wrapping a towel around my shoulders, he forces me to face him. "What were you thinking?"

I stare at him, but his face comes with no thoughts, like a nameless tag, and I can't process anything he's saying. Everything that has just happened feels dreamlike. Had I been underwater for seconds or minutes? Floating, flying, or drowning?

"Raven," he says forcefully.

I clumsily stumble to my bed, perching on the end and rubbing my temples as if trying to stimulate my brain cells into action. "I-I don't know. I just wanted to... get away. Things seem simple down there... *under* there..."

He shakes his head, eyes wide and terrified. "You're... you're just tired, Rave. You aren't thinking. Sleep, and we'll talk tomorrow. I don't know what's going on inside your head at the moment, but you're scaring me. I thought you were alright, you know? Just like I thought Wynn was better and I was better. But it's all so f... None of us are, not really. I mean..." His eyes dart from side to side. "What am I even supposed to do? About you, about this, about everything? Should I... do I need to *sleep* in here? Is that what it's going to come to? Can you not keep yourself alive for five seconds?" It is the true, solid terror in his eyes that brings me back to reality.

"I'm sorry," I say quietly. "I don't know what's going on in my head right now, either. Every time Spok mentions Frost or... or Willows... it just reminds me of what's out there. And it's as if I completely shut down. I get scared. I don't want to leave."

"You're only seeing the dark, Raven. You have to remember there's a brighter side to this world. And I'm going to take you there, okay?"

"I can't see it. You said it yourself— home isn't good. It's not safe, and the people are awful to you," I stress, waving my arms about.

"Because that's the way things are! Nowhere is a utopia, Rave. You can't make the world safe and happy for everyone all the time. I'm a human, and you're a Flai. We were never going to be skipping across the Flai Realm together, and if you thought we were, then you need to empty your head, alright? It's all fantasy!" he finishes heatedly.

"Then you shouldn't have befriended me in the first place!" I retort, my voice wobbling.

Under his spotlight-like glare, my senses itch to life, and I'm suddenly more aware of everything— of the slight hum created by air ventilation, of the taste of chlorine on my tongue. It's all coming back now. I'm back in the real world.

"Why, Sparrow?" I demand, "Why do you want to have any kind of relationship with me? I hated you. I gave you every reason to despise me like the rest of your species."

"They're not *my* species. I don't belong to anyone, and neither do you. Can you please get that idea out of your head? I know I keep saying that you're Flai, and I'm human, and that that fact exists as some kind of barrier between us... but it only exists because everyone says it does! Even we do! I'm saying it right now, see? But we could go off together if we really wanted to. There's just... nowhere to go. A-And I don't think you would —or you should— ever choose me over your mother, anyway."

"I never *knew* her, Sparrow! I don't even know what I'd lose if I refused to go home. I knew who I wanted Mother to be. And quite clearly, she's not that person because she'd hurt you. She's... she's just..."

His eyes are wide and searching, locked on me and hooked onto the end of my sentence as I fumble for words.

"She's just a stranger. And you're... not."

That pause.

That *pause*.

You're... *Pause*. Not.

What fills in that pause? What million words am I refusing to say to not only protect him from Mother but to protect me from myself?

"What am I?" Sparrow asks, deflated. His voice is trembling now, too. "'Cause I really don't know."

I drag my fingers through my wet hair, pressing my lips tightly together. "A f... a bloody... a human."

"Oh."

It's the falsest truth, the dividing line between us. He's everything humans aren't: compassionate, selfless, patient. A boy working hard to save a girl he barely knows. And yet, he's human to the core. Human in a way that only matters physically and on an island called Evrilore. But with me, with only me, he's not the slightest bit human at all.

He knows what I mean.

He knows he's human because it's all he *can* be.

And the worst thing is this: he doesn't care, and he'd take every criticism of Evrilore and of nature just to be with me.

"Human," Sparrow repeats. "What does that even *mean*?"

I raise my head to meet his eyes. "Nothing and everything."

"What does it mean to you, then?" he asks, reapproaching.

I've no response, so I simply shake my head, blinking away tears, and gulp, "Things used to be simple."

He crosses his arms and looks away momentarily, deeply contemplating something. And then he hesitantly turns to leave.

I pull the towel tighter around me, my heart pounding as if to push me forward, push me towards the one boy on Evrilore who's keeping me sane.

"Don't go," I whisper. I swallow, forcing down the lump in my throat. The lump that says I'm stupid, small, scared, and afraid.

I push it away because that's what I am. My teeth are chattering, my hair is in rats' tails, and my cheeks are pink with cold. I'm pathetic. Weak. Helpless.

I raise my head, my eyes desperate, as my knees come close to buckling. "Please. Don't go."

CHAPTER 23

BOOM!

I sit bolt upright, the speed of the movement causing the bedsheets to tumble off my bed and crumple onto the tiled floor in a heap. Sparrow's no longer curled up beside me, but there's a significant dip in the pillow where his head was last night. I frown, opening my mouth to call for him—

BOOM! Yelping, I stumble over to my dresser and throw on a blue shirt and a pair of black pants before stumbling over to the lift doors. My clothes from yesterday are in the sodden heap where I left them, and when my eyes stray to the open bathroom door, the boy in the bird mask is nowhere to be found.

BOOM! The impact of this noise reverberates through the floor, sending me crashing into the wall. "What the *hell*?" I cry to myself, pounding a fist onto the elevator panel. The doors slide easily open, the lift lit up by the warm glow of the chandelier. "THIS BETTER NOT BE SOME KIND OF JOKE!" I call up the shaft, then clamp my lips tight together, remembering that revealing my location to anyone other than Sparrow, Spok, or Bronwyn is a death wish.

I am greeted with a ding as I step into the -2 floor corridor, a place that is always shadowed and dimly lit, much like the backstory of its main inhabitant. Today, I am in total darkness. A blackout?

"Spok?" I whisper hoarsely.

No reply. But... perhaps something. When I turn, the shadows on the wall look slightly different, as though they are hitting a different spot or being altered somehow. That is when it occurs to me that I shouldn't be able to see at all due to the complete lack of light. Then I notice it.

Right at the end of the corridor, a single candle's flame still flickers. And beside it, reaching out from the dark, there is a hand poised to extinguish it with one pinch. "Bronwyn?" I say weakly, rigid with fear.

The flame disappears with a hiss. "Guess again," a voice growls, and a moment later, I am being sized by the neck from behind, fingers crushing my windpipe.

I gasp, which is not a wise decision as it loses me most of what little oxygen I have. "S-Sparrow?" I choke, turning my head as much as I can.

His eyes are wide and mad like a rabid dog's, the black pools dilated with adrenaline, his face concealed by black, waxy feathers, and his hair is in a bedraggled mess, but as soon as he hears my voice, his pupils shrink with relief in recognition. "Raven?"

"Hi," I wheeze.

He releases me almost instantly. "Raven! I thought you were a guard, I— I'm so sorry!"

"Where did you *go*?" I hiss, "I woke up, and you were gone!"

"I heard—"

BOOM!

"*That*," he finishes.

"Well, you could've— hang on. A guard? Why would I be a Guard?"

BOOM! "You hear that? Those are Zeun," Sparrow interrupts, cutting across me in a frenzy.

"Zeun? Like the animal? But those aren't... those aren't real..." I begin.

"Oh, they're real. And they're here. Along with two hundred Ra and Frost soldiers, rounding up everyone from the inn upstairs to take into custody," he says. "I've got three guns and a couple of throwing stars, but I left the weapon sack downstairs. In short, I've got nothing that even compares to them. We've got to get out."

My breath is cut short, blood rushing to my ears. Zeun are animals like eels. Except they aren't one of nature's creatures. If they were, they'd have destroyed everything on the island by now. They eat everything, and nothing eats them. In many ways, they are like Flai: unexplained beings which just appeared someday, leaving scientists to unravel the mystery.

As one story goes, an eel wormed its way into the Flai Realm, absorbed the powers of a dying Flai, and since then bred magic into the next generation of what would've been snakes or eels. Their priceless intelligence, precision during attacks, and loyalty to one master are widely known as treasured by the Sun Queen; she keeps them as pets.

Another story tells of mad scientists who played with nature in the worst ways. There are only about ten Zeun left alive on the island due to poaching. Now, Zeun are locked up and allowed to breed annually. The uncaptured were either stolen by Floodonora and ill-kept or destroyed by fearful guards.

It's rumoured that, at first, Flai tried to kill the Zeun because they were never meant to exist and they were a threat to the balance of nature, and that it was the Sun Queen who saved and mothered the creatures, half out of curiosity and half because the unknown is feared, and fear is power in her eyes.

Nobody knows when they're about to suffer a full-scale Zeun attack, for the creatures are silent and genetically modified to be so. But when Ra wants their target to know they're coming, the Zeun make deafening noises that send shockwaves through the earth.

Undoubtedly, I'll be featured on the news over the next few days to send people into a whirl of terror and triumph. They'll capture my helpless body being dragged out of this building and show the rest of Evrilore that Ra and Frost will forever overrule Flai, forever be able to exterminate whoever they wish... The fact that they are now being used to find us displays just how desperately the King and Queen are competing to bring home our heads.

The election mustn't be wavering in either of their favours, but our arrest could turn that all around.

BANG! And as for what the Zeun do to their victims... Attempting to disguise the fear in my voice, I straighten up, turning back to Sparrow. "Are they... can they get in here?"

He ignores my question. As if I need an answer.

"The Zeun won't take long to find us. They detect heat. Body heat. From miles away. And if they know we're here, they'll find the trapdoor. When they find the trapdoor..."

"We're dead, dead, dead."

"And dead," he adds, for good measure.

"Alright. So, what are we going to do about it?"

"Well, first, we're going to find out how they know we're here. And second, we're going to decide what to do with them."

""Them"?" I repeat.

"The traitor. There are four of us in this building. I didn't call those guards, and neither did you. We were together last night, so we both know that for certain. Also, you wouldn't be yelling up elevator shafts if it was you," Sparrow mutters.

"So, are you saying..."

"Spok or Bronwyn. One of them did this," he nods.

"B-but 'Nora! She could've easily... Bronwyn and Spok wouldn't..."

"Let's not assume what people would and would not do, Raven. It's you and me right now. We can't trust anyone."

"I-I trust Spok. I know she's innocent."

"Then where is she, and why didn't the Zeun wake her up, too?"

"She's on sleeping pills to help her rest," I say defensively. "We were talking about it the other day, and I saw a jar of them in her room. Listen, Spok's extreme generosity may be... questionable, but this? This isn't her doing."

"Let's find out, shall we?" he says darkly, melting back into the shadows of the corridor like a shark's fin slipping under the waves.

My stomach churns as I follow him, half with panic and anxiety, half with guilt. Spok is innocent... I *know* she is. She would never do this to us. But if she didn't... Peter's large, desperate eyes flash across my mind. Then the dark circles under Bronwyn's eyes... then Spok's fake accent the first time we met, and finally Sparrow's anger on the beach. That feels like forever ago.

He still hasn't told me how he came to wind up in the Flai Kingdom. Spok hasn't explained what drives her to help Flai. And Wynn... who knows what she's been thinking these past few days. Everyone here, including me, has a veiled life, one the others have yet to see. My eyes widen as I realize.

Everyone could have done it.

We all have a reason to, don't we? Spok'd be killed if someone found out about us. If she turns us in, she gets one hundred thousand shackles and evades a death sentence.

I killed Bronwyn's best friend. If she hands us in out of vengeance, she can finally live the normal human life Peter deserved.

Sparrow can escape his oppressive leaders in the Flai Realm and start anew as a human boy. And me…

I guess there were times in these past few weeks when I thought that I deserved to be humanized and locked away.

"How did they find us!?" Sparrow demands, pummelling Spok's door.

I cringe at how loud he is, but it isn't as though it matters now.

"Is it you!? Did you tell them!?"

There's no reply, so he continues to shout and hit until there are rustling sounds from the bedroom. Spok doesn't take two seconds to hear the Zeun, hear Sparrow's furious tone, and put two and two together. "No, no, I swear!" she exclaims.

I can hear the Innkeeper rattling around with keys on the other side. Neither of us has time to utter a word before she appears beside us and presses two cloaks into our chests. She strides down the hall, and we hurry after her. "Come on. Follow me. You kids shouldn't have wasted your time getting me. You need to learn when to get yourselves out of danger and who your real enemies are. Do you think I called those guards? The Zeun may not be the most dangerous thing in this building at this point. God, I was so blind… I should have seen it earlier…"

"Seen what!?" I press.

"That one of those stupid traders at the inn was bound to find us out and—"

"Spok, we don't think it was someone from the inn," I interrupt.

"We thought maybe it was you for a second, but…"

Sparrow begins.

"*He* thought it was," I cut in sharply, throwing him a look. "Anyway, I explained about the sleeping pills, and then—"

"Both of you shut it. Now isn't the time for petty disputes. There's no way either of you are getting out of this without me," she snaps, rounding the corridor and slamming a fist onto the elevator panel. It arrives in a matter of seconds with a mechanical woosh, and she ushers us inside. "Wait a minute... where's Bronwyn?" Spok asks.

"Still in her room, I think," I reply uncertainly.

"You sure about that?" the small girl asks, panting as she dashes down the corridor. "Don't worry, I heard the Zeun. I'm all filled in. Do we have a plan?"

"It mainly involves not dying."

"I like that plan," Bronwyn nods breathlessly.

Spok gestures for us to join her in the elevator and hollers. "Floor 3!" The lift doors close as it follows her instructions.

Sparrow's still glaring at the innkeeper.

"Quit it. She's doing everything she can," I whisper to him.

"For all we know, she's leading us right into a trap, and she called those guards," he shoots back.

I shake my head. "Look at her. She's just...*her*. She's not evil nor deceitful, and she cares about us, Sparrow. Plus, there are other possibilities. The guards could've followed the carriage tracks we left on the way back here after Spok rescued us."

"Our tracks would have been buried in snow by now!" Sparrow argues.

"DNA, then. Hairs or something."

"I agree with Raven," Bronwyn cuts in, "Spok's nice."

"We can't trust her, Raven. We can't... trust..." Sparrow's

voice cracks away into nothing.

I seize his arm and force him to meet my gaze. "Then trust me."

The lift slows, and Spok glances back at us. "Sparrow, Raven, Bronwyn, hurry! We don't have much time."

As we jog, I can't help noticing how she puts his name first. In the brightly lit underground hallway, as they run side-by-side with Bronwyn a few paces behind them, it's startling how similar they look.

Both have chocolate-brown hair, tanned skin, and slightly hooked noses. Both have strong, smooth jawlines... The more minor details come to my attention. Details insignificant to the naked, knowledge-deprived eye. But mine are like hawk's trained by paranoia to notice how Spok continuously glances down at him, concern darting across her furrowed brow. And then I recall how the Innkeeper reached out for the elevator panel with her right hand, picks things up with her right, but always cooks with her— My eyes widen. *Left hand.*

Spok is ambidextrous!

In a flash, I understand. Spok is Sparrow's *mother*! Sparrow is Spok's *son*! It was obvious, yet I was too blinded by Peter's death and Bronwyn's despair to see it. Even Sparrow seems oblivious.

What would happen if he found out? Surely Spok knows? But then why did she abandon him— *did* she abandon him? Why was he taken in by the Flai Realm? My head spins with questions.

Jogging to catch up with the two of them, I reach the entrance to my room. Spok awaits my arrival, and almost immediately, I catch her eye. Perhaps it's better if I say nothing. I can't confront her here, now... can I?

But it's too late to act innocent of the knowledge because my eyes, accusing, alive, and shocked, have already deceived me.

Catching sight of my enquiring, calculating gaze, Spok gives me a very subtle shake of her head. *Not yet.*

Why? I silently communicate.

He won't understand. Not yet, but someday, she replies, as I gaze at her in wonder and befuddlement.

It takes a forceful thud of an army on an elevator door to bring me back to my senses.

As the echo runs past us, raising the hair on my arms, I look wildly around.

"There's nowhere to go," Sparrow whispers, eyeing Spok, "You've led us here on purpose, haven't you? We're finished. You're the traitor, aren't you!?" His eyes are wide. Wider than I thought eyes could possibly be.

"No! Sparrow, I'm not a—," Spok begins pleadingly.

"You *are*!" he roars, "I-I trusted you! *We* trusted you. I slept in your beds, ate the food you cooked me, and brought Flai here because I thought you were safe. I-I endangered my friends for you, and you're a liar! Because of you, we're dead!"

He lets his palms fly out, shoving the woman backwards while insults pour from his mouth. I have to hold him back as he runs at her, tears glistening in his eyes. Hurt and betrayal cannot describe the expression written across his face. It's more painful than that. It's a cut deeper than that. It's two years of gradually sinking deeper and deeper into the comforts of this inn and its landlady, seeking refuge in these walls and allowing himself to feel mothered by a guardian.

"Sparrow-calm-DOWN!" I struggle, wrenching him away from her. I've never seen him behave so violently. It erases every moral he's stayed true to for the past month and digs darts out of bodies, replacing them with lethal bullets.

Fists flailing, he struggles, wrestling to escape my grasp. "Don't you dare, Raven! She cheated you, too, you know. She played you like she played all of us," he says bitterly, dark eyes fixed on his mother. "And now, they're going to kill us! They're going to—"

"Can you *swim*, Sparrow!?" Spok gasps exasperatedly.

"What?"

"Your leg. Where you were shot. Can you swim?"

He's purple with rage. "I- *yes*, but—"

"Follow me!" Spok says determinedly, striding forward and pulling off her hat, jumper, and shoes. Then she wades into the pool, calling back to us to follow suit.

Bronwyn is the first of us to dive after her, the small girl questioning nothing.

Sparrow shakes his head in disbelief. "What is she trying to do, drown us?"

"Maybe. Maybe not. But I'm not sitting here waiting for a public demise at the hands of Perseus in a village square. It's a chance. Take it or leave it," I answer, stripping down to my trousers and a bra that Spok lent me. In any other situation, I would be terribly embarrassed, but at this point, embarrassment isn't a word in my vocabulary.

"Perseus?" Sparrow asks.

"The guard Captain who stole my friends and cornered Peter and me at the Berg. He's out to get me. I'm certain of it," I explain in a rushed breath. "He's a horrible, horrible man, Sparrow. Every time I see him, every time I look into his eyes... It's like there's dark greed there. Greed that won't stop until he wins." I shift my eyes to spok. "That's why I'm going to trust that woman with my life— at least while it's in Spok's hands, I'm still here. I'm still alive. With Perseus, the moment he has me, Sparrow... I'm already dead."

BOOM! This one is louder and closer. Ear-splitting. The

others glance back at us as the ceiling shudders. "Are you coming or not!" Bronwyn yells.

Slowly, silently, he nods, and I drag us both into the water. We plunge in feet-first, and I can hear Sparrow's groan even when he's underwater as a stream of bubbles emits from his mouth. I instantly hoist him up to the surface. "Sparrow? You okay?"

He takes in a few deep breaths, eyes squeezed tightly shut. "Just... just stings... ahh."

"Let me see it."

"It's fine. C'mon," he says dismissively.

"It's not. Let me help you," I plead.

With his arm around my shoulders and my legs kicking to propel us both, we reach the edge of the other side of the pool, and I'm about to ask the Innkeeper where we're going when she disappears below the surface and presses a complex pattern onto the tiles in a weird sort of underwater dance.

Then I realize the wall is opening up. Opening up to... possibly reveal something else, something beyond it.

"In here," the woman rasps, resurfacing, "Quickly, quickly!"

I narrow my eyes, trying to see past what first meets the eye. This entire building seemed like a mask at first, but now it goes deeper than we ever thought. Maybe this secret underground house is only hiding another building.

Come to think of it, everything here could be a lie...

We splash our way inside the passage, the pool water pursuing, but as soon as we've scrambled inside, a series of metal doors slam shut behind us, cutting off the torrents of water and leaving us in total darkness. I feel my way around in total darkness. We're in a long, tight metal box.

"I can't see anything!" I hiss.

"Shh! Just because the guards can't see you doesn't mean they can't hear you. Now, follow my voice," Spok instructs.

I feel around for the walls in the black void as my eyes adjust. Instead, my hand lands on flesh. "Bronwyn?" I whisper hoarsely.

"No, Sparrow. And that's my *foot*."

"Oh! Sorry!" I whisper, drawing away and feeling the rest of my way along the tunnel. The hem of my trousers is damp and dripping with water, and my senses are on high alert.

Every time I hear a drip on the metal floor, I flinch, looking back for signs of unwanted pursuers. I think I must have crawled past Sparrow because two people are behind me now, from what I can hear.

At last, my hands find the tunnel's edge, where the floor plummets down into a pit. Crying out, I move away and call back news of the hazard to the others.

"Are you sure?" Bronwyn peeps. "It could just be a step. Are there more?"

"Try jumping down," Sparrow offers.

"Alright, alright. Keep your hair on," Spok grumbles, and the way her voice reverberates upwards instead of from behind suggests she's already reached the drop at the end of the tunnel. "It's, like, a three-foot drop."

"Oh," I say, almost disappointed, then pause. "But... I still can't see," I point out.

"Sit on the ledge before you drop, then. What do you think you'll do, twist halfway down, defy the will of gravity, and crack your skull?" the woman snorts, "Just say, "Lights on"."

"Lights on," I echo.

Suddenly, all along the ceiling of the passage and the void

CHAPTER 23

beyond, a strip of humming lights flickers to life, illuminating my surroundings in a cold but wonderfully bright glow.

Spok stands below me, looking up, her feet firmly planted on a simple metal floor that's divided up by small grooves into little squares.

"Question— why didn't we do this before?" Sparrow asks.

"Because these lights are running on emergency generators, as is the lift, and therefore are extremely short-term. The soldiers must've blown up the mains. The inn is probably already a wreck... We need to save the electricity. Just get down here and do it quickly so I can turn them off."

Sparrow crawls up to my side and hops down easily before turning back to face me and offering his hand. I scoff and jump with far less grace than him but land on my feet anyway. He rolls his eyes, muttering something about how chivalry is dead. Bronwyn is the last of us to scuttle out of the tunnel's mouth and land on the metal floor. A small amount of the water that swelled and burst through the tunnel entrance is dragged along with her heel, splashing down into the room where we stand.

Her shoe hooks the edge of the ledge, and she tumbles clumsily down, unharmed but still allowing a scream to slip past her lips.

Bronwyn looks at me. I look at Sparrow. Sparrow looks at Spok.

"Oh, for crying out loud," the Innkeeper yells, barging past Wynn as the girl climbs shakily to her feet. She's so weak and timid these days. Maybe after seeing just how quickly we lost Peter and how easy it is to die, she's afraid it will happen to her, too.

"I've done it, haven't I?" Bronwyn whispers, timid and anxious. We all ignore her.

"Uh oh," Sparrow gulps, as the frantic words of Frost soldiers shoot along the passage from outside like a knot of ravenous snakes.

"Did anyone else hear that!?"

"Go, go, go!"

Spok quickly contradicts my earlier statement with a simple "Lights off", which I can only assume is an attempt to delay our discovery with the help of darkness's cloak. Then she moves over to the left wall to grasp a wheel I hadn't noticed before.

"There's a panel!"

"Something's moving!"

Now, the door that seals the tunnel off from the saltwater pool is slowly sliding open. Dread leaps up my throat like a pack of hounds.

"Hey! Help me!" Spok yells as she tugs at the wheel.

The oncoming group of soldiers wades along the passage, quickening their pace as they spot us, and with their reopening of the entrance comes an enormous wave of water, crashing down and spiling over my feet, dousing their heads.

"Sparrow, Wynn! Come on!" I shout, frantically dashing over to the wheel and grabbing it with both hands. Sparrow follows suit, not questioning my leadership for one second, but Bronwyn does nothing, hanging back.

She stands there, eyes calculating as they flick from the guards to the three of us.

I watch her closely, watch her thick brows pull together like velcro. Just like that, she makes her decision.

And suddenly, I realize what a large difference there is between us now. Sparrow and I have grown close without realizing it because we've relied on one another so much throughout our journey.

However, my relationship with Bronwyn isn't like that. Not anymore. She doesn't need me anymore, and, really, that's all our relationship ever was. We stayed together because we needed to survive. But now... Now she's human. Now, she doesn't need anyone.

She can have a normal life. She can go to school and make friends. She can't relate to me or pity me. She's human filth, like the rest of her new species.

The taste of sick and blood fills my mouth. Bet they'll be nice pals now. But me? I'm not one of her kind, not someone worth staying for.

Even so, it takes one snip to sever a rope and another to pull one end from a tight fist. "WYNN!" I yell, not bothering to lower my voice.

I seize her hand, rushing forward, and pleadingly force her to meet my gaze.

Maybe there's hesitation in her eyes, I think. That'd make it bearable.

Or maybe you're a fool.

"Wait! Wait!" she cries out, "Wait! Help me! Help! They're kidnapping me! *Help!*" Then, for extra measure, she splashes up a great mouthful of water into her jaw, making herself look weak and helpless as she stumbles towards them, reaching out, gurgling. "I can't... I can't breathe!" she gasps.

"Bronwyn, what are you..." I stare at her in disbelief for a moment, but Sparrow pulls at my arm firmly, yanking me towards him as if to tell me that it's over, that we've lost her.

"Don't even try, Raven," he says darkly, "There's no time."

The soldiers have grasped Wynn's collar now, and I watch as they hoist her up and send out a spray of bullets to keep me at bay. Sparrow's quick reflexes save me. He sees the men loading their guns seconds before they open fire and dives forward, his fingers locked around my arm, to send us both crashing onto the floor and out of range.

Meanwhile, Spok flattens herself against the wall and continues concentrating on the wheel. If only a door, or a wall, or *something* would just *close!*

"Come on!" Sparrow yells, leaping to his feet once more. I hastily rise and stumble over to the pair of them, desperately tugging as the guards prepare to fire again.

With our combined efforts, the wheel finally turns a few inches, and a panel begins to slide over the tunnel exit. It'll not only seal off the soldiers from us but will seal off the passage from the chamber, disallowing any more water into the room.

Upon realizing we're on the verge of shutting them out, the soldiers furiously hurry to reach us, causing gushing, twirling ribbons of water to flood the floor of the room.

Robotically, the men at the front raise their guns, barking at one another.

The panel groans slowly shut, but not slowly enough. As I lean slightly to the left, I'm unexpectedly rendered eye-to-eye with a soldier.

He raises his pistol, wiping his trembling wet fingers on his armour, and meets my eyes. The man is shaking at the sight of me. Of a *child.* What does that mean? What kind of a person does that make me?

I'm reflected back at myself in his pupils, staring at myself, at the child who destroyed a fortress and killed a thousand prisoners who never escaped before they were flooded. I realize I'm quivering, too.

I can see it now. What they see in me: a monster.

And I wonder for a moment if I'd call for my own blood had one of those prisoners been family.

And then I remember that one was.

"I—" I sob, my voice emerging as a rasp. I have to look away for a moment, "I'm sorry," I whisper to the soldier.

Sparrow sees my face. Understands, I think. His jaw sets, and he seizes me incredibly sharply, as though I'm his own sanity. "Those depths aren't for us. Not yet."

He's referring to a certain lake.

For a moment, with my heart pounding in my ears, I have a flashback to a fortress that floats no more. Ice and death on the ocean floor. I can remember so clearly how I looked back at Sparrow that day as he pulled at the iron chains around Bronwyn's wrists, attempting to free her limp body while seconds that could've saved us —and Peter— slipped by... and now look at her. Now look at what she's doing to us.

"Why... why would you do this?" I splutter, not even to Wynn but more to myself, to try and understand... and I think my words somehow reach her for just one second because she pauses and turns her head ever so slightly to face me.

"Raven," she says softly, and *she* even sounds sorry and irreparably broken. "I'm *tired*."

And then she's gone, clambering up the ledge and to soldiers lifting her to what they assume is her safety.

It isn't like they recognize her. It isn't like they know what she used to be. And no one else will, either. The Berg is gone, the documents destroyed, and after what she's "been through", her fake story of a kidnapping, a tragedy, or whatever she can pull out of her twisted mind will be passed down in history.

And what will I be? I grind my teeth together in fury. I'll be the fugitive who kidnapped her.

I'm propelled back to the moment I realized that Peter was never coming back when I was locked in Sparrow's arms, my eyes never leaving the empty doorway where a ghost boy is sure to now hover above the shimmering water.

And now, with the same liquid that killed him swathing over my feet, the same panic overwhelms me, and I shut out the quiet peacefulness that comes with imminent danger, imminent death. I can't end up like Peter, I can't!

"RAVEN, *snap out of it!*" Sparrow cries.

I fall sideways with a yelp as water attacks my feet, making the final tug at the wheel. The panel slides shut with an echoing bang, a twin to the reverberation of a single, collective round of gunshots.

We all fall about, panting and gasping with relief and exhaustion, like fish out of water, as the furious military monsters verbalize their fury on the other side of the wall through a vicious string of curses and yells.

My eyes weakly scan my friends. Each person is relatively unharmed. Spok clutches her side tightly, and Sparrow limps, but we're okay.

I closely inspect the panel before flopping onto my back with relief— it's bulletproof.

"You know, I think I've had just about enough water for a lifetime," Sparrow says faintly.

CHAPTER 24

"That," Sparrow gasps. He's regained his energy and angrily paces the room, shaking his head in disbelief. "That- that liar. That snake! How can she do this to us after everything?"

I groan, curled up in a corner. "Sparrow, please. I'm exhausted. You aren't really angry; you're just in shock," I mutter.

"I'm in shock because your friend tried to murder us."

"She didn't try to—"

"What if I hadn't jumped to the ground, Raven? Those men pulled their triggers on us because of her. Do you never think about how you affect other people? What if you'd *died*? I could've watched you die." He stops abruptly, composing himself, and simply shakes his head bitterly.

Blood is still pounding in my ears, pounding like the hooves of a thousand horses, pounding like the fists of men on metal walls. "We can't stay here," I mumble quietly.

Nobody hears me, for Sparrow is still yelling and swearing, and Spok's trying to calm him down. I want to interject and redirect the conversation to our current situation, but what can I say? Really, my newfound hatred of Bronwyn and feelings of bewilderment are just as hot, fresh, and searing as Sparrow's. The only difference is that I'm fighting it back to think logically.

"Maybe she was just... delaying them. Trying to help? You

heard her: she said, "Wait", and they stopped to help her up, remember?" I say, my tongue dry with scattered remnants of dissolving hope and faith. It's difficult to talk. My voice is raw and beaten down to something thin and powerless from screaming. Screaming at the Berg, wailing to Sparrow on the rooftop... I've screamed a lot lately.

I look to Spok for reassurance, but her head's deep into her palms, and she's unmoving, making no attempts to support me or hush Sparrow. She looks defeated now, too focused and distressed to worry about petty teenagers' quarrels.

I momentarily wonder if it's truly the headache of exhaustion and stress that silences her or if she disagrees with me. I like to "simplify" things, don't I? I Like to break people down into chunks I can understand and interact with instead of their daunting wholes?

Am I doing that to Bronwyn in my search to justify her actions?

"Wynn loves me," I continue shakily.

"Oh?" Sparrow interjects heatedly, "'Cause you'd know what that feels like, right? You'd know, yeah?"

That physically hurts. It stings. I stare at him, at the Boy in the Bird Mask, who I thought I'd seen every side of, and the flinch starts in my eyes and works its way down to my drooping, wordless mouth. I duck my head and rock back to sit against the wall.

"She didn't leave us to help. She left us because she doesn't care anymore," Sparrow continues.

I cast my eyes to the ceiling. It's difficult to keep them open even under the blinding glare of the lights. "Who's to say she's not going to come back? Come to her senses?" I ask quietly.

But a word burns through my heart, red-hot, painful, and

silencing: *vengeance.*

Some people never forgive. Some people never forget.

Sparrow opens his mouth to respond, still fuming, before Spok cuts across us both. "Listen, we can discuss this later. Right now, you should both be worried about what we're going to do." Face shadowed, the Innkeeper's monotonous voice hangs alone in the air. Usually, it's accompanied by a flood of body language and facial expressions. But she's straining, and I can hear the panic and concentration in her voice. Neither Sparrow nor I even begin to interrupt.

"Here are the facts: We're in here, and they're out there. They can't get in right now, but that doesn't mean they won't be able to. Knowing Frost, they'll have a bomb down here and ready to blow that door open in about an hour flat, and this won't be the kind that was in the Berg. That bomb was highly destructive and unstable, but the kind that they'll use will generate a far more concentrated explosion. It'll be strong, it'll be dangerous, and it *will* kill us. So, here's what we're going to do: either break out or stay here and argue about Bronwyn, knowing that, sooner or later, we're all going to die. Which will it be?"

Silence falls as though a great shard of glass has descended from the sky, cutting us off from Spok. That's the reprimand I've been waiting for. A calm, clear slap to tell us we've much more important things to do than bicker.

"Do you have a plan?" Sparrow finally asks, his temporarily tamed voice thick with rage.

"I'm Spok," she replies.

"So you have a plan?"

"Of course I have a plan."

❋ ❋ ❋

"This saferoom is located under the west side of the inn. That means that if we can find a way out, we can use the side alley to escape to the stables. If the ground is covered, we can use the drainpipes and scale the rooves of the neighbouring buildings. I have a stash of weapons hidden at the Old Mill that we can use to fight across the village or drop from the rooftops onto unsuspecting soldiers. Raven will cover us from the Zeun with her sixth sense. As for the start of my plan... well, for that, we need to get out of here. Obviously, we can't leave the way we came, but the Inn's original owner wouldn't build a safe room like this one if there were no emergency exits."

I nod quickly. "Right. That makes sense. The pool, the safe room— it all seems like a collective effort made over time. And since it's old... Maybe the exit is sealed up? We can try removing the wall panels. The water might have loosened the bottom ones."

"It's worth a shot," the woman observes, eyes scouring the room. "Okay. We'll do that. Worst case scenario: you use your magic, and we force our way out."

"But I'm a fire Flai," I say anxiously, "My powers aren't centred around earth. How am I supposed to blast us out?"

"So far, you've frozen a lake and set a room ablaze. Plus, the former was an accident. I think you'll manage."

"Flai are only supposed to have one elemental region in which we can cast spells. Sure, loads of Flai are born with some level of control over all four of them, but we gradually lose three until only one power remains. I'm lucky enough to still have power over water and earth, but only very little. And now I'm somehow supposed to use it?" I gasp, exasperated.

"We don't have a better option, Rave. You can do this. You *have* to do this," Sparrow says, sliding grumpily back into the conversation to reluctantly give encouragement.

I sigh, nod, and crouch down, flicking water away with my foot, and begin running my fingertips along the underside of the very bottom panel. It's loose enough to get a hand under but firmly nailed into the wall above. And just under the panel, attached to the wall... the cold, hard, smooth feeling of metal below my fingertips.

"Hey, I found something! Give me a hand!" I call out to the others.

Spok rushes to my aid, and Sparrow begins yanking at his own discovery across the room— a series of loose tiles. I glance over my shoulder to briefly study the section of wall he's hacking at. "I think you have something over there, on the third panel up, far left."

"Maybe," comes his stiff reply.

I turn back to the innkeeper as she kneels in the water. It's at least half a metre deep. She doesn't seem to care about her clothes, though, so I don't mention it and instead drop to the floor beside her to converse. "So, if you can help me pull this off—"

"It's got screws," she frowns, interrupting me. "You're going to have to melt them away before we can do anything."

"I'll try," I answer, tentatively bringing two hands up to each screw.

"Remember your training. Just focus. Channel your emotions. No pressure."

Yeah, no pressure, except for the fact that I have less than an hour left to live if we can't find a bloody door.

I close my eyes, feeling only emptiness in my hands, and flush with embarrassment. *Come on, Raven.*

"Hey," Spok says.

"Mm?" I open my eyes.

"You seem distracted. Don't worry about Sparrow, okay?

He's just upset because you almost got hurt," she says kindly. "He cares about you very much, that's all. Just focus on this. He'll come around, I promise."

"D'you think I should apologize?"

"What I *think*," she sighs heavily, rubbing at the bridge of her nose, "Is that Sparrow's far too good at being calm, and now he's facing the repercussions. Have you ever seen him cry?"

I think back to the Berg, to Sparrow sobbing in my arm as his chest rose and fell rapidly, his rattling lungs sucking in breaths as exhaustion and pain choked him, and his ribcage failed to shield his heart from what nothing can. Even Spok's compassionate eyes don't feel right scouring into that scene.

"No," I lie.

"Explains a lot. By the way, I couldn't find him last night. Were you two—?"

"Spok," I snap, trying to focus.

"Sorry. Use some of that annoyance to melt these screws, eh? Emotion is magic."

I nod, taking in a deep breath.

Emotions, emotions... What am I angry about? Bronwyn, obviously... I glance at my palms. Still nothing. I'm angry with... myself for letting Peter die and for being blind to Bronwyn's pain. My palms are tingling now, ever so slightly. I'm angry about my mother, about what she might do to Sparrow. Heat. I'm angry about my lack of understanding. I want to know who the Boy in the Bird Mask is and where he came from. I want to know why he thinks he's an orphan when his mother is right here...

"Atta girl," Spok grins. "What were you thinking of?"

"You," I say. Almost instantly, I'm stunned by my unfiltered honesty.

Her brows draw together. "*Me?*"

"You and Sparrow," I continue, sneaking a look over my shoulder and lowering my voice so that he can't hear me. "There are lots of things to think about, aren't there?"

She swallows, but her expression of puzzlement only makes me sure she knows I've latched on to who she is and exactly why she's been caring for Sparrow all these years. "I thought maybe you knew... back in your room when I saw your face... And I must've been right. So you *do* know."

"Why aren't you denying it?" I frown.

"Would you believe me if I did?" she asks coldly.

A small smile tugs at my lips. "So... you mean to say you'll tell me the truth?"

Spok avoids my eyes now, but her own have glazed over with memory. "Honestly, I don't know yet. I still hadn't decided if I'd ever tell Sparrow when I realized you knew. Our parting was a long, long time ago... I hardly even remember —"

"But you *do*," I snap, "So what did you do to him? Did you abandon him?"

She tugs, and the bottom half of the panel between us breaks loose. Then, her arms become limp and hang weakly by her side. She sighs deeply. "Yes... No... sort of. There's more to it than that."

I shrug. "I'm listening."

"I just don't want you to misunderstand. You won't believe—"

"Try me, Spok. I'm fifteen years old, and I blew up a prison, shot a man dead, drowned my best friend, emotionally wrecked a thirteen-year-old girl, and did all of the former whilst running for my life away from a travelling market. On foot," I say stubbornly.

Spok fixes her gaze on the floor, her face rigid. "If you ever tell him what I'm about to tell you... I'll rip the tongue from your throat, Raven. He's my son, and you do not have the right to take that away from me. D'you understand?"

"No, I don't understand. And he doesn't either. He doesn't know who he is, Spok! And neither do I. So, who the heck is he? Tell me."

Spok closes her eyes, almost as if in pain. "He's Flai."

My heart thumps as I process this information. Sparrow!? A Flai? "He... he what?" I whisper.

Spok pauses, her lips sinking into a very uncomfortable smile. "Sparrow's father was Flai, and Sparrow is, too. Half, technically, but there's magic in his blood. At birth, we christened him Armos, after his father."

"A-And you are—?" I stammer.

"Human, yes," she nods.

I stare at her in wonder as though she's a beacon of light in an abyss. A world where Man and Flai married? Had children? What must it be like to look around and see someone like me as your... your *equal?*

"That's impossible," I murmur.

Spok shrugs. "It *was* possible. He was just a small boy in a happy, peaceful family when it happened... the Fall. So many of us were just normal households. There was nothing special about us. We were average people living average, acceptable lives. And then... suddenly, we weren't. I know it's hard to believe, but you weren't always the victims, Raven. Humans suffered too. So much," she adds. Her dull tone loosens, cracks of emotion showing through, and she composes herself.

I carefully distract my eyes from the Innkeeper, blazing through metal while she regains the strength to speak.

"When the war began, there was no real warning

beforehand. Tension had been around for years, but it wasn't supposed to just break like that. We'd all grown used to it, so war was abrupt, and we were unprepared. Just like that, it suddenly wasn't safe anymore."

"But *humans* turned on *us*," I say, selecting my words carefully. They emerge with an unintended harshness that makes "humans" sound targeted at the innkeeper, as though the word ought to be "you".

Spok nods. "Yes, but we turned on ourselves, too. I used to drive Armo- Sparrow to the park, but then the King banned cars for interspecies families. I used to hold his hand and walk him down the front porch stairs because he couldn't get down on his own, but soon, my neighbours threw me dirty looks every time they saw me even touch him, as though I was... conversing with the enemy or something. *Touch* my own *son*. Can you imagine how that feels?" Spok continues. "I carried him in my womb, and I birthed him and cared for him, and not once did he harm a soul, but he'd grow up despised by those who once asked what trimester I was on."

"I'm really sorry," I breathe.

The woman gazes at me long and hard. "Do you know why Man stopped trusting Flai? Why the Fall happened?"

"They just... fell out. Got scared of each other," I answer, but upon seeing her face, my tongue turns to dust, and I realize that not once have I discovered those facts for myself. Out of mouths, into others' ears. Intercepted like a phone call, and yet I'm still only hijacking somebody else's line. The real truth is gone. Vanished from history. Was I ever taught a sensible reason for the war?

Spok sighs. "Falling out? That's what they want you to think. That's what they taught you in school. Because really, they're the reason it started and the reason the Willow district, Ra, and the Isles of Sun are still recovering from poverty while the Moon King ensures his kingdom is highly funded and protected."

"How? What *happened*?" I blurt.

"There was... a plague. An outbreak. A highly contagious disease, spreading rapidly through the kingdoms. Although I wasn't there to witness the beginning, I did see the end. And it was terrible, Raven. It attacked the brain, making you vulnerable to manipulation, and stopped you from thinking logically or having complex thoughts. There were theories that the disease didn't come from nowhere and that it was around centuries ago— which helped people draw conclusions about why the Far Lands landlocked us. Another theory was that Flai brought it when they came here and were biding their time, waiting to unleash it..."

"But... but..." I sputter, struggling to find words. "Why would they lie? How would they? You can't just... cover up the past. People talk. People passed things down... you'd have to kill the whole island to..." I trail off, my mind whirring. "But only if the island knew!" I finally gasp.

Spok taps her nose. "Exactly. Frost couldn't kill the whole island. However, they *could* infect it. If one person gets it, they infect their neighbour. Their neighbour has a kid. The kid goes to school, watches a movie, and the next thing you know, the child has a gun and thinks terrorism is great. It just grows and spreads, bleeding from one town into another. If you can gather that town and tell them all a message at once —"

"You can make them forget all at once," I finish.

Spok nods, tapping a panel to remind me why we're here, and I lean forward eagerly to melt more screws while she continues.

"As you can imagine, Frost wanted to experiment with the disease, to find its power and use it to make themselves practically undefeatable."

I sway where I crouch, my hands sizzling furiously through more metal. "Mind control?" I ask. It's not even a question.

She nods slowly. "Lucky for us, their attempts failed, and they destroyed the evidence so that no one else could finish what they started. It's why they don't teach the history of the disease to anyone today. Mind control alone is enough to overthrow Frost. The only problem was they'd already tampered with nature, and nature bites back. A new strand of the virus had developed in the labs, one that thrived in the heat."

"Ra..." I whisper.

Face after face strikes me. Men bent double with age, women having their clothes torn off by families with no roof to shelter under. My fellow outcasts, my fellow survivors. The dust under the throne awaiting the swift sweeping brush of extermination. Poverty kills them, and hope and community keeps them alive.

"Most of the kingdom was struck, and its population took fatal blows. That's why its people are so spread out across the huge country today. Fortunately, most of the population became immune after a year or so. But the same can't be said for the rest of the island."

I draw away from the panels, resting my hands on the damp floor. "Then how'd they stop it?"

"I'm getting to that. Eventually, the disease drove people to be so stupid that they'd stumble right into their own deaths. My mother... she got sick when I was six or so. I barely remember... these men —traders— stopped by our home one night. Nobody else was awake. Nobody heard her leave. She unlocked the door, and they said something to her. Not even something persuasive, just... asked, I think," Spok says softly, "We woke up the next morning, and she was gone. They'd carried her away in their carriage, and the authorities couldn't prove the culprits took her. She climbed inside and tied herself up, the police said." Spok's voice turns shaky. "Found her body in a ditch, they did."

I prise up the corner of another panel in solemn, commiserating silence. Tears shine in the woman's eyes, and she lets out a choked sob, falling quiet.

"Are you two alright over there?" Sparrow calls to us.

I nod, struggling to produce words. "We've almost uncovered something."

"Need a hand?" he offers.

"We're okay," I whisper back. It's not directed particularly at anyone in the room. It's more of a general statement, a desperate wish.

Spok takes a few deep breaths, not wiping the tear from her face, and resumes. "After another ten years, Flai were the only people who had successfully developed a cure for the disease. But to manufacture it on the mass scale required, Frost needed factories. Land. Supplies. It would cost millions of plants and entire habitats. The extinction of several species was Flai's main concern. When the Elders of the Flai Realm said no to the Moon King's requests, he saw it as a great insult to Man."

"That's kind of fair. Control is his whole image," I reason.

Spok side-eyes me. "Yes," she says slowly, "But I think the whole genocide thing was a bit of an extreme response."

"What I don't understand is how he did it," I frown.

"Easily. The Moon King used the Mindlocus to his advantage, targeting certain towns to infect and using propaganda to frame Flai as monsters who wished to exterminate the lot of us and abandon humans while they roamed uninfected. After that, it wasn't long before humans turned on you. And you know the rest. Eventually, slowly, through cunningly small laws and acts of oppression, war broke loose."

"And what did he do to protect humans from Flai propaganda? Anyone infected would've been vulnerable to both sides."

"Flai couldn't create media. Where are the phones, the laptops, the televisions? All gone, and for one purpose."

"So... everyone's... still infected?" I ask, puzzled.

Spok shakes her head, tucking a strand of unkempt brown hair behind her ear. "Everyone's immune. They bred Raes into Frost and Willows and then covered their tracks. The whole island would be weak if not for Ra— and now the Queen wants compensation. Her people saved ours, and not once did the king send his men to their aid. Only recently did the League rise to power, allowing her to seize the men, women and children whose genes run like blood vessels back to her castle."

I clamp my teeth together as my hands burn with fury. "He left the Raes to die and then demanded their help?"

Spok nods silently and helps me tear away the next panel. We've uncovered a square of metal nailed to the wall— an exit for sure if we can break through it.

"If the Raes made the Willowfolk and Frostborns immune, why did they need a cure from Flai?" I pant, sitting back on my heels to give my hands a break.

"The Raes didn't come in until much later, after the war, and after the Elders' refusal," she explains.

"So the king just sent diseased men to war?"

"Would you put it past him not to? The king's image is "whatever it takes", and his brainless brutality is why, at first, Flai had good odds against the Frost Guard. The problem was that although Flai could defend against the army with their powers, it wasn't just the king who was furious. It was the people. In protest of their lack of assistance to humans, there were mobs, campaigns, robberies, and murders. Flai's houses were burned down, Flai's rights were revoked, and they were rounded up and exiled to the Flai Realm by communities across the entire island." The pain in the woman's voice escalates now, and I can almost feel the rush of the flames of grief that consume her on my skin when she tells me the next chapter of her life. "My high school sweetheart —Armos— and I became engaged when I was just nineteen years old. We wanted a quick marriage and a private ceremony, and we were married at twenty."

"Then did you remarry? Sparrow's too young for him to have been Armos'—"

"I'm not pretty enough to be married twice, Raven," she snorts, "And besides, I was too old by the time everything ended, so there was no point trying to remarry and start a new family. See, the reason I'm an old sack of onions and Sparrow's only sixteen is that we were afraid to have children, fearing I'd end up like my Mother. Even so, parenthood was something Armos and I both desperately wanted. So I eventually travelled to the Willow District, the only place where Flai were still somewhat safe and extreme violence had yet to blossom. I was a late mother, but a mother nonetheless. When I was thirty-nine, we had a son."

Wrenching another panel from the wall, I peer at the metal square, confounded. There are no grooves in it where something ought to open and no hinges, either. I'm beginning to wonder if we're wrecking the wrong wall.

"So what went wrong?" I ask, choosing my words carefully. It's already obvious what the fate of her husband was, and so now I must speak delicately.

Spok's eyes mist over, remembering a brief period of bliss in her married life, and her face illuminates with a bright, fond smile. "For a short while, everything was perfect. Every morning, I awoke beside a perfect husband and a beautiful boy— and a coffee, if Armos was up early for work. He always added too much milk," she laughs, shaking her head. The light in her eyes quickly flickers out. "Then... then it just *happened.* One night, a group of teenagers set fire to my house. They stood outside my window laughing and shouting swear words. They threw eggs and watched as I coughed and grabbed Sparrow from his crib."

I silently prise up another panel, giving her a moment to calm herself.

"His father... he.... h-he didn't make it. The house collapsed in on him before... And when I realized that Armos, my husband... my love..." her voice cracks with emotion, "Was dead... I just sat there and wept. Sparrow was crying, too, that day. Wailing for food, safety, or both. I held him in my arms on the scorched, blackened steps up to what was our porch, waiting for help. But who would ever aid the mother of a Flai? I went to the Frost Guard, the Willows Guard, begging for help, pleading for protection... but they did nothing. And that's when I realized I was on my own. It was just me and my boy. So I did something that I'll forever regret."

"What?" I ask softly.

She turns to me, her eyes miserable and tired, full of forgotten regret that's only now rising from the depths of her heart. "I thought I was doing the right thing." Her voice is flat again now. Dull and yet so thick with the emotion bawled tightly up behind her dark, glinting eyes.

"What did you do, Spok? You can tell me."

My voice quivers as she turns to me, the demons leaping out of her eyes. "I humanized him."

"You... You what?" I splutter.

Please.

Anything but this. Spok's not that evil... Surely...

I turn to face her, and she smiles sadly, every wrinkle in her face a river of regret, "Please don't overestimate me. There's no such thing as a good person." She stops tearing tiles off the wall and closes her eyes, pausing.

I take the opportunity to leap onto her with accusation and outrage. "He lost his father, his home, everything! And you took that away from him, too? That wasn't your choice to..." My volume escalates dramatically. "You're just like... like them! Like every other human!"

"Shhh! Please, Raven. Please don't let me lose my son again!" she gasps.

"Lose him? You took away everything that he is!"

"Just let me explain myself... just let me explain..." she pleads.

I fold my arms, my lower jaw trembling with the effort of hiding the intense terror surging through my veins. She's just a human. This whole time, it was all she was and all she'll ever be.

Spok lips her licks nervously. "A-After I did it... I realized that despite being technically human, Sparrow would still never have a normal life. His shoulder blades, our neighbours, the records... the stain of magic remained a shadow hovering over us.

"I was staying in a cheap hotel with my friend Suzanna when a bullet shot through the window of our room and almost killed me. I knew, right then, that harmless little Sparrow could never be cleansed in the eyes of the public. There was only one place left for him, and as a mother, it was my duty to do the unthinkable. To leave him so he'd have a better life," she explains, "And, I know, I should've gone with him to the Realm. And I know I shouldn't have humanized him, either. But I was scared, stupid, and irresponsible. I blamed myself for what happened to Armos. And then I started drinking. Cards. Drugs. I plummeted into a downward spiral, surrounding myself with plastic joy. I thought it'd kill me eventually, living like that. I deserved as much."

She nods profusely as though reassuring herself that her past self-hatred was entirely just. But —and I know I'm only fifteen, and I know I don't know much, but I do know this— her loathing is stacked layers of the same revised, deep, and unchangeable desire to fix the past. She hated herself, but at that hatred's core was a single wish to change one action.

I reach out and awkwardly pat her. We both cringe at the gesture, but I have to find some way of showing I understand. "You assume there's something wrong with you because you made a mistake. When the consequence outweighs the action, you carry it for life. You tell yourself you should've known, even though you were only being stupid and making a mistake. *One mistake*, like everyone else does, every day. But they've got families and happiness, so clearly, you're being punished for a reason. You're fundamentally evil. Your crime is the worst. That is..." I look at Sparrow. "That is, until someone proves to you that you've something left inside you that's capable of being... liked," I finish flatly.

Spok stares at me, and I turn away, suddenly dizzy with the realization that I've just opened my heart to an innkeeper who humanized my friend.

"Um.. what did you do after the hotel?" I mumble quickly, feeling quite hollowed out.

Spok hesitates before continuing. "One day, I was visited by an executor who told me I'd inherited a building in the Frost Wilderness. And I suppose, for the first time ever, I knew what to do with myself."

Her voice is strange as she finishes her story. It's a tone I've never heard before, a tone of absolute calm, absolute certainty. It is as though the innkeeper has explored every aspect of her past, every factor and blemish in her flawed actions, and she's at peace with it. "Two years ago, someone walked through my front door. Someone I thought was gone forever. And so I had a second chance. I could be a mother again. I showered my son with hospitality, advice, and kindness, keeping a spare room for him, always. I could raise him from the outside as an influence and a caregiver he'd never suspect to be more than a kind landlady."

"But you still didn't tell him who you were. He thinks he's an orphan," I point out.

"He won't forever. But I want to fix our relationship first. Right now, he barely trusts me. And I can't lose my son again," she whispers, her voice cracking.

"You won't lose him, Spok. I promise. I'll do whatever it takes to bring him home to you. When all of this is over."

"Please don't make promises you can't keep," Spok says miserably.

I flick a spark at her from between my fingertips. She yelps, brushing it hastily off her shoulder, and turns to throw me a look. I'm already awaiting her gaze, serious. "*Listen to me.* I'm a bad liar. A bad friend. Maybe even a terrible person. But I can at least promise this to you, Spok. I'll bring him home."

"Even if it kills you?" she demands, and there's suddenly a nasty, selfish edge to her voice.

There's no such thing as a good person.

I look deeper, holding her gaze. Beneath it all is simply a widowed mother. "Maybe. I don't know," I say weakly.

The answer frightens me.

INTERLUDE

The ceiling sags with the weight of last night's downpour, and the frayed old tapestries strung from upper corner to upper corner of the room bulge downwards with the rain's produce. I tread carefully around the collection of buckets and towels laid out on the wooden floor— our pathetic attempts to limit Food Tide's impact on our home. The roof's wood is already rotting, though. This old shack won't last much longer.

It's a mere leap, and a short one at that, to cross the room, but the wood might cave in beneath us if we stomp too hard, so I creep, shoeless, over to Peter's bed. "Peter!" I hiss, shaking him gently. "Wake up."

His eyes flicker open, illuminated by the weak moonlight streaming through the paneless window. He jolts to life, already reaching for the emergency wooden panel that slides aside to reveal a secret passage in the walls. I cover his mouth as he struggles, waiting for the realization to calm him.

After around ten seconds, his body relaxes under me, and I flash him an affectionate smile. He jerks his head to the floor, and I nod. Silently, he slips out of bed and kneels beside me on the wood. I kick a crumpled shirt to one corner of the room and dig my fingertips under a plank. Its nails came loose ages ago, so now it's another emergency hatch. Or, for Peter and I, a secret hideout.

Peter helps me lift the plank, then places it neatly to the side to reveal a gaping hole in the floor. His eyes, glinting with the delight of familiarity and tradition, meet mine. I swing my legs over the hole and drop down onto my stomach, using my arms to crawl forward, then scurry deeper under our shack to make room for my friend.

I brush away cobwebs and then push a swinging window out of my way— a feature of the other side of the upturned carriage that has become our home, acting like a catflap for small children. I hear it groan again as Peter follows suit, and then the ceiling of the passage rises into a tunnel that I can crawl comfortably through on all fours, and I stop.

Fog, drifting in from the alley ahead, nips at my arms.

"Quite a night," I whisper, hugging myself as I awkwardly manage to shuffle into a lying position on my front.

"Quite a *silent* night," Peter adds purposefully.

I flash him a half-smile that radiates disapproval, sternness, and uncloakable fondness. If a window opens, Peter's ready to climb. If a lamppost's glow shudders out, it's a passage of darkness free from prying eyes, bridging our world of rags to the inviting homes stocked with food and tradeable goods. *Stealable* goods, to rephrase.

"They'd hear... not a thing," he adds, leaning his head back against the wall as he grins to himself. "That Maure family've plenty to spare, and they're far from home..."

I shake my head, pressing my lips together to hide my smile.

"Don't you ever get bored of the same old marketplaces?" Peter sighs. "Don't you ever want to... I don't know, do something different?"

"We've travelled all over the island, Peter."

"I wish we could *leave* the stupid island," Peter says, slumping. "There's a whole world out there, and everyone hates us here!"

"*I* don't hate you," I say pointedly.

Peter groans and puts his face in his hands. "You're not *supposed* to hate me. You're family."

I reach for his hand and crawl slightly forward, into view for passersby, further than I ever would've dared to before, and his face lights up as the sky comes into view, speckled with stars. His fingers squeeze mine as the breeze ruffles his curls, and he beams at me. "Thank you, Raven," he whispers.

"Just for tonight. Then we're hiding again properly," I say sternly back.

He only moves closer to me, shivering a little, and leans his head against my shoulder.

"You okay?" I breathe.

Peter shrugs. "I don't think anyone is, really. Bronwyn's angry all the time when she thinks we can't see her. She hates it here, and so do you. You look at those guards like they aren't even *people*," he observes.

"Bronwyn and I just get... frustrated. *I* get frustrated because I want to fix everything for you."

"Nothing's broken, Raven."

I only smile sadly at him. The night sky's reflection twinkles back at me in Peter's thoughtful eyes.

Peter lays his chin gently down on the earth and exhales softly, the sound mimicking a butterfly's fluttering wings. "I'm happy right here," he whispers. "Right now, right here, I'm happy."

I can't help but turn away from him, swallowing guiltily.

"Stop it," Peter says.

"Stop what?"

He pulls his jumper sleeves down over his pink fingers, shrinking into his clothing and away from the icy draft. "You're thinking about what we don't have again. Food, water, proper clothes, parents... I *know* you are because I know you, Raven," he adds, stopping me before I can deny it. My bother stares at me, urging me to listen. "Raven, I know things are quite bad. I didn't always, but I do now. So I can understand why you and Wynn are always like that. But I do think we have something you forget sometimes. I've got *you*. And I think you and Bronwyn are... wonderful," he finishes sleepily, settling on that last word with his big, blue eyes fixed on the stars.

I process his words for a long time, then finally squeeze his hand. "I love you, Peter."

He's already fast asleep.

PART 2

CHAPTER 25

We've removed around nine panels so far, and the only sounds are our pants and the muttering of soldiers on the other side of the wall. I can't help wondering exactly what will happen to us if we do eventually break out.

If we can make it back up to ground level, will Zeun be zipping through the village in search of us? Is the perimeter of the inn guarded?

Spok is watching me melt the screws with interest, as though fascinated by it somehow. "Can I help you?" I manage to get out as politely as possible.

"It's just interesting. Nobody knows how you do it, but it's amazing." She clucks her tongue. "It's such a shame. What happened to you, I mean. And all Flai. You didn't do anything wrong."

"We call it life where I come from, and it's generally not in favour of my happiness or well-being," I snort.

"Don't put the world on your shoulders, Raven. Not everything and everyone hates you."

I stare at her. "Um... Not that I don't like our... *conversations*, but is this necessary? Now, of all times?"

"Yes. I'm tired, and I need a distraction from my aching arms. Besides, who cares what's necessary? I could say the same to a pair of wings that don't fly," she says, the impact of her statement feeling like a slap.

"Touché. My parents left me on a doorstep," I shrug. "I grew up on a farm in the Willow District, fluxed when I was six or seven, and I've been on the run ever since."

"Where're you running *to*?" Spok laughs. "It's not like any of us have anywhere to go."

I nod to her in acknowledgement, then pause. "Home, I s'pose. Why're you looking at me like that's a bad thing? Sparrow's the first person to point me towards anything. Before that, I was just... here."

She sighs. "Just promise me you'll remember what's important."

"Enlighten me."

"Love. Freedom. My Sunday roast. Don't forget it. It's all you'll ever need."

"If you say so. But it's not like you can just have those things. Lots and lots of bad people are working together as we speak just to ensure I'll never have freedom."

"And their actions come from fear, Raven. Fear that we humans acquire, keep, harvest, and then breed into our children. You see it in every man's eyes these days. Some of them, your species has never left a mark on, and yet Flai are still their biggest fear. That's why it's so important to face and overcome our fears, whether it's heights, spiders, Flai, or even death."

"I'm not scared of death, and I don't even understand why people are. I just don't particularly want to die— that's what the fear's of. I swear I've told you that before..."

"No one wants to die, Raven," she says calmly.

"Doesn't mean I'm afraid of it. It just means I don't want to die. Is that so wrong?" I point out.

"And why don't you want to die?"

"Because my life only just *started*," I say, and as the words flow from my mouth, it feels as though I'm truly realizing it for the first time. I turn to look at Spok, suddenly aching all over. "I had a life here, with you, Bronwyn, and Sparrow."

"You've a life back home," Spok points out.

"It won't be the same, though. Not without my friends," I mumble.

Spok takes a breath, as if deciding to voice her thoughts. "The most difficult part of losing my husband, Rave, was realising that nothing could be done. A part of me died that day, and I could never, ever get it back. Everything was over. And things that are over are simply *gone*."

"Is that supposed to be comforting?" I snap.

"It's *supposed* to be closure."

I open my mouth to respond, but before I can, the sound of metal screeching along metal echoes through the panel and into the saferoom. Bomb, Sixth Sense whispers.

"How much time've we?"

Right, Sixth Sense replies, ignoring my question. I trace my eyes to the wall at my side, my eyes running along the grooves seperating panels. And suddenly, I know. "Dumbwaiter." I blurt.

"What?" Sparrow says from the opposite side of the room.

"Dumbwaiter. That's it. I know how we're getting out," I say quickly. "Listen, we've questioned why this place was built, but have we questioned *how*? How did they transport anything down here into this room? And how did they test this room to see if the mechanisms worked if they couldn't get back out? How did they transport food down here for workers building the saferoom? There has to be a dumbwaiter or a lift big enough for a full-sized adult. It just makes sense."

"Well, that's true, but wouldn't we have noticed it before?" Spok asks.

I consider this for a second. "When Sparrow and I were sneaking out to sail across the border, I did see a small metal door on the side of the building."

"That's a rubbish chute," Sparrow laughs.

And where's its entrance? Did you see any chute inside the building?" I challenge. He falls silent, his mind whirring.

"I think you're right," Spok chimes in, "So let's get out of here. If your theory is correct, it should be... this wall."

We dive in simultaneously, eager to break out of the room. Now that I'm more determined, more hopeful, and more pressured to bust us out before Frost blows us out, I tear away at the panels with maximum force.

And at last, the corner of a metal square behind the wall reveals itself. "Look! I told you, didn't I?" I grin, wrenching a piece of silver panel aside, causing a large spray of water to splash up onto my back.

"You got the DHQ17?" a voice demands suddenly from the passage beyond the saferoom.

"Yes, sir. Locked manually by Mr. A. Seven minutes to detonation. We received urgent news from Frost. The King wants the girl. He has a hearing tonight with the League."

"Start the clock anyway. If they want to live, they can pull back that panel and hand over the girl."

My triumph at having my dumbwaiter theory proven right is short-lived, giving way to sheer stress. "That doesn't sound great," I whisper to Sparrow, face paling.

"You *think*?"

"They're gonna blow us up. They're *actually* gonna blow us up," I whisper in disbelief.

Spok's expression is grim. "Three panels left. Let's get them over with," she interrupts.

"Yeah, three panels with 6 nails each and seven minutes! We're never going to make it!" Sparrow gasps.

"I don't like your negative attitude," Spok says.

"I don't like your *plans*."

"And I don't like being blown up," I yell, freeing another panel. They both fall silent, rushing to assist me.

"Raven, hands!" Spok exclaims.

"Which screw?"

"Bottom left."

I push my palm onto the screw, silently begging for my powers. They come in a sudden rush of electric blue flame, sizzling and hissing away at the metal panel until the whole thing melts away.

Just one panel, and we're out. The handle of the dumbwaiter is visible now, promising an escape. I hardly dare to believe it. We're going to live.

"Come on! Both of you grab a corner, and we'll all pull together. Three…" Spok instructs.

"Two…" Sparrow says.

"One!" I shout, and we all grapple and tear at every side of the last remaining panel.

Just like that, it's detached from the wall, leaving a shiny square door fully exposed.

Both Spok and Sparrow insist I escape first since I'm the smallest of us all, so I can fit the easiest. "Are you sure?" I ask doubtfully, eyeing the tiny space.

"You'll be in there for a few seconds at most. Relax," Sparrow says.

"Do we even know if it works? Why me? I don't want to die in a dumbwaiter," I reason.

"Well, neither do I!" he retorts.

"One of you get inside, or I'll make you go in together," Spok warns. I obey pretty sharpish after that.

"I don't think we've thought this through very well." I wheeze, squeezing myself inside the stuffy box. "People on this island used to be a lot smaller."

"You fit. That's all that matters," Sparrow shrugs, reaching for the button that will send me flying up through the shaft, "Better tuck your hair in."

I do—just in time for the door of the dumbwaiter to slide shut, leaving me short of breath, cramped, and squashed as I rocket upwards.

Nothing feels better than pushing open the hatch on the wall of boots and Shackles a few seconds later and taking in a large inhale of beautiful, fresh air.

I fall immediately onto a cushion of rank-smelling bin bags. The dumpster is right below the dumbwaiter door, breaking my fall. Grimacing, I stand amongst the rubbish, taking in the scene around me.

Snow covers almost every surface that hasn't been trampled. All the guards must be inside Boots and Shackles because there isn't a soldier in sight. However, the destruction the military caused upon arrival at the inn is evident. Enormous footprints created only by their metal-studded boots are everywhere, and loud, distressed neighs ring out from the village stables.

I cautiously look around for any sign of villagers. Even a normal citizen of Evrilore could be a great danger to us in a situation like this. Unfortunately, it'll not be long before the soldiers realize we're no longer in the building, and by then, we have to be far away from here. "Guys, come up!" I call down the dumbwaiter shaft, sticking my head down.

A mechanical drone sounds as the lift is summoned back to the safe room. I wait in a crouch beside the dumpster, scanning the street. In my clumsy discomfort, I'd forgotten all about the Zeun.

"They're just about to blow it," Sparrow gasps from above the bin, heaving himself out of the dumbwaiter. His appearance makes me jump, and I let out a little gasp.

"Oh. Hi. You scared me. Is Spok coming? Is she out?"

The dumbwaiter shoots back out of sight. "She is now, apparently," he says, "But she'd better hurry. We haven't much time."

I nod, and we both fall into silence while we wait. "Hey, Sparrow?" I ask suddenly.

"Yeah?"

I shift around so that I can face him. "Have you thought about... what this means for Spok? I mean, those guards saw her face. They *know* that she's helping us. What if she can never come back here? What if... it's not safe for her anymore?"

"There's plenty of room in the Flai kingdom."

"Yes, but she belongs here. This is her home. You've seen how they treat humans in the Flai Kingdom. Do you truly think she could ever—"

Ding. Spok crawls out of the dumbwaiter, beginning to say something along the lines of, "Hey, I'm here—", but before she can finish, Sixth Sense interrupts.

LEFT!

And in the next moment, I am throwing all three of us out of the path of a Zeun.

The eel-like creature is black as ink, the edges of its figure smoking and flaring. Its tip is razor sharp, its sixteen eyes glinting like beads along its spine, and a hundred little legs wriggle beneath its belly, scrambling along a road of invisible air.

My hands are shaking as I cover Sparrow's mouth, eyes scanning the pavement as it slithers up to us.

"Don't move. Don't breathe. Don't speak," Spok whispers.

For a moment, I think that perhaps it will pass us, keep moving, keep seeking out whatever its target is... But Zeun aren't designed to have weaknesses. Zeun are designed to kill.

It lurches towards us and overestimates the angle needed to reach us, screeching as it smashes into the top of the dumpster, making an enormous, ground-shaking boom. Then its eyes lock with mine, and it comes to a sudden halt, absolutely motionless in mid-air.

Somehow, the stillness is more terrifying. "It's alerting the guards of our presence. They're coming. Right now," Spok gasps, pulling me off the bin. "Come on!"

"But the Zeun will never let us leave—" I begin.

"They've been instructed not to kill us. Not yet. They'll hurt us if we try to leave, but to hurt us, they have to catch us. So here's what we're going to do: not get caught."

I'm not so sure about that. It's chasing us at least twice as fast as we can run, hot on our tails as we sprint.

"It's catching up. What do we do, Spok!?" Sparrow gasps.

"Split up and confuse it. I'll meet you two in the back alley next to the stables. If I can."

Sparrow nods, taking me by the wrist. "We'll go this way. If it gets you, try and lose it, okay?"

"I can handle an oversized eel. Just stay safe," the Innkeeper says, then disappears behind the back of Boots and Shackles. As she predicted, the Zeun chases after her, then screeches to a halt, furiously calculating which of us to follow.

We're pretty much equidistant from the Zeun, but somehow, it must have sensed that we're a less easy target because it goes after Spok.

"Do you have a plan now? For getting us out of this village?" I splutter to Sparrow.

"No, but I'm guessing that Casper might come in handy."

"If you say so. Let's head to the stables like Spok said."

Listening carefully for soldiers, we dart from street to street. A deafening wave of bangs announces the arrival of a wave of Zeun, summoned by the single eel that found us. They're leading guards out of the building now, flying towards us with glee.

And, knowing that we have outsmarted them, the guards certainly won't be happy. Suddenly, I catch a glimpse of a black flash on the other side of the alley. My fist closes around the hood of Sparrow's cloak just in time. "Not that way. Back," I hiss, beckoning for him to turn.

"What about that one?" he whispers back.

"What one? Where?"

In response, he points to an eel sliding along the gutter of the rooftop behind us. I whirl around, but two more Zeun are snaking along the floor, closing in on us from either side.

Panic claws at my throat. "W-We...we're trapped!"

"And about time," a sinister voice agrees.

"Who is that? Show yourself!" Sparrow commands, but the man's voice only chuckles.

"As if you're in a position to be ordering me around."

That voice. I *know* that voice.

"At least I'm not the one hiding like a coward!"

"Sparrow, stop!" I beg, gripping him tighter.

"She's right, you know," Perseus seethes, appearing right beside me from seemingly nowhere. "*Women.* Always smarter and stronger than we think."

CHAPTER 25

His silver chest plate and cold eyes haven't changed one bit since the last time we crossed paths. Disgust and horror bind my mouth shut as he reaches out with his spider-like fingers and strokes one hand through my hair. I stiffen at his touch but do not resist, for I know the consequences.

Next, his eyes move to Sparrow, who stares him down with smoking eyes.

"Tut, tut, tut. You children must learn to show your superiors some respect." Back to me. Then to him. Back to me. Toying with us like a cat batting a mouse between its paws. "So, you think you can get away with sinking the Iceberg? The King isn't too happy about it... but after all, who could have possibly predicted that the little, timid mouse would turn into a snake? And then, who do we have here? The snake's boyfriend?" he grins wickedly. My cheeks flush a furious red, and I grit my teeth. He smirks at my expression. "Oh, yes. He is, isn't he? Look at those wide eyes! You obviously care for him a lot. Mm. How... *tragic*. If only he hadn't already mouthed me off... then I might have let him live."

"We don't want your mercy, Perseus. What do you even *want?* Why are you here? If you want me arrested, fine, but leave my friends alone. You win, alright? Isn't that what this is about?" I manage to get out.

Perseus freezes momentarily, anger flashing across his eyes at the mention of his name. He holds my stare before calmly continuing. "Dear girl, you've escaped me, humiliated me, and committed treason against Frost. This isn't about winning. This is about justice. Do you know what we do to reasoners and traitors?"

"Do you know what we do to humans? Do you know what I do to liars? Just admit it! You're obsessed with the seven-year-old child who escaped you all those years ago. Well, that's not me anymore. I'm older, smarter, stronger," I retort, fire sparking between my fingertips. *Come on, come on...*

Perseus surveys me with great interest. "I did promise the Moon King a good show— a nice, clean public execution. But I think that I might just have forgotten my little arrangement with him. I'd rather watch you bleed out myself. Try anything, and fifty zeun'll rip your throats out," Perseus says casually. Too casually.

I know as his hand emerges from the folds of his cloak and endless plates of armour that I have only seconds to make a move. Zeun are slithering across rooftops, shooting through the air towards us. Each one is poised to strike, to kill. Their metallic scales glint, their tiny legs scrambling over thin air in clumsy excitement. Their eyes fix on us, scanning, calculating each jerk of their manufactured limbs.

"Sparrow..." I whisper shakily, "Sparrow, there's so many of them..."

The Captain looks almost amused. "This is priceless."

"I could still kill you," I stammer, "If you don't call them off."

"And who'll defend Sparrow?" he grins at me.

Raven! Sixth Sense says urgently. *Behind you! You can—*

"Kill them," Perseus commands, and at least twenty Zeun hurtle toward us from every direction.

Face drained of colour, Sparrow meets my eyes and moans with annoyance. "Oh, why are these stupid creatures letting him tell them what to do!?"

One zeun opens its flat, wide mouth with a screech, its lips transforming into two needles, and I trip over my feet, stumbling backwards. Sparrow and I crash to the ground.

"STOP! We-we're just like you! She's FLAI!" Sparrow screams.

A needle penetrates my shoulder as a howl escapes my

throat—

As though a switch has been flicked, the terrible ring of death surrounding us freezes. Sparrow grapples for the hem of my collar, pulling my ear to his lips. "What's going on?" he stammers.

"I don't know... but whatever you just said, I think it ... somehow it stopped them," I answer, two twin fireballs ready in my palms.

"I asked them why they were taking orders from the Captain," Sparrow says blankly. "But— I don't know, almost as a joke, a complaint. Not an order."

"No, after that. About us being like them. Sparrow, I-I think... they understand us. They're smart. Maybe you should try to... negotiate with them? Reason with them? I don't think they're like the zippers, Sparrow. I think they *feel* somehow."

"They're *machines*, Rave."

"They're also genetically altered— *and* they come from the Flai Kingdom."

The Zeun are twitching now, resisting the urge to shoot forward. They're awaiting Sparrow's next words. I clear my throat loudly in his direction, and he awkwardly props himself up with one arm. "Uhm... you're all from the Flai Kingdom, right? Well, so is she! Raven is treated like an animal, and her kind is traded in by Floodonora and Merchants. Everyone wants to capture her, yet they're afraid of her. So you and Raven are very alike, huh? Misunderstood? Mistreated? Nobody respects Zeun. They're just afraid of you. If you kill us —*her,* I mean— it will be like killing one of your own kind. And... and, why do you even take orders from Frost? Why do you take orders from anyone?"

"Sparrow, that's enough. Come on, they'll become self-aware," I hiss.

He falls silent, and we wait for the Zeuns' verdict. They quiver excitedly now, passing messages I cannot understand between them. Then, like a storm passing, the mob disperses.

I nearly collapse in relief, stumbling back into the wall. Perseus seems to be weighing up his chances of fighting both of us. A revolver is at his side, but he has no idea if we're armed, and two guns versus his single one won't give him the better outcome. *Go on. Flee, you coward.*

Sparrow and I collapse in an exhausted, bewildered heap. "You do realize what this means?" I ask him shakily.

"You can control them, Sparrow. You can speak to Zeun. You were amazing!"

He nods slowly as though struggling to comprehend it.

"And you know what else? It means you saved me. So I owe you my life again," I sigh, gingerly pressing two fingers to my shoulder. They come back dotted with red. "We still have to find Spok. She could have run into trouble," I say, wincing. "The Zeun may not be after us now, but she's in danger…"

"Don't say that. I'm sure she's fine, and she's waiting for us at the stables."

"There's only one way to find out."

We exchange cynical glances and set off again, dread pooling in my stomach as a series of scenarios flash through my mind. Spok dead, Spok arrested, Spok tortured. The carousel is infinite.

Down the street. Up the cobbled road. Past Boots and Shackles. And finally, into the courtyard surrounding the stables.

"Spok?" I call out hoarsely.

Behind you, Sixth Sense snaps. I whip around, eyes sharp, expecting a soldier—

But it's only dishevelled, kindly smiling Spok, breathing heavily as she yanks a Zeun out of her stomach and crushes it in her fist, "It almost impaled me," she mutters, lifting her shirt to inspect the scratch. The familiar old twinkle in her eyes is the most comforting sight I've been greeted with in the past hour.

"We're so glad you're okay. I thought something'd happened—"

UP! Sixth Sense screeches.

My head snaps skyward, and I reach out to pull Spok away. But I'm too slow. The loop of rope swings neatly over her head and around her waist. She looks up in alarm, her mouth wide open in a silent "O".

And then she's yanked violently backwards, and the story falls full circle. I'm back in the woods, alone with the Boy in the Bird Mask. No brothers. No friends.

Most certainly no innkeepers.

CHAPTER 26

Sixth Sense yells for me to duck, but Spok's muffled cries, strained to audibility through her gag, distract me. Her eyes are locked on her son, and she's screaming "RUN!" at the top of her lungs, lunging for us again and again, a mane of windswept brown hair slicing across her wide, distressed eyes. Thugs beat her away from us, their merciless fists slamming her to the ground. A pair of surly, muscular arms seize me without warning, binding my hands before I can react, and a gag is pulled painfully tight between my lips, jerking my head back so hard I fall, smashing my head onto the cobbles.

Sparrow whirls around, frozen, and I'm already yelling, "BEHIND YOU! BEHIND YOU!". My words are muffled and go unheard. My heart seems to break itself into two pieces as he's dragged backwards, kicking and screaming, by the guards.

Next, Spok's hauled forward face-first, her hand over her stomach as blood oozes out of a fresh slash in her side.

Spok is strong, and she can surely break free. Years of heaving laundry piles and plates around the inn will assist her...

But she's too weak, and the soldiers' grip holds firm. The innkeeper is wrestled into a carriage, and the door is slammed shut. She presses herself against the windows, and Sparrow starts screaming. *She'll be fine, I repeat to myself, they won't kill her... they can't kill her. They need her for information, right?*

But what happens when there's no information? What happens when she doesn't give us up and she won't tell them anything? Torture? Prison? Will she ever return? Is her life's work at Boots and Shackles about to be obliterated?

I can't bear it. I can't bear to watch as they take her... then again, what else am I supposed to look at? I can't tear my eyes away. Even Sparrow seems to be in complete shock, paralyzed, his eyes filled with terror. Sparrow, who always has a plan, confidence, and delusional optimism.

It's the unmistakable smear of black across my vision that brings me back to my senses. I look down and glimpse a Zeun slicing through the binds on my wrists, silently hacking the rope away.

Sparrow's desperate eyes find mine. He opens his mouth to say something, but then he, too, is gagged.

Just a few more seconds... Wait... I try to communicate with him, but my efforts are fruitless. He's crying out to me through his gag, telling me to use magic.

I don't need magic, I want to say.

Before they can stop me, I bolt to my feet, turn and throw open the door to Casper's stable, and tear the gag off my face. Casper bucks with joy in recognition. "Alright Casp, c'mon. Steady, boy." I mount him, running a hand along his warm neck. "Let's see how fast you can run," I whisper.

Instead of going after me, the soldiers surround the only leverage they have left: Sparrow. In response, the Zeun envelop him in a protective stormcloud and easily bear his weight, interlocking to form a sturdy net. Spok hurls herself against the door to her carriage, yelling. "GO! DON'T WASTE A SECOND, RAVEN! GO!"

I reach for the horse's reigns, then hesitate, looking back at her.

My promise rings through my throbbing head. *I'll bring him home.*

Even if it kills you?

The innkeeper's eyes lock with mine. "You'll save him, Raven! YOU'LL SAVE MY SON!"

I tear my eyes away with a scream of frustration, seizing the reins and slamming my boot into Casper's side. The Zeun quiver excitedly as Casper retreats from the stables, his rapid, muscular legs making for a slim exit between two buildings.

"Thank you," I whisper to the eels, pulling Sparrow safely onto the horse as they finish his delivery, "For everything."

Enraged, the guards begin to hack away at the shield of Zeun surrounding us, but the creatures only hiss, undamaged, with rage, and whizz from man to man, carving a passage through flesh towards one particular Captain, who stands defenceless, his men slumped at his feet.

Perseus gives a final cry of fury before the Zeun encircle him, and the last place his eyes settle is upon my face. Upon my victory.

"I win," I mouth to him.

I know he understands me. I know it.

At my command, Casper trots forward a little and the Zeun part so I can lower my face to eye-level with the man who has tormented me. "You will never hurt my friends or me again. And if you try, I will kill you. Again." I emphasize this last word as the dusk of outrage on his face shrinks away, and the realization dawns on him: a million Zeun are poised to tear out his throat.

"Kill me? Is that what you'll do?" Perseus says, his jaw trembling.

"You're just a man, Perseus," I spit at him, "But a *human*? My brother, who you arrested, and my sister, who you tortured, were more deserving of that word than you'll ever be. I finally know what it means now."

His eyes bore into mine. "Don't," he says.

I don't know if he's talking to the Zeun or me, but if he's addressing the Zeun, that means he's not asking me for his life.

So it's not my responsibility to save it.

After all, what did Spok say? *There's no such thing as a good person.*

I steer Casper away from the shrieking, writhing, bloody sight that is the Captain and towards the nearest available alley.

"What are you doing!? We can't go, Raven!" Sparrow hisses into my ear, returning to his senses. "We've already lost Bronwyn and Peter, and we can't lose her as well!" he begs.

"We were going to lose her right from the start, Sparrow. We were going to cross the border into the Flai Kingdom, and we were going to leave her behind. It was always going to be just you and me in the end. We have to finish this the way we started it."

"But they'll kill her," he says, his voice cracking with emotion.

"They won't. I won't let them. We'll go back for her. Didn't you say my mother has an army?"

"Big enough to defeat the Frost Guard? I'm talking hundreds. The Moon King's talking thousands." His eyes are pools of despair and desperation. "Please, Raven. I didn't want it to be like this. I didn't want this to be the way we split up. What happened to all those fantasies back at the inn? About staying there, about living there? What about that?"

I stare at the ground and tear away from his gaze, the wind blowing cool air across my face and drying the tears that glisten on my cheeks. "That's the problem with fantasies. They're that and nothing but."

"RAVEN! RAVEN! No, we can't leave her! *Raven!*"

It's too late. The remaining soldiers are finally slaughtering through zeun, their faces slashed open, and there's only a small group of eels left. Spok's carriage is directly opposite us, beyond that wall of guards.

The Innkeeper's looking at me sternly.

There's no such thing as a good person.

I kick down hard on Casper with the heel of my boots, and he gallops away from the inn as I've never seen him gallop before, his tail streaming out behind us like a ghoul waving distantly in the wind. The colour is whiter than snow, whiter than my skin after fluxation. It flutters out like a flag of surrender hoisted high into the air, displayed proudly for the distant approaching army to see. And they *will* see it.

No more hiding, now.

Let them come.

✣ ✣ ✣

Don't think about Spok. Don't think about Spok.

This simple thought allows me to survive the next few hours of constant travelling. Never looking back, never knowing what will happen to her, even though both Sparrow and I truly do, and never daring to imagine.

Sparrow is silent, his face stone, as the horse gallops tirelessly. Somehow, somewhere in Casper's eyes, I sense that part of him knows what's going on. And he wants to help us, so he's using every last bit of stamina in his legs.

My heart still leaps up my throat even though we're away

from danger. Every time safety greets us, it only eventually reveals itself to be fake. Evil and peril always find us— and in this case, it was already standing amongst us, unsuspected behind a mask of thirteen-year-old innocence.

I pause, frowning to myself. But Bronwyn isn't evil. She's... there's almost no world for it, so I select one carefully. She's incapable. Too young to cope with her trauma, so she's building a pipe to funnel it away.

And, I suppose, so am I. But mine takes the form of hope now, branching away from an original, toxic self-isolation.

I've begun to shed old skin and accept that I'm changing in ways that are out of my control— I know for a fact that every second of every day, a part of me is dying.

The part of me that grew up in the Willow District with friends and a life and a family, and the part of me that once sat down at a dining table and scrawled images of the Flai monsters in crayon onto napkins. The human part of me.

But that's okay.

I don't want it, I realize. *I don't want those memories.* That childhood was fake, and those memories are plastic. That's not what I am. It's not what matters anymore.

I glance behind me at The Boy in the Bird Mask.

Sparrow hates me for what I've cost him. I'm sure of it. And if he doesn't, I know he will now. He was already an outlaw of sorts but not a criminal. Now, his name will be known to all. Now I've dragged him down with me and destroyed his reputation inside and outside the Flai Realm.

He said it himself— he can't come back with me without endangering his life. Everyone, everywhere, intends to cause him harm... because of me.

Strangely, I'm dreading the day he realizes it. I know it's selfish how much I don't want to lose him and want him to stay at my side while his name is stained with blood and charred by magic, but I've never wanted someone so badly before.

I've never wanted a friend in the way that I want Sparrow, and the unnerving part is that I'm beginning to question if I want him at all or if I, quite simply, selfishly need him.

"I don't hate you," Sparrow says suddenly as if reading my mind, breaking the heavy silence between us.

"You do," I reply glumly.

"No. Storming an unarmed inn, sending zeun after children... You're not the monster. They are."

"Monster?" I reply. "Not human, but not quite an animal. What else am I, if not a monster?"

"A person."

"Sparrow..." I whisper. "*Stop.*"

He can't say anything, can't reassure me it's alright. I yank Casper to a halt and turn to face him. "What we said at 'Shackles, on that rooftop... we need to stop, now. We were just playing. Just making things up. And now we *have* to stop. Everything about me is a lie. Not just a lie from me, from my deceptive appearance that could paint me as an almost-human, but *your* lie, too. That loving sister trying desperately to save her family? She doesn't exist, Sparrow. You made her up, alright? You made her up because my skin is chalk-white and my veins are filled with blood that will never be human. I will never be human. We will never be anything more than a human and a Flai. Spok could die, all because of our pretending. We *need*," I repeat, one final time, "To stop."

Sparrow calmly meets my gaze, exhaustion glittering in his dark eyes. "Raven, you haven't lied to me. Flai are... beautiful. All humans can do is destroy."

"I'd rather destroy than be what I am," I say quietly, trying to conceal my shaking hands inside my cloak.

If only he knew... knew what he used to be... Despite losing his powers, he still somehow ended up here with me. What kind of message is the universe trying to send? That we should stick with our own kind? Does life have a way of sending you right back around the circle, of guiding you to your roots, even if it means prising you, finger-by-finger, off of your branch? Sparrow has no safe home to return to, and his only former guardian is now in Frost's hands because I wasn't brave enough to save her.

I yank on Casper's reins and dismount, turning to face Sparrow. He jumps off, inquisitive. "Why'd we stop?"

As I step closer to him, crunching snow under my feet, the air nips at my skin. The short winter day is drawing to its end, and night is coming, moving in in its royal blue glory to take the sun's place. I sigh, knowing darkness will bring haunting nightmares. But tonight, I won't sleep. I'll stay awake watching and waiting. I will do it for Spok— to protect her son and ensure he does not meet the same fate as Peter.

And I will continue to protect him, even if it means going to extremes, even if it means catching a million stars, even if it means it kills me. I know that now. I know my unspeakable promise to Spok was true. But perhaps, I realize, I made that vow not for her but just for the Boy in the Bird Mask.

Sparrow clears his throat loudly, but I don't even look at him. I think for a moment that he's going to grab my hand and force me to meet his gaze, but instead, he just leans back against Casper's back and exhales softly, saying four words that revive me. "It isn't your fault."

Face softening, I let my eyes float up to his. He still trusts me and still wants me. I know I should be blamed, but he doesn't blame me. He blames the world. The world he once loved, his eyes full of wonder and compassion for people who do not, and will never, know him. I've poisoned that innocence and stolen that love, selfishly bundling it tightly enough to fit inside my cold, cold heart.

I need to say something. "Thanks"? Too little? "You mean everything to me, and I don't know what I'd do without you because before you walked in with your ridiculous, unrealistic ramblings about my Mother, my life had no meaning"? Too much?

Just one word, I think. Just "goodbye".

"Sparrow—" I begin tearily.

Cutting me off with a desperate embrace, he crushes my hopes of leaving him and finding the strength to do so. He tightens his arms around me and draws me so close that you'd think the wind was trying to sweep me away. He shakes his head frantically. "Not you, too," he whispers, burying his head into my shoulder. "Especially not you."

I gasp, choking on tears and icy breath that steams up before my watering eyes. "I do nothing for you. Nothing."

"You can't leave me alone, motherless and homeless."

"You'll be safer if I just... go."

Stop it. This is enough. This is forgiveness, my heart says.

I gently push him away from me, reach out for his hand, and press my fingers into his closed fist, asking permission. He relaxes his fingers, taking my hand in his, and I close my eyes, savouring it.

"I couldn't hate you. Not even if I desperately wanted to."

"Even after Spok—?"

"No," he interrupts firmly.

"Truly?" I ask, eyes wide and searching.

"Truly," he whispers, leaning forward to press his forehead to mine in an embrace.

"I've never done anything for you. How can you be like this? I don't understand," I say miserably.

CHAPTER 26

"You don't have to," he says simply.

We ride through the day and deep into what feels like a never-ending night. I constantly twist back to peer at the tiny village in the distance, at the inn and the stables speckled like dust on the horizon. From afar, enormous problems seem so small and insignificant, like something you could brush away with a spare hand. The scenery that envelopes us is barren and silent, save for Sparrow breathing deeply in and out, his body loosely swaying to and fro to disrupt my view.

I rub my sore throat and stuff my hands into my pockets. It's freezing and dark.

And I'm *lonely.*

"Please wake up soon," I say in a child-like voice. Then— "I'm sorry."

It's a very loose, untargeted apology like a dandelion's white, tufty head breaking off into seeds as the wind carries it away.

Sorry for Spok. Sorry for what happened to you. Sorry for accusing you, distrusting you, and pushing you away.

I open and close my fist, striking up tiny fires at the edge of my fingertips and then extinguishing them repeatedly. I fling the flames forward onto the wet grass, and they sit there dully for a moment before dying. Then, I begin to aimlessly fling more all around like fireflies, planting seeds in the wild. I leave some on the ground and some floating in the air, creating a tunnel of light that we ride through.

I create Floodonora, imitating their carriages with little beacons of light that stretch across the countryside on my command.

I sit back and admire my work, my fire multiplying without my permission and uniting land and sky with tiny green flashes. *These powers that I bear,* I think, *are so heavy and yet sometimes make me feel incredibly light.*

Using them is a moment of freedom, a breath that reminds me what I am. And my relationship with them is so, so, indescribable, swaying uncontrollably and inevitably between hatred and wonderous love like the changing of seasons. Magic is a vine that bears fruits of unbelievable rarity and beauty, but the thorns protruding from those vines make their harvest impossible.

My abilities create such a strong fear in me.

As a sudden chill creeps up my spine, I realize that I'm alone again for the first time in weeks. Yes, Sparrow is behind me, but there is no one to see me, hear me, or judge me. And so I can face disregarded ugly truths.

Something that's been playing on my mind is how strong I've become. I could kill someone. My fire can't hurt nature, but anything that takes unfair advantage of it is at risk. If I wanted, I could engulf entire cities in flames and scorch innocent children in their cribs. I could be a monster if I wanted to.

But I don't want that.

There's a bitterness forming on my tongue in admitting that to myself because while I don't want to hurt, I don't want to help people, either. I'm unlike Sparrow, who still, despite his fixation on me, has so much love to give. I've nothing left for anybody. I find that I can choose myself now, and there's no shame in that.

And there's no guilt, either.

The world has robbed me of so much. I've been unguided, unsupported, and uneducated. Nobody has told me who to be, and so I've had to do that by myself. I've had to figure out what's evil and what's good. I've had to somehow discover empathy, grief, love, and befuddlement. And most of those, I achieved through suffering. Others, through people like

Sparrow.

The thought pricks my eyes to tears because it makes me wonder who I'd be if I were normal. If Raven Asgard would exist at all. *Why* Raven Asgard exists at all.

And as much as Spok soothed me and Sparrow reassured me, I still desire most desperately to understand why someone as bright and kind and selfless as Sparrow can care for a person like me. I'm a person who's barely even that, barely complete.

I've so much anger, hatred, and fury, and it leaks out of my eyes now, seeping away to carve rivers of glistening, star-speckled woe in my cheeks. The hatred is so strong it terrifies me.

I'm a child and ruined in every way, but I still have to carry this burden. There's no mercy, no limit. I'm a statue with no foundations, crumbling and cracking into weathered ruins strewn across the ground.

The worst part is that I feel unfixable. I'm such a mess of a person, a mismatched bundle of homemade morals and biased views based on scraps of newspapers and shreds of conversation. I feel finished. Over. As though there's nothing I can do to progress, to change, to be better, or to somehow justify Sparrow's feelings.

And so I sit back, and I soak up every drop of moisture in the air until I am the darkest, heaviest cloud. And then I cry.

I cry until I've exhausted every drop of energy I have left.

My shoulders rattle with sobs, and my breaths emerge as fractured wails. I wrap my arms around myself, cradling this body that I despise so much.

I just can't put myself back together.

CHAPTER 27

Satisfied, I sweep out my arm, efficiently extinguishing the forest fire which I successfully commanded across three acres of land like a blazing army. As a limitation of nature itself, a Flai's magic cannot make permanent biological changes to the world around it—only temporary alterations to the plants and animals. So, though my fire can damage men, it causes no harm to me or the trees I send up in flames.

However, it can harm humans. Even those that were once... my eyes flicker to Sparrow.

Us.

I swallow my discomfort at the thought of his humanization and how it blanketed him from nature's keen gaze, depriving him of all the magic and safety he deserves to possess. He'd certainly use his gifts more responsibly than I. More responsibly than anyone, perhaps, because he sees what the humans who hunt us can't, and the Flai who'd kill him for simply existing refuse to: Everyone, everywhere, is so obsessed with the great divide between two species that we've forgotten that people are simply people.

Even I fell into that trap. That detest. That burning fury for people who I'll never know.

But not the Boy in the Bird Mask.

Somehow, he escaped. He got out. He's not human, nor Flai, nor mine, nor Mother's, nor *anybody's.* He can't be categorised, which is what makes him so dangerous. And yet, here I stand, turning to him for approval, my palms dimming to their usual skin tone as the last green flashes disappear.

"You're getting stronger," he assesses, "It won't be long now before you're home, and then you'll be able to use them whenever without being afraid. And if Flunters ever come to get you, you can just zap them like some sort of mad, power-crazy goddess, and..." he trails off at the look on my face. "What?" he says, frowning.

I shrug. "Nothing. I was just hoping that if it ever came to that, you'd ninja-whack them for me. Like you shot those guys with a dart gun at the Iceberg," I grin.

He groans. "Why do I always have to shoot people? You never shoot people."

My face melts into a warm smile. "I have a reputation for keeping a clean record," I shrug.

He gapes at me, and I burst out laughing. Now that it's just us again, I can almost pretend that we're back at the lake, back before everything was complicated, and I wasn't grieving for my best friend and the only mother-like figure that's ever been in my life.

But the thought of Peter hits me in such a brutal, melancholy wave that I slump miserably onto the grass.

"Raven, your record is about as clean as a rhino's— Raven?"

I grunt in acknowledgement.

"What's up?" he asks.

I still haven't told him about my breakdown last night, instead choosing to adopt delusional optimism and fake a newfound enthusiasm to practice my magic, claiming it to be Spok's final wish before she was arrested. Sparrow'll never know her real one, never know what I agreed to do at the cost of my life, should it be the scenario. Truly, even Spok didn't hear me say those words.

But she knew.

I look back up at Sparrow. "Just thinking. I don't know. Bad stuff popped into my brain again. It keeps doping that," I mumble.

"You have a brain?"

"Let's not," I groan.

"Let's not what?" he frowns.

Sighing, I raise my head just a little. "Let's not pretend. I'm really tired. We've been through absolute hell, Sparrow. You lost Spok, the only parental figure you've had consistently in your life for the past two years. You're doomed to be punished when we reach the Flai Realm, 'Nora... well, who *knows* where she is! Oh, and my best friend died, Bronwyn turned on us, we turned an intelligent life form —Zeun— against humans, and the king hates us. So, please. Let's not. Pretending is exhausting."

"Well, yes, that's all true. But... I mean, here we are, right?"

"Here we are," I repeat miserably. "We just keep... getting out, don't we? Somehow, it's always us who survives and someone else who gets hurt... and I just... why? What did we do to deserve it?"

"Maybe you're overthinking it. It's not our fault we're lucky."

"This isn't luck. This is twisted. What are we, Sparrow?" I gasp. "Because we're not special. We're not saints. Don't you see? Our "luck" will run out eventually. How do we know that this won't continue forever? How do you know that bringing me home isn't a death sentence to the village, or—"

At that precise moment, an unfamiliar sound reverberates through the trees, far off but moving closer.

He offers me his arm, and I take it, hastily leaping to my feet, my eyes narrowing.

"Ah..." I wince as a sudden dull pain flares outwards from what feels like the centre of my skull. "AH!" Clutching my head, I stumble backwards, my hands reaching to cover voices only I can hear.

Sixth Sense is bellowing a series of repeated overlapping instructions, growing appallingly loud.

LEFTRIGHTUPDOWNRUNSTAYLEFTRIGHT

"Raven? What is it?" Sparrow asks, lowering his voice. I reach up slowly and tap my ear with a shaking finger, trying not to scream.

In the frenzy of terror, my eyes meet his, and the pain pauses for just a moment. "I can *hear*," I whisper.

And then the aching in my head explodes outwards, and Sixth Sense engulfs everything.

"What? What can you hear?" Sparrow asks desperately, supporting my shoulders as I'm thrown backwards with agony again.

My skin's paling, veins of ice rising to the surface of my arms, and I can feel the bones unfolding themselves from my back as my wings fight to be released from my shoulders. "Listen!" I cry, my hands helplessly batting at my ears.

At first, it's a single, collective rumble of thunder, and then the thunder becomes rain, pounding down onto the earth like a hailstorm, each droplet grouping into one ongoing sound. Except it isn't hailstones, it's... Footsteps. It's *footsteps!* And... I listen harder... Not all human ones.

Sixth Sense is suddenly quiet, and I collapse in an exhausted heap with relief, frantically straining my ears against the silence.

Sparrow's looking at me. I'm looking at Sparrow.

"RUN!" I bellow, making for the horse. But Casper is stumbling around in a circle, neighing loudly in distress. He can see something we can't, and his panicked limbs trip over themselves as he spins around and around in terror.

"What's wrong with him?" Sparrow cries.

"He doesn't want to go forward, but he won't go back," I reply, both hands out in front of me as I approach the horse, "Hey, Casper…"

With a final shriek, the horse gallops away, leaving us alone. Moments later, a single bang rings out across the plains, and whether it's the thud of Casper's body hitting the ground or the collision of A Floodonora carriage with a boulder, it means death.

I whirl around, staring wildly about in every direction. And then I see them and realize there's nowhere to run to.

Closing in on us from every direction is the Frost Guard, undefeatable and inescapable.

They've finally done it, I realize, paralyzed. *They've realized their mistake, and now they're surrounding us.*

There are soldiers, uniformed and brandishing gold swords and pistols that are already swinging loosely and unlawfully from their fists. Then there're seven-man guard units, who travel with their captain upon a mighty steed, leading.

Protecting the soldiers are traders hired from 'Nora. While her dealings are mostly legal, there are still some foul exchanges hidden from the public eye. But the Frost Guard turns a blind eye to them in exchange for a thousand extra men. Besides, the Flood Market is a force to reckon with. Friction between the Frost Guard and Floodonora would shake the entire social culture of Evrilore.

Marching grimly before the traders are the last part of Frost's army: Flunters. Take notice of the S. Not Flunter. *Flunters.* Hundreds of them, all with the same shortly cropped spiky hair, thick fur coats, heavy leather boots, and blood-red cloaks. Most possess huge, snarling dogs bounding along beside them, poised to shred us apart on command. And, of course, thick, loaded fluns.

These aren't the men who can't swim, who blunder blindly in bewilderment through the Frost Wilderness in teams of three or four men. These are trained, professional Flunters.

I'm too paralyzed to think, terror clawing its way up my throat. The overall effect of the entire assembled Frost Guard is of a well-oiled machine put together with spare parts from the most powerful contraptions of all time. A range of weapons and talents, of great minds and wicked ones. Some men on foot, others ordering their horses onward. Captains conduct their troops as though each one is a vast orchestra, slotting cogs into place with other units to move forward as one entity towards their prey.

Sparrow calmly passes me a pistol and the throwing stars, withdrawing an enormous black gun from his cloak. "I've been waiting for an excuse to use this one. Spok's finest," he grins, and there is something in the confidence of his voice that makes everything slightly less terrifying. He takes both of my hands in his. "Listen. They don't know us. In reality, we're nothing compared to the Guard. But they think we are. We're the kids that blew up the most powerful fortress known to man, right? So if they want "Raven and Sparrow, the deadly criminals", let's give it to 'em. You and me, yeah?"

I swallow my fear, resist my instinct to run blindly into the arms of a hunter, and stand my ground at his side. The odds are a thousand to one, but what else is there to do? I've no other option.

So I suppose it is okay to fight back sometimes when they leave you without a choice. It is okay to be the monster they have labelled me as. Because I'm not going to die today. I've one life left to protect— and it's not my own.

I step forward abruptly, my eyes flaring a bright emerald green to match the fire in my palms. It comes without command, and Sixth Sense's voice is in perfect unison with my thoughts, merging two consciousnesses into one stable, determined mind.

Spok's training. Eight years of terror and oppression. I inhale it. Exhale it. I let all of that trauma and guilt and hatred leave my body. None of that matters now.

It's firewood.

The army halt about two hundred meters away, forming a dividing ring of untouched grass between us and them. The no-man's-land.

One of the soldiers opposite me glances at the man beside him, who shakes his head. A captain and a flunter step simultaneously forward and glare at one another. Eventually, the flunter falls back in line.

The captain calls across to us, his voice tinged with human pride. Frost pride.

I shake my head bitterly. Where do men acquire the audacity to believe they're entitled to anything simply because they're humans?

"Raven Asgard," he sneers, "One hundred thousand shackles... to think how much you're worth! And you gained quite the publicity in Frost..." His eyes flash with excitement. "I imagine your death will only maximize your... fame." He chooses his last word carefully as it rings out across the grass.

Then—

"*WHAT?*" Sparrow yells from beside me.

The captain freezes, glances about him self-consciously,

and clears his throat before continuing, drawing himself up to his full height (an intimidating five foot two). "I-I SAID RAVEN HAS GAINED QUITE THE PUBLICITY IN FROST!" the captain bellows back, his voice barely audible.

Pause.

"WHAT?" Sparrow repeats.

The captain blinks, then clears his throat. "YOU HAVE GAINED PUBLICITY! WE ARE HERE TO KILL YOU."

It seems the whole Frost guard is holding its breath as we wait for the drama to escalate. Every pair of eyes is fixed on Sparrow, weapons at the ready as they await our reaction and retaliation.

Sparrow glances at me. I only shrug.

"DIDN'T CATCH THAT," he hollers, shrugging apologetically.

Everyone freezes, unsure what to do.

My eyes move over to the lump on the horizon that is Casper, but neither Sparrow nor I dash for escape. Nobody's attacked us yet, after all.

A short, nervous-looking trader steps forward, his face gentle. "Listen, we don't want to hurt yeh. Yeh just kids, and we want yeh to be safe. Yeh ain't safe out here by yourself, are ye? And yeh aren't safe for other people. Even Flai have an awkward growing-up phase. Yeh must be feeling very confused and scared. But we can help. We can take all this confusion and danger out of yeh system for good. How about that? And I'll tell yeh what, eh, if you come quietly, we can make sure ye get to live the rest of yeh days as a normal kid. We don' have to kill you, do we? C'mon. Yeh've caused us all enough trouble. Don' cause it for yourselves, too."

Another man yanks him backwards. "Don't even try. She may look like a little girl, but they aren't like us, Drake. Not until they're purified. She's more manipulative than you think. Don't you know that Flai have mind control powers?"

I arch a brow, folding my arms with mild intrigue at this new knowledge, and he loads his rifle with suspicious eyes screwed onto me.

The captain speaks again, and I make a mental note of Perseus' absence. Looks like I truly ended my enmity after all.

"Alright, gentlemen. You know what to do. The elites will be here in a few hours to pick up the parcels, and they won't be happy unless the girl is in tip-top shape. You can leave the boy, but cut out his tongue so he can't sell us out to whatever gang of traitors he's from. Don't want some treason-committers crashing the execution."

Execution!? I look at Sparrow, alarmed.

"I like my tongue," he whispers weakly.

"So do I, so let's come up with something sharpish."

"Can you use your magic?"

"I can try, but that could end very badly for everyone."

He stares at me. "Would you rather die at the hands of some overpaid git employed to kill you?"

I cock my head to one side. "Good point."

"Get the boy first. He'll be the weakest," the captain instructs, aiming his gun at my feet. "If she tries anything, shoot her ankles."

Three men break loose from the crowd, wolves creeping behind them like silent, stealthy shadows, and I know the little time we've had to formulate a plan is up.

We back into each other until Sparrow and I are pressed tightly together. My hands are burning up, but not enough. That's the trouble with magic. When I don't need it, it's there, and when it's not there, I need it.

"You! No sudden movements!" A guard barks at me as I writhe my hands together.

No sudden movements!? You're the ones trying to kill us!

The three men pounce on Sparrow, seizing him, and two more I didn't see before grab me from behind. I cry out, wriggling, but their grip is almost inhumanely strong.

"Hold his mouth open," a flunter instructs, withdrawing a small, sharp blade from the depths of his huge fur coat.

Sparrow kicks at the man's shins, turning his head as much as he can to look at me. "Raven! NOW!"

One of the men grabs his jaw and twists his head back around sharply, snatching his mask with one hand and tossing it to the floor. The other Flunter lowers his blade, and Sparrow cries out in distress. "RA-EN!" he says again, unable to speak properly.

That's the last straw. How dare they? How dare they hurt him? *My* friend? I bite my lip with fury and dig my elbows sharply into the man behind me. The other still clings to my arm, so I kick his legs out from under him. Then I turn to the flunter with the knife and raise a throwing star.

He notices me and freezes as I hurl the star, jumping aside a second before he would have been slashed open. The star opens a cut along his cheek, though, causing him to release Sparrow in an attempt to stop the blood gushing from his face.

More Flunters advance on us, each preparing to shoot, their guns loaded. I take a deep breath, crouch low, and dig my fingers into the earth. *Spok is gone. Peter's gone. And now they're trying to take Sparrow away from me, too...*

Fuelled by anger, flames slide stealthily off my fingertips and spread across the grass. At first, none of the men notice, and Sparrow has to yank me a few meters left by the collar to avoid a spray of bullets.

Then, the flames grow higher than the grass, and the men's faces are overcome by sheer panic. Fire rips out across the field in an emerald river of heat, sizing up to greet anyone who attempts to cross into our little island of untouched land in the centre and preventing them from getting close.

I carefully weave my way over to Sparrow, watching the fire slowly flush the guards out. Most flee in terror, and some try to fight. They fall to their knees one by one, and suddenly, I notice Sparrow gaping at me and lose my concentration. "Why have you never done this before?" he whispers.

"I didn't know I could," I admit. "Not before Spok taught me."

"Well, it's pretty awesome. Whatever brought it on, I'm glad it did. We should probably clear off, though," he adds, "Can you fly us out of here?"

I stare at him. "I can't fly yet. I'm a fledgling. You know that, right?" I ask. He says nothing. "*Right*?" I repeat.

"Raven, we're surrounded by fire," Sparrow says.

"I can see that."

"So how do you plan on escaping!?" he cries.

"Well, it won't harm *me*!"

"Oh, well, that makes it a whole lot better! We might as well have a tea party! Let's just forget the part where I'm human."

"I'm SORRY! I'm kind of making it up as I go along!" I yell, running my fingers through my scalp.

"Well, can you make it up a little *faster*? I don't wanna get toasted!"

I'm suddenly aware of how the flames around us are no longer keeping the Flunters out but keeping us in. I flick my wrist to keep them at bay, but it does little. The fire has grown out of my control, and little by little, the heat is closing in.

Sparrow backs away, a bead of perspiration trickling down his forehead. Our biggest obstacle now is perhaps not the fire but the smoke rising from it. I drop to my knees, coughing.

"Raven—" Sparrow begins.

"I-I don't know why this is happening! It shouldn't be able to hurt me. It's my fire," I gasp.

It's my fire. I can control it... It's my fire...

Except it's *not*.

My fire doesn't harm me. My fire is under my control. My fire doesn't produce putrid black smoke. My fire isn't tinged with blazing reds and violent oranges.

The shock hits me like an icy slap, stealing the words from my mouth and the air from my stomach. My eyes have gone wild, searching, searching... There, on the other side of the wall, I make out a faint silhouette, smudged at the edges but absolutely, certainly there.

I know my eyes do not deceive me, for everything is beginning to make sense now, all of it linking perfectly together in a complex web. She could be a dead tree ablaze, the way she stands so perfectly rigid, except I know she's not. And I know it's not a guard, either.

Because a human would writhe and shriek in agony. A human would run for its life. And a Flai would move its limbs, open its mouth, and show dominance over its powers.

And so now she stands on the border of both worlds. Not quite Flai, not quite Man. Now, she is one of the in-betweeners, one of the prisoners of the berg whose souls are so torn between wings and impure blood that it drives them to madness.

My stomach lurches. Now she's like... like Sparrow.

Sparrow...

SPARROW! I wheel back to him, shouting at the top of my lungs over the roar of the fire. "Bronwyn!" I cry.

"W-What?" he sputters.

"Bronwyn! She's here! She's doing this! She's started her own fire all around us, and whatever she's using to fuel it isn't just wood. This smoke is poisonous, and this fire is *real*."

He meets my eyes for one terrifying second. "Raven, you're going to have to fly."

And then his body is lost in smoke, clouding my vision, and I begin to retch as it makes its way into my stomach. I desperately try to change into my Flai form, but I can't. I'm retching too violently to do anything. Sparrow grasps my hand, and I take it, covering my mouth with my sleeve.

It's not enough. My body inhales gasps of poison faster than it rids itself of it. The edges of my eyesight crumble in both eyes, darkness burning away the streaks of fire all around us until there is only smoke and darkness. Darkness and smoke.

Sparrow falls first. He lets go of my wrist and slumps to the floor. Suddenly, fear strikes the deepest part of my heart, and my head spirals into a dizzy frenzy. Now Sparrow is gone, and I am back in that dark place in the Frost Wilderness a year ago, with wet, shining blades of grass tickling my ankles as the wind dries my tears.

I'm alone. The word echoes through my head. Alone, alone, alone. Sparrow has died, Sparrow has left me, and now I'm going to die alone, as I always feared.

As the wall of smoke descends ever lower, I let my palm fall away from my face and onto solid earth, overcome by drowsiness and burning lungs, my organs crumbling to ash.

Except my palm doesn't hit the earth. Because the dirt melts away instantly below my oddly tingling fingers, falling in on itself under Sparrow and me until there is simply nothing left. The ground caves in, and we fall through it, my fire exploding out in all directions to slash a blazing network of passages into the earth.

CHAPTER 28

I sputter and cough up a mouthful of dirt, rolling over onto my back.

Black surrounds me. Am I dreaming?

No— every part of me hurts.

Dead?

Again, this seems foolish, but the only way to get answers is to explore and discover. And so, willing myself to take another breath, the first thing I do is light a fire in my cupped palms to illuminate my surroundings.

Above me is a ceiling of earth, and below my body is cold, compacted soil. I guess I've been lying here for a while.

Very carefully, I rise to a kneeling position, testing each part of my body for injury. My lower legs appear to have suffered minor burns, but they only sting a little. It's my head that worries me. A thick, deep gash sits upon my hairline, leaking blood, and if I prod very gently, I can feel that my hair is matted with it.

The rest of me aches terribly, but there's nothing more than bruising, so I set about crawling through wherever I am. A tunnel, probably. Whether I opened up an entrance to a pre-existing passage or created my own, I'm unsure, but I know Sparrow is down here somewhere, and I have to get to him. Calling out his name is certainly a gamble. What if soldiers were also caught in my accidental trap?

What if there are animals down here? Zeun?

What if, what if, what if...

Water, a voice whispers. My throat is parched, my body is weak. *Water*, Sixth Sense says again, *We need water.*

Maybe a little stream once ran through the ground and eroded soil until it formed a tunnel. But nothing looks wet. Perhaps I'm miles away from a true source of water.

Get out.

"How?" I breathe.

You fell. So if you came down, the only way out is-

"Up! Of course!" I gasp, sitting bolt upright.

I toss my fire to one side, where it blazes weakly, before reaching up and clawing away at the compacted earth above my head. It is not the soft, crumbly earth you find in a rich trader's vegetable patch nor the nutritious grounds in the north of Ra.

This is clumpy, and areas of it contain small stones that attack my wrist like razors. Perhaps it was a particularly large rock that hurt my head during the fall that landed me here.

I can't think about that now.

Calm down. What do you know?

What do I know? My fuzzy thoughts can't even string together to form one long, continuous train. My name is Raven Asgard, except maybe it isn't. I'm friends with a human boy named Sparrow, except he's not fully human. All the facts swirl together, and I realize I just don't know anything.

I carefully unpick every scenario I can conjure up in my mind, analyzing the flaws and weighing up the risks.

But it's hopeless: there's a strange sensation of dullness in my brain, as though I've reached the end of a path, and there's simply no road left to leap onto. It's an emptiness, a kind of stupidity, and it gives me a headache if I try to concentrate.

I'm trapped somewhere... somewhere between Frost and Ra. Frost and Ra... somewhere... *Focus.*

The Willow District is the centre of trade. The farming kingdom. Its lands are rich and fertilized, perfect for crops. If this is the kind of earth I have to dig through, for possibly kilometres upward, then how far away am I from the battlefield we just left?

I remove another layer of soil, the gritty stuff getting under my fingernails, and observe the uncovered earth. It's thin, bone-dry powder. And it spikes panic in my chest.

Stopping to rest only when it's absolutely necessary, I dig with haste. My arms soon begin to ache from reaching up, but I persist.

Soon, the ceiling is too high, so I dig out hollows in the wall of the passage and use them as footholds. The roots of vegetation are beginning to appear, and hope rises in my chest.

As the minutes (or maybe hours, as without the sun's guidance, I lose all sense of time) pass, it's harder to climb up repeatedly into the dug-out ceiling and more challenging to think clearly.

Not to mention the significant lack of oxygen, which seems to be becoming more of a problem all the time. As the roots go up, the soil becomes more crumbly, raining down over my head in worryingly large chunks. Several times, my fire is smothered, and I'm left in terrifying, empty darkness.

"Come on, Raven. You can do this," I whisper to myself. "Just dig."

Dig like you're not going to die.

As if reading my thoughts, a huge chunk of earth shudders and breaks off from the ceiling, crashing down.

Then more.

Then more.

CHAPTER 28

A chain reaction.

I shield my head, but my body is the least of my problems. When the hail ceases, the tunnel is blocked up all around my feet, trapping me in this tiny space with very little air. The tunnel below is completely inaccessible.

Suffocation claws at my throat, but I can't stop. Not now. I have to dig my way out of this...

Four or five minutes later, I'm choking, gasping, dying. As I fight back invasive darkness in my vision, my limbs grow weak, and my brain turns to mush.

As I fork handful after handful of dirt away, I find myself drawing in bigger breaths, but there's still not enough air.

Up, up... *There's more oxygen up*... And, indeed, I'm so close to breaking into fresh air.

The roots are thick and long, even damp. If I can just get out of this bloody tunnel...

And suddenly, I don't care what happens next. All I want is to live, and I'm beyond rational thought, and I'm so desperate it's destroying me. There's only one name left, one person I automatically cry for.

"Sparrow! Sparrow!" I scream. "Sparrow! SPARROW! HELP!"

My muscles are screaming with the effort of holding myself up by clumsily dug, crumbling footholds. I let one of my hands go free and seize a thick, sturdy root as though it's an artery, the ceiling bleeding the colour of Sparrow's eyes as soil hails on me.

The last memory I have is of the world fading away as a pair of warm, steady hands break through the dirt and pull me out of the dark, just as they have so many times before.

CHAPTER 29

The long grass tickles my thighs, and the cool night air rushes across my exposed back. I can feel the cool night air running its hands along my feathers even now when they're folded back under my flesh. The wind is fierce, but there's nowhere to shelter. Sparrow has nothing of use in his weapon sack, which he's miraculously managed to keep throughout the ordeal.

We're in the middle of nowhere, near the heavily guarded border. All alone and as good as dead.

I have no idea what to say. No idea what to do. No energy left. Spok is gone, and our time at Boots and Shackles is up. We're back out in the open, exposed and vulnerable. Where the wild things are.

I start a small fire, but its emerald flames will never be as effective as real ones, bright and streaked with orange and red like rejected paper streamers lying abandoned on the street after a celebration. Mine bring momentary warmth, momentary relief, and then sigh out of existence to crawl back into my flesh. Flai magic can't last without its caster or their strength. And right now, the flames mimic my weakness.

A snowflake flutters down onto my arm, and I curse under my breath. The air is heavy with the threat of rain, and a weak flurry has already begun. It's going to be an uncomfortable and miserable night.

"So... what now?" I ask, hugging myself to battle the cold.

Sparrow looks up at me. "We cross the border and... and go home, I suppose."

"What about rescuing—"

"No. Don't even say her name. She's gone now," he interrupts, teeth gritted.

"But, Sparrow, she's your Mo—" I have to stop myself. "She's our friend. We should at least try," I say in a small voice.

"And who takes the next blow? There's only two of us, and there used to be five. Every time we try something stupid, someone goes. So what happens when one of us is next? What happens when *we* go? We need each other, Rave. We'd be killed by ourselves."

"That's not going to happen."

"And how can you know? How do you *know*, Raven? How do you know it won't be you that's next? I thought you were dead. I thought I hadn't made it in time to save you. I crawled through a tiny tunnel in the ground that you created and trapped me in, found my way out less than a minute later, and then sat there for hours, all alone, waiting for you. And then you crawled out of that hole, limp, still, and good as gone. I don't want to go through that again! I can't lose another friend!" he shouts, his voice breaking. His face seems to be crumbling and cracking under his charred mask, and there's visible pain behind his eyes. "I know what you and Spok said— that we weren't a family. But that was the damn closest I've ever gotten, okay? And it fell apart overnight. *One night.* With the rise of a tide, we both lost what could've been really special."

"Friends protect each other. As we will," I say, trying to sound confident.

"Friends aren't always enough."

"Then we won't be friends at all! We'll just be... us," I

finally manage. I'm pleading now, almost begging him. "Raven and Sparrow, yeah? You and me. A team, whether we like it or not, like we were back in the Frost Wilderness. Rely on each other and trust each other just because we simply have to in order to survive. No attachments. We don't have to be friends. We can go back to the beginning. Please, Sparrow. We've got to keep fighting, even if there is a chance of losing each other. We've got to fight for Spok."

"Then what about... us?" he gets out, "What about whatever it is that's between us? I've never had a friend before, never had anyone like you before. I don't want to throw it away now. You can't always just resurface, Raven. Sometimes you're already in too deep."

"You know I hate metaphors," I groan. "But for the sake of continuity, I'd rather not be friends than drown at your side."

"Well, say what you want, but we're not just "partners", and we never will be again," Sparrow snaps. "Friends don't throw away friendships because they're scared. Which is what this is— you're just *scared,* Raven. Friends don't *leave.*"

"What, like how I left Peter?" I cut in sharply.

"That was different."

"Was it? Really?" I demand, "Why wouldn't I do the same to you? Why do you want to be friends so badly after seeing what kind of a person I truly am!?"

"Because I was *there!*" he yells, "I held you back! I saw your face. And— and because I *like* you, okay? Not everyone has to look at you and think, "Oh my gosh, a Flai, EWWW!" You're loyal and brave and funny, and I—" he stops abruptly and slumps onto his back in frustration on the grass, at a loss for words.

The wind sighs in harmony with my exhale, and I lie down beside him, nodding slowly. "Friends, partners, enemies whatever. Just... just take me home, Sparrow," I whisper, curling up on my side to sleep. "Please, just take me home. Whoever that is, wherever it is. I just want to be safe and— and *happy*. And I want that for you too. I'd risk everything to give you that."

"I know. But I'm trying to focus on one happy ending at a time."

"I know you are. And there are a thousand reasons we aren't there yet, me being one of them. I'm just... I'm so sorry," I say shamefully.

"*You're* sorry? Sorry for *what*?"

"Sorry that I set off the bomb. Sorry that I couldn't stop the fire. Sorry that I let them take Spok. Sorry for everything."

"Hey, it's not like I haven't messed up, too."

"Yeah, but I've messed up more. Because I have no idea how to behave around... well..."

"People?" he offers.

"Yeah."

With weak heat on my back and my eyes fixed on the landscape beyond our little camp, I take Sparrow's hand in mine, trying to shut out the world.

Even in my thick cloak, I'm just about freezing. The sky is clouded— no sign of stars to help us tomorrow. It's not fair. None of it. Why do we have to be the bad guys?

I know the answer: because we're different. And different is bad. It has always been that way, not just because of someone's species but because of the smallest details about them. In school, it was the girl with red hair, then the boy with dark skin whose family was from Ra. I just never noticed the bullying because I wasn't taught to.

To think, I could have been born as a merchant's daughter, happily tagging along behind a group of traders as they travelled all over Evrilore.

If I close my eyes, I can even visualize myself behind a stall or getting up when the day is so young that the sun has not yet risen to collect gems and shells.

Around ten o'clock, I would return my findings to my parents and be praised and appreciated for my efforts.

Maybe I would have a friend who did the same, and even though our families would be rivals in trade, we would secretly swap our best findings. I could have a boyfriend or a girlfriend right now.

If I wasn't Flai, there are so many things I could be doing.

And yet, here I am, silently weeping under a sky that is home to a merciless god, weeping for everything I will never have.

It is no good praying. It is no good asking. I just have to be grateful for the people that do appreciate me. The people I *do* have. *All* I have. I take Sparrow's hand, my face slumped into a stubborn, unmoving expression of sorrow. "Is it going to be like this forever?" I ask.

My tone is blank and emotionless, and I can see Sparrow considering his answer, trying to understand exactly what I'm looking for, what I want to hear. Something to equip me with hope? Validate my grief? But I don't want to hear anything but his opinion. I want to know him. Know his heart like I know my own. Know it inside out because... Well, there is no "because". Why does there have to be?

"Maybe. Maybe not," Sparrow says at last, "Forever is a long time. Someone could bump off the Moon King. He might kick the bucket. Laws can change, and rebellions can spark."

"And... and if things do change, what will we do?" I ask hesitantly. "What will we do in a world where it doesn't matter that you're human and I'm Flai?"

"Does it matter now?" Sparrow asks quietly.

The fire crackles through the silence, and I find myself smiling in its emerald glow. "Not to me, Sparrow. Never to me."

And then we roll over and fall asleep with our hands still touching.

CHAPTER 30

Over the next couple of days, all the emotions that were previously stewing in my stomach dissolve into intense concentration. My powers, my Mother, and most importantly, Sparrow. I learn to control my magic for Sparrow, become adequate in the use of every firearm for Sparrow, and march us on in our grim advance towards the Willow District *for* Sparrow. For the next few days, we live like robots, travelling at a sluggish pace in the general direction of the border. Everything I do, I do to make sure my companion survives.

I stop laughing at Sparrow's jokes, stop smiling. My attention turns to only the tasks that need to be done, and when I'm not doing them, I feel distant from everything, as though I'm floating out of my body and my limbs are moving in an unconducted blur. My mind wanders constantly to the horizon, and every night, I lie awake in terror and suspense until darkness bleaches away my vision, sinking into a pit of nightmares.

It's Sparrow or the sunrise that gently awakens me, assuring me not to move with haste, for there isn't a threat in sight— it would seem we've killed most of them, actually. In the morning, I gather small, tasteless berries, earthy-tasting vegetables, and bark, which we clump into meals and force down our throats, chewing in miserable silence. I light fires and catch stars, but my wishes don't work.

They're all the same, anyway: "Bronwyn, come *home.*"

We've not a house, not a brick, but I'd labour at the earth and trees around us if it meant I could save my sister from the grasp of humanity. By ourselves, we could still be a home. She could still forgive me someday.

Sparrow makes weapons and cooks any food worth cooking, watching my back when I climb trees to retrieve eggs from birds' nests. At night, we either take shelter in the thick branches of trees or lie out in the open, gazing dreamily up and exchanging almost no conversation.

Misery envelopes us both. We both digest it rather differently. Sparrow tries to disguise his mounting confusion at what's happened with bad jokes and small talk, neither of which I dignify with a response. On the other hand, I have accepted that the world is the way it is, and people are the way they are, and maybe that I am the way I am. I don't bother unpicking things and mulling them over like Sparrow, whose eyes never leave the saferoom where Bronwyn left us.

No, I'm more accepting. There's no plan and no hope. There are still potentially two armies in our way. Sparrow's unsafe everywhere, even at home, and he may not be able to re-enter the Realm at all. Me, on the other hand? I might be unable to protect him from the threats within those walls. From my own people. From angels. What kind of angels'd kill someone simply for wearing different feathers?

Would I fight my mother and my species just to protect him?

I suppose he did the same for me, but lumping Sparrow in with humans just because that's what he technically is feels wrong somehow.

He's not one of us, and certainly not one of them. Which opens a million doors and obliterates a thousand stereotypes, assumptions, and conclusions.

It shakes my world, and it'd shake Evrilore's, too.

If the world knew Sparrow and I were working together... what'd it even *become?*

On one particular night, as dusk is descending in its thick and heavy glory to smother the hillside, the inky outline of a wolf appears on the brink of the horizon, its silhouette smudged at the edges where fur refuses to stop rippling in the wind.

It doesn't approach me— it doesn't move at all, in fact. After an hour, I question if I'm just going mad, but it seems to be waiting for me, morphing and melting into the darkness like an un-moulded ball of matter awaiting the verdict of its existence, with two glistening black eyes at the centre of it.

Sharp, defiant knives of fur spike up from its head like the mountains on the horizon, and whenever I move, its patient, dark eyes follow me. I don't know how or why, but its presence is comforting. Being preyed on and spied on by a hungry creature is soothing because it's awaiting our deaths with infinite patience— and our deaths are an event that will not arrive in the near future.

The hunger in the wolf's static observation reassures me of the strong, steady life in Sparrow's eyes, burning bright. We're not being passed down from layer to layer of kelp by twisting ribbons of green, lowered into a riverbed coffin. Not in that place where the Iceberg and my best friend once stood.

We're here, and for that, I am grateful.

I turn away from the wolf, shaking my head in sympathy. There's no prey for miles yet, except maybe Casper.

Casper, I think... I hope someone killed him properly. I hope he didn't lie there bleeding.

❋ ❋ ❋

"Hey, Raven! Does this look burned to you?" Sparrow calls from the fire, turning to me with a blackened rabbit leg skewered onto a twig.

I want to laugh, but the task seems impossible. It doesn't help me get to the Flai Realm. It doesn't protect Sparrow, resurrect Peter, help us cross the border, or save Spok. There's a cord knotted tightly around my stomach, restricting me. "It's burned," I state simply.

Sparrow sighs, "That was the joke. It'll still taste good, anyway. Sit down, will you? I was hoping we could talk over dinner."

"About?" I ask stiffly.

He fiddles with the skewer. "You seem off again."

"Again?" I prompt.

"You've zoned out like you did at Boots and Shackles in the pool. And don't pretend you don't know what I'm talking about."

I stare at him as though he's mad. "*That's* what you're focusing on? Excuse me for not laughing at your jokes, but I'm trying to focus on living. You *do* realize that our actions won't go unpunished? Two kids, all alone, with hardly any weapons, breached, robbed, and single-handedly destroyed the most secure fortress in the Moon King's ownership, defeated his army, and managed to get out of it all unscathed. What kind of a King allows that to happen? A king with the world wrapped around his little finger like a ball of string? Because of us, that ball of string is now unravelling rapidly, and he needs a turnaround if he is to win the election. And he must win. My public execution is his vitality now. My chances of getting to peace and safety are almost nonexistent. So, yeah. Sorry for not smiling much. May the flood bring you good fortune, but I'm gonna pack up and leave with Floodonora before the waves swallow me," I finish with a sharp glare and a bite of rabbit.

Sparrow blinks, taking in my rant, and eventually, he shrugs. "The moon King doesn't *have* to kill you, so technically, our lives aren't in danger. All he has to do is convince the League to vote for him. Plus, I don't think the King could've just refused an election. It was always bound to happen as the Sun Queen rose to power."

"Yeah, but we aren't helping him. He's angry, Sparrow."

"He's an old man with an army. A battered army, at that, thanks to you," Sparrow adds.

"Doesn't change the fact that I ruin his image. A protector, a peacekeeper... and now, look what's happened. He can't protect any of them." I frown, licking my fingers clean of grease. "What's the Sun Queen's deal, anyway? She has Ra already."

"Ra has been second best for a long time, but I suppose the Sun Queen is tired of it. The capital of Ra is well-fed, and the buildings are well-constructed. It's a big hit for 'Nora when it's a good Stone Tide. See what I mean? It's all *good*. But nothing's changing. The rest of the country is either poor or unoccupied. They aren't like Frost, all secure and tightly packed into one kingdom, growing steadily through the gradual domination of the population. And because Ra doesn't have the right conditions for growing tradable goods, like Frost has its fish and Willows has its crops, it's not like that's going to change anytime soon. If the Sun Queen rules Frost, she can divert funds and resources to her own country, and the League will be right behind her to help with the governing."

"Still, why now?" I press, "There must be a reason."

Although there's no one to hear us, he lowers his voice. "The Moon King and the Sun Queen had an argument, I reckon. A big one."

"Why would they argue?" I whisper back.

"Ra and Frost have been enemies for a while now. The day Evrilore was landlocked, they turned on each other, and after that, it wasn't long before Frost tried to overthrow Ra because they were so weakened by the Mindlocust virus."

"Wait... you know about that? About the Fall and the disease and stuff?"

"Of course I do. In the Flai Kingdom, they straight up tell you the facts, no matter how dark. In human schools, though, they normally wait until the seventh year or something, and even then, they cover most of it up. But of course, you didn't do your seventh... I only mean to say... I mean, you..." He coughs loudly. "Forget it. How do *you* know about it?"

"Spok told me. It doesn't matter. What were you saying? About... an argument?" I reply, waving him away. I don't want to even think about that Innkeeper. About what Sparrow might've heard, about what he might know that I've no right to tell him...

"Yeah. Back then, it would just have been too easy for Frost with the disease and the Far Lands no longer aiding with resources. Something happened, something they never filed or documented, and something that everyone conveniently forgot. A part of history is missing. They call it the blackout years in the Realm, a decade when the timeline just... stopped. They destroyed everything. Records, documents, diaries. There's something about the Fall they don't want us to know. And now, some old grudge has returned to haunt them, and the Sun Queen wants revenge," he says grimly.

I shrug. "'S all guesswork. They used the disease, Spok reckons. Made everyone forget about it... I still don't understand how it could be that simple, though. An election that will change the lives of more than a million people just so that Ra can get even with Frost? There's got to be more to it. Raes aren't vengeful people, anyway. Convincing them to abandon centuries-old traditions of peacekeeping..."

"If there *is* more to it, we'll likely never hear about it," Sparrow says firmly, licking his fingers clean.

I return to staring, glassy-eyed, into the distance. The wolf is still there. "Do you see it?" I ask slowly, allowing the previous conversation to slip away like water through cupped hands.

"See... what?"

I nod directly ahead, and he follows my gaze to the figure prowling atop the hill.

His hands reach down to his feet, to the weapon sack, and I stop them with my own.

"He won't hurt us," I say sharply. "Just... oh, just *look!* Isn't he beautiful?" I whisper.

"He's a *wolf!* Keep away from him, or he'll try and take a bite out of—"

"*Sparrow*! It's harmlesss!"

"It wants to eat you!" he protests.

"It's. Fine."

Sparrow can't take his eyes off it, all tensed up. "We haven't eaten properly in *weeks*. You need yur strength for the border. You need your energy for... everything. You're already exhausted all the time, and, excuse me for saying so, I don't blame that totally on our diets."

I turn away. "Sparrow, you need to stop trying to make me happy. I know I'm not myself. I don't feel like myself. But I lost my best friend, and I let them take Spok, and I... I want us to be... I want you to be safe! If I can do anything at all, it's that. Sometimes, you just need to let people be messed up."

"And for how long!? We can't do this forever!" he exclaims.

"You think I don't know that!?"

He stands up and tosses his skewer aside. "What I *think* is that you're so focused on keeping me alive because you're scared of every other thought in the back of your head! If you die protecting me, it won't repay anything. It won't change what happened! Just because things are bad doesn't mean your delusions of a noble sacrifice are completely called for! I've still got nowhere to go, and Peter's still dead, and Bronwyn's still busy being a traumatized thirteen-year-old, and Spok's—"

"*Noble sacrifice?*" I finally blurt, cutting him off.

"*Please*, suggest a different choice of words!" he snaps.

"How about being willing to protect you no matter what because I care? That fit the bill?" I fire heatedly back.

"If you care about me, why'd you almost drown yourself?"

"That wasn't on purpose!"

He throws his head back in fake, nasty laughter. It doesn't suit him at all. "You ran back to what you knew: isolation, darkness, and fear."

"I have as much to run back to as you do, and you know that," I retort, stung.

"Yeah, but we have nothing to run towards, either."

"My Mother—"

"Is just like everyone," he interrupts.

"You mean the rest of humans—?"

He grips me by the shoulders. "*Everyone*, Raven." He stares at me, locking his eyes into mine, and waits. And then releases me, looking utterly agonized. "But you still can't grasp the concept," he whispers softly.

"HUMANS AND FLAI! That's what we are!" I scream, but my words betray me, and I'm stumbling, fumbling, scrambling over them.

Sparrow inhales tightly. "Right."

I feel my face soften. "Sparrow..."

He turns away from me, seemingly close to either terrifying fury or hot, overdue tears. "Don't do this. Don't... don't say things like that. I really thought you were dfferent, Rave. I really *hoped* you were..." he trails off, his voice crumbling into pain.

I stare at my feet.

"Look, I... Regardless of- of everything." He throws an arm dramatically to one side. "Forget what we just said. The point I was trying to make is that it's like you're here, but you're not," he whispers, "Stupid people do stupid things, Raven. And you aren't a stupid person. But sometimes... sometimes even intelligent people do stupid things, and you can't save them until it's too late. I don't want you going down that path, Rave. Promise me you won't."

"I—"

"Promise!"

Eventually, I nod. "I promise."

He exhales. "Good. You've had me really worried recently. You're hardly sleeping, hardly talking... but I do understand why you're like this," he adds. "And you have every right to be after losing someone so close to you. I should've been a better friend. That's the simplicity of it."

As I open my mouth to protest, his eyes suddenly widen. "Wait! That's it!"

"What? What is it?" I press.

"Simplicity. What if that's been the answer to everything this whole time? We've been overestimating our enemy and underestimating ourselves. We just took out an army, for God's sake! So maybe that's just it... instead of trying to get around Frost, we just have to go right under their noses... but it will be dangerous... and it all depends on... so it'll have to be..."

"Yes, yes, what is it!? Go on!"

He screws up his face, his mind whirring. "Floodonora are definitely ahead of us by now. We spent a fortnight at Boots and Shackles, and it's been just under a week since then, not to mention we spent a night at the cave, a night in the blizzard, and a night at the Berg. Floodonora has passed us for sure. I bet they're arriving in the Willow District as we speak. And you know them. "May the Flood bring you Good Fortune"!? I mean, c'mon! There's always one that lags behind, one that's too greedy. Their stall is caught in Flood Tide, and their trade is completely ruined. Happens every year without fail. They'll also be lagging well behind the rest of the Flood market. Well, that trader —whoever they may be — is our ticket right into the Willow District."

My eyes widen. "What are you saying? We pay them to smuggle us? But we have no money, or...."

I trail off at his expression, and he laughs. "You aren't the sharpest tool in the shed, Raven, are you? What I'm saying is that we'll sneak into their cart. It's brilliant. They won't bother checking the Trader because they'll be well known and have been in Floodonora for years. The traders are good mates with Willow and Frost guards. Well respected. That respect is shown through trust in a lot of situations. Situations like wagon searches. Even with Flai on the loose, they'd still do a semi-thorough search, but if we hide well enough, they won't find us. It's just common courtesy not to open all the crates and things. It's like the unspoken rules of the traders. Did you hear the story about that fight way back in 2051? I was... what? Twelve, then. A guard tried to search a trader like any other citizen and pat him down, and the trader got so annoyed that he *hit* him. There was a big news coverage on it."

Just as I'm processing this information and mentally listing absolutely everything that will inevitably go wrong with his plan, the sound of wheels grinding against the ground and horses neighing in distress rings out like a wind chime through the trees.

Sparrow's smile only widens, and I know exactly why. "Ah, here we go. Speak of the devil."

I arch a brow at him. "That could be literally anyone. Y'know, I *hope* it's anyone. I hope it's a random traveller, and this is really humiliating because you just tried ridiculously hard to look all intellectual."

Sparrow stiffens. "I *am* intellectual."

"Just watch it be a random traveller," I scorn, shaking my head.

"*You're* here," he points out, "A fugitive who blew up and infiltrated a fortress is on the run. 'Snot someone on holiday."

"My *presence* is a holiday."

"Hm," he says.

❈ ❈ ❈

"Go! Go! Go!"

I hurry to the cart, breathless from the past ten minutes of chasing the vehicle across the grass and, being careful to make as little noise as possible, clumsily clamber up into the wagon's back.

The trader must have driven along the plains about twenty miles behind Floodonora, going very slow to avoid damaging the cart, but now it seems she's stopped, allowing us to sneak in.

I crawl forward, inspecting my surroundings. Just as

Sparrow predicted, her cart must have been caught in Flood Tide because all the items in the back are wet and squashed. From what I can see, I guess that she specialized in trading groceries —a member of the outer circle of traders, the kind who don't deal in rocks or gems but prey on 'Nora's customers instead— and so there's bound to be a crate or a box of fruits we can curl up in.

"Apples, oranges... bleugh. It's all mushy and disgusting," I say, making a face.

"It's not as bad over here. Right in the corner, it's dry. The poor girl must have been trying to drag her cart out of the sea but didn't get there in time," Sparrow says sympathetically.

"Well, that's what she gets for being greedy. Hey, there's a bunch of polystyrene in boxes over here. In the crate that says "Fragile contents"."

"What do you reckon? Can we make a bed in there?" he asks, peering at where I kneel.

"Sure, but we'll have to remove what's in there to make room."

"We'd better hurry. She's bound to be on her way back by now."

"Okay. Give me a hand. I think these are vases. Heavy vases," I wheeze, heaving one out of the polystyrene. "Where should I chuck it?"

"Dunno. Burn it?" he suggests.

"Alright," I reply, and the vase crumbles to a thick pile of ash between my hands. "Now what?"

"Cover the ashes in fruit. But don't burn all of them."

I stare at him. "Why not?"

"Bit suspicious, every single vase disappearing."

"Blame the Tide," I shrug.

"But they're..." he stares rather sadly at the vases. "Okay.

Burn them."

I blink at him, legitimately impressed by his care for something so inanimate. "You're so Sparrow it hurts."

"Did you just use me as an adjective?" he asks, offended.

"I didn't take my sixth year. Shut up and help me cover these ashes."

Just as the remnants of the china have been covered by squashed grapes, footsteps fill my ears.

"She's coming! Get in the box!" I hiss, turning to Sparrow, "Quickly!"

"Oh, it *stinks* in here," he complains.

"It'll get worse now you're in it," I grin before sliding in next to him and pulling the cardboard flaps down just in time to hear the trader return to her seat.

The box's interior is a claustrophobic rectangular space, but cool air slips in between the wood, and if we nestle down on our sides, we can both fit.

There are tiny gaps between the planks of wood that allow me to see outside, and judging by the pace at which the cart is travelling, with the wheels groaning like wounded animals, I guess we'll be here all night. "You do know that if it rains, we're screwed?" Sparrow whispers to me.

"Oh, we can handle a bit of water."

"I'm talking more about the fact that if it rains, the crates will flood, and we'll have to get out. When we do, the trader will see us."

"Let's just hope it doesn't rain, then," I mutter.

"Since when has hoping done a whole lot for us?" he chuckles. Then— "Ow. You're squashing my hand."

"Sincerest apologies."

He pauses. "That was insincere, wasn't it?"

The typical flat landscape of the plains between Frost and Willows stretches on for miles in every direction, with occasional hills or valleys and patches of trees dotted around. It's a fairly warm day, perfect for travelling, so we move quickly, and it's not long before grassy hills fade into merry, continuous woodland. Plants of every kind thrive in lush, green glory, and the chirps of birds harmonize into one beautiful song.

Due to continuous panic and paranoia, I've never truly appreciated the lands still unclaimed by humans on Evrilore. I'm lucky the King hasn't invaded paradises like these yet with ever-growing, ugly cities.

As morning rolls into a breezy afternoon, the sun turns gold and sinks lazily toward the horizon. I settle down with my knees up to my chest and try to make myself comfortable. Sparrow, too, lies down in the polystyrene and shuts his eyes. Apart from the occasional jolt of the cart, the rest of the ride is smooth and carries me off into a soft, hazy world of dreams.

CHAPTER 31

My eyes snap open because of the viciously cold air crawling up my flesh and raising the hairs on my arms like men from the dead out of their graves. Having grown used to curling up beside fires at night, the bite of the night's chill feels suddenly far harsher than I remember.

I sit up in the crate and push the flap open just enough to peer through. My limbs become stiff with fear as I realize I'm staring directly at someone's chest. The hot breath from their mouth steams up, but I can't see their face. They're saying something in Sun Tongue, in a deep voice, which I assume to be male. "*Fier do'suk,* brother. *Fierrace?*"

Another voice responds, nearer to me, and I guess from the tone that it's the trader who owns this cart. "*La'ra fierra?*" The trader sounds considerably upset and almost offended, but there's a light-hearted humour behind her words. "I should have known better than to pack up at two," she says in rough English.

The man chuckles. "*Fier. Maximo riefrakinranohce ra adneibo.*"

I adjust my position to glimpse his attire. A belt is looped around his waist, and on it is a long plastic stick with a flashing green light. I've heard about these. Flai detectors.

"*Reifdahadnoece quence'ra haja!?* Look at my trade!" The woman replies angrily.

The man only continues to laugh and moves around to

the back of the cart. I can hear him shifting through bags and crates, occasionally raising the stick and waving it about before sliding it back into his belt.

I squeeze my eyes tightly shut, holding my breath.

Pleasedon'tfindusdon'tfindusdon'tfindus. I know exactly where we are: the border.

Sparrow said they wouldn't search Floodonora carriages as much as regular ones, but what if he was wrong?

The guard continues sifting through things, reaching for the larger items at the back, and as I watch the trader's face, she grows visibly impatient and thoroughly offended. To calm the situation, the guard exchanges casual conversations with her, discussing Flai, the Berg, and other things I can't understand due to the complexity of the sentences.

Finally, one of his large, meaty hands lands on the roof of our crate. I hold my breath as he hooks his fingers around the edge and begins to open it, sliding the detector out of his belt.

"What's that stupid stick for? *Riefrakinrace wellvar?*" The trader's voice again, and amused this time.

Don't you have a gun? I translate.

There's a pause in which the man draws away from the carriage, and I exhale sharply, relief flooding my body.

"*La riefrakinra wellvar?*" he repeats back to her, mocking. "*Dah la reifrakinranoh raspece?*"

Why do I need one?

Then, in a slightly poor accent, he adds, "You have something to hide, huh?"

"*Rief quence'ra guard? Peo quence'wellvar?*" the trader teases.

You're a guard, no? Where's your gun?

"*Fier, la rakinra wellvar. Ad... wanato la'ra e quence'ra!*"

Yes, I have a gun, and... a pause. *I'll... kill you!* It only occurs to me now that the man's voice is slightly slurred, and a silver flask is fastened to his hip. Which explains a lot.

More laughter, several sounds of people mocking the firing of guns, then—

"Astaar! Back to work! Stop babbling on to your friends, and, FOR CHRIST'S SAKE, PUT YOUR GUN BACK WHERE IT BELONGS!"

Heavy breathing, the click of something sliding into place.

"Good. Now, did you find anything, or is she clean? And if she is, hurry up and move on."

"No, sir. Yes sir. Sorry, sir," the guard replies hurriedly.

The sound of scuttling feet.

"*Hi'ra efpaldun!*" the trader sniggers.

"Shhh! You will have me in trouble!" the guard hisses back.

"Whatever. Can I go?" she sounds genuinely impatient now, as though demanding, not asking, and I understand what Sparrow means now. The light-hearted banter encouraged by alcohol does not even overrule the underlying expectations of trader-sentry interactions.

The guard straightens up and nods. "*Fier. Poefkince.*"

Okay. You can go.

After a moment, I hear the neigh of a horse, and the carriage begins to move again. I practically collapse with relief. We did it. We're across the border.

CHAPTER 32

I sit sleepily up, stretching. My tangled limbs feel like cardboard, and my face hurts from sleeping on my side. One of my arms is trapped beneath my body, devoid of sensation except a sharp, unpleasant tingling. I shake it back into use and then compose myself, flattening my hair, cracking my stiff knuckles, and yawning loudly.

Almost instantly, Sparrow's hissing in my ear. "Raven, get up! We have to go!"

"Alright, *Alright*!" I grumble, "Are we in Willows?"

"I think so."

"You think so?"

"Just get out," he mutters.

I mutter something under my breath and push the lid of the cardboard box up, freezing for a moment as I survey my surroundings, checking for humans. "Looks clear. C'mon," I say, crawling tentatively out onto the cart's back. He follows suit, and we hop off simultaneously, sneaking glances over our shoulders to check we've left no obvious signs of our presence.

Polystyrene is littered all over the cart's contents and dotted on our clothes, but there are other explanations for how it could've gotten there.

I turn my attention to where we are. The carriage is parked in a small side street between two picturesque, ivy-throttled cottages. We cautiously follow the alleyway out into the main road and halt suddenly in our tracks.

"Sparrow," I whisper, "I've got a feeling we aren't in Boots and Shackles anymore."

"Okay, Dorothy. Go off," Sparrow says.

I ignore him, lost in wonder.

We're in the very heart of the Willow District, where the streets are jam-packed with villagers hurrying in a bustle to attend to their business. People rush in every direction, crisscrossing and apologizing profusely for collision after collision.

I urge Sparrow to stay close to me. In Willows, if you step ever so slightly away from the flow of foot traffic, you're sucked into currents going the opposite way and must fight against the crowd to be released. The streams of villagers sweep things up like a tornado here, spitting them out at random locations.

It fills me with delirious happiness because Willows is just as chaotic as I remember it as a child, and I'm momentarily overcome by brief joy.

The chattering is so enthusiastic that it'd be impossible not to be elated. Excitement and apprehension for the upcoming Stone Tide flits through the air like a disease, bouncing off shoulders and exploding like firecrackers in the air. Floodonora bathes the kingdom in eagerness and anticipation, popping up on street corners and plastering pamphlets to your doors. Everything is made out to be refreshing and new when, in reality, it's the same every year.

The festive brilliance is absolutely infectious.

Sparrow nudges me. "Look. Two fugitives on the loose, a ten thousand shackle bounty on your head, and they're inviting us in," he marvels, pointing.

I follow his finger to see that every door on the street

opposite us is wide open. Children race in and out, yelling and whooping.

Straight ahead, I can only see more houses and shopfronts forming the front wall of the square, with an occasional tiny cafe asphyxiating between buildings.

Stalls are set up in every available space, like islands in an ocean, poking their heads out of the crowd to advertise everything from traditional Willow District treats, like cider and meat pies, to leftovers from Frost and goods collected from 'Nora's travels across the country.

Because Frost's final Stone Tide of the year (a Tide Cycle year lasts from November to August) was around a month ago, Willow's annual Stone Tide is due to arrive in May, two entire months away, but of course, that won't stop Floodonora trading in advance regardless.

The celebration of a Stone Tide is marked by a day off school in the Willow District, and the Flood Market will do absolutely everything in their power to ensure Willowfolk don't miss it. Therefore, advertisements begin almost instantly after Frost's Flood Tide. Though, of course, the market's arrival was delayed by their short stay in the Frost Wilderness, thanks to Sparrow's genius.

I whirl around to take in the bustling roads that lead away from the square into a maze of cottages, my eyes eagerly drinking up familiar childhood sights.

Already, parents dressed in the most atrocious shades of pastel green and yellow drag their children out of sight of stalls to avoid them seeing sweets, yet they're still caught by traders lurking on the outskirts of town.

And, yes, there are the restaurants, being forced to stock up more than usual to feed a population suddenly concentrated in one area of a kingdom. Their owners will be forced to turn to traders for supplies that farmers cannot give, extra staff that just can't be hired as everyone wants to spend the Tide with family...

This is the art of trading: Nobody escapes 'Nora. She extends outwards like a carefully designed web, beginning from a core of traders and growing through tiny, unnoticeable threads and piggybacking salesmen that are sly, tricky, and unnoticeable enough to entangle a kingdom. Ordinary townsfolk don't pay attention to the tiny details, like the "free" charms given away to entice more customers that suddenly cost money or the buy-one-get-one-free offers promoting products twice their usual price.

When the whole thing comes together, it's really quite formidable and magnificent.

Sparrow taps my arm, looking sheepish. "Raven? Can we buy a hot dog? We'll share it, I promise. It's just that I'm so hungry, and they look delicious."

I sigh. Maybe *too* magnificent.

We both jump as a nearby door slams unexpectedly, and a gnarled hand reaches through the window in it to hang a sign on the wood. It reads:

INN FULL!

The hand is replaced by a beady, narrowed eye surrounded by wrinkles and loose skin. "Oi! You kids! No loitering."

I stammer a flushed apology, but Sparrow casts him a dirty look and leads me away with his nose held snootily in the air. We both crack up at that and begin to strut around like posh ladies from Ra, twirling and bowing to one another with enormous imaginary diamonds strewn along our necks.

At one point, a couple of mothers holding infants begin to watch us and chuckle, but thankfully, their babies get restless and begin to wail, so they hurry away. One woman presses a few shackles into my hands as she passes. "I loved the dramatic arts at your age. Funny performance. Get yourself something nice, dear. Share it with your young man. Get him to buy you dinner," she teases.

I thank her profusely and then turn to glare at Sparrow. "Yeah, Sparrow, buy me dinner. C'mon, be a gent."

"Shove off," he mutters, rolling his eyes.

We loiter a little longer, my head swirling with memories as I take in familiar sights, and eventually, we find a modest little stall selling meat and groceries run by a shy, red-headed teenager. She must be new to the Flood Market, awaiting acceptance from the rest of the group. The kind of trader that piggybacks onto the customers of the larger stalls.

We exchange a handful of coins for the cheapest stuff: three potatoes, dried fruit, cooked chicken, a block of cheese, and a few apples— and she insists on pressing a few free lumpy carrots into our hands as well. "No one buys 'em 'cos they look unappetizin', but they taste good 'nough," she explains glumly.

"Oh, but- well, are you sure?" I stammer nervously.

"Of course she is. Thank you very much," Sparrow says quickly, pocketing the goods.

I glare at him as if to say, "We didn't pay for those!". He only shrugs and begins to stroll away.

We sit on the rim of a nearby fountain, absent-mindedly watching a couple of kids as they splash about without a care in the world. My eyes run over their clothes. Fairly new, well-weaved, and soaking wet. The wool drips water miserably onto the cobbles, and the children's hair falls to their shoulders in sundried straw-like clumps. One of the girls has a bag slung over her shoulder, and a small hole scatters glittering pennies into the fountain.

"Look at that," I murmur to Sparrow, gesturing to them, "Their mothers throw money at them, and look at what they do."

"They're just kids," he reasons back.

"So were we."

Sparrow falls silent. I shift my gaze up to the sky, where smoke stumbles higher and higher from countless chimneys' roaring fires.

"Imagine having all of this to grow up to. I mean, they don't even know how much they have. Don't know what's out there. Don't understand who they'll be. They turn into their ignorant parents, who became *their* parents, and every man who ever turned a blind eye births a generation of copies, each one's hatred slightly lesser, slightly weaker than the last. And they're all so happy about it. It must be true, mustn't it? Ignorance is bliss," I say sadly.

Sparrow shrugs. "Dunno. Is it? There's a difference between being uneducated and being ignorant. If I knew my views were poisoned, I'd rather know the truth. I'd be happier with the truth," he argues.

I turn to face him. "Are *you* happier with the truth?"

"I don't know it," he replies honestly. "Nobody does. All I know is that I've figured things out for myself. I know what things mean to me."

You still have a family. A mother who loves you and a father who was a hero. Your real name is Armos. You know nothing about yourself.

I cast my eyes to the floor, shameful. "How can you be sure? Say you had a family... s-say you weren't actually what you thought you were..." I stammer.

"I don't want to talk about Spok. What she said... the last thing she called me... whatever that was, *I don't want to know.* And you're wrong— ignorance isn't bliss. It's just procrastination for something that will eventually bring you the liberation you seek. Would you rather ignore Bronwyn or actually know what was going on inside her head so you could help?"

Just the mention of Wynn's name creates a sick feeling in my stomach. "Enough deep conversation. Let's go," I say, though, in reality, it's more of a beg.

"You just proved my point."

"Let's *go*, please."

We have to be careful to keep our faces shadowed for fear of being recognized, but generally, our spirits are high. The Willowfolk seem much too occupied to care about us, or any criminals, for that matter. I must remind myself several times that the Willow District is not as safe and kind as it seems.

No, I've seen the transformation happen before. When the sun begins to dip below the horizon and the branches of trees shroud the last droplets of its glow. That's when the walls rise up to enfold you, and the side allies become death traps. Sweet and innocent places are almost always infiltrated with wicked people if you're willing to see them.

We walk in the general direction of the Flai Kingdom, and it's obvious we're headed to the correct place because the number of tourists almost doubles, and it's impossible to stay together. I'm forced to yell over people's heads and fumble for Sparrow's hand in a sea of confusion, losing my grip on him several times. I eventually give up and wait for the crowd to stop swirling like disrupted correlations of stars spiralling out of orbit.

There's a heavenly smell nearby, which I impulsively trace back to a bakery teeming with customers, and although

I've no money, it's impossible to resist lingering at the door. My eyes rake over the tarts, sandwiches, shortbread, and pies, and I'm reminded of the money we wasted earlier on cheese.

If only I'd saved it for something less sensible.

"Excuse me? *Excuse* me." A man. Old, angry, and wrinkled up in suspicion. "You look rather alike... doesn't she, Margie?"

He taps his companion: an old, smiling woman with a long, thin smile and badly applied lipstick.

"Margie," he repeats, "Doesn't she look like that Asgard girl?"

Margie laughs. "In a bakery, of all places? Do not be cruel, Archie. What's your name, love?" she beams at me.

"Ra... Ro... Rosanna. My name is Rosanna," I lie.

"Don't take any notice of my partner. He's quite the accusatory sort."

"But... but Margie!" the man persists.

"May the flood bring you good fortune, my dear," Margie addresses me, ignoring her husband dismissively and touching my shoulder as she leaves the bakery.

"Raven? Raven! I've- been- looking- everywhere- for- you," Sparrow wheezes, stumbling inside the bakery.

"What's the blooming hurry?"

"Come see for yourself. We're *here*," he gasps, turning to hobble back out the door. I follow him reluctantly, taking one last glimpse of the mouth-watering treats.

He leads me forward, pressing himself against walls to squeeze through the crowd and issuing several flustered apologies.

Finally, the crowd swells, forcing Sparrow and I shoulder-to-shoulder as people press in on all sides. The current bursts into a giant expanse of people in a wide outdoor space as the street opens up. I stop dead in my tracks.

CHAPTER 32

Ahead is a gargantuan mountain, one that disappears into wide valleys, sparkling rivers, dense forests, and huge, limitless plains of wildflowers, their petals spanning out like wings for meters long, visible even from miles away where we stand. The landscape mimics a snow globe or an overly saturated photo produced by Frost's fake media centres, intensely detailed yet so fake, bright, and unrealistic that it looks utterly believable. No man's hands have stained these lands, and no traces of them have been scattered like Autumn's leaves to remind people who owns them. Even Sparrow, who knows what punishments await him within the kingdom, is delighted to see it, his chest swelling with pride. I shake my head to check I'm not dreaming, and my feet slam back down to earth on solid cobbles, but my eyes are no traitors.

The Flai Realm glows with magic, drawing me in like a thousand fingers to a gaping mouth. This is a sight I've purposefully distanced and torn myself from for fear of being caught by the mob of tourists and traders. My parents always forbade me to see it when I was younger due to their extensive hatred of Flai.

But now, brought here by my own stumbling, fighting, and determination, no one can shield me. No one can pull me away. That kingdom is *mine*, and no hands have even neared it to pull it from under my unsuspecting feet.

"Oh," I whisper.

"Yeah. Oh," Sparrow says, but when I turn to him, the joy and recognition of a wondrous place that is plastered across his face melts into a melancholy longing, as though he wishes that the Realm could belong to him in the same way it does me.

I wish so desperately to tell him that it does, and no one has the right to take that from him, especially not my

Mother, and *definitely* not just because he was unwillingly humanized as an innocent baby. His detachment from his magic doesn't sever what he once was. He's still Flai, even if he can never be in anyone else's eyes.

I touch his arm lightly, and he turns to me, his gaze enquiring.

"You're coming home with me," I say pleadingly.

He nods, but his eyes are empty.

Surrounding it all is a ring of Stone, as tall as a hundred men. It's evident that the land around the kingdom has been purposefully lowered as if to outline the differences between the land of men and the land of Flai. Several complex pathways, stairs, and ramps lead up to a great arch in the wall, which seems to be almost alive in an inexplicable way. Swirls of colour melt together and turn over themselves inside the doorframe, blocking what lies beyond it from clear view. *The shield that covers the Flai Realm*, I think, *the boundary between safety and danger.*

If only we could just walk right through it and into refuge...

But we can't, for what blocks our path is a force greater than magic itself: an army. Two armies. Three.

My mind wanders back to the Berg and the scattered Frost Guard dashing from my fire on the plains between Frost and Willows. How much more can the Moon King possibly hurl in my path? How many lives can he risk, and how many guards can he promote to Captains to compensate for lost lives?

My demise is suddenly almost more important than his protection, and it forces me to confront the extent of my significance to his political safety.

My eyes move over the sentries' guns, and my lungs seem to freeze in fear, twisting in my chest until I forget how to breathe. The Flai guns are huge. Bigger than any I've ever seen before. They look so heavy that I would bet my life they only hold one bullet. One bullet, one shot. One shot, one man. Ten thousand men... And one *me.*

"Sparrow," I croak, grasping for the hem of his cloak at my side. "Sparrow, there are thousands of them... we'll never get past! They even have Archers."

"We'll think of a way to draw them from the border so we can get through," he assures me.

"It's impossible."

"And once, you said the same thing about a human and a Flai being friends," he reminds me. "Trust me. We'll figure it out."

I nod, taking deep breaths to steady myself. We're so close. We've come all this way, after all, and if Sparrow can get *out* of the Flai Kingdom, then he can get *in.*

My shoulders relax slightly. "So, what's the—"

"I haven't got a plan," Sparrow interrupts, "Usually, the guards only block the entrance, not the whole border. I'd bet they've lined the entire perimeter, and we need to get to the woods on either side of the kingdom."

"So how are we going to draw them away? How are we going to get near the secret entrance?" I press.

"What, was I supposed to think of everything?" Sparrow blinks.

"You might have at least prepared a plan B for what would happen if we had company!"

"We *did* have company! At the Berg! And then we blew it up, remember, which was supposed to *solve* that problem! But ohhh no!" He waves his arms about. "It turns out— I have another army *not* at the most dangerous fortress in Evrilore, 'cause *that* makes sense, and by the way, remember all those guys you toasted on the plains? Nu-uh! Army number three is here to make your life hell again because I'm the Moon King, and I'm a t—!"

"*Sparrow*," I say, staring at him.

He clamps his teeth together, exhaling sharply.

"I'm not completely sure how to respond to that," I admit. "But I think you should sit down."

"No. We need a plan," he says, waving me away. "Let's get closer and see what we're dealing wi—"

"Hey! What are you kids doing? Where are your parents?" a sharp voice calls from behind us.

I turn to see a guard standing there, his eyes narrowed. That's when I suddenly remember that I match the description of a certain wanted Flai girl disturbingly well.

"School trip?" I offer meekly, distracting the guard.

The guard glances sideways at Sparrow, then at his mask. "Take that silly thing off," he demands.

Sparrow and I look at each other. "What was plan B again?" I whisper.

"We don't have one," he replies.

"It's a good thing there are twenty-four more letters, then, isn't it?" I say sweetly.

He pauses before speaking, trying to decipher my facial expression. "Whatever you're about to do, I strongly disapprove of it."

The sentry steps closer to us, impatient. "I said, take off that mask. And you, girl, remove those silly contacts so I can see your eyes. Dressing up as a Flai 'round here ain't a good prank. Not with that dirty fugitive on the loose."

Sparrow silently opens the sack of weapons and passes the throwing stars into my waiting hands. The guard opens his mouth in alarm, grappling for his pistol, but I'm already centimetres from his face in seconds, my weapon raised.

"Dirty fugitive?" I repeat.

CHAPTER 32

"She took that personally," Sparrow informs him, shrugging apologetically.

The guard gowls with pain as I deliver a satisfying thump to his ribs with my knee, and he doubles over. Sparrow and I dash forward, making for the exit.

"H-hey!" the guard wheezes, "Get those—" He stumbles forward and falls unconscious.

Exclamations of shock and loud, gruff orders echo from all around us as we dart through blockades of guards and hurry through the crowd down the nearest alley, sprinting east until the streets are reduced to dirt paths and the farmhouses and abandoned barns thin out. We reach the woods in minutes, with a wave of footsteps right behind us and occasional arrows and bullets whizzing past our ears. I take a moment to hurl a throwing star over my shoulder, and a man cries out in surprise as it slashes into his stomach.

"Raven!" Sparrow gasps, yanking on my cloak as he skids into a sharp turn, changing direction abruptly.

Smashing face-first into the earth, I cry out in surprise. The guards yell to one another and hurry after us. Terrified, I stumble to my feet with the help of Sparrow's outstretched arm, and we barrel on through the forest side-by-side, swatting branches from our faces.

"They're gaining on us!" Sparrow gasps.

"No, they're not," I say through gritted teeth, swivelling around and slamming two hands down onto the forest floor.

The earth beneath my flesh shivers, pauses in a pathetic attempt at resistance, and then falls, splitting into a bow to create a deep, violent crack that snakes toward our enemies, throwing them off-guard as they shriek and leap aside. The hole widens to swallow up the unsuspecting, dividing the pursued from the pursuer and chasing the guards back several more meters for good measure.

A few men have the common sense to stop running and fire more bullets, but we're too far ahead to be properly aimed at, and soon, the commotion dies away. I catch Sparrow gazing at me with a mixture of shock and praise. He shakes his head, panting. "I-I k-*knew* you took it personally."

We continue running until my muscles cry out, and our lungs fail us, collapsing in an exhausted heap at the base of a tree.

I glance sideways through the trees, scanning the bushes all around. If someone managed to follow us all the way here, they're being quiet about it.

After a few seconds, I flop decisively onto my back. "Can we rest now?"

He shakes his head. "We need to find somewhere where we'll be hidden. If we're not found tonight, they'll dispatch new soldiers first thing tomorrow for this area. Most likely, Ra soldiers— and we don't want to be anywhere near *them*. I'm going to take us to the secret entrance, but getting through their defences won't be easy. We have to draw the guards away from the wall. The entire perimeter watch has tripled in guards, weapons, and, unfortunately, trained wolves. Those wolves hate Flai, you know."

I raise an eyebrow. "Wow. Do they? Never knew. If only I was Flai, and we could all find out."

He eyes me wearily. "What is it with you and the sarcasm? *Always* you and the *sarcasm!*"

I shrug. "I don't know. Comes naturally, I guess. But you signed up for this, and unfortunately, there isn't another me to complete your mission with. Mind, I suppose if you could find another Flai girl with black hair and green eyes, you could just take her to my mother and pretend—"

"Forget that," he interrupts, shaking his head. "There's no one else like you."

CHAPTER 32

He picks up the sack. "Let's get going. I know a good patch of trees around here somewhere. We can probably scale a trunk and set up camp high up where no one can find us. It might be a bit of a squash, though." He looks at me. "Well, get up, then!"

I groan. I'm beginning to feel like a bear, sleeping in caves here, trees there, constantly crawling into new dark and desolate places as though I'm about to hibernate. Maybe one day I'll step into direct sunlight and burn to ash, turned into a vampire from years of living like this.

We trudge through the forest until we discover a large, thick-trunked tree. Its wood is dark, firm, and streaked with raindrop-like moss drizzling down the bark. It's rooted at the base of a stretch of grassy hills, and I figure it's safe enough. The best thing is that thanks to many fingers of crisscrossing, intersecting branches, once we've hoisted ourselves twenty meters up, we're almost completely shrouded from view.

After a quick inspection of our chosen accommodation, we unload our things on the ground and spent the rest of the night checking through our weaponry over a weak fire, with the distant calls of guards to one another and clinks of metal growing ever-nearer in the distant background. I fiddle with the daggers and spears as we quietly suggest plans of action for tomorrow's impossible feat until the flickering orange flames give a sigh and extinguish.

Once the moon is at its peak, it's less than minutes before the search parties descend upon us as naturally as fog, with no more citizens to interfere with our demise.

The men scale trees and command their wolves upon our scents. Yet somehow, the violence is muffled and distant, as though the clouds have snatched us up here on the lightest, most delicate branches that sway under our bodies.

When they finally reach us, we've erased any traces of our fire and hoisted our things high up. We melt into the darkness as they shove through it, pressing ourselves into the wood until you wouldn't know where a body ends and a branch begins.

"You think they'll find us?" Sparrow whispers.

I press a finger to my lips and nod towards the floor, where a guard marches through our clearing, her fist tight around a torch. She moves the beam upwards, illuminating the branches of our tree, and then mutters something in annoyance, swiftly swiping her gold rapier through a patch of flowers.

Petals spill out onto the grass, scattering in the breeze as the plant bows its stalk. And then the woman grinds it under her heel and carves a swift X into our tree before slithering away into a patch of bushes.

I look grimly back at Sparrow. "A brief check, that's all. They can't climb every single tree on Evrilore."

"They will, though, if it's to find us."

"No."

"To find *you*, then," he corrects, and, this time, I don't disagree. Sparrow sighs. "It would be comforting, Rave, to know that someone else realizes how much you're worth as a person, if only they didn't see your extensive value as a tool for the King's failure. All of this is for you. Everything he's doing is for you. He cares so much, and yet he's got you so wrong. No one sees you're a person. They just see you."

I stiffen at his reference to my confessions at Boots and Shackles. "Tonight, this forest will bleed more than I would've," I mumble.

Sparrow nods solemnly, and we both lie back onto nets of branches and prickly leaves.

I try to allow the soft grumble of clouds overhead to help

me relax and sift through today's events, processing each moment, but it's impossible with the slaughter below.

Bushes trampled, habitats perturbed.

Instead, I focus on the boy lying next to me. I find this helps due to the simplicity of it. He's just another person lying there, attempting to fall asleep. He's one thing that doesn't want my life.

And maybe it's just my body playing tricks on me, but I feel a little warmer tonight despite the harsh weather conditions.

"There's no one else like you".

The intentions behind his statement might have been to simply state a fact, or... *well*. I don't know. I won't ever ask, and I'm not sure if I want to. But still, I feel a little warmer, smiling against wet bark in the moonlight. Not much, but just a little.

CHAPTER 33

As time peels layers off the leathery night sky, the moonlight-dipped treetops become encased in swirling fog that rolls in from the north, peppering our branches in cool air.

I invite the fog in to kiss my palms, warm air rippling around me in the dark. It distorts the clarity of my vision to mush as particles ripple and science is overridden by magic, but it's better than the shivers that engulf my companion. If I could share my talents with him, I would, but the level of extreme control over magic required to not burn him alive lingers in the back of my mind and presses down like a weight. No, it's better to let the night chill him than my fingers cook him.

Even in my bubble of heat, I don't seem to be able to relax. I'm exhausted, but my mind still whirrs, and nothing I do seems to put it to rest. Then, just when I'm ready to give up on the prospect of slipping into sleep, I hear the creaking of branches as Sparrow rises to a shaky crawl and clambers to the tree's uppermost branches.

Cautious, he finds a fork thick enough to straddle and balances his weight, brushing hair from his face.

"Can't sleep?" he asks quietly, looking down to address me, and I freeze for a moment, wondering how on earth he knows I'm awake.

"Yeah," I reply, my shoulders relaxing, "Busy mind. You too?"

"Mm-hm."

I roll onto my back so that I can see his figure, silhouetted against the moonlight. "I've been thinking a lot. It's going to be really different in the Flai Realm," I say. "Isn't it?"

"It won't be... you know. Like this. No more nights together. No more hugging or holding hands. No more fighting or teamwork or rescue missions, and—"

"No more Raven and Sparrow," I finish. The stars rush to fill in the pause between my words, and when I try to find them again, they emerge damp and heavy, sucking in all the moisture from the air. "Every time you speak of that home, it becomes more of a stranger to me. You described it like paradise, but they'll kill you for what you did. For simply acting suspiciously. And humans aren't welcome there, so, in reality, it's no different at all from what's out here. Except everything's messed up. It's inside out."

Sparrow hesitates, and when he speaks, his voice is funny. His lips reject it as though it doesn't belong to him. "Raven, I'm your nightmares. I *should* be your nightmares. What divides Perseus and I? For all they know, I'm kidnapping, killing, or selling you. Don't you understand that? There's nothing I couldn't do to you if I wanted. I'm not trusted. Sending me out here to retrieve someone as important as you... that isn't trust. It's just putting me in danger so that they don't have to be. If you want the truth, that's what it is. In that place, humans are treated no differently than how Flai are treated here. We can't be... this. There's nothing left for this beyond that wall!" he gasps in exasperation, and yet there's a melancholy acceptance behind his words, as though he already understood that this would be the end of our friendship right from the moment we met.

"This?" I repeat.

"Us."

My tongue feels heavy, and my throat is sticky, as though the words trying to clamber out of it are glued inside. "And what... what about outside that wall?" I ask quietly.

"Raven, no."

"But—"

"No! Don't you dare! Don't even..." He cries out in frustration. "We didn't come all this way just to get killed! Just to give up! I have a mission, and that mission is to get you home," he says, his voice cracking. "It's all I'm good for. It's all I want. Isn't that... isn't that what you want too?" he turns to me, eyes locking into mine, and in this moment, it's so incredibly effortless.

All I have to do is say it. Let the words fly off my lips and change my fate. All I have to do is say no.

And I hate him for it. I hate him for being so incredibly selfless that he would erase everything we worked for, lied for, and almost died for just to keep me happy.

And I hate that he knows the reason I'd be happy would be because he's safe and with me.

And I hate that he wouldn't do it for anyone else.

Only me.

"To take me home...is it what you really want?" I ask.

The air is freezing, and a flurry's fluttering down, but the shame on my burning cheeks keeps me warm. After everything, I'm forcing him to admit his true desires? After my best friend died, my sister was humanized, and Spok was arrested? Now, I wish to turn back and to carve a different path into the promising hillsides of these woods?

For just a second, as I'm staring up at him and he's gazing down at me, we're one another. I'm finally not cold, impulsive, or distrustful. I'm selfless, and I'm offering him a chance to tear open his chest and display his inner workings, to unmask the direction of his heart's fateful compass' needle. Sparrow's thinking only of himself and the girl he wants to be with— the girl he wants to be with more than he wants to protect.

The right thing is to take me home, where I'm safe and have a family. But to take me home is to give me up, and Sparrow's genuinely considering opposing that course of events with his own dream of a human and a Flai being friends.

He says nothing— he can't admit that to himself.

So, I fill in the gap. "That place... may be my home. But it's not yours. I don't think so. And I also don't think it's humanely possible for you to be so selfless that you can't consider it. That you haven't considered it already."

"It doesn't matter what I want. I'm just a homefetch," Sparrow finally says, avoiding my eyes.

"More importantly, you're Sparrow. And I am *not* going home if it means something awful will happen to you. Aren't you worried at all? Even if not about Mother, then about the guards? Losing Peter wasn't bad luck or recklessness. It was just *easy*— killing is easy when you're as powerful as Frost. They design mechanisms that drown children and systems that murder a species... And it could happen again. Killing, I mean. It *will* happen again. I have a feeling... a terrible feeling."

"Don't talk like that. I'll ensure nothing happens tomorrow because if your mother's right about anything, it's that I've been too careless, prioritizing your mental health over your safety. I shouldn't have taken you to the Iceberg or Boots and Shackles. Raven, I'm going to keep you safe from now on, whatever it takes. That was my task from the very start, and so far, I've failed it... and I've failed you, which makes it a thousand times worse. I let you get into too much danger, and I'm so sorry."

"You can't protect me from myself, Sparrow," I answer softly, "I know I'm reckless. I know I'm destructive. But I try. And things are better when I'm with you. *I'm* better when I'm with you."

He hesitates. "Are you? You almost drowned yourself at Boots and Shackles. Another time when I just wasn't careful enough... nd it very nearly killed you." The self-blame in his voice turns to certainty as he adjusts his position. "Listen. If I can't protect you from yourself, I'll protect you from everything else. I promise," he pledges, and I almost believe him for a second.

But complete safety and protection? It's something we both know is a fantasy. "Please don't say that, Sparrow. This world is too cruel for such things," I say in a small voice, watching as he climbs back down the tree and edges along the branch to sit beside me.

"Then I'll build a new world and take you there instead," he says firmly.

This is his final word. His true promise. There's nothing I can say to doubt it, for his tone is so steady, strong, and confident that the only thing I can possibly do is trust.

"Okay then. Build your world and take me there," I smile.

It's the first genuine smile I've given him all night. Not a smile because I'm laughing or because I need self-assurance, but a smile because someone else has made me feel good about myself, and I want them to know it.

"And we'll go to Japan?" I add, stifling laughter because it's such a petty addition to demand from his vow.

"Sure. We'll go to Japan."

His head turns my way, and our eyes meet in the dark, the moon reflected in his pupils. I reach out for his hand, my worries and fatigue reducing me to a small, scared child, curled up and afraid of being alone in the dark. He takes it, looking just as young and vulnerable as we both feel, and I'm a little more comforted.

"I know it sounds crazy. But one day, Raven, I'm going to do it. You'll see. I will," he says, settling down into a lying position, "You can say it's impossible, but I'll do it for you."

I curl up as my hair, peppered with white snowflakes, spreads out beneath me like a spillage of ink, his voice sending me off to sleep at last. Carol singing echoes through the trees from the Willow District, it's lights twinkling on the horizon like fallen stars. My eyelids grow heavy as I watch them blink out, the Willowfolk retiring for the night.

"The knife that harms us has a beautiful blade," Sparrow murmurs.

"Come the morning, it'll melt, though. As will the snow."

"I'd give anything to keep it. To save everyone. Anything."

The moonlight's silver glow basks him in light as the clouds part, and the sky pauses to beam down on us.

"*Anything?*" I repeat. "Even to save your oppressors?"

He stares straight at me, his eyes mournful of the world that's already dead, and yet continuously dying. It is in this moment that I begin to understand a part of Sparrow's selflessness— he loves humanity. Loves the world, and wishes to correct something so deeply rooted, so complicated, that others shy away from the thought.

"Anything," he breathes.

CHAPTER 34

The following morning, the combined efforts of the Frost Guard and Willows Guard have reduced the forest encasing the Flai Realm to a bloody field of fallen soldiers. Trees with snapped, half-sawn branches bear deep slashes in their bark, and the guts of a thousand roses paint the trampled grass red.

The soldiers are gone, but deep footprints remain.

Occasionally, we find bullets, torches, or a dead rodent speared by a frustrated hand's rapier. Discarded flasks and rusty weapons hang from trees and penetrate bushes like darts thrown carelessly onto a board. The remains of fires are scattered throughout the trees, materialising as blackened stains creeping up cracked, weary bark. Sparrow walks closely behind me as I inspect the damage, crouching low to press my hands to the earth. The soil's ragged breaths refuse to answer my call to magic, and even as I send a blaze through the ground to scorch the roots awake, I'm ignored, shut out. Blamed, almost.

The soil is icy cold with rejection against my fingers, shooting my magic back up into my fingertips like venom. It's unnatural and absolutely shocking to my limbs. I jerk away, gasping.

"Raven, are you okay?" Sparrow frowns, concern creeping across his furrowed brow. "What happened? What did you feel?"

CHAPTER 34

There's a sharp stab of weakness in my muscles, and suddenly, I'm thumping down onto the grass, my hearing growing gradually more muffled until only my heartbeat thumps in my ears.

It's all black after that.

I've passed out before, but not like that. Not in a way where the darkness that blinds you also reaches out to bind your thighs to your stomach, to curl you in on yourself until it's impossible to breathe. This unconsciousness cuts deep through your bones, overwhelms your nerves, and clasps around your heart like a forbidden, shameful ribbon stripped from a medal and repurposed as a restraint.

This is punishment.

For the first hour after I wake up, I refuse to speak. It's as though my vocal cords were left behind, and only flesh and bones awoke.

Sparrow simply holds me while I stare at the survivors of the mindless violence of last night. It casts a dark shadow upon me, knowing the intended receiver of the slaughter.

It's all for me. Everything the King killed, everyone who died at the Berg... it's for *me*.

I snap a flame to life between my fingers. Extinguish it. Light it again.

"Do you feel okay?" Sparrow asks, sitting down behind me to lean against a tree trunk.

I don't reply, staring blankly at my hand. He shuffles closer to me and gently takes my hand in his, pushing it down and pushing the sight of my withering fire away from my fixated eyes.

"It's cold," I mumble miserably, on the verge of tears. "The air's cold, even though I'm heating it. It's rejecting magic. My magic. It's rejecting me," I finish with a dull stare at our intertwined fingers. The soil is cold and wet against my palm and utterly lifeless.

And I can't even blame nature's absence on the fact that a human's flesh is so calmly placed on mine. It's not humans, and it's not Sparrow that's making the earth repel me.

It's me, and it always was.

It was always everyone who ever thought like me— the fools who couldn't see past the winged and the not.

"The air's rejecting me," I repeat, crestfallen.

I can feel Sparrow raise his head, his chin brushing my shoulder. "Then the air's a fool," he whispers.

I lean my head back into his chest. "As am I and the island. I didn't realize that until now. I was too focused on sides. Rules. Systems. Limitations."

"I... Where'd this come from?" Sparrow frowns.

I glance back down at our hands and stiffen. "Forget it."

He notices.

"What if they knew?" I say suddenly before he can mention it, "What if everyone knew a Raven and a Sparrow existed... that we *can* exist... what'd the world do?"

"Hypothetically? Burn. Tear itself apart. Probably have another war. Speaking of which, we can't stay here. The armies'll return," Sparrow eventually says. His fingertips run lightly up and down my arm, tracing the moles there like constellations of stars. His skin is incredibly warm.

Good, I think. My fire's absence is a wound that needs cauterizing.

"Your mother's men are picking us up at 12. All we need to do is stay hidden until noon," Sparrow continues.

I nod, my hands writhing as I struggle to find my voice

CHAPTER 34

amongst the pile of ashes and chalk dust that is my throat. "Okay… yeah, that makes sense. But I need to do something first," I sigh, bowing my head.

Sparrow makes an inquisitive noise.

I'm hesitant to say it. "We've done everything together up until this point. But there is something I have to do. And alone, if I must. The only thing is… I want you to be there."

"Where?"

I take a deep breath. "Ever since I left home, there was one thing that gave me hope. One thing I simply can't forget. And I need closure. I need to tell myself that those childhood dreams were nothing but. It's immature and desperate, but before I can re-enter a new world, I have to rid myself of the poison of this one. This is my final obstacle. This is my last test. And if it means I charge into my own death, then at least I tried to free my people. At least I'll know I didn't turn my back on an opportunity to right an ancient wrong."

He arches a brow, and I continue awkwardly. "It's the prophecy. I know it's stupid, and I know it's bait for people like me, but I have to see… I have to try… I can control all four elements. I am a fire Flai, but I'm exceptionally good at mastering earth and air. My connection to the other elements should have withered ages ago, but Spok helped resurface it, and now I'm stronger than ever. I've felt different these last few days. The closer we drew to Willows, I could feel the kingdom reaching to me," I explain.

Sparrow's hand freezes, then draws sharply away from me. "So, you want to go to the gates," Sparrow says slowly, dragging his hands over his face. "Of course you do. Fancy blowing it up, too? Raven, you've got to be kidding me…now, after everything? Now, after we were sighted yesterday, and two armies're looking for us?"

"I have to know, Sparrow. I have to know if it's real!" I plead imploringly.

He sighs heavily. "Raven, no. You're not the chosen one. There is no prophecy. C'mon, you aren't stupid. You know this is a trap!"

"Maybe there isn't, but that prophecy is one of the only things I've ever had to pin my hopes on, and—!"

"What did Peter die for?" Sparrow asks suddenly, and his voice is overwhelmingly close to me. Closer than I'd realized. His cheeks are flushed with a slight tint of annoyance, and his hair is ruffled in the breeze. "What did Spok get captured by those barbaric men for? I'll tell you what: nothing. We're here because we're damn lucky to be. Don't you see? It's just a stupid story, Raven! A story designed to change that luck."

"It may be just a story, but it matters to me! Just like that song I sang in the hollow. A stranger wouldn't recognize it, nor its meaning. But I do, and if it matters to me, it should matter to you too," I gasp.

Sparrow stares at me, eyes aflame. "Blimey, Raven, what the hell does that even *mean*? Everything I *do* is for you! Everything I think and feel is somehow associated with you! If you're sad, I'm sad. If you need something, so do I. If you're grieving, I must be too. I came running back every time you pushed me away. I sat with you and talked to you even when I had my own problems to deal with! And now you're acting like I don't care how you feel?"

"I never asked you to do any of those things for me!" I say heatedly, moving away from him to rise to my feet.

"No, you didn't. But I still did them because I wanted you even if you never wanted me!" he yells.

I stumble back, eyes wide. "Sparrow... that's not true. I-*Wanted* you? We... this... We're... we're friends," I stammer.

"Yeah, 'cause *you* would know what it's like to have a friend!" The moment the words roll off his tongue, his glistening eyes soften, and he knows he's said too much.

CHAPTER 34

Silence swells up between us, my throat stiff and unable to form sounds. My insides are on fire, as though someone's roasting my heart, my lungs, and my ribs, taking everything I've learned over the past few months and reducing it to ashes in the pit of my stomach.

Sparrow climbs to his feet and marches past me, face conflicted between expressions of anger, regret, frustration, and guilt. Then he snatches the weapon sack and slings it over his shoulder. "Let's go to the blooming gates."

"No. You were right. I'm sorry. We-we don't even need to go. It was a stupid idea, and I—"

He cuts across me. "We need supplies, anyway. You want to go, so let's *go*."

❊ ❊ ❊

As we walk through the withering wasteland, my mind fixates on anything other than Sparrow's words. The landscape, the demolished forest. Anything that can distract me from the terrible, terrible pain.

I glance at the boy beside me, the boy who built me up for months and then tore me down in a sentence. Is it in his nature to destroy everything in his path? To reach for my neck, to snap every bone in my body, and yet to somehow also sob afterwards, consumed by grief and remorse?

Humans are cursed with killer survival instincts but complex emotions to question their decisions and blame themselves for wrongdoings. So, what exactly is nature trying to achieve with that partnership? What are humans here for? Why do they fight everyone and everything so hard when they're already destroying themselves anyway?

I gaze ahead, sighing. Someday, these woods will be cut

down, cement laid, and houses constructed, the wildlife butchered. Even though they don't need it, they'll expand, grow, spread diseases, and turn animals into coats.

I hate myself for admitting it, but if it was discovered that Flai genuinely came to Earth to destroy humans, I don't think I'd be quite as devastated as I like to think.

Sparrow doesn't say anything for a long time, his eyes unfocused and hollowed out by despair. Eventually, he gathers up his vocal folds and slowly says, "When we enter the Flai Realm... you should forget about me. It's for the best." It's achingly slow but business-like all the same, produced in a practised, melancholy tone. He's been mulling this over for some time.

"No," I sound pathetic. Like a child refusing to give away her favourite toy.

"That's the way it must be."

"Are you serious?"

He inhales sharply, closing his eyes as he slows to a standstill. "I'll deliver you home safely. I'll stay by your side until I physically must leave for my own safety. And you can fight, and defend, and try to make them see sense, but in the end, I'll have to leave. And I'll leave you behind when I do. Then, Raven, you must forget."

"If we just explain to them... if we just *try*..." I beg.

"There's nowhere for us, but there's still somewhere for you. I refuse to take that away from you."

"You're taking yourself away from me!"

"I was never yours! Don't you get it? I don't normally form relationships with the Flai I rescue. You're different. This is different. Yes, you feared me and hated me when we met, but there was also a fatigue, a loneliness, and I knew you liked me. You pretended not to, but we got along. It kind of just happened, like a weed growing in a cracked pavement.

I never intended it to. I never wanted to build something only to destroy it."

"You'd need a bloody hefty sledgehammer," I snap.

* * *

The key to entering Willows undetected is simply stealth, this time. So, we lay a few ground rules: no interaction with anyone other than one another, no transactions, and no straying from the crowds. As for disguise, I chopped my into a short blunt cut that falls to just below my ears, and I wear Sparrow's eye-dimming blanket as a sort of headscarf, twisting it into a style popular in the southeast, near Ra.

Sparrow's considerably less wanted than me, so he simply bathes in the closest river we can find, removing conflict's signature of blood, dirt, and leaves. Then we scrub the soil from our clothes and leave them to dry in the sun. He leaves his bird mask behind.

Once we're both ready, we hike west until the woodland whittles away into village paths and enter the heart of the Willow District around lunchtime.

Sparrow leads, creating distractions while I swipe food from the market. It's a tricky business, ensuring we aren't seen, but so long as we keep to ourselves and blend in with the crowd, following the flow of traffic, we're practically invisible.

Guards search for us everywhere, posted outside shops and questioning citizens.

Celebrations are still in full swing, and fiery red and bronze (The official colours of Ra) streamers hang from many different stall roofs and windowsills to push the election in the Sun Queen's favour. I spot a poster plastered onto a wall.

It reads, "TWO DAYS, THE ELECTION OF A DECADE", and proudly bears an illustration of two silhouettes striking poses, with a crown hovering between them. One of the silhouettes is a woman, her waist slim and her curves accentuated. Long waves of hair cascade down her back, and she's tilted to one side so that we can see a playful smile and long, thick eyelashes. The Sun Queen.

Young, charismatic, and absolutely gorgeous. She's known for being so earth-shatteringly stunning that people have genuinely fainted upon setting their eyes on her for the first time. Her beauty goes unmatched throughout all of Evrilore. As for her leadership... well, no one has eyes for that, do they?

Two days, I think to myself. Two days, and the world could change forever. New laws, new policies. Two days and the fate of all Flai is in one person's hands for eternity. She could free us with the passing of one law or order our deaths with a simple command of those painted glossy lips.

It sends a wave of anticipation along my limbs and makes me pull the headscarf tighter around my face.

Pushing down our nerves, we stroll further into the heart of town. While the crowds grow and countless traders appear on the streets, the attentions of vendors are briefly diverted, and I manage to swipe several more pocketfuls of food, a loaf of bread, and three rolls, all of which are freshly baked. Once we've stashed everything in the weapon sack and found a doorstep to duck under, we split the rolls between us, munching silently.

When his bread has completely disappeared, Sparrow brushes the crumbs off his palms and mimes, pressing a microphone under my face. It's not exactly the best way to approach me after our row, but it's a joke. It's a start. It means he's sorry, and that counts for something.

"So, today, you're going home. Thought about it much?"

I shrug. "Don't want to think about it, in case we fail... in case I fail. It won't be your fault, of course," I add quickly.

"I think it would. It's my job, isn't it?" he says, arching a brow.

I sigh, pushing away his pretend microphone. "Your job was to get me home safely, not to help me blow up the most heavily protected military fortress in the world. It's my fault it even happened because I set off the bomb and, therefore, led to the bounty being placed on our heads and the maximized border security. I don't want you to get punished for something that wasn't your fault."

"Let's not talk about it anymore. I don't want to think about what'll happen to me any more than you do."

"Sparrow, please look at me. I will protect you. They can't do anything while I'm there. And I have my powers now," I add.

Silence falls once again, both of us unsure how to break it. Thoughtful, I gaze at my feet. "It's just weird, isn't it? That I'm going home, that my entire life is changing, and if I hadn't taken your hand that day in Frost and jumped into that lake, everything might be different."

"It wouldn't. I'd have swum after you."

"Really?"

"Definitely."

I turn my gaze to the sky, pensive. "Sometimes I wonder if everything's all decided. If certain things just happen because that's the way it is."

"What d'you mean?"

"I mean, what if Peter would've died regardless of what I did? What if that was never my choice to make? I don't know. Maybe I'm just making things up to feel less guilty. You said it yourself: I don't know what a friend is. Coping with losing Peter and Wynn all by myself... I-I don't know if it drove me to start imagining—"

"I never should've said that," Sparrow interrupts, sharp as a razor blade. And I know he truly means it.

Another pause. "Come on. It's time to do what I've waited fifteen years to do," I say firmly, ducking out from under the doorframe (Willowfolk are ever so short, and their architecture reflects it) and beginning to walk.

We reach the entrance to the Flai Kingdom at ten o'clock, giving us time to hike back to the woods and meet my mother's workers.

Thinking about the journey inside the Flai Kingdom floods me with a mix of indescribable emotions, so I decide to set it aside for now.

I've better things to focus on.

The entrance to the Flai Realm is built on an elevated platform, with a series of intersecting ramps, stairs, and paths leading up to a small space big enough for about four people, and in between the roped-off paths are little patches of grass littered with wildflowers stretched out leisurely under the sun.

There's an enormous queue of tourists, old and young. The youngsters are giddy with excitement, the children are screwed up and impatient, and the elderly are quite content; most of them have visited before. We join the back of the line without fuss, ducking our heads.

"I suppose you think you're the "chosen one" then?" Sparrow says, leaning casually back against the rope divider.

"Hey! I'm counting on this a lot. This prophecy is something I always relied on when I was younger... it was my last hope, especially after I lost my friends. If I get up there and nothing happens, I'm sure I'll still feel more connected to my origins."

He eyes me sceptically. "Uh-huh. It's a door. You know

CHAPTER 34

that, right? Yeah? Just checking. Well, let's get you up there, your royal hopefulness."

I scowl at him. "I thought you dropped that?"

He grins. "I did, but annoying you is fun, and I'm bored."

"How long are you gonna keep that up?"

"It's a long line," he states simply.

I give him a friendly shove into the nearest thornbush — all just banter, of course— and trot merrily up the cobbled path. The guards standing on either side of the queue are dozing lazily in the warm midday sun and pay little attention to me.

What I'm actually worried about is the small troops of guards marching around. They're disguised in normal clothing, but it's obvious from the stone-cold faces and dominant stance that they're no ordinary civilians. Sent here to search for us, I suspect, as a backup.

I turn away from them, pulling my cloak tighter around my shoulders despite the glowing sun. We've just got to pray that the crowd stays thick and thoroughly buzzing with excitement.

Over the next half hour, the queue whittles away until we reach the front. Up close, the details spring to life, just as I dreamed. The arch bears intricate carvings portraying hourglasses and the four-pointed star that now represents Frost. A threat, a legend? All the contextual history is gone, of course.

But they can't lay a finger on the arch. The Realm is untouchable.

"Go on, then. Try and open it," Sparrow says, nudging me from behind.

I take a deep breath, chewing on my lip. "I'm not sure how... what if it's electric or something? What if—"

"Touch it, Raven. It doesn't matter what happens," he says calmly. "But if you don't do it now, you'll regret it forever."

"W-will you do it with me?" I blurt.

He blinks, surprised. "Yeah. Alright."

Sparrow moves closer to me, pressing his chest into my back, and reaches out to mirror my hesitated arm. We're so close that my heart is thrumming uncontrollably. "Sparrow?"

"Yeah?"

"Let's not fight again."

"You're procrastinating." He gently takes my hand in his and places my palm on the arched invisible doorway to the Flai Kingdom.

I hold my breath, my stomach plummeting, my heart racing. My fingertip touches the spectrum beyond the stone, and a rush of electricity flies down my arm as the shield greets me.

The magic concealed within the walls seems to be trying to get to me, throwing itself against the wall, demanding to be released. Blood courses rapidly through my veins, rushing to my palms, and my heartbeat sings in harmony with a twin one, as though the Flai Realm is... alive.

I let my whole palm fall onto the surface, and the soapy bubble beyond the arch responds, thriving with the knowledge that Flai still live. Suddenly, The kingdom seems to soar into the air, wings beating against the sky.

Harder, harder, until a force so great is released that it throws everything back a thousand miles except me. It is just me and my powers. Flai and I. "We're the same," I gasp.

"Raven..." Sparrow whispers in disbelief, taking a step back. His hand leaves mine.

CHAPTER 34

"Yes?" I gasp, enchanted.

"It... the power... it's too much. Oh! Oh! I... I think I might just have a nap. Can you hurry up, please?" I turn back to the arch to discover, with shock, that nothing has happened at all.

"What...?" I whisper. "This doesn't make any sense, it... it..."

My mouth is dry. Even if nothing happened physically... Spiritually and emotionally, something inside me is different.

I take one last bewildered look at the door before drawing away. "Woah... guess I'm not "The chosen one"."

"You can still be a princess, your royal disappointed-ness," Sparrow offers.

"I'm kidding. Of course, I wasn't expecting anything to happen."

"Then let's go, people are staring."

We shove through the sea of crowds and retrace our footsteps back to the roads that trail off into the woodland, navigating the hundreds of unexpected guards lurking around corners.

The birds are chirping merrily, and beams of sunlight shine through the trees, creating an almost glowing effect on the smooth, dark curve of Sparrow's cheek to frame his face like an eclipse.

Voices fly past us as guards march through the woods, undoubtedly searching for us. But there are so many couples and giggling children walking or having picnics that we look no more suspicious than regular citizens of the Willow District.

Sparrow keeps glancing to our left, towards the wall that

frames the Flai Realm. And this time, I'm not too emotionally self-absorbed to let it go unnoticed.

His words from Boots and Shackles dance through my head like a carousel. *"Do you know what happens to people who threaten the Flai Realm?"*

He had seemed so distraught that day. Since then, we've had bigger things to worry about, but now I can see the same panic and stress written plain across his face.

"They'll kill me."

I clear my throat, stop walking, and turn to him. "Sparrow... Listen, I know I've acted awful in the past. I've been so neglectful, untrusting, and cruel. I can't even describe how sorry I am. I wish I could erase everything I've ever done and said to hurt you... But now I promise I'm ready to listen and to look out for you. So... can I please ask you something?"

"'Course," he shrugs.

I take in a deep breath. "Why are your hands shaking?"

"They are?" he asks, surprised.

I slowly nod, but he says nothing. "Is everything... okay?" I ask hesitantly.

He finally turns to look at me, and I'm stunned to see that, for some unspoken reason, his eyes are filled with tears. "Only when I'm with you."

CHAPTER 35

With a full stomach, it's easy to walk for the next hour, and the sun is high and pleasant in the sky, beaming on my neck.

While the weather glows, however, our spirits are low. A sense of dread, unease, and tension hangs about the air around us. Uncertainty leads the parade. What will happen to Sparrow? Will he be accused of traitorous actions? Trialled? Killed? Can I protect him if he is? Will he be forced to leave me to save his life?

To march on towards the Flai Realm is only natural. Only normal. It's just a destination, a pre-paved stone to walk upon.

But now I realize this journey was never about reaching a location. It was about family— about my mother.

The woman who oversaw, commanded, and will ultimately end my time with Sparrow is a mere shadow, and the promise of her role in my life seems suddenly pathetically insignificant compared to the friend I've made. To forfeit Sparrow for a fantastical goal is delusional.

And yet we walk on in solemn acceptance of the way it is. The way it must be.

I begin to craft things. Maps, plans, dreams. There are places we could go. The Isles of Sun were said to have homed the largest Flai population after the Willow District. There could easily still be huge underground communities there. It's not impossible, is it?

If not the Isles, then the wilderness. A mountain. There are places they wouldn't look. Places we could hide if we tried.

"It's a big island," I whisper to myself, digging for the courage to say the words aloud to Sparrow.

It's a big island.

The further we travel from the heart of Willows, the more healthy the vegetation becomes, springing up in lush sprouts of bushes spotted with vibrancy. These areas were not quite as disrupted last night as the woods closest to the Willow District.

The secret entrance into the Flai Realm is located on a peninsula far east, so enveloped by the ocean that the slap of waves against rocks is audible even kilometres inshore. As we near the wall, keeping a cautious distance from the surrounding army, I notice that the trees are a little greener and stand a little taller and prouder, as though some of the Flai Realm's magic has bled through into the land around it.

We set down our things in a sparse clearing just far away enough from the wall so that we can't be spotted by sentries.

Our plan is for me to send a signal to the Flai Realm, whose ariel spotters will retrieve us. There's no hope of fooling the entire Frost and Willows Guards with a distraction, but there's a chance we can be escorted into the Realm unseen.

"What should I send them?" I ask Sparrow, flexing my fingers as magic hurries towards my palms, eagerly burying itself into my skin.

My hands feel stiff from a lack of use since this morning, and the magic that was happily fizzing inside my blood is muted and exhausted from its connection with the Flai

Realm. The shield should've charged my abilities with energy, but instead, it seemed to fuse me to my home, and the further we walked away, the weaker my limbs felt— my body yearns to turn back.

"Fire?" Sparrow offers flatly.

"Well, yes, but *what* should I send them? What shape?"

"A Raven. And don't mention me." He sits down against a tree, looking expectantly up.

"What, right now?" I ask, rather surprised at the alarm in my own tone.

Sparrow stares at me. "When *else*?"

I shrug, folding my arms. "I don't know, I just didn't think we'd..."

"Raven."

That's all he says, and rather heavily. He looks at me. Just looks. Not gazes, not glances, not scrutinizes... just looks, as if only to give tired eyes a place to rest.

"Okay," I say, raising both my hands, but they're suddenly like bricks, and I can't. I *can't*. "Sparrow," I say, dropping my arms again with a sigh.

"What?" he grunts, burying his head into his knees.

I hesitate. "I want to tell you something. And I'd like to say it now, just in case I don't get the opportunity to speak to you alone for a while."

He drags his hands over his face. "Don't do this now."

"I have to," I say, shaking my head apologetically. "Because I've been stupid."

"Raven—"

"I've been stupid," I repeat, growing more sure of myself now. "You were right. Every time about everything, you were right. I'm sorry!" I gasp. "I tried so hard to make you something just because of what you are— just because you're human, I mean. A hunter, a manipulator, a liar... I was awful, and I'm *sorry*. I'm *so* sorry, Sparrow," I say again, "Because I know now. I know what you are and who you are, and I wouldn't change a single thing about you. Not a single thing. In fact, I think you're... you're... I mean—"

"What do you want me to do?" Sparrow interjects, hopeless and deflated. "Say it. Tell me. What should I do? What's the *right* thing to do?"

"Oh, "right"!" I snap. "So, there's a *right* thing, now, is there?"

"Maybe!"

"Isn't this... aren't *we* right?"

"I..." He forces the words out. "No. We're not. And... and that's truly what I think."

"Uh-huh. Sure it is," I retort bitterly.

"You wanted a home. *You* wanted this!"

"And look at what my "home" is doing to us! We're fighting, again. We're fighting like Man and Flai!"

"*This* is your home!" he continues, ignoring me.

"Well, then, I'm *sorry*." My voice cracks this time. Just once, as I push that last word through my lips. "I'm sorry I can't be what you want me to be. I'm sorry I'm not like everyone else. But... but *you* changed me, Sparrow. You made me different. So don't you dare act as though I ought to hate you like an angel would. Angels don't even *exist* to me anymore."

After several seconds of heavy silence, I offer my hand to him, and he stares at my open, outstretched invitation. "Don't do this," he says again. His voice is softer this time as he reaches out and gently pushes my hand into the air, towards a sky full of particles awaiting instruction. His eyes lock with mine.

"Send them a Raven," he whispers.

Uncommanded, a green spark flares up at my fingertip and then runs down to my palm. The air around me tightens as magic is sucked into my hand and released again, transformed into a green inferno, growing rapidly into a blaze that spills out from my cupped hand to mimic the physics of water and pools at my feet, surrounding me.

I close my fist just once, and the fire remodels itself, dancing and dashing and bounding with energetic ease into clumps that slot together to form a bird. I lift both my arms to toss the shape into the air, and it disappears in a millisecond, soaring into the clouds above.

When the fire's gone, there's a strange absence left in its place. I look to Sparrow for comfort, reassurance, or perhaps praise, but his head rests in his hands, and his body's fatigue-stricken and hopeless, curled into a ball with his knees up to his chest.

"You shouldn't have made me do that," I say before I can stop myself.

He doesn't say anything at all.

"How long do we have? And how will the guards not trace them back to the Realm if we're spotted?"

Sparrow slowly uncurls himself and replies in a very monotonous, masking voice. "The shield over the Flai Realm has weak spots— I already told you that. Weak spots where we can get in. But knowing they exist isn't good enough. It's a bit like catching stars— you have to know exactly how to use them."

"We can't just walk through, surely?"

"No. There's still a wall in the way, regardless of the shield."

"Are we going to... climb?" I ask tentatively.

"We're going to fly."

"I can't fly," I say, "I can't seem to stress that to you enough to you, Sparrow."

He points up, and I follow his finger to the huge glimmering dome surrounding the Flai Realm. The surface looks undisturbed, unchanged. I look back at him, confused.

"They can."

I arch a brow. "They?"

A rush of air passes over my face, and I look up again, stunned.

Nothing, then another swoop.

"What's going on? Do you feel that?"

Above, a gap of sky peeks through the net of branches. Then it's gone, cloaked by something else, something bigger.

"That was quick," Sparrow murmurs. "Too quick. I wonder if something's wrong."

"*Who's* quick?" I demand, striding forward.

"You might want to hold onto me for this," he says, ignoring me and climbing to his feet, motioning for me to come close to him.

I nod and step forward, awkwardly taking his waist. "So now wha—?" I begin, but almost instantly, I'm interrupted by the sound of wings as two figures descend from the sky, circling us rapidly.

Air whips my hair into my face, and it's difficult not to scream as we're encased in a tunnel of blurry figures with indistinguishable faces. Round and round, faster and faster, until the force generated by their wings lifts us off the ground.

I look down in fascination as my feet leave the grass, and Sparrow gives an involuntary chuckle at the look of utter delight on my face. It's incredible. Magical.

The Flai circling us begin to fly left, moving us towards

CHAPTER 35

the huge ring of stone surrounding the Flai Realm, and we continue rising until my feet skim the brick and the shield nears us, the treetops below shrinking to a plethora of green raindrops. The soldiers below us are specks of dust, indistinguishable as they stand uniformed and unaware of their targets as we soar over them.

As we head towards the shield at an alarming speed, I instinctively cover my face.

"Open your eyes, Rave."

I keep my eyes tightly shut, awaiting the force of the impact, but there is only smooth soaring.

"Raven, *look*," Sparrow insists, gently probing my fingers away. "Trust me."

We're flying through a kaleidoscope, surrounded by blotches of ever-moving colours and blurry, flitting shapes. Nothing is ahead. Nothing is behind. It's as though we've slashed a hole in the universe, and the flow of a million thoughts, feelings, and species has spilt out into a river of undefined matter.

I can make out green vegetation ahead and the bleak forest far behind, but somehow, we don't seem to be drawing nearer or closer to anything at all.

It suddenly occurs to me that we're inside the shield. It's much thicker than I would've initially thought but just as glamorous as it looks from the outside. Everything seems softer here, blurred at the edges as reality remoulds itself into a place where ordinary laws of science cease to exist and anything is possible— where *magic* is possible.

Sparrow's voice is muffled and far away yet calming. I know without asking that space and time do not exist here. This is a wonder of the world created to protect and save, and no evil can penetrate it. Inexplicable relaxation overcomes every inch of me.

"This is crazy," I whisper.

"It's like a dream, isn't it?" Sparrow says, "Nothing quite makes sense, but it also does in a way you can't describe." Unhooking an arm from around me, he reaches up and lets his hand soar through the air. His fingers stretch, twist, and dissipate before my eyes before returning as easily as they came, carried through the circuit of the shield's magic in less than a moment.

"Pinch me," I whisper.

The cotton clouds all around begin to thin out, and the rosy discolouring of the air seeps away. Suddenly, the wind feels much colder, alerting my senses to fire, water, wind, and earth as reality slaps me.

There's a moment of intense pressure all around us as our transporters struggle to fight against the force of the shield before we finally break through and emerge in a new place.

"Raven Asgard," Sparrow says, with a grand sweep of his arm, "I believe I have officially delivered you to your destination. Welcome home."

My stomach seems to soar out of my chest. The fire in my palms no longer feels restricted but natural. It leaps out as uncontained, separate entities, bounding off my skin and thumping down with ease onto the ground to nuzzle away into the earth. The oxygen rushing into my lungs is speckled with the same substance that resides in my bloodstream, waiting to be commanded and unleashed. I'm more powerful than ever, charged up by the environment.

I'm *free.*

Forests and hills stretch as far as my vision and even beyond. There are cliff faces, like the one surrounding the lake in the frost wilderness, except these are a thousand times bigger. I imagine scaling them, flying up there when I'm older, my wings unfurling as I am lifted into a self-conjured spiral of wind. And then, perching atop, I will spread my arms out on either side of me and dive forward into the tangle of gorgeous, undisturbed nature below.

My heart flutters as I recognize the legendary Jade Palace, its pillars penetrating the clouds. This is the temple where the elders once met to discuss the most important and pressing issues of the Flai Realm. This is where the cure for the horrible disease was created.

And now shame presses down on my heart, for how could I ever have been ashamed of them? My ancestors. My origins.

My home, I realize.

The pair of Flai that took us through the shield gradually lower themselves, the torrent of wind disappearing. I turn my head to thank them, but almost instantly, they fly away as though in an enormous rush. I frown but don't think much of it, for, light as a feather, the wind gently caresses my face, tilting my gaze to observe my surroundings.

What I saw over the top of the wall back in the Willow District was nothing but a sliver of the Realm.

I gawk in fascination at people engaging in everyday tasks, the mundanity of farming and weaving drowned out by magic. One man is chopping wood outside a cottage nearby using blades of invisible wind. A teenager weeds a bed of plants to my right, ordering stalks to rearrange themselves. Nearby, a group of women busily craft tools out of foraged metal, blazing away at the scraps until molten silver drips onto the earth.

Food's teasing scent tumbles from chimneys, and a freshwater stream runs past our feet at a child's command, snaking into a nearby cottage.

The atmosphere of the community is startling— and its

effect on me is, too, because I'm not throwing petrified glances over my shoulder or gnawing at my nails in anxiety. I'm utterly ordinary, and my heart sings.

Everything shimmers here in the same way my eyes do. Men and women with snow-white skin surround me, their veins protruding, and although I have always thought Flai to be ugly, I realize that amongst this new herd, there is no such thing— standards of appearance were created *by* humans, *for* humans. It shouldn't surprise me as much as it does, but even so, my eyes struggle to adjust to the sight of people who are impossible to judge due to a complete lack of understandable human context.

I've so much to learn.

Closer to us, the unpleasant smell of fertilizer hangs in the air over crop fields, and all around us, and a little bit further up winding paths carved into the untamed growths of the Realm, are clusters of small houses built into a grassy, gradually steepening hillside, their walls overcome by vines and flowers in heavy bloom. The nature's takeover almost masks them entirely.

Above them is a newly built stone castle, the walls smooth and rising to dominate the hilltop with sand-coloured brick.

My lips droop from their wonder-struck smile as I settle my gaze upon it. Everything about the huge building screams human, from the stained glass to the sentries stationed at every corner. The land on which it sits is also bare, save for a few lonely flowerboxes, levelled out to meet the requirements of a construction site. It's unnatural, ugly, and absolutely mismatched with its surroundings.

"Want to let go, now?" Sparrow asks casually, cutting across my train of thought. "I mean, it's no skin off my nose. But, y'know."

My cheeks turn scarlet as I apologetically release my hands from his waist.

"Everything ok?" he asks, noticing my frowning face.

"Oh... yeah! I was just lost in thought," I lie, but my tone wavers, not the slightest bit convincing.

Sparrow's eyes drill into me. "Is it not what you thought it'd be?" he asks quietly. "I *tried* to warn you."

"It's everything I wanted. It really is!" I say quickly.

"Then what is it? Why are you not happy? Did I do something?"

"What? No... *No!* Honestly. It's just that everything's so... efficient? Systematic? I don't know. I thought there would be more of us, I suppose. There's barely anyone around," I sigh, and suddenly I realize how much the seeemingly fake excuse bothers me.

Rolling hills, golden sunlight refracting and reflecting off every surface... yet, how many Flai have I seen? Maybe a hundred. So much land and so little of us. It shouldn't be so empty.

"There *are* more of us, Raven. They're just inside their homes, in other parts of the Realm, or hiding in other kingdoms of Evrilore," he says confidently.

"Yeah, but are they safe, and if they are, will they be for much longer? You've seen what the Moon King's doing, and with the Sun Queen rising to power, who knows what new rules she'll enforce? Already, they're raising the bounties and thickening border security... and that'll only get worse with a new leader, especially a leader of the kingdom which suffered the most because we didn't cure its people! How will any of them ever get here alive?" I reason.

"Well, of course, there's me and others like me. Everyone contributes to bringing others here— and there are people like Spok —good, honest people— who put efforts towards helping Flai even on the outside."

"And where do those people end up? The same place Spok will. In a cell."

"There are no more cells. We blew them up, remember?" he points out, bowing his head a little to whisper it to me as though it's a secret.

"If there's a darker place to put people, they'll find it," I persist, deadly serious.

He sighs. "You're still only thinking negatively. It's all going to be alright, Rave. Spok's going to be alright. So are you. So am I. You can relax now, yeah? Look at where you are. Okay, maybe there aren't many people out there —and in here — that will make such bold sacrifices to rescue a few of their own kind. But we'll figure it out like we always do. We really will. For now, just look at what we've got. Enough to keep us all going and enough to keep everybody happy. The Queen — I mean your mother— is even developing a new plan to help us grow the population faster."

I press my lips together, unconvinced.

"We're going to harvest more food, and each family is now being encouraged to have at least two healthy children. Your mother has big plans for our kind as well. She wants to free the Flai Realm eventually and make a peace deal with the League. Of course, I'm not allowed to know much, so what I'm telling you is mostly gossip, but—"

"Our kind?" I interrupt. "After everything you've said to me this past day, you refer now to a kind to which we both belong?" My eyes drill into him, burning with hurt. "Sparrow, if there was ever an "our kind", we're the sole remnants of it."

"I didn't mean... I'm sorry," Sparrow says.

"You're not sorry enough," I whisper. "That's kind of the problem. You say things like "forget me", and then you group us together as one "kind". And why, Sparrow? What is it that you still allow yourself to hope will change?"

He turns away to hide the tears of anger in his eyes. "Everything. I wish I could change *everything*."

My shoulders drop, and I force myself to admit my next words. "I know it's awful, because it'd mean I wished a war upon you, and endless suffering, and torture and gold and hatred... but I wish you were Flai."

He hesitates. "I wish you were human. Perhaps your being one of us'd make Man a little less disgusting to belong to. Make me less of a... let's see... genocidal sadist? Ignorant imbecile?" It's supposed to be playful, but his tone is thin, and the same anxiety and exhaustion from earlier poke through it. He sounds as though he's lost a long, draining fight.

"Don't say that," I plead. "You *don't* belong to them."

"Sorry. Not far, now."

We set off walking through the village.

There appears to be another family with another small child jumping up and down and waiting to greet me at every doorway and alleyway possible. I'm not sure exactly what they're so excited about, but I suppose it's nice whenever they see a new person joining the community. Another Flai returning to the Realm is another victory for them and another sign of hope. Hope for change, hope that things will get better.

If only they knew what was happening outside of their optimistic bubble. If only they knew about the election, the growing security, the iceberg being blown up and the killing of prisoners who were potentially their own relatives.

Not wishing to reveal the darkness spreading across the outside world, I greet them with my kindest smile.

Overall, this doesn't take very long because there aren't many families to greet.

Sparrow doesn't say much— he just stands there casually,

leaning against walls. I figure the villagers and Sparrow aren't very devoted to acknowledging one another's existence.

They pass each other when the inhabitants scramble out of their huts to excitedly speak to me, and I can almost hear their thoughts: *I'll pretend you don't exist, and you pretend I don't exist, and that way, nobody gets in trouble.*

Of course, I don't like it, but who can blame them? We were forced out of our homes, killed, hunted, and taken as prisoners during the Fall. They stripped us of our magic, and despite this all happening about fifteen years ago, why should they trust any human even now?

Because not every human is the same, that's why. He's one of us.

A part of my heart wonders if he would be accepted if they knew about his past, about what he has been through, without even knowing at such a young age what was happening to him... But no, my mind tells me even that would never convince them. At the end of the day, he's still human. Still an enemy... And yet, how strange it is that I made a promise to that enemy. A promise to protect him from my own species.

Some enemies, we are.

Sparrow greets the guards at the castle with a terrible attempt at Flai Latin and presents a small black paper crescent to them with trembling fingers. I take his spare hand reassuringly, but he releases me instantly as though I've electrically shocked him, shaking his head frantically.

"You're granted access," the guards finally say, addressing Sparrow. "And what about the girl? ID?"

"She's not a citizen here," Sparrow says quickly. "She's been requested by the queen herself."

Clearly, these particular guards have not been very well

informed of the current situation. The girl on the right of the door steps forward so that her face is millimetres from his. "You better cough up some ID or else—"

"Or else what?" a voice says silkily, the doors to the castle flying open with a flick of her wrist.

The woman is cast in shadow for a moment before she steps gracefully forward into the sunlight. The sheer size of her aura causes the men on either side of the entrance to step back several paces and hurriedly lower themselves into bows, each one folding like creased cardboard.

I gape, stunned, at the lady before me. Ebony hair cascades down her forearms in thick waves, her eyes are brighter than the lush greenery of the landscape beyond the village, and her height and large, set shoulders overpower those of the castle guards.

She's a mirror image of me, except... older, majestic, more extravagant, powerful, beautiful, and dominant.

The differences between me, a filthy, exhausted teenager, and my mother, a calm, confident adult, are hardly significant.

Under my grime and wounds, and even with her dressed appropriately in a royal gown made of the finest silk in Evrilore, I look nothing short of her daughter.

"Mother?" I whisper, almost afraid to believe it.

The guards draw weapons and move to shield her, facing us with eyes narrowed in suspicion. "With all due respect, we must protect you, and these children may be dangerous. The princess was due to arrive over a month ago, Your Highne—"

"I am aware. I have been in contact with the boy. Please do not interrogate them any further. Thank you for your rational concerns, but I shall take it from here," Mother says dismissively. She looks down at me with a warm, welcoming smile. "My daughter. At last, you have come *home!* We have waited... we have all waited... so long..." Her eyes scour into me, taking in every detail of her child's face.

"I'm your daughter?" I repeat, the words echoing off my lips and ringing through my head as I try to adjust to saying it. *Daughter...*

"Indeed," she nods. "My Raven. My beautiful girl."

"Fifteen years... it's been... fifteen years..." she says slowly.

"But I came back. I'm here now," I say, attempting to steady my clumsy breaths.

"You're here now," she echoes.

"And I am never leaving again. We're together for good," I say firmly, beaming. She nods and takes my hand delicately, leading me forward and leaving the boy in the bird mask behind.

I'm ushered inside by castle servants and maids who are eager to meet me and showered with affection.

"It's the princess!"

"Oh, she's gorgeous!"

"What a darling!"

"Alright, Alright! Clear off, give the *Aalipa* some space!" a girl snaps at them through the crowd. "She's reuniting with her mother for the first time in her life! Come on, now, clear off! Hey, you, with the rag on your head—!"

"It's a bonnet, Misstsu! For the humidity—"

"I don't blooming care! Come on, now!" she cries angrily, ushering the girl away from me. I can't help but giggle, and she throws me a look, her narrow eyes sharp with concentration. "Something wrong, Your Highness?"

"No, I was just laughing. Are you... uh... are you a maid?"

She folds her arms sternly, towering over me in a way

that suggests he's not quite accustomed to her height, and under the hard glare of her piercing eyes, I can't help but feel intimidated. She reminds me of Spok in how she holds herself, and something about her youthful face gives me the impression that she's been forced to grow up far too quickly.

She brushes a stray strand of jet-black hair from her face. It's cropped into a short bob and twisted into a firm bun at the back. "I'm the High Supreme Maid Ultimate, if you please. Head of Housework, Royal Bed-maker, Soldier, Chef, Sister, Advisor... whatever you wish to call it. These staff members answer to me either way. I also work in the military, help out in farming, and lend a hand to the locals doing this and that. Name's Tsubasa, but you can call me Tsu," she says with an authoritative, no-nonsense tone, "And I already know you, of course."

"I think everyone does," I say with a weak smile. "Why did that woman call you... what was it... Misu?"

"Misstsu. Miss-Tsu. Miss-Tsubasa. In Flai Latin, you combine someone's title with their name, usually with an apostrophe in-between. The locals around here speak mostly Flai Latin and English, so they picked up a few things, and in places, the languages mesh together and things. The correct word is really "Mij'tsu" or "Mij'Tsubasa", but don't worry, you'll get used to it, *Aalipa*," she adds, laughing light-heartedly at the look of befuddlement on my face.

"Ally-*what?*" I blurt.

She chuckles again and shakes her head, sending ripples down the straight black, shoulder-length hair framing her face. She seems stern, but her eyes are kind, young, and adventurous. She draws herself up to her full height, giving the impression that she is someone who carries a great amount of responsibility on their shoulders. "It means "princess" in Flai Latin. The maids speak it quite often, but you don't have to. Anyway, welcome to the Realm, kid. You might see me around the castle quite a bit. By the way, if you have any questions, I'd be happy to introduce you to any of our... ah... customs," she says. The young woman then turns to the Queen and bows respectfully. "Your Majesty, I believe you wished to take the princess on a tour? Unless you'd like an escort, I have duties to attend to."

"*Uvalyna*. You are dismissed," Mother nods, then gives a start. "Oh! Sparrow! Dear me, I forgot you existed. Tsubasa, please ensure he... finds his way to the servants' quarters. Leave them to deal with him."

I don't like the way that sounds, nor do I like the way he shuffles forward without a complaint.

"Where are they going?" I ask, trying to keep my voice casual.

"Just down to the dungeons, which also happens to be where we train our homefetches. There are certain procedures we have to do to ensure the safety of my people. He'll be searched and then receive extra training as punishment for his actions. Training is rather intense but beneficial. It'll do him well," the Queen answers.

"But... they won't hurt him?" I press.

"He endangered you. He will face the consequences of that. The only pain that human will feel is the pain of resistance to training. And who in their right mind would do that when they're learning new skills? Is there an issue?"

"Right... but can't I at least say goodbye? I'll be spending the next few days with you, after all."

She inhales sharply. "Surely you've spent enough time together already?"

"I know, but still... He told me we might not get to spend much time together now. I'll miss him."

She scoffs. "If that boy knew what was good for him, you wouldn't. You shall soon learn, Raven, that humans are manipulative no matter their upbringing or education. The lot of them are rotten. Please don't forget that. It puts every man, woman, and child in this Kingdom in danger."

I don't reply to that, only turn to face Sparrow and creep over to him. "I suppose this is goodbye for now."

"Yeah. I'll see you around the palace... maybe," he nods.

"Thank you for bringing me here."

"Anytime," he whispers, lowering his voice so that only I can hear.

I lean my head closer to him and lower my tone to a whisper. "You'll be okay, won't you?"

"Of course. Trust me, it's less bad than I thought," he says, smiling reassuringly. "I can take some extra training. It's no big deal. We'll both be alright. We always are. We're Raven and Sparrow."

Mother clears her throat loudly, and Sparrow quickly moves away from me. "Goodbye," he mumbles, avoiding my eyes under Mother's intense gaze.

"Wait!" I gasp.

"Raven, I have to *go*!"

"I-I'll miss you," I finally get out. Then I grip his arm tightly. "Sparrow, if they do anything to you... anything at all..." I take a shaky breath. "We'll leave. I promise. And I'll... I'll destroy them. I'll *destroy them*, I swear it."

He can't look at me. "Until Japan, Asgard."

That's good. It's an agreement of sorts. A pledge to flee to safety with me, even if that safety is inaccessible and unrealistic.

"Until Japan," I whisper back.

Mother sweeps me up with her dress and her charm, placing a hand on my shoulder and beginning to steer me out of the room. But as we walk away, I turn and catch a final glimpse of the boy in the bird mask. Silent, timid, scared. Ducking his head and being marched away forcefully.

We'll both be alright. We always are.

I'm not convinced.

CHAPTER 36

It's impossible not to gawk at everything. Even the entrance hall we stand in is a thousand times larger than my old shack in the Frost Kingdom, and the walls are patterned with intricately carved diamonds and squares, painted perfectly without a patch or a scrape. The ceiling rises into a beige dome painted with vibrant flowers.

The room branches into two passages on either side, leading to long hallways bathed in glorious candlelight. A window of interlocked blue and silver glass shapes allows screened light to beam onto my mother's face. She's captivating as the filtered colours dance across her skin, rippling like water.

I try to imagine her in Flai form for a moment... how would she look with wings? And what kind of Flai is she? Do my powers stem from my father, or is Mother a Fire Flai, too? Like me, does she possess at least a little control over all four elements?

"I know you have so many questions," Mother says, as though reading my mind, "But the day is growing old, and we have so little time, so let's begin, shall we?"

"Begin what?" I frown.

"The tour, of course. Naturally, we're starting here. Or, I should say, right through that door."

I follow her gaze to a set of double wooden doors that lead into the next room, and she nods encouragingly. I stride forward and cautiously push them open.

I previously thought the foyer was impressive, but this is a dream. Golden arches separate the wraparound corridor from the rest of the chamber, and seemingly unsupported floating staircases wind up to a balcony that extends over my head and disappears out of sight.

An enormous, deep, indigo rug obscures the stone-tiled floor, silencing my footsteps. There are bookshelves and armchairs everywhere, making the palace feel homely yet formal simultaneously, and the wallpaper is the sort you get only in the richest houses of Ra, soft and smooth to the touch, with absolutely no gaps between the sheets and raised areas mimicking the shapes of blooming roses that you can trace for hours.

"What... how did you build all this?" I breathe, fascinated.

Mother only laughs. "We can fly, Raven. There's almost nothing we can't do."

I smile in sheer dumbfoundedness.

"Upstairs, we have guest rooms and army commanders' offices. There's also a lovely little library and a study for my personal use— of course, you are welcome anytime, but knocking is always polite. Let's see... we have the map room, where you can find a scale model of the kingdom; that's on the third floor. And lastly, your room is straight through those doors ahead, to the double doors on your right, left, right, and last door on the right of that corridor. But if that's too much of a trek, you can always go back into the foyer, right, left, straight on, right, last door on the right at the end of the corridor."

"Am I expected to remember all this?" I ask sheepishly.

"Don't worry, you'll get used to it," Mother chuckles.

"That's what Tsubasa said about the language here, and I don't think I'll ever grasp a word of complex Flai Latin. I can only have a basic conversation in it."

"That's more than what eighty per cent of Evrilore can do. I think you'll manage. She's quite a handy one, that girl, but she comes across as stony. It's a responsibility thing, I believe, to do with her role in her family. She looks after her sisters alone." Her words wither into a thoughtful silence. Then she looks back at me and smiles, snapping back to reality. "Anyhow, don't be discouraged. I'm sure you'll be speaking fluently in no time. I can tutor you myself. Anyway, this is the throne room, where you'll find me most of the time," she says casually, opening the second set of double doors.

Now, we enter a room that stretches up to cover the height of three floors, with a hall running around the room separated from us only by marble pillars that support a balcony above. At the back of the room, seemingly miles away, a grandfather clock ticks with another stained glass window above it, depicting emerald ropes with snake heads intersecting as they attempt to unknot themselves.

But the real centrepiece of the room is the throne itself. It's just the same as how they describe them in fairy tales, only grander and better. Golden and cushioned with typical red fabric that looks thick enough to drown in, it's elevated on a platform high enough to require three steps to reach it.

While I gape at her side, she struts calmly onwards, announcing her movements. "Next, I'll show you the dining room. Right through here," Mother smiles, gesturing to an arch on the west side of the room.

Through it, I can see a large table, already set for dinner, the silverware polished and pristine. There are three knives and forks beside each plate, three napkins, two spoons, and four neatly stacked plates. *Four!* For someone who's crammed food into a starving stomach with bare, grimy hands, it makes me dizzy beyond belief and wild with childish excitement.

I find myself smiling uncontrollably at the thought of dinners with Mother. I trace the smell of food back to a half wall, which I can only assume acts as a staircase's bannister. I stroll over to it, taking in the beautiful artwork hanging on the walls depicting the wondrous beauty of the Flai Realm, and then peer over the side.

"You won't find much down there, just a few staff and the kitchens," Mother shrugs.

"Can I see?" I ask.

"Do you like cooking?" Mother enquires.

"I just want to see everything," I explain.

The kitchen is a bustling underground chamber with steam rising from pans everywhere and divine scents dancing, untamed, through the air. The maids are running around calling to one another, preoccupied with cooking, but quickly desert their posts to hurriedly welcome me, introducing themselves one by one.

"Hello," I whisper, looking down at a small child who looks no older than six. "What are you doing here?"

"I'm on a special school trip," she giggles, "They're teaching us to make bread. I'm Lily-Rose. You're the princess!"

"That's right!" I nod, pretending to make a disapproving expression at the sticky dough on her hands. "Bread, huh? What kind is this messy dough meant to be!?"

"What *kind* of bread? It's bread!" she exclaims, frowning as though I'm ridiculous.

"Oh." That's all I can say. *Kids.* Then I notice the rounder shape of her jawline and the bright, frosty blue of her hooded eyes. "Hey, Lily, are you related to Tsubasa?"

"You know Tsu? She's my sister!" the girl squeals, "And I'm

going to be big, big, big, someday, just like her. Wait 'till I tell my friends the princess knows my sissy! I'll be famous!"

"Bet you will," I say with a wink, grinning at her. "Well, you keep working hard, alright? Bread won't bake itself. The dough looks delicious, though."

She nods, flushing with pride, and then begins to file back into the depths of the endless kitchen with everyone else. I chuckle as Lily walks away. "She's cute. I like her. Do they come here often? Kids, I mean?" I ask, turning back to my mother.

"Regularly, actually. We try to train them young, not just in one speciality, but in lots. They'll come to the kitchens for a day, work on the farms for a day, try safety patrols, and things like that. That's one of the good things about being such a basic town here. We don't do anything unnecessary. There's no point teaching kids maths they'll never use, for example. Instead, it's better to prioritize life skills and an understanding of Flai anatomy. We have farmers to produce food, castle staff to run the castle, an army to protect us, and the Highest Order. Everyone does their part, even the kids, and we all enjoy doing it."

"What's the Highest Order?"

"Think of it like the League, except they answer to me, not decide who takes my position. They're appointed by me, and they have the most crucial roles here. The army advisors, the squadron leaders... other people."

"Like?" I prompt, but she waves me away, unrevealing and cool.

For the first time, she appears almost intimidating, and when she speaks, her authoritative tone sends a shiver down my spine that makes me feel as though I ought to snap my lips shut. "Irrelevant. Now, where would you like to go next? Outside?" she asks.

"No, upstairs. Please," I add. The stiffness in my voice as I awkwardly attempt to stop her from derailing the light-hearted mood doesn't go unnoticed.

"Sorry for being cold," Mother says quickly. "It's just that... Raven, you already know I created my throne and claimed a position of power when the people of this realm were vulnerable. And I know how that looks, and I know how it sounds. I don't want to tell you anything that will give you the wrong impression of me until the time is right. I can and will answer all your questions, but first, I want you to feel comfortable here. To dump politics and complicated matters of power on your shoulders is not my intention. I want to mother you above all."

I gaze at her with newfound understanding, seeing for the first time not a leader nor a secretive, cool persona treating me like a fascinated, innocent little child. I see a parent trying desperately to entice her daughter into her world. I see someone gripping onto something.

"I lost my friends and watched them destroy my sister. Whatever you've done, I've seen worse. You don't have to protect me, Mother," I whisper. "I understand what you're trying to do, and I understand what's at stake. I won't judge you for trying to save what you love because I did that over and over again. I always will. We're Flai. It's what we do."

Her face lights up, and she nods. With me latched onto her arm, we set off going back the way we came.

As we walk, I notice that some of the furniture that lines the walls is obviously and shamelessly unused and newly crafted, worth at least seven hundred shackles apiece. Once we reach the top of the staircase and I have the opportunity to peek inside each door, I also spot countless four-poster beds, all made yet unslept in.

"How did you afford all this?" I splutter.

"Not all of the Realm was destroyed in the Fall, you

know," the Queen replies, but she catches the sceptical look in my eyes. "And we... borrow a few things."

"Borrow?" I repeat with an arched brow.

She sighs in brief annoyance, but her lips still curl up in an undeniable smile. "I can tell you're going to be a handful, Raven."

"Wouldn't dream of it," I grin.

The first room we enter is The Map Room. From its state of intense disorder, I can sense almost the moment I cross the threshold that this place is always in use. Even as we enter, I must duck to avoid a web of papers strung together. Desks hidden beneath stacks of books and illustrations are crammed into every corner, and above them, bright colour-coded pins hold files together on the walls.

The questions begin to spew almost immediately from my mouth, thrown so quickly at Mother that they could be an onslaught of archers' arrows. She laughs throughout my breathless gabbering of observations and inquiries but never grows impatient, describing things to me vividly and animating her face to bring it all to life. I eagerly listen to tales of squadron leaders and Air Flai, who prevented others from being crushed by landslides. She tells me of hidden ancient houses at the bottom of rivers, and hammocks strung up between trees by the river bordering the southwest side of the realm.

The centrepiece of the room is quite possibly one of the most amazing things I've ever seen. Sculpted from real moss, leaves, twigs, mud, water, fur, and flowers, it's constructed onto a clay base that perfectly mimics the relief of the landscape, an immaculate model of the Realm, lifelike to the touch. I stare in awe at the Jade Palace, small enough to hold between my finger and my thumb. A real waterfall trickles from its base, joining a larger lake at the bottom. Every tree is carved individually, and every blade of grass is sharpened to perfection.

Eventually, Mother draws back from the table and gestures to the door. "Wouldn't you like to see everything for yourself?"

"In the forest?" I ask, surprised.

"Yes. I've arranged for us to have lunch in the gardens overlooking the northeast forest, and then a fleet will transport us to the north of the kingdom. Or, if you wish to bathe and get dressed first, that is fine."

"No, thank you. I'm really hungry. But..." I'm hesitant, suddenly worried that amongst so many adults with fully developed powers, I should be embarrassed. "When you say "transport"... You do know I can't fly yet?"

"Naturally. Most Flai only develop the ability to fly at sixteen or seventeen. And you are—"

"Fifteen just a few months ago. But I don't celebrate my birthday," I explain.

"Oh?"

"Bronwyn's idea. We celebrate —well, *celebrated*, I suppose— *Deittae* instead."

"Is that Sun Tongue?"

I nod. "It means union— *Deittae* celebrates life and the infinite flow of energy between all things. People choose when to celebrate their own specific existences, so it's more personal. Why celebrate an uncomfortably hot summer's day when you love nothing more than to watch the graceful descent of snowflakes onto the earth? It's about choosing something —or somewhere— you love and celebrating your coexistence with it. I chose the bluebells in the Frost Wilderness when they open their petals just after Ice Tide."

Mother pauses, taking in my words, then beams. "Well, that's *quite* delightful. May I ask why you chose the bluebells?"

"They remind me of a very special moment I shared with my best friend in the whole world. Something he showed me about resilience."

"That's lovely. But... Raven?" she says hesitantly, looking uncomfortable. "I-I really am so sorry about what happened to your friends." It's the first time she looks genuinely uncertain of herself or what to do. The first mark of a crack in her grand facade.

I offer a strained, thin smile in reply.

First, we cross the palace gardens to make our way down the hill. It's a beautiful array of orchards and melting frost, a rainbow of flowers and fruit. The majority of them are still buds, just beginning to spread out their petals after winter. In spring, it'll be truly lovely.

We chat about the palace, my childhood, and how I survived all these years. I explain the full story of the Berg to her, stopping abruptly at Peter's death. I know she'll surely disapprove of betraying him the way I did, and if she was aware that it was Sparrow who held me back, he might never see the light of day again.

However, that doesn't mean I'm shy about Wynn. Every word I speak is carved out of spite, out of anger, and, eventually, out of love. While the Bronwyn who abandoned me and hates me roams vengeful, the little sister who I met in a marketplace in Ra is stained into my heart. I know who she is, beneath the trauma and the pain, and I miss her so much it physically aches.

When we reach the gardens outside of the castle, a table is already laid for us with a pretty, delicate cloth and polished silverware. My fork looks wrong in my grimy hand, clenched by bruised knuckles, and my self-cut hair is jagged and ugly in the reflection.

"What are we having?" I enquire, looking around. There's no food in sight.

"What do you like?" she prompts, expectant.

What do I like? I don't like things. I'm Flai.

"Um... tea?" I guess, vague.

Almost immediately, a server appears beside us, balancing a china teapot and two mugs.

"*Aalipa,*" she says, bowing respectfully to me, and then she rubs her palms together slowly to my mother, bowing her head.

Mother returns the gesture, and I stare between them with fascination. "What's that?" I ask the girl.

Her head snaps up, her expression quite startled, and she almost drops the tray.

"S-Sorry," I say quickly, "If I startled you."

Speechless, the server hurries away. Perplexed, I turn to my mother.

"She doesn't speak much English. And we don't tend to speak to the servers much," Mother adds, lifting her teacup and taking a delicate sip. Her lipstick leaves a tiny red blotch on the rim.

I stare at her until she meets my eyes, then clear my throat loudly. "So... How did you find out about me?"

"You're forward," she laughs, her beautiful dark locks bouncing off her shoulders.

I raise my eyebrows, and she clucks her tongue at my impatience, then reaches for a packet of sugar. I watch as it hisses softly out of the paper sachet and disappears into the drink. Then Mother selects a spoon to stir her tea with, taps it against the side of the mug, and sits back, satisfied.

"I always knew you were out there. Always. It's why I sent

spies and homefetches to find you. Nearly three years ago, when we first discovered the holes in the shield... It was the first time I truly considered... I mean, I never thought I'd see you again..." she pauses in something close to confusion, as though she's still rather dumbfounded by the fact that I am here, and I am alive, and we are together.

"I'm sorry for what happened to us. Sorry that we never knew one another," I whisper, and she nods. "But I also need an explanation. Why did I grow up away from you? I have to know."

She sighs. "I was worried about this. Worried that you'd be angry at me. I mean, a homefetch coming to find you after fifteen years with wild claims about still having a family? And then everything with your friends. I should've done something... should've been there."

"I don't care about that," I say quickly. "Peter had nothing to do with you. Don't be sorry." I change the subject. "Why didn't you come for me yourself?"

She stiffens. "I can't abandon my duties here. The homefetches bring back somebody new every week, and almost every person is alone. These people need me to reintroduce the concept of community and trust into their lives. For some, a leader's all they have."

"Duties? I'm your *child*," I blurt, stung, before I can stop myself.

She reaches for my hand, which I reluctantly give. "I know. I'm really sorry for forgetting what's important. I should've just come myself, and I admit that I was a coward."

I can't meet her eyes. "Why did you leave me? All those years ago... why did you *go*?"

Mother diverts her eyes from me, wiping her mouth with a napkin, "Before I say anything, I just want to tell you that I had you at a ridiculously young age. I knew almost straight away that I couldn't raise you, couldn't protect you. Your father was violent, and we had arguments almost every day, especially as the Fall neared. He wanted, having already drained himself of magic, to humanize us both and move out of the Realm. One night, I returned home to find his bed empty and his belongings gone."

"He left us?" I ask, horrified.

"Yes. But I don't believe it was entirely his own choice. There was the mindlocust, of course, which I trust you know of?"

I nod, struggling to find words. "Do you know where he went? Where he is now?"

She laughs. "Of course I know where he went, Raven. He took you with him."

I frown, leaning forward on my crossed arms. "But I was adopted. Why would he take me only to abandon me?"

"*Abandon* you?" she repeats, disbelieving, "He- He had a second wife, Raven! A second family. A human one. No one ever abandoned you— that family was yours."

My mouth is a desert. *Papa.*

"I don't... why am I not... why would he leave me like this?" I cry, gesturing to myself, "If he wanted a human daughter, he should've had one! He could've!"

She thoughtfully spoons a mouthful of soup between her lips. "I think that perhaps he convinced himself, with the help of the disease, that you were human. You have half-siblings, don't you?"

"Louis. Chloe," I reply flatly.

She nods slowly. "And I'm guessing you've not seen them since—?"

"No," I reply sharply.

She sighs sympathetically. "Your father may not have

been entirely truthful, but the rest of your family was innocent, Raven. And even your Papa didn't know what he was doing. You can't blame the people who only ever tried to love you."

"Is that what that was? Love?" I ask quietly.

"Raven—"

"He was alive and well for six years, Mother. If he had the virus, it would've killed him."

"Not everyone died. People like him crafted their own realities and drove themselves crazy... but it didn't kill them. And your father, whether humanized or not, was Flai. Which meant he was always stronger against it than others."

The distorted, forgotten faces of Tata and Maman drift through my memory, swirling like disrupted water in a deep, long-forgotten well. My family, who I blamed and hated... and yet, a family who were all blinded by one manipulative man.

"The shield didn't appear until 2040. For at least a year, you could've found me. Taken me back," I whisper, barely able to string words together.

Mother tears her gaze away, nodding to herself. Eventually, she speaks softly. "Was she kind?"

"Who?"

"His wife."

I blink, trying to summon memories I've tried to forget. "She was."

"And good?"

"Faithful," I nod.

"Then I am glad I did not come for you. You deserved at least a good mother."

"She's not my mother," I say coldly.

"She's as much as I. And even then, a finer woman. I

hope…" her voice turns wobbly and thin, "I hope she was very beautiful." Then, Mother turns back to me. "And I hope you were happy."

"I was a child, confused and terrified. And she- she *cowered*," I gasp. "She may have raised me, but she wasn't there."

"Was I?"

"At least you looked," I choke through thick, hot tears. Then curiosity spikes me sharply. "You… you *looked*… But how? How did you know where I was? Know I was alive?"

"Frost Flood Tide of February 2053," she recites.

My jaw sets, and the warmth leaves my blood. I know that date off by heart. I can remember every detail and look back through my own eyes without a single imperfection in my memory.

It's the day my friends were arrested.

There's something no one ever tells you about adrenaline. I mean, real adrenaline. When you know you're under the cat's paw, and no matter what you do, it still has your tail.

All your senses are amplified, and your peripheral vision kicks in. Every breath that streams from your mouth tickles the hairs on your upper lip and communicates with the rest of your muscles. And you *store it*. You store the moments of absolute terror. The memories never turn hazy, never fade.

They just rot.

Slowly.

"The reports… they had a description of me?" I ask steelily.

"They hide everything from the citizens of Evrilore. A Flai escaped, and she's running wild? Does that sound like control to you?" she asks.

I press my lips together, my eyes wide and immersed.

"The problem with hiding things is that they still exist. The past still happened, and not everyone was quiet. When you were spotted fleeing Frost by eyewitnesses," she continues, "I knew I had to send someone to find you. But you were tricky. Almost impossible to trace."

"How many people were looking?"

"A team of twenty. When the time came to confront you, a few volunteered. Others wouldn't do the job. Not on a Flood Tide. I thought your timing of leaving Frost was very clever, by the way. To use Floodonora as a cover when nobody would suspect a Flai to even set foot near the market? It's brilliantly stealthy."

The server returns with fruit, cheese, and a scalding bowl of soup. Mother pours me more tea, muttering that it has gone cold.

I wait until the girl disappears again. "Do you know how the Guard found us? It was such a specific location, and I didn't leave any trails. At first, I thought maybe Sparrow—"

"It *was* someone on the inside," she nods, confirming my thoughts, "I suspect it was one of our spies who knew the plan. Or, there is indeed a possibility that..."

"He wouldn't," I interrupt quickly.

"I said the same about your father."

✱ ✱ ✱

As we stroll through the village, I notice multiple construction sites and gathered piles of wood, nails, and tools.

Small children are climbing on some of them, waving happily at us as we pass. The sun beats down hot on my neck, the weather reflecting my mood, and I know that the only thing that could make this moment better is if Sparrow could be here with me. Walking beside me and telling me about each person. Mother can do it, too, but it just isn't the same. She's not one of them in a way that I can't quite explain.

"I still can't believe how far we've come since the Fall," I say, "You definitely had a lot of cleaning up to do."

"Well, it took time, but we're getting there," she smiles. "What the people needed after the Fall was a leader, something to hold on to and have faith in, and I gave them one."

"All the houses you're building... it's amazing," I grin. "But... what's it for?"

"Well, the revolution, of course," she says matter-of-factly.

"What?"

"Driving this kingdom into a new age," she continues.

"Oh... Sparrow told me about your plans to make peace treaties, but it didn't sound like a... revolution."

"Well, it's going to take a lot of fighting to get the king to see sense. But don't think of it like a second Fall. Hopefully, everything will go smoothly, and there'll be no physical fighting. It's the laws preventing us from having rights to safety and life that need to be changed so we can finally come out of hiding. And to change the law, we're talking about meetings, parades, propaganda, debates, bargaining, and maybe even threats... But we'll never attack first, Raven. It's not who we are. We are peaceful people— that is the most important principle we hold ourselves to here."

I exhale, relieved. But the concept of human massacre leaves my muscles a little tensed even after the moment passes. "You must be excited, of course," Mother goes on, "Finally getting exactly what you always dreamed of."

What did I dream of? Freedom, a normal life, and

acceptance... Sparrow's face flashes across my mind. Then Boots and Shackles.

"I don't know," I say quietly.

"Hm?" Mother frowns, turning to me, "Whatever do you mean? Flai are going to be free."

"No, it's not that. I was just thinking... things here are great, but... I don't know how we could ever make everything normal again. Sparrow said that humans aren't welcome here, and that just made me wonder. He said that because there was a chance that he put me in danger... you might... hurt him," I finish, guilt fizzing in my stomach. "And if that's how things'll be after your revolution... still abiding by the same old rules about sticking with our own kind..."

She stares at me until I trail off. "Raven. We are not going to hurt Sparrow."

"He seemed really scared," I say quietly, "Like it'd happened before. *Has* it happened before?"

She draws herself up to her full height and lays a hand on my shoulder. "I didn't want to be the one to do this. But I must because actions of love are involuntary."

"What are you talking about?" I mutter.

"You told me to stop trying to protect you. And I will agree to stop now because what I am about to reveal to you will hurt you a thousand times less than Sparrow can. He's been alone with you for almost three months. You've fought together, saved your friend together, saved one another. That's what you think. It's what you saw. But was there ever anything else to see? As I said, you were alone."

"Sparrow is my friend," I say coldly, glaring at her.

"Sparrow is just a man, as I am just a woman. He is not incapable of wrong, no matter what traits he displays under your gaze. I wish your experiences and revelations were true, Raven. I wish for you to connect and laugh and cry and love.

I *do*. But the hunters in the Frost Wilderness did not just happen to stumble upon you, and Sparrow did think you couldn't enter that lake. I understand that those facts alone are cause for only brief suspicion, but his behaviours proceeded to grow questionable beyond logical explanations. Tell me, Raven: who stayed healthy during a blizzard while you almost died from hypothermia, forcing you to rely on him, trust him, and sleep beside him? And how did he stay so pristine?"

"He's stronger than I am. He eats well," I blurt.

"Or," she says gently, "He had something. And he didn't share it with you."

I stare at her, shaking my head slowly.

"Oh, Raven... Open your eyes! He led you into the most heavily armed prison in Evrilore's waters and killed your best friend, cornering you into emotional vulnerability, weakening your defences. He slept in your room at Boots and Shackles, did he not? You didn't even question the rapid development of physical closeness."

"You don't know that," I breathe, "*How do you know that?*"

"Forget *me*. How did *Bronwyn* know your location on the plains? Why did the Zeun not kill Sparrow? How, why, where, who? So many questions. I have the answers, Raven. I *had* to have them because I almost lost you again. Please just understand, for one moment, that I'm protecting you. I'm your mother, and I want you to be safe," she says desperately, taking my face into her hands. "*I* let this happen. Do you understand? This is *my* responsibility. And it hurts me to see that you were hurt. It hurts me to see that familiar sheen of naivety in your eyes that *I* once possessed, because I was hurt my by youthful hope, too. You were right about humans and right about him. He convinced you that your suspicions were unjust, cruel, and a result of paranoia, but your heart knew, Raven. You always knew."

"I-I don't believe you," I stammer.

She's relentless, listing every one of Sparrow's unexplained actions that my heart blockaded. "You made peace with Bronwyn, didn't you? She seemed like she'd be okay with your support. But he got into her head, and she left you. *Spok* left you. Once again, it was you and Sparrow. That was the way it had to be. The way he made it. Don't you *see*?"

"Stop. *Stop!*" I cry.

Mother runs her hands down my jawline and strokes her thumbs on my shoulders. Back and forth, gently. "Spok is a good woman. She made you stronger. And he took *her* away. Bronwyn made you a stronger team, so he took her away. And then, finally, he could get you arrested and be rewarded with anything he wanted in the world. Nobody could help you. *No one*," she breathes, letting the word hang in the air.

"That's not true!" I'm helpless, a spectator of time, as I plummet and spiral, trying to catch my stomach as it leaps wildly out of my chest, making my head spin. "T-The guards. We fought them off at the inn and on the plains, though. We did it together," I whisper, grasping for something to believe in.

"Yet, *you* started the fire. *You* saved yourself."

"Why didn't he get me arrested at Willows, then?" I demand. I'm half-shouting, terrified.

"He tried. You climbed into a cart, Raven. A Floodonora cart that just *happened* to pass you. My spies watched you do it. And why?"

There's only one answer.

"Because he told me to," I reply numbly. "A-And in Willows?" I ask, afraid to hear the answer. All the torn scraps of mistrust and biased filtered reality fit together now. The truth dawns on me before I'm even given a reply.

"You're so lucky that the guards didn't find you. The

guards that *my* spies drugged. That trader was never an alcoholic, nor were the guards. Any good, life-saving coincidence you encountered was the craftsmanship of me. Of Flai. Of "the bad guys who'd hurt Sparrow"."

"How did you..." I shake my head as my insides knot themselves.

"When Sparrow failed at the border, he staged the fight between you in the woods and destroyed your self-confidence, eventually insisting on taking you to the gates even after you said it was a stupid idea and a child's fantasy, to get you back in the town centre. Don't you see, Raven? Your safety is owed only to the Flai who picked you up and my underground intelligence network. Not to that boy. You owe nothing to the traitor who only used you as a tool for his fame and riches. And he..." Her facade slips for a second like a flickering lightbulb. Through the cracks, I can see only blistering rage. It's fresh. "He will pay for what he did to you. For what he did to my child."

I take deep, heavy breaths to steady myself. "Tell me how he did it," I say slowly.

She presses her lips together anxiously.

"Tell me! How did he lie? How didn't I know? Who did he contact!?" I shriek.

"Raven—"

"NO! I-I don't understand... how could this happen to me? I was so... so *cold*," I gasp. "I did everything to push him away... I left him to die... and yet he still found me, which means he had people posted, watching me... he knew where I was! TELL ME HOW!" I bellow.

Her eyes glitter with tears. "It happened because he was genuine. It was all genuine in his mind— the friendship, I mean. He simply inflicted the wound and plastered it with kind hands. He's a psychopath with empathy. He fell for you, knowing what he was going to do to you. Knowing he'd stray from his mission and have you arrested. Human or Flai... whatever he is, he's dangerous."

A long pause in which I compose myself and shuffle through my millions of thoughts. "You *will* hurt him," I state quietly.

Mother looks down at me, surprised. "How can you care for him, knowing all of this? He doesn't care about you, Raven. No matter what he said to you... words are just words. People lie and steal and kill and hurt. People do love, but that's not what this is. He isn't your friend."

It cuts into me. Deep. Cruel.

I open and close my mouth but can't find a response.

Mother sees it in my eyes and sighs, hanging her head. "This... this is wrong. I should've waited until you were ready."

I look up to the sky, then down at my feet, my eyes wide and accusatory as though I expect them to crumble into lies, too. "How can you... how can you possibly know all of this?" I ask weakly, my eyes stinging with tears.

"I wouldn't have had you followed if I trusted that boy," she replies.

I'm speechless, as though someone's torn out my insides, and my vocal cords refuse to produce sound. I simply stare at the floor, unable to make any sense of the world around me.

Who's real, and who is not? What feelings from the past three months were real, and which were manufactured by a manipulator?

"Mum," I whisper.

"Yes?"

"Can we go to the forest?"

"What?"

"I think..." I say slowly, testing out the stepping stones of a new worldview. "I need to be with my own kind... for a while," I nod, becoming more sure of myself. "I think that'll make me feel better."

Mother lowers herself onto one knee and takes my face in her hands again, her eyes flitting from side to side as she takes in every inch of me. She looks deeply sorrowful. "I need you to promise me that no human, no man, will ever take from you what your father did. And what Sparrow did. Let me assure you that there is nothing more painful for a woman than watching her sisters be crushed by soulless, shallow men." Her eyes are wide and desperate and absolutely aching with regret. "Letting either of those people touch you was the worst decision I ever made."

"Maybe I am," I mumble.

"Hm?"

Maybe I'm the worst decision you ever made. "Forget it. It's nothing," I reply

She stares at me for a long time. "I love you, Raven. I *love you*. I'm *real*."

"But how would I ever know? None of it— none of *him* was," I whisper.

Her arms are around me in moments, her body failing to shield me from the agony. Even so, I bury myself in her perfumed chest.

Hiding.

We set out for our destination with the air all around me suddenly so heavy with deception and lies that it's crushing me.

I press myself so closely to my mother that I disappear, enveloped by the folds of her dress.

It's no place we can easily access simply, no one-mile walk, so several adult Flai are summoned to fly me across the land. We make our way up a hill to what Mother refers to as the "Drop-off zone".

For a moment, it's just the two of us, and the silent rustling of the trees sounds toxic and aloof in my hyper-vigilant ears.

I almost want to sink my head into Mother again and cry, but surprisingly, that thought conjures up another image in my mind— another woman entirely. "Spok," I whisper.

Tears prick my eyes the moment her name is carried off my lips. Where she must be, what awful punishment she'll be facing, all for my actions, all for Sparrow's manipulative, deceptive trickery.

I can't seem to settle on an emotion, can't seem to process what's been done to me. Manipulation, platonic infatuation? The world spins on a thwarted axis.

I'm thrust back into reality at an alarming speed, my thoughts dying, for all of a sudden, I'm surrounded by unexpected beauty.

If the village alone impressed me, this is something of a dream.

Spilling into the clearing and preparing to transport Mother and I are men and women of all shapes and sizes, all in their full Flai forms, unafraid and unashamed, in a neat diamond formation, their wings spanning out and sweeping air toward me.

Each Flai is unique. I have known this since I was a toddler when they taught us about the opposite species in school. Every Flai has something that can be used to recognize them individually. Whether it's the shade of their feathers (females are naturally darker) or the bright colour of their eyes, they all look different.

They ruffle their wings casually as though it is no big deal at all, and I watch them prepare to take flight in awe. One day, I will be able to stand amongst my fellow Flai and do what they are doing.

One day, I will not be ashamed to be who I am.

"We call this a fleet or a squadron," Mother says proudly as the Flai rise into the air. "The ones at the rear are the strongest, and usually Air Flai, so they help everyone stay in flight when we get tired. At the front are Earth Flai, to push through the undergrowth when our fleets do daily perimeter checks in the dense jungle at the edges of the Realm."

"You do perimeter checks?" I frown.

"Of course we do. With every Flai's death, the shield grows weaker, and we never know when a new weak spot may appear."

"There're... more than a few?"

"Unfortunately, yes, at least ten now... but we cross those bridges when we come to them. For now, our population is relatively stable, and it is not a major issue, though many Flai did die on the Berg, and so the villagers are being quite pressured to have more children. Ah— here we go!" she says brightly, turning back to the fleet, who are all flapping in perfect unison and slowly rising into the air. The fleet is now complete. "Alright, everyone, as you will know, this is my daughter, Raven. She can't fly yet, but I trust you will be able to handle her. If everyone is ready, then let's go!" Striding into the middle, she lets her own feathers unfold behind her, and her skin turns an identical chalk white to my own.

I hurry after her, and the diamond of villagers encloses us. I catch sight of Tsubasa and smile warmly at her. She returns the gesture with a respectful bow.

"So, er, how exactly does this work?" I ask, glancing up at my mother as she stands directly in front of me. The villagers all smile kindly at me and bow before shaking my hands.

One by one, they pass me in a perfect pattern of swapping and replacing the empty spots of their friends, hovering above the ground before retreating back to their positions. I enquire again about the process, and in response, the villagers sweep up into the air in a sharp, steep curve, and I'm caught in the gust of wind generated by the sheer force of their bodies rocketing up like shooting stars.

A scream escapes my mouth before I can stop it, and the fleet laughs as they twirl and spiral, rising higher and higher above the trees. "Why are we going so fast!?" I cry.

"What? You want to go faster?" Tsu grins from beside me.

"NO!" I yell.

"What was that? I'm sorry, I can't HEAR YOU! Come on guys, she says *FULL SPEED AHEAD!*"

Terrified, I cling to the billowing hem of my mother's dress as the fleet dips, and I plummet with them.

"Open your eyes, Aalipa!" Tsubasa calls to me. "Come on! Fly with us!"

"I can't fly!"

"Says who?"

I open my eyes, half expecting to see myself still being thrown around, but the fleet is gliding smoothly now, occasionally dipping so close to treetops that our feet skim the branches.

The Flai at the front and back are passing commands to one another, and the Flai at the sides of the fleet control whether we fly left or right. In the very distance, a great cliff awaits us, with a shimmering waterfall running through its centre. Above it, sitting on top like a perfect crown, the Jade Palace. My true origins.

"You like it now, huh?" Tsu smiles.

"No. I love it," I gasp, extending my arms out on either side of me, pretending to fly with them.

I'm higher than stars, more weightless than wind.

I soar away from icebergs and manipulators and my father, leaving my past behind. I glide as easily and naturally as a bird.

No.

As a *Raven*.

CHAPTER 37

Dizzyingly high, the fleet twirls and dips, spiralling upon invisible currents of air as we slice through clouds and descend dramatically to skim treetops. As we near the Jade Palace, the scenery thins out until the forest disappears entirely into rocky terrain that rises like stone giants into towering cliffs, water splashing grandly and violently down into huge lakes between boulders. The Flai rise sharply upwards into an almost vertical acceleration, and air rushes along my body, raising the hairs on my arms.

We rise higher and higher, shooting like a bullet toward the sky, and despite the enormous rush of air propelling me, I can feel gravity tugging me fiercely downwards.

"I'M GONNA FALL!" I scream.

"Hang on, Raven," Mother shouts calmly back to me. "Things are about to get a little steeper!"

"HOW CAN THEY POSSIBLY BE STEEPER WHEN WE ARE FLYING AT A ONE-HUNDRED-AND-EIGHTY-DEGREE ANGLE?" I cry, terrified. Then I catch sight of Mother's face. "Oh... no," I whisper. *"Surely* not."

She throws her head back in a laugh as the Flai begin to tilt backwards, flying with their torsos bent away from the cliff face. I scream again, but I'm drowned out by the rush of air that encases us.

"ALL OF YOU... ARE *CRAZY!*" I yell as the fleet flips completely over, rushes over the cliff's top, and flies upside down. I cling to the nearest Flai for dear life.

"It's quite alright, Raven," Mother calls to me, "We're landing."

What a comforting statement that is when your head's hanging backwards over a cliff in mid-air.

"*HAEKKUT!*" a woman behind me commands.

The fleet calmly bends into a perfect sweeping curve until my feet are facing the earth again, and I'm dizzier than I ever would've thought was possible. Just as my toes brush the floor, the rush of air all around me suddenly disappears, and I slam face-first into the grass.

"Ow," I say, muffled.

A sharp tug of air lifts me off the ground, dusts off my clothes (courtesy of my mother), and sets me gently back on my feet.

Before I can thank her, she turns to the Flai.

"Wait outside and line perimeter. Follow *gefokah*," Mother instructs to the fleet. "Raven and I shouldn't be more than half an hour, but you know how time can be in there. Should you receive a distress call, attend to it on my orders. Remember to prioritize the west quarter and the school."

I'm half-listening with interest, but the trickle and splash of the water running off the cliff face occupies my thoughts. It is so pure, so clear. How can water be magical?

Everything fascinates me here.

Tsubasa talks to my mother for a short while, and then, at last, the troop spreads out to surround the palace, and Mother turns back to me.

"What was all that about? What's *gephoca*?" I ask.

"*Gefokah*. It means "give and take" in Flai Latin," she explains, "It's of one the three military rulebooks here. Each set of moral principles is designed for a certain scenario. For emergencies, for safeguarding... that kind of thing. It's all about exactly how we tackle an attack. We give some, and we take some."

"Give what? *Lives*?" I splutter.

"No! No, goodness! Give way. Give... compromise, I suppose. To the enemy. It's about how much force we put towards attack and..."

"Defense?" I offer.

"Exactly. Should there be an issue, I was instructing them to follow a specific set of rules regarding the amount of resources and force we attack the enemy with and whether or not to respond to the distress calls or let the other troops do it. But you needn't worry about it because nothing will happen. These are just precautions."

"Then... what are we waiting for?" I breathe.

She sweeps an arm out to the side. "By all means, you know where the door is."

Smiling from ear to ear, I dash up to the entrance to the building, pausing at the door to lift my head and take in the sheer size and otherworldly nature of it. A hexagonal room of pure sea-green glass forms the ground level, and arches and pillars surround a cubic floor on top, reaching up to at least three times my height.

Above the second level is a cylinder-shaped room with no walls at all, just columns and open sides like large windows devoid of panes. The green tone of the walls is darker there because golden beams stream into the room, illuminating certain areas, but the rest is swallowed in shadow.

I catch a glimpse of a great spiral staircase winding up into the rafters, thinning as it reaches the top; each floor is slightly smaller than the one below it.

Sprouting up from the balcony of the flat roof of the ground floor are two curls of glass, both shaped like a backward Ss, connecting directly to the fourth and final level: a triangular-pyramidal room topped with a huge, towering roof and walls eaten away at by a hundred different plants.

It is a place where nature and Flai have both taken their course, crossed paths and emerged as one beautiful product.

I feel my joy deflate slightly. Why can't the rest of Evrilore be like this? Why can't every human on this island see what I'm seeing now and understand why they need us to save their lands? Even if Flai were sent here to destroy humans, we don't necessarily still carry that purpose in our instincts and hearts. We genuinely want to restore nature's balance.

Mother strolls up beside me, releasing a deep, satisfied sigh. "It means everything, Raven, to see that expression on your face. A longing. A drive. You are young, naive, and hurt, but you maintain a most respectable will. A drive to spark change and build something new. Tell me: looking at this building, how do you feel?"

"I can't believe it. I feel like I'm insane."

"Is it what you imagined? Is it what you hoped?"

"Everything. And more," I whisper in awe.

Her lips curl into a proud smile, and she lowers herself to eye-level with me, reaching out to tuck a strand of hair behind my ear and caress my face. "And now, I gift it to you on loan, just as it was loaned to me, your grandmother, her mother, and every Flai, ever, by these lands and the magic they hold for us. It is what we guard, what we steward, and what we fight for. A heavy burden, I know, but this palace is yours to use as you wish. To stand here alongside you and present this burden is all I have ever wanted. It means you have been reunited with your spirit, Raven. It calls to you. And I hope that you will protect it just as it has sustained the lives of Flai for thousands of years."

I nod, my jaw set. "Of course. This... this is ours. This can't be conquered, can't be overruled. This doesn't belong to Man."

The Queen gently places her hand on my shoulder. "There's a reason I brought you here, you know. And it isn't just to show you what we have to fight for. It's more than that. All your life, you've been longing for a home. You finally have one. With me and with the castle. But this, Raven? This will always be your true home. Your true origins. This is the heart of Flai. It's in me, and it's in you.

"Yes, nobody knows how Flai first came to be in this world, but there are theories. Tales as old as the rising sun. And almost every story of how we came to be on Earth starts here, Raven. This place is believed to be the bridge, the pathway, the corridor between mortals and... and *angels*. Magic and science. Humans and Flai."

Our eyes lock, me hooked on to her every word.

Mother raises one hand, and a blossom of fire sprouts from her palm, growing to dance around her fingers as she talks. "If we *do* originate from a bigger place— a different, higher place, as they say, we were bound by that place's laws of science. It's own forces, physics. Now that we are here, we are under the rule of different ones. The gravity that keeps us glued to the ground, for example. Does that exist in this different world in the sky? Nobody knows. However, we do know that magic isn't real. Not here. Not on Earth. Not while we're under its laws and facts."

A new fireball sparks to life on the floor between us, directly below Mother's outstretched hand. "My theory — what I choose to believe is correct— is that when we... *fell*, shall we say, we made a puncture in the fabric of the universe." She draws her hand away, but the fire remains in mid-air, the centre of it caving inwards as though pushed by a great force.

Suddenly, the force smashes through, and there's a

gaping hole in the fire like a devil's screeching, blazing mouth.

"Magic was attached to us, the same way we're attached to earthy by gravity. And, quite simply, it wouldn't let go— bonds of nature, bonds that made Flai what we are, couldn't be broken. So we pushed, and pushed, and forced our way through this barrier between worlds, creating a tunnel. A tunnel that we fell through, and in doing so brought our magic with us."

A tornado-like spiral of fire extends out downward as though the flames have grown a new limb, connecting to the fire on the ground, and with a crackle, the two are suddenly one mass, flickering and dancing through the dirt. "That is why we can use magic here on Earth. It is sitting on you right now, sprinkled like salt or dust. Invisible to the eye, yet most certainly there, and attracted to you like a moth to a lamp. It was brought to Evrilore —to you— by me, and my parents, and their parents, and every Flai right back to the beginning. The only problem with any of this is that magic exists *with* Flai. It cannot be without us or something from its world."

I open my hand and Mother's fire dances into my palm, attracted to me like a magnet. It recognises me— as did the shield when I touched it in Willows.

Mother's fingers sift through the air to send a current of air up my sleeve, inviting the fire to spread up my arm. It's eager, and much more so than the magic outside the realm.

"Why's it so... energetic?"

Mother smiles. "The magic you're used to is mostly recycled, consisting of not fully charged particles drifting about you like snowflakes that cannot melt, and it has passed through you many times. Here, the air is rich with magic swirling about the breezes and racing with the rivers. Consequently, the magic we use *here* passes through us, leaves, and, after quite some time, is drawn into another Flai

— meaning that it has time to rest while its unused brothers replace it. On the outside, where there was only you, there was less use for magic, so only the same old particles stuck to you while the rest thinned out over the landscape. As a result, you were weaker. But here, magic will rush to replace those old particles. Here, you will unlock your true abilities. All I ask, in telling you this, is that you use this newfound strength responsibly and that you help us save it. Once every Flai perishes, so will the magic in Evrilore and the passage that we created in coming here. Why? Because once we are all dead, Raven, there'll be no one left to return to our world. We will have failed, and magic will die."

The branch of fire connecting the top and bottom flames flickers out before my wide eyes, and the fire on my arm melts away into nothing.

"I don't understand, though. Why can't we all just use the tunnel and go home? Be *safe*?" I ask.

"The passage is... blocked. We have made attempts to leave and have been unsuccessful," Mother explains, smiling mysteriously. "I believe that we have something to prove— and that proof will act as a key. Nothing ever happens without meaning. We were sent here with a duty. And either we complete our mission, or we die trying. I choose to believe that if a certain Flai is alive, their life will be the key: there is one person who is unlike the other Flai. One person who has been born into every generation so far. They are special for a reason I cannot imagine, but if we can prove to this realm that they are alive, we prove that we have not failed. We go home."

"The prophecy child," I whisper.

"Maybe," Mother shrugs. "Perhaps we shall never know."

I frown. "But if this place is a tunnel... how come no one leaves the island?"

"People barely set foot in this palace. Once a year, maybe,

when somebody dies, or they have a crisis, or they miscarry a baby. When people are desperate to understand their suffering or life's great mysteries. Aside from that, people do not volunteer to search the place. Even if they did, their efforts would be pointless. The Jade Palace is like a maze inside your brain. It's incredibly easy to let your thoughts wander and find yourself lost in memories, questions, answers, and imagination. Navigating the palace requires enormous concentration and energy. But never fear it, Raven. Never fear something that cannot hurt you unless you allow it to. Command it. Command the magic you command so frequently with your bare hands. You are powerful. You are worthy."

"Are you sure I won't get lost?" I ask nervously.

"I am positive. Now, are you ready?"

I take a deep breath, excitement and nervousness bubbling up in my throat. "I've never been more ready for anything," I answer, and without a second thought, she strides forward, flings open the doors, and we cross the threshold.

※ ※ ※

Light. That is the first thing I notice. Blinding light in every direction.

The walls all around are narrow yet somehow big, warping and changing like a large, soapy bubble before my eyes. A labyrinth of magic, so mind-boggling that I must take a moment to find my feet again. "It's... weird. But beautiful," I laugh, and my voice bounces off every surface it can, echoing down endless halls and passages and then somehow making its way back to me in an uncanny loop.

The walls are mirrors— long, tall shards of glass. Then I realize that, in the mirrors, Mother is no longer with me.

CHAPTER 37

"Hey! Where did you go?" I frown, looking all around for her, but she only chuckles softly, her laughter reverberating into a wind chime.

"Follow my voice."

"Your voice is everywhere," I point out.

"Is it?" Her words echo. *Is it, is it, is it?*

What does she mean, "is it"? Of course, it is... everything is.

And yet, as I walk forward, the confusing display of bodies, eyes, and light seems to melt away.

The walls part and fracture and shrink until the air around me is completely clear, and I have stepped into a new place entirely. Here, there is a high, arched ceiling, wind chimes hang from every available surface, and right from the centre of a diamond-patterned floor sprouts a pure white tree, its gnarled trunk snaking up from out of the ground. White tiles, scattered and chipped by roots, surround its base.

I tear away my gaze, ignoring the temptation to blindly clutch and follow coils of truth, turning myself to the tree once more. It bears branches of a silvery colour and leaves of bright jade green, giving the palace its name.

Light dances and refracts off every surface, and I notice that the way it's reflecting doesn't quite make sense. All the shadows seem to grow and shrink simultaneously, and every surface I can lay eyes on is moving in indescribable yet fascinating ways.

"Welcome."

I'm so lost in wonder that the soft chiming of the overhead ornaments nearly masks her voice.

"What just happened?" I gasp as the Queen steps out from behind the trunk of the tree.

"You're in control," she says, beaming at me. "This place is different for every Flai, and only you can control what you see. For some, it'll be a foggy, cloudy field the moment you step inside. For others, it will be crystal clear. All you have to do is master the art of calming the mind and deciding exactly what you want. And I, Raven? I know who I am, I know where I am, and I know exactly what my goal is. That is why I arrived here much more easily than you did. You had to focus on the fact you wanted to find me, didn't you?"

"Oh, yeah, I suppose I did," I say, slightly befuddled, "But if I control this place and everything in it, is this version of the palace real or not? What does it look like?"

"Do you want it to be real?" she prompts, and as I think, the illusion all around me seems to ripple, ready for my next command.

"No, I want to see what's really here. Show me the truth," I say clearly, not speaking to her but more to the building.

"Ah, the truth. What a complexity of life. Everything began as truth, but then everything lied. Flowers that looked innocent sent humans dropping dead. The sky displayed a bright sun, and even so, it rained. Truth grows as we evolve, but it branches out into lies and manipulation. So, to see the real truth, you must trace your tree right back..." She drums her nails on the bark. "To the roots."

"And what if I say you're lying?" I challenge. "How would I know?"

"I am not lying, and I believe that with every fibre of my being. That is my truth. Your truth may be different."

I arch a brow. "That's completely absurd. I'm dreaming," I say, shaking my head. Then I catch her eyes. "Aren't I?"

"Why don't you take a climb and find out?" she suggests, and in the blink of an eye, the large white staircase appears before me, winding up into an eternal hazy shaft of colour and light until it disappears out of sight.

"Alright then," I decide, straightening up. "I will."

※ ※ ※

Have you ever been climbing stairs so absent-mindedly that you lifted your foot even at the top and ended up falling over your own feet when you realized you were already there?

Well, that's how I feel after the first twenty stairs. I never seem to put my foot in the right place, but I never fall. I'm determined to reach the top of this twisted dreamland and get out of this hypothetical palace into the fresh air.

The very topmost branches of the tree always seem to be just a few steps away, but how to get to them when the stairwell does not stop? It only occurs to me at least two minutes later that I could just reach out and pull myself off the staircase, and after I have that thought, I act on mere impulse, deciding (without a good reason) to climb the tree.

Taking a deep, nervous breath, my lungs stuffy and thick with magic and truths, I place one foot on the bannister. Another. *Steady, now.*

I raise myself to my feet, somehow feeling no force pushing me down even though I'm standing on a diagonal curved surface. I bend my legs, spot a thick branch, and leap.

Nausea creeps over me as the wood groans and sways under my weight. But it doesn't give way, so I take that as a cue to scramble forward and hop onto the next thickest branch I can find.

Instead of landing on it, however, I just plummet *through* it and rocket down, the scent of lush greenery encasing me, and then I'm falling straight through it, right into the endless darkness of a hollow trunk.

With a thump, I land on my back, lying on the hard, cold earth for several seconds while I recover my breath.

I think it hurts. I think my legs hurt. My brain says they should hurt, but then my brain is adrift, sending complex signals, communicating with the environment that entraps me, and... perhaps connecting, bonding with something else.

I immediately feel that I am not alone from the creeping sensation on my spine, so I sit sharply up, my vision rippling and distorting, and take in the scene.

Everything is quiet here, quiet and calm and not entirely real. I think something's creeping up my arms, something like fire, but it's not painful. It's just a pleasant tingle.

I try to observe my surroundings in the black abyss. It stretches for miles as far as I can see, with not a sight of life. It's unnerving but also familiar. I can see my own body somehow, but nothing produces light except three small leaves curled up in my palm, pulsating an odd, unnatural glow.

"Hello?" I call out uncertainly, "Mother?"

No response.

Your truth may be different. Why don't you take a climb and find out?

Suddenly, staring at the leaves in my hand, I know exactly what I have to do.

I look back at the leaf in my hand, sitting there patiently.

It's incredibly simple— just like stars, except I'm not making a wish this time. I'm asking a question. I take the first leaf and hold it up to my lips, closing my eyes.

I search for something that disturbs me, something in the back of my mind. I settle on the castle and its man-made, ugly glory. "There's something wrong with this place... isn't there? Something that isn't quite right and something that shouldn't be happening. It's unnatural for us to live like that. It isn't healthy," I whisper. "The castle— tell me about the castle. I-I want to know about the castle!" I finish firmly, squeezing it tight.

For a moment, nothing happens, and then it flutters out of my palm like a butterfly, landing delicately and weightlessly on the floor.

As its tip touches the ground, it sends a ripple through the air, the kind I saw earlier when the temple transformed from the hall of mirrors. This time, however, the room does not transform.

Instead, the leaf appears to be spinning and darting all around, its tip dragging on the floor and spilling out golden patterns to write frantic words: *The sightless one is upon these lands. Return their eyes.*

My heart thumps against my ribs. "Sightless? What?"

She's undone and re-spun, but this future is unmovable, and the sin will still come, the leaf says.

"Who's undone? What sin?" I press.

Pause. *Can't say.*

"Why?"

The leaf crumbles away into dust.

Okay. Very helpful. *But you still have two left*, I remind myself. An eerie calm overcomes me once more. I know exactly what to do, and without movement, without thought, I blink, and the next leaf is between my thumb and finger.

Alright, next question. I know what to say, even though I've every reason not to. "Is Sparrow safe?" I hold my breath as the second leaf springs to life.

No.

"Is he... alive? Is *Spok* alive?"

Both are alive.

I feel momentary relief as this information washes over me, but not for long. "And Spok's unsafe, too?" I push, pleading for more details.

Obviously.

My mouth turns dry. "Will she ever be? Is there a chance we can rescue her?"

It writes more urgently, lines spilling from the tip. I know instantly from its manner that I am running out of time. *You'll stop the burn, but far worse fires blaze unseen.*

"Burn?" I repeat.

She and she are driven by love. Only one means death and destruction, but both will fall.

"Who's "she"... Mother?"

You know the truth already.

My mouth goes dry. "I... what? I have no idea who you're talking about. My mother wants to help. To rebuild the Kingdom!"

Do you want to see the Kingdom now?

"What do you mean, "now"? Now is... here. Now is now." Every moment I spend here seems to fracture what I know to be reality.

Perhaps to you, but to me, now is whenever now is. And my now is not yours.

I stare at the leaf. "What." Drawing back, I drag my hands over my face, feeling momentarily disconnected. How ridiculous does that sound, just by itself?

"I stare at the leaf".

I'm talking to a bloody leaf. Normal people don't talk to leaves!

Raven.

"Shut up."

Raven.

"I-I want to leave now," I stammer.

Raven, observe.

"I said I want to leave, I—! Observe *what*?" I frown.

In response, it begins to draw a picture, with me at the very centre, painting a moment that has not happened yet. Or at least, it's not a moment that I remember. The glassy stillness of the black walls and floor is completely removed in a matter of seconds, turning into diamond-shaped fragments that grow smaller and smaller, revealing a new landscape behind them.

Finally, the land under my body is painted over, and then, just as the final pieces of the photograph slot together, the scene thrusts into motion.

I'm in a field of leg-tickling crops, barefoot. The sky is blood-red, its clouds like pathetic tissues mopping up a battlefield. Blazing fires and putrid smoke smother the valley to my right, and a thick, dense wood lies ahead. The air is thick with the choking, eye-watering stench of burning material, and I can hear faint screams and crashes echoing through the trees below.

I am sure I remember this from somewhere, but the memory is slippery and unfixed, leaping from my fumbling fingers as though not bolted to my senses. This feels like someone *else's* memory.

"Is she safe!? Where is she!?"

I whirl around, searching for the source of the voice. My eyes land on Sparrow. He's facing Spok, except... "he's" not Sparrow. This boy is older, his mask is gone, and he looks as though he's seen a ghost, his calm expression completely lost to distress.

His clothes are torn and his face is bloodied and bruised. I want to help him somehow, but the second my fingers stray too close to his skin, the scene breaks a little, cracking into diamond-shaped crumbs.

I am not allowed to be in this moment. I am here to observe. Tendrils of darkness seep from the cracks between fragments in the air, threatening me. Their message is clear: *Watch.*

I'm overcome with a wave of nausea as I realize. This isn't a vision nor a fortune-telling. This is actually happening right now, somewhere along a timeline that could be the same as mine or different.

It's so tempting, though. I know he can hear me. Or at least that he could if I wanted him to. And he could feel me, too. Feel as I took his hand. Hear as I reassured or scolded him, feel as I blamed and punched and kicked and unleashed all my fury on the boy who blinded me with fake friendship. But not Spok.

Her eyes are glued ahead, her movements like that of a wax figure, strained and calculated. She is focused on something else, unaware I'm here. Why can only Sparrow feel me? This doesn't make sense.

"I don't understand," I whisper as loud as I dare. "I don't know what this means!"

Something is triggered in my memory, sending me shooting back to... Boots and Shackles? *Try harder.* Think *harder.* A... book? Or rather, its contents? A page I memorized.

"We call this binding. All matter in our universe is bound, and binds cannot be broken unless newly formed by physical beings.

Binds are pure energy, and they come in two types: Fundamental Binds, which fix us to one reality and one timeline, and

Smaller Binds, not formed by the greater powers that hold us here, but by the living things in realities themselves. A binding could be manually formed between a father and a son, two best friends, two enemies, or two lovers.

The most powerful passion known to man, whether that be passionate love or passionate hate, is needed to form a bind. While soul-binding beyond physical, observable science is often dismissed by experts, the theory of binding suggests there is more to love than simple chemicals. Love — real love — is all bound. Bindings such as these are not limiting for they do not fix us to time and space, but to one another. And, why, if there was a binding powerful enough, it could tear a hole in the universe, uprooting Fundamental Binds as two beings gravitated towards one another despite their time and location!

These binds of passion mean that no matter how far you may stray from one another, no matter where you stand in life or death, you'll never truly escape one other. Nature will draw you together inevitably, and at times, it may even seem as though..."

The words float off the page, intertwining with my senses, until they seem to be spilling from my lips themselves, and I can hear them loud and clear in my ears. "As though you are together when you are not. Because your subconscious is reaching out for them in a place beyond the mortal world, beyond the world of physical beings. Somewhere deeper, you're following the bind, as we all do, all the time. Every decision you make in life is simply following the bind... wherever it may take you."

I close my eyes, allow it all to wash over my face, and fall away. This isn't important. This isn't *it*. There's something deeper here, something the Jade Palace wants me to see.

Follow the bind... I grab each fibre of this scene with my hands and sift through it and everything I'm experiencing. *Follow the bind.* "What are you looking for, Raven Asgard?" I ask myself.

The truth, I think. *I want to find my truth.*

Then look, and you will see.

I'm drawn back to the scene as all my senses are suddenly on fire, and it all feels horribly real.

"Find the others! I'll lead the villagers to the Palace."

Thick with terror and panic, Spok's voice rushes towards me, and my eyes shoot open. Everything has returned to its place except me: I'm directly in front of the innkeeper now, and their conversation is clearer than anything else, unlike before when their words were distant.

Panic envelops me despite the obviousness of my safety and distance from the scene unfolding before me. I'm still in the Jade Palace, yet my feet are stumbling over themselves, and my chest is knotted with anxiety. It's as though Sparrow's senses are intertwined with mine.

I can sense him.

But can he sense me?

Observe.

I will the Boy in the Bird Mask not to hear me with everything I have. If Sparrow notices me, it could... Where *is* Sparrow? I whirl around to discover him mere millimetres from my face, and it takes everything in me not to scream with shock. I'm directly in between the two people.

"I FELT SOMETHING! Something is WRONG! What's going on?" he demands.

Spok grips her son's shoulders, visibly trembling, and her arm rushes through me in a sweeping curve of freezing air. It makes me gasp. It *hurts.* I'm like a ghost. A ghost to everyone but him because he could really, truly see me if only I willed him to.

CHAPTER 37

The pain suppressed in her voice is almost unbearable to listen to as Spok pleads with her son. "Sparrow, please calm down! We're running out of time— they took out the northeast settlement and are advancing across the valley. The fighting's ceased at the border; we need to find S.P. and Nosoyeong and get to the Palace. Soon, this will all be gone. There's only one last exit they haven't secured, and if we can't leave through the bridge now, everything and everyone will die. We have to get them out! They'll follow your lead, Sparrow. Lead them to safety. They trust you."

"No! You're not LISTENING! Something's *WRONG*!" Sparrow cries. "I- Why can't everyone meet at the Palace?"

"Stick to the plan!" Spok hisses.

"We won't HAVE a plan when we're dead because *you're* being stupid! Something is very, very wrong."

Sook ignores him, glancing over her shoulder. "I-I have to get the children from the Amazon settlement. It's the last one I haven't covered, and then I'll come straight after you, I promise. But those children can't fly yet. They need me."

"*I* need you!" Sparrow gasps, tears pricking at his eyes. Spok takes his face in her hands and plants a kiss on his forehead. And it's the softest, gentlest kiss I've ever seen.

I desperately want to break free from the cruel rules of whatever dark forces are restricting me and find out what all of this means. I've only ever seen the expression on Spok's face before on one other person, and his name is Peter. If I'd realized that fact at the iceberg, I'd have forced him to stay with us.

Spok's saying goodbye.

If this is the future, I can't let it happen. I *won't* let it happen!

This is the future. You already did.

"I-I don't understand!" I stammer, "What is this? What's happening?"

The scene plunges into darkness like a light being snuffed out, offering no further insight, and the second leaf vanishes.

Sparrow's face remains, though, carved into my mind forever. It's an hourglass, a prophecy, an assurance of evil yet to come.

Trembling, I slowly move my gaze back to my palm, where the third and final item sits. One leaf left. One truth left to tell.

I press it to my chest, squeeze my eyes shut, and whisper my final question. Better to make it count.

This time, there is no painting, there are no conversations. There is only silence, darkness, and somewhere in it... there is truth. I take a breath, dare myself to look— And my racing heart stops.

The answer is yes.

CHAPTER 38

With my hands scrambling for something to clutch onto, I'm involuntarily lifted out of the darkness, my body weightless in the clutches of an otherworldly force that propels me into the light. I can't stop it, nor can I return to the roots— I've had my share of secrets. Three and only three. That's the way it goes unless you're lured into the infinite halls and interconnecting passages of this place.

I grapple for the stair bannister, my eyes adjusting to the light. Something about what I have seen feels forbidden, harsh, and unreal. No one is supposed to see the future. I have broken unspoken rules.

Why would the palace bestow this kind of information upon me?

My mother gives me a questioning look when I step off the final stair, but she doesn't attempt to prise any information out of me. I gratefully nod at her, and she wraps an arm around my shoulder and lightly presses her lips to the top of my head.

"Well done," she whispers, "Well done, my Raven. I knew you were strong enough."

"It was terrible," I confess.

"Yet beautiful?"

"Yet *perfect*," I say, shaken. "Beauty isn't real. It's a perception, a construct, and subjective... but somehow, this was real, and it *was* beautiful. I just don't... How can it be pure and unmanipulated? How can something hold all the answers to everything? Every question I had had a clear answer, and it wrenched me apart in all directions, tugging me towards different truths. Even so, I learned very little. It was as though my heart knew what was too much. I was still so fragile against it, though... I don't know if I could do it again," I admit.

Mother offers her other arm, and I bury myself into her as she speaks softly. "Whatever you have seen, it was entrusted to you because you have the strength to hold it. I'm so proud."

I'm hesitant to voice my thoughts. "After everything..." My throat feels raw. "It was easy to fantasize about you. About lies and manipulation and running away with Sparrow. But then I thought, and I wondered why you would give me access to this place if you had something to hide from me. You wouldn't. What I'm trying to ask is... are you using this to gain my trust and, in turn, me?"

"Yes, but also no. I am using the palace because I believe, with absolute confidence and good intentions, that I am in no way any harm to you. I want you to see the truth of this kingdom and your mother. If that tree told you I wished only to use or abuse you, it'd be news to the both of us."

I stare at the ground. "You said that about him, though. That Sparrow thought he was being good. That he genuinely wanted to be my friend in some kind of sociopathic way. I've no way to tell you apart. You could be just like him," I finish with a shaky breath.

"Sparrow is a human," Mother says simply.

"What does it matter if that wasn't enough to stop me from liking him?"

She pushes me gently back to take my face in her hands. "It matters because you're one of us, my beautiful Raven. An angel. A fairy. We are incapable of self-created illusions of fondness. We're not that tricky. We love, and we heal, and we catch falling stars in our palms. When we were forced against our nature into war as an act of self-defence and lost, that became obvious, didn't it? Violence isn't in our instincts."

"We can still hurt people if we want to. I have," I murmur.

Mothers waves away my comment. "As a response to an attack, violence means nothing. But for humans? It's wired into them. Bred into them, waiting to be unleashed. And we are above such limitations of our abilities. It's time to learn who you really are. Time to let Sparrow and every seed he ever planted inside your head go. Humans are, most tragically, only that. Not angels. I'm sorry— I know you wished so desperately for something else. But we must mourn our dreams of equality and freedom so long as those monsters have power. There's no such thing as "Raven and Sparrow", and you have strayed most hazardously from your flock. There are only humans and Flai. What Sparrow showed you is fantasy. It's not real, Raven. Neither is he." She gazes at me with eyes full of tears and despair, shattered by her child's heartbreak. Her hand slides down to my chest, and she feels my heart as it tears itself apart with another heavy thump. "It'll pass," she finally says.

❋ ❋ ❋

On the flight back to the castle, Tsubasa's eyes never leave me as she attempts to decipher my expression—she's already sensed something is wrong.

I can't talk to her yet. Even if I do, what am I supposed to say? Have I suffered some great trauma? No, because it isn't a great trauma. It's just something that left me feeling panicked and out of place. I have suffered and survived worse than this, haven't I?

The Berg... Perseus... Bronwyn... the Frost Guard...

Sparrow.

It feels strange to say I've survived Sparrow because, truthfully, I feel quite defeated, quite lifeless. A thick scar tissue of shock seems to separate me from what he did, and if I attempt to tear through it, the anguish is simply unbearable. So I stand numbed, chilled to the core, and to begin to dismantle my emotions is simply not an option. How long will it be before I can function again? How long before the memories of strikingly true, clear happiness I experienced at his side begin to fade into sharp moments of vulnerability? Everything I felt with Sparrow was so undoubtable. *He* was so undoubtable.

Am I really that easy?

Once Squadron 13 lands and guides us to the castle doors with armoured men, Mother tells me I should bathe, dress for dinner, and settle into my quarters.

Thankful for an excuse to avoid questions, I plaster a smile onto my face and hurry along the corridors of the castle, leaving smears of grassy mud on the marble. They no longer feel fun and mysterious, and I no longer feel silly and explorative. Instead, they just look dark. Dark and secretive, a maze of infinite rooms with no meaning and no inhabitants, abandoned webs.

It's easy to understand what my Mother said about the Jade Palace becoming addictive. When your entire perception of humankind and Flaikind shifts irreversibly, and the one person you trusted is proven a manipulator, to flee the castle and return to that tree seems the only sensible thing to do in the world. The scariest thing is that, as I look out over the black sea of dusk-kissed treetops through the bathroom window, I know I'd do it. I'd drag myself mile after mile, over cliff after cliff, for just one silver of truth. And I can feel its eyes on me.

I can't wash or can't prepare for dinner in this state. Once I've locked myself inside, I switch on the bath tap, unplug the drain, and then let it run, watching the water trickle wastefully down the gold-rimmed hole with my arms wrapped tightly around my stomach like restraints, my nails digging into my sides. The pain helps. It separates truth and lies and tells me my senses are working.

The trickling tickles my ears, reminding me of my countless days on the run, my countless days in hiding. Back then, a source of fresh, clean water was perhaps one of my biggest concerns of all, and now here it is —galleons of it!— at my disposal.

This must be what it is like to live in luxury, I think, *to live as a king or a queen.* Can I imagine the rest of my life as one? "King Raven" has a nice ring to it.

I close my eyes and visualize the Willow District, fantasizing about myself striding down the streets in wonder, letting the scents of the strange world of Man wash over me. Pastries, pies, exotic fruits, and freshly made tunics and jumpers, and spices! Bright puffs, explosions of eye-watering, mouth-watering scents and colours.

So many items from all over Evrilore, brought to Willows by traders and relatives.

The time I spent exploring its streets with Sparrow feels like so long ago now, but I can still remember it clearly. Everywhere was overwhelming and wonderful— wonderfully *ordinary.* I remember the exasperated (but not really, only in a parent-ish way) adults pushing through the bustling crowd. The joy on all the children's faces shone and bounced off strangers as their parents pointed out new traders arriving for Floodonora and explained everything about them.

And those children were *happy.* They were happy to see their parents educate them about a world they knew nothing of.

At least, growing up alone, I had formed my own opinions about the world.

But even then, I'd foraged in bins for newspapers. Hidden and awaited strings of gossip to slip from keen mouths. I sought out someone to form my judgements for me, too.

At what age did I start to question everything I decided? All my hate for humanity and the simple, widely accepted cock-and-bull version of the Fall?

I suppose it was when Sparrow showed up. And then my worldview was knocked out of orbit once more by Mother.

Mother, I repeat thoughtfully in my head.

She doesn't seem like the type of parent who would let me do that. Everything she says has an edge of bitterness to it, as though it should be confirmed as a fact. Her opinion is the only opinion. Nobody else can have one, and if they do, it is simply incorrect.

It is funny how she assumes that a bed and a castle will satisfy me, make me compliant, and turn me into an easy daughter. If I get what any girl dreams of, I'll just nod and smile and agree with everything she says. But that's the thing. I *don't.* Now that I reflect on it, nothing she tells me about her visions for the Flai Realm feels right, and nothing aligns with my morals.

I know her intentions are good. I truly do. I just worry that we Flai are stripping ourselves of everything that makes us special— everything except our powers. And even then, the reason we keep our magic is for power and protection, but being Flai isn't just about that. It's about beauty, too.

All I ever truly wanted was to live like a normal Flai girl, before the Fall and in harmony with humans, but now I'm not a normal girl; because of Mother, I am a princess now, and not even a real one, because we aren't supposed to have royals. Flai are supposed to work as one community.

In the past, we often had elders, but they weren't chosen because they were elegant, or posh, or because of their wealth. They weren't self-elected like my mother is. They were chosen because of their knowledge and their honourable work ethic.

As the air all around me steams up, I realize with a pang of hopelessness that I hate it here. I hate it in this castle, full of pointless things for pointless people. This place, a place I once dreamed of, is just turning into a combination of Frost and Ra.

And now I have no one at all. My best friend is dead, my sister humanized and overwhelmed by hatred, Spok captured, Sparrow locked up somewhere, and I don't even have my mother. Not really.

I want desperately to believe Sparrow, and for our relationship to be genuine. But the truth is raw and sharp like a fresh wound, and my mother bears the knife that inflicted it.

Sparrow was trying to sell me, have me arrested, and ruin me emotionally so he could save his handcuffed damsel. Everything he ever did was for himself.

And I was a fool.

Even worse, I was *his* fool.

Owed simply to that fact, I can't seem to reach inside of myself and harness the boiling rage I once felt in his company. The rage that I couldn't be kind, selfless, compassionate, and loving just like him. All my anger at the world has disappeared, only to be replaced by pain and solitude. Sparrow changed me in ways I didn't realize, ways I didn't always want.

He stripped me of my armour, and now I'm naked.

I turn to the mirror, surrounded by golden-flecked tiles, and study my reflection, sizing myself up. I don't match the pure gold tap behind me. My feet feel awful on the cream-white, polished floorboards. This is not where I'm meant to be. Here, the walls press in on all sides.

I'm used to a house without bricks. I'm used to the smell of ferns, animals, and trees, and here, the air smells too clean, intoxicated with chemicals, fresheners, filters...

Sometimes, change is good. Sometimes, you just take time to adjust.

But how can I ever adjust to this? This is hell.

When it seems as though twenty minutes or so have passed, I turn off the tap, wrap my hair in a towel, and palace guards almost immediately "escort" me back to my quarters.

As the bedroom door clicks shut behind me, I explore the place that will now serve as my bedroom. There's a four-poster bed with long, sweeping curtains tied neatly to the posts by red ribbon, several silver cushions, and violet throws. Folded. Washed. Devoid of smell and personality.

I creep soundlessly over a plush rug to the window. I kneel on the cabinet below, climb onto the sill, and press my fingers to the glass. Triple-glazed. Thick. Almost unbreakable. And the frame? The handle? Gold.

Collapsing onto the floor with real panc, now, I crawl over to the cabinet and raise my knees to my chin, squeezing my eyes tightly shut. This can't be it. This cannot be the Flai Realm. My home. My life. I have not mentally watched Peter and Spok die a thousand times in different situations, each more horrifying than the last, for this.

Even thinking about my perilous journey here unnerves me, though. Sparrow's smile, Sparrow's eyes, Sparrow's distress, and Sparrow's lies. It's all just a blur, snowballing into a heavy weight that presses on my stomach. The feeling of betrayal has intensified into an ache, a puncture in my lung that makes me feel as though I cannot breathe without screaming or sobbing.

I climb to my feet, throwing my hands out onto the dresser to steady myself as I hyperventilate. The Jade Palace's glare burns into my neck, and Sparrow's name is burned into the back of my eyes. If I close them, he's still there, and the world's still madness, and everything, *everyone* is lying.

A knock.

"Come in!" The first time, my throat is so dry the words are barely audible. I have to try twice more before it rings out loud and clear.

Tsubasa enters the room carrying a tray laid out with tea and several rich breakfast foods. "Hello, Aalipa. You look a little stressed, your highness. Everything okay?" she asks, setting the tray down on my bed.

I inhale a deep, calming breath and allow her presence to wash over me. Another Flai with memories, thoughts, and feelings. She's no blank page like this castle. She's the same as me. She's trustworthy. "I-I guess I'm just adjusting to how things work around here. It's... difficult, you know? I always had the freedom to move around and go wherever I wanted. Guards were something to fear, not here to protect me."

She smiles reassuringly. "I understand. When my sisters and I were rescued by a homefetch, it was all a strange new world, and... I'll be honest, you'll feel uncomfortable for a few weeks. It takes time. This isn't... it isn't the Flai Realm I dreamed of. But the world is changing, and we have to change with it so events like the Fall don't repeat themselves.

Even if it doesn't seem like those changes are good ones. This place isn't about what we want— it's about what we need. It's all we have, Aalipa. That's why the villagers complied with all the changes your mother installed, like having a Queen, a castle, and an army... She's the last person most of us have to turn to. We're the survivors, Raven, and the sole inheritors of our ancestors' legacies. We need a leader, and your mother is that person. She keeps us all strong."

She pours me a glass of orange juice and places a hot roll in my grimy hands. I stare at it.

"Eat. You'll feel better," Tsubasa encourages. "Listen, I know it's hard to be thrust into a new life like this and suddenly have so many eyes on you, but it's exactly the opposite for us. We tried for years, Raven. We really did. Long before my sisters and I were rescued by a homefetch, they were trying. Your mother never stopped fighting for you, and now the people want you to fight for them, too. So, in your own time, please do try to settle. Be our *aalipa*."

I nod, hesitant to say it because the question is out of context and sounds utterly wrong in this room, in this castle. "Tsubasa, speaking of homefetches... where's Sparrow?"

"Training," she says instantly. Automatically.

"No, he's not," I say softly, "Is he?"

Her eyes are wide, pleading, suddenly flooded with fear. I realize with a start that I was wrong earlier. She's not like Spok at all. There's shiny, raw fear in her eyes, a weakness behind her hardworking, helpful exterior. A terror that establishes the difference between her and the formidable innkeeper.

She mimes a finger to her lips. "It's not a good idea to go asking people things or investigating around here. U-Us maids... us castle workers... we know what we're told. What we're told is what we know. Understand?"

"I don't want to do anything rebellious. H-He wasn't my friend," I say quickly. "It's not like that. I don't want to speak with him, secretly meet him, or anything. Not after... anyway. But will he... will he at least get a fair trial?" I stammer out.

"That depends on what he did."

"He was a double agent. Working with the Frost Guard." Even saying it makes me feel sick.

"Then, I don't know," she replies honestly.

"What's the worst... I mean, is there a chance that—"

"Killing as a punishment is authorized by the Queen," Tsubasa interrupts stiffly.

"Is there anything I can do? At all? He hurt me so much, and he lied and betrayed me and killed my friend... but I don't want him to die."

Tsubasa stares directly into my eyes, then finally whispers, "Why are you asking me this? Why are you telling me this?"

I inhale sharply. "Because you have a sister. And I have... I *had* a brother. His name was Peter, and he was everything to me. I was the eldest in my family, so I understand the need to pretend you can look after everyone. To be the strong one, even though, on the inside, you don't feel strong at all. I guess I felt like because we have at least one thing in common, maybe I can understand you. And you can understand me, too," I finish, hopeful.

"I'm just a maid," Tsubasa finally says, smoothing out her dress again, and makes for the door, her face considerably flushed. At the last moment, she turns her head. "I... I love my sisters more than anything, Raven. We don't have a mum or a dad, so I'm the only parental figure they've got. And it's my job to keep them safe. I'm their guardian. So if something were to happen to me... If it was to be discovered that I had told you certain facts that I wasn't supposed to..."

"I understand. I won't say anything," I nod, my face set, but she only grows more urgent, pleading.

"Don't go sneaking around, Raven. And if you do... For your own sake, for mine and my sisters' sakes... do not get caught," she says before shutting the door.

The moment I hear the footsteps dying away, I stroll back over to the door and rattle the knob, intending to stride right back out and sneak into the servants' quarters to see Sparrow. With the new knowledge given to me, I don't believe he's "training" anymore, and I want to hear his manipulation from his own mouth. Get a confession and hear an unfiltered account of what he did to me.

But it's locked.

The door is locked.

And it doesn't even surprise me, which floods me with terror.

Something tells me I'm being watched. I'm supposed to do something, and if I don't, I'll never be released. I'm on some kind of schedule, a planned routine. My eyes wander over to the bed, now the seemingly only escape from the bundle of tangled influences that is my fractured reality, and I realize that that is just it. Sleep. Get out of the way. Wake up later. And do whatever it is Mother has planned.

Right now, I am an unwanted pawn on the board, but at any moment in time, I could be roused from sleep and shoved back into one of her schemes, right back into a game I didn't know I was playing.

I am just a piece in her plans, like everybody else in this damned castle.

I didn't know that until now.

Momentarily, I'm disgusted at myself. Why are my thoughts suggesting such a thing? Mother has been compassionate and gentle, and everyone here seems to share the belief that, though extreme, Mother's changes have proved to be good with time...

But what about me?

Do I feel safer? More secure? More comforted?

I'm forced to sit down by the weight of my befuddlement, and I look dully at the pillows.

Something about sleeping is so inviting, now... the satin sheets, the fluffed pillows... even the scent, as a hazy mist drifts through the room from such fresh laundry detergent.

My eyes snap open. What am I *thinking*?

Fuming at myself, I hurry to my feet to search for an alternative exit to my bedroom, running my fingertips along the walls and knocking on the floor for trapdoors.

I'm delusional. Dramatic. Over-impressionable. Pathetic.

I smile, almost wildly.

And I'm running right back to the Boy in the Bird Mask, which is what I should've done since the start. I have to find Sparrow.

The longer I search, the more hopeless my situation seems to become. There is no way out, and it was always made to be like this. I march over to my en-suite bathroom and drag back the blinds, inspecting the window frames lined with gold.

I march back out, more desperate now. Examine the chest, searching for tools to pick the lock.

There's nothing. It's all designed to trap me.

Light streams through the thick panes behind me,

creating a pillar of gold inhabited by swirling dust. And... maybe something else. The same hazy fog I saw earlier...

Ah, yes, the fog. The fog...

My eyes widen, blotches of darkness creeping stealthily into my vision. The *fog!*

Covering my nose with my arm, I cough and splutter, fighting back the darkness that threatens to consume me. All of a sudden, adrenaline is rushing through my body, and I am aware of it all around. Gas. Weaving, snaking, rushing through the air.

Whirling around in desperate confusion, I keep searching for refuge. But where to go? There is no escape.

With no better option, I bolt for my en-suite, the only place that the mist hasn't yet penetrated. I can lock myself inside and line the cracks between the door and floor with towels—

But before I even make it six feet across the cream rug, the knockout drug grasps my final fibre of willpower, and I slump to the floor, my eyelids fluttering closed and cutting off the world.

CHAPTER 39

Something's boiling.

I can hear the kettle's soft hiss as water bubbles.

Uncommanded, my arm reaches for its sleek handle. I fumble for the mug.

What mug?

The mug.

With trembling hands, I pour the water. A single drop sloshes over the side and rolls miserably down onto the table.

What table?

The table.

I stare at the drop as it melts into the wood below, and fury surges through my blood. *I didn't say you could fall.*

I rise to my feet, yelling at the mug. "I DIDN'T SAY YOU COULD SPLASH!"

I didn't say you could run your cold fingers over my exposed skin. I didn't say you could paint my lips. I didn't say you could remove my—

Peter materialises, picks up my mug, gulps the contents in one swallow, and then raises his head to look at me as an endless supply of water gushes from his nose and mouth. "Something's boiling," he says.

"There's no steam," I point out.

His dead eyes meet mine as his features collapse into ocean, overcome by water pressure. *"Something's boiling."*

※ ※ ※

I sit up, my chest rapidly rising and falling. I'm lying across my bed with my hands folded neatly across my stomach.

You didn't go to sleep on your bed, my mind whispers.

I don't even remember falling asleep, I reply.

And why do you think that is? It asks sinisterly.

Since I have no good answer to this, I push these thoughts away and swing my legs over the side of the bed. Thankfully, the rug is soft as a cloud and disguises the sound of my footsteps in its thick fibres. At least nobody will hear that I'm awake. *But maybe...* My skin crawls, my eyes scouring the highest and uppermost corners of the room. *Maybe they can still see.*

Deciding to play dumb and ignore the strange series of events that have followed my abrupt slumber so far, I set about doing whatever it is "Normal" people do.

First, I pull on the dress that was laid out for me. It's a long, silky, sacramento-green gown with golden embroidery, oversized sleeves that drape graciously off my wrists, and a small band around the waist. Now what?

If I go now, will I appear too quick? Too desperate to escape from... something. If I wait, will I appear scared and hesitant? It is all a game of presentation. All a game of show and tell. But how to win it?

Lost, I creep over to the large, polished mirror beside the swept-back curtains, noticing how the beams of light that slice through the air from the window are no longer odd and hazy. Then I straighten up and frown at my own thoughts.

Odd and hazy? What am I talking about? Firstly, was it odd and hazy in the first place? Now, come to think of it, I can't remember. And secondly, why does the sun, hovering over the castle, look peculiarly bright and oddly high today?

Unnaturally high...? It hits me.

It's midday, I realize.

What have I been doing, asleep until midday? Was I not supposed to have dinner with Mother?

Dinner... 'Shackles? A peircing ache slashes through my head as I attempt to recall the recent months of events. And trying to recall last night's is even worse. Peter's face is amongst the milky complication of tangled threads of memory, but all he does is remind me of the blood. Inspecting my hands, I realize all the mud that was hiding under my nails has gone. Not only that, but my nails have been cut, filed, and polished with delicate rounded tips.

These are the hands of fine rich ladies in Ra, not an outlaw.

I quickly kick off my dress and crawl tentatively over to the mirror to see my full body, my arms already creeping around my ribs in a protective cage as I brace myself for what I am about to see.

Raven Asgard has gone, and a stranger now stands in her place. My hair has been cut shorter to disguise my jagged self-cut waves from before, washed and brushed free of leaves and earth; now, it is silky, wavy, and darker than ever, styled into a sleek ear-length pixie cut. My emerald-green eyes bear elongated lashes and seem to have even more of a magical sheen than before, causing them to stand out and look full of intelligence and confidence. I can understand what Sparrow means now about our eyes looking different from human ones. They're always just too bright.

My eyes trace my reflection to my cheeks, tinted with a light, rosy touch that only makes them stand out more. I think something happened to my whole body, too— though my skin is still the same pale shade of zombie-like greyish white, it looks warmer.

The only explanation is that I've been thoroughly groomed while I slept. But surely I would've been awoken by the feeling of scalding water when I was bathed? Or the tug on my scalp as maids and Palace workers combed my hair?

Have I been *drugged?*

My panic escalates with every thought. Why would they need to wash me again? How could they have known that I hadn't bathed before being escorted back here? More cameras? I gag. In the bathroom? It disgusts me that someone could invade my privacy so shamelessly.

But then I remember.

There's no such thing as a good person.

I hit the floor so hard that a bruise swells up instantly. My body is on its side, caving in, but I force myself to move into a sitting position, putting my hands in my lap and taking deep breaths.

Mother isn't what she seems. That's the first fact I can confirm.

Secondly, Sparrow's real. At least, he's the most real thing in this kingdom, and possibly on this island.

Thirdly, my mother lied about him. Simply looking back on my memories confirms this much. Her declarations of love and the rapid changes in her formality and facial expressions as she flicks on like a switch any emotion she likes to provide a calculated effect on the onlooker. Desperate parental despair, compassion, sympathy... *Lies*, Sixth Sense whispers.

I've been so naive. So stupid out of desperation to be loved. How could I possibly have thought that this place would be a haven? Nowhere is a haven. Everyone in this world has something to hide. Everyone has their secrets.

CHAPTER 39

I have become another piece in a larger game— namely, my Mother's. But what's even worse is that I have been moulded into exactly the right piece by heaven knows who without my consent. Somebody —possibly several people— stripped, clothed, and bathed me. Touched me all over, threw products and water all over my skin.

I have no freedom in these walls. I am not in control. Not *really.*

And even if Mother is no liar, and I'm merely crawling back to the boy who blinded me with his affection and appreciation with ill intentions, I'd still rather die a bound and bloody fool in Frost's torturous hands as a Raven —as *Sparrow's* Raven— than live as a miserable, infatuated Flai grovelling at my Mother's feet, preaching about my hatred of Man because —what? Because somebody told me to?

Scoffing at the concept, I compose myself, concentrating on my breathing and climbing steadily to my feet. I am fifteen, and I have hated, loved, feared, and been convinced to avoid at all costs, humankind.

Now, where do I stand in that great debate about species and their defining characteristics? I must make my own observations, I suppose. Start all over again.

Sparrow and my Mother stand on shared land— I'll place no trust in either of them until my eyes tell me the truth.

Striding to the wardrobe, I find my old filthy jacket hanging inside. Reaching into the pocket, I find what I'm looking for and slip a handful of something into the shoes waiting patiently for me at my door.

I dress myself in the gown again and make for the door.

This time, it swings open easily.

"*Oh, Mother,*" I whisper to myself, "Always no surprises."

❋ ❋ ❋

I rush down the corridor, away from the dreaded chamber that is supposed to be my private space, and just as I turn the corner of the hallway, I hesitate, then look back for whichever pair of eyes is sending a shiver up my spine.

But the only shadow is one of a candle wick's flame, dancing and flickering in a pool of gleaming wax, growing and shrinking on the wall like a monster from hell.

I tear my eyes away from the distraction. What did Mother say again? Straight ahead, right, left, right? What's that in reverse? Can I retrace my steps back to the throne room?

Just as I'm about to step in the opposite direction, the distant sound of sharp, serious voices echoes along the passage, and I follow them after a hesitant pause.

Ahead, the hall opens up into the throne room entrance, but one of the marble pillars blocks my view of the enormous room.

Glancing over my shoulder, I realize there are no guards in here. There are always guards— Mother said it herself on the tour... So, where else could they be if they aren't here? Who else are they protecting?

Sixth Sense sends a shiver down my spine. Not speaking, just... warning. I frown.

"Something is... wrong?" I guess.

Nothing.

"Something is...missing?"

Not that. But I'm close.

Voices float down the hallway, reeling me towards the throne room. "Just another week! Surely, we can wait that long!" A man.

"Why should we wait!? She is here, the army is ready, and

there is nothing in our way!" Mother's voice.

"Please, miss!" the other voice trembles, "Our spies have returned with reports of carriages from Ra crossing the southern border of the Willow District. And Frost carriages from the West. They're meeting up— the Sun Queen and the Moon King are deadly enemies. There's clearly more to this Flood Tide than we know. Something is *happening*! And this election—"

"You say something is happening?" Mother's voice cuts across him, seething, "Then *stop it*. I have a thousand troops. I have been waiting for this day for years. You will prepare them, and you will do it now. Do I speak Flai Latin to you? DO YOU UNDERSTAND?"

"No, miss. Yes, miss!" the other voice squeaks, then there are more footsteps, and the man is gone.

I press myself against the wall and listen to the sound of my breaths, trying to decide my next move.

There's a very elongated sigh from my mother, and the shadow of her figure briefly flickers in between the pillars as she crosses the room. I hear a door click as she opens it to speak with someone.

"Bring him in. And, for crying out loud, get me something to drink."

Sixth Sense flares again, more desperately. *Someone is coming.*

Now, noise floods my ears once again. I creep silently forward through the doors into the throne room, leaning back against the wall, and drop into a crouch, intending to hide behind the pillar and eavesdrop.

Mother is standing at the left side of the hall, and now I can see that she has changed into a sunset-orange dress, complete with fiery makeup to match. The whole look is unnervingly similar to the Sun Queen's. She moves like a swan, but a sinister one. Again, I have the feeling that something isn't quite right. Something about this place...

My train of thought is frozen as Sparrow is thrown onto the floor by two guards who disappear almost as soon as they arrive. He struggles to his feet and hastily bows to her. "Your majesty! I apologize for my entrance. If I had known sooner of your request for my presence, I would've made a better attempt to appear presentable."

Presentable? He doesn't look presentable; he looks half-dead. His eyes are large and fearful, and his stance weak. And what are those bruises scattered across his limbs?

The smirking, triumphant "manipulator" from my journey to the Realm is gone. The vengeful, furious, failed hunter who tried desperately to get me arrested is nowhere in sight.

Perhaps those versions of him are carved out of fear and puppeteered by... someone else.

I have to make my own judgments now.

Despite everything, despite peeling layers and adding them in an attempt to find the truth of our relationship, my heart sings to see him.

No matter his true intentions, the Boy in the Bird Mask was real to me, at least for three months.

And that's blinding, overpowering my mother's judgments. If Sparrow really did manipulate me, I want to find out and bear the despair alone. Whether fake or not, our relationship bombarded me with uncontainable happiness. It's not for my mother or anyone else to take that from me.

"Oh, Sparrow," I whisper, delighted to see him and terrified for his wellbeing all at once. "What did they *do* to you..."

My brain tugs my heart sharply back from its attempt to leap out of my chest. *And what did you do to me?*

CHAPTER 39

Mother holds up a hand gracefully. "Ah, please! You are pardoned. If anything, I should be blaming my staff. They seem incapable of bringing my guests to me in a reasonable state."

"With all due respect, Your Majesty, I don't see why you feel inclined to care," he says honestly.

"Truthfully, I am only now realizing that I strongly prefer not to hire thugs. Everything should be exercised with grace within these walls. Really, they have no manners. Speaking of which, for the sake of manners, I wanted to thank you for bringing my daughter home to me. After fifteen years, nothing made me happier than to see her again. Your volunteering is the sole reason I have my child back. Thank you."

My shoulders drop, and relief washes over me. Maybe she is just thanking him, and that really is it. The cameras everywhere are just a precaution, and this castle really is my new home, and I will be happy here for the rest of my life...

Then, it strikes me. *Thanking* him? She *knows* —or at least claims to— that he was secretly calculating my arrest! Why does she need information if her spies already reported back his trickery and deception? Is this a forced confession? A testimony? The final proof?

My heart thumps with excitement. Perhaps while I was asleep, Mother had a revelation. Perhaps Sparrow was truly not lying!

"...But."

Oh, God. There's a "but". Why is there always a "but"?

"I do have some concerns about your delayed return and the..." Mother purses her lips. "*Unusual* methods you used to get her here, shall we say."

I'm certain I can see Sparrow's adam's apple bob. "A-As you wish. Ask me anything," he stammers, and I flinch away from the picture.

What's wrong with him? Why is he so posh, and such a pushover? This is not the Sparrow I know. Where is the Boy in the Bird Mask who faced an army and fought Flunters in the Frost Wilderness?

"The Iceberg," Mother says matter-of-factly, getting straight to the point, "Why did you go there, and how did it result in a pile of wreckage on the ocean floor?"

Sparrow clears his throat. "At first, we were going to sail across the border between Frost and Willows because the border on land was too risky with all the tightened security measures, and I figured that once we arrived at the port in the Willow District, everyone would assume we'd come directly from Frost port, and that we'd already been stopped and searched. Mountains and blizzards cover the northern coast, Your Majesty. It wouldn't have made sense that we managed to travel there during Flood Tide and depart alive. But then I began noticing things. Things about Raven that..." his forehead creases. "...Weren't quite right. She was alert but distant simultaneously, constantly distracted by something. I soon learned that two of her very close friends were in the Berg, and I guess we just... took the opportunity."

""We"?" Mother repeats with an arched brow. There it is again, the tone that suggests her opinion is a fact.

"I," he quickly corrects himself, flushing. "I took the opportunity. Unfortunately, Raven set off a bomb, which was entirely my fault for not realizing and warning her, and a security mechanism was triggered. The Berg flooded and then exploded, killing one of her friends in the process."

"But the other survived?" She addresses him with the same sharp tone she used to tell me the truth about Sparrow's intentions. Accusatory, blunt, and seemingly truthful. The atmosphere is heavy with something that ought to be released, and whether this is Sparrow's confession or something else, it stirs up great anxiety in me.

I can't decipher Sparrow anymore. His generosity, selflessness, and politeness to my mother, whom he informed me would have him killed, all lead me to different conclusions about his personality.

Nothing about this is like the boy I knew, and it's terrifying to confront the fact that perhaps I don't know Sparrow at all.

"Yes, Bronwyn survived," he replies.

"And where is she now?"

"We... don't know," Sparrow admits.

Mother's eyes run over him, dark and unimpressed.

"I never meant for any of it to happen. I only wanted to help Raven," he adds quietly, "She was distraught, completely wrecked. You have to understand... I- It was *killing* her, Your Majesty, knowing her friends were in there while she was about to go home to a family and safety. Killing her worse than any soldier could."

"So, you care for my daughter, then?" Mother asks casually, her calm tone returning.

"Very much," he nods, "She means a lot to you and the villagers, and your priorities are my priorities."

"Yes, yes, I've heard all that formal rehearsed hogwash, but you and I both know that that is not the answer I require. So, I ask you again." Her voice is dangerously low now. "Do you care for my daughter?"

Come on, Sparrow. Just say no. Say no, say no, say—

"More than anything," he replies, raising his head to meet her eyes.

As much as this makes my heart rise into my throat with hope and elation, I cannot shake the feeling of how horribly wrong his face is. His eyes are pleading, not wide and confident, and his position suggests a puppy awaiting orders from its master.

Mother's eyes darken now. Her face remains steely and calm, with her lips slightly pursed so that she could have just finished speaking or just be about to. Her brows draw together, and as she surveys him, a flash of alarming rage darts across her expression. "You will not touch her," she whispers, her fingers making as though to caress the air. Her voice has changed now. It perfectly mimics rustling leaves, so gentle it's murderous. It's so harmless it's horrifying.

"Yes," Sparrow breathes.

"You will not so much as meet her eyes. If you do, I'll destroy you *and* your species."

Sparrow swallows. Hard. "I want to assure you that nothing would ever, ever happen between—"

"Do you know what happens when humans mix with Flai? Do you understand what chaos ensues when we meddle in one another's business? My child was stolen from me by a father with no love left in his heart for the woman he married. All because he was human. The price I paid for staying in his company was losing my daughter. But I lost her once, and now she is found. *Don't* let it be twice."

"Yes."

Mother glowers at him. ""Yes" will not suffice. At Boots and Shackles, you shared Raven's bed. You chose, just now, to withhold that information from me. Why?"

His voice wobbles. "Nothing... nothing happ—"

"I am perfectly aware that nothing took place that night! You dare even *suggest* such an event?"

Quite suddenly, Mother outstretches a hand, and he is thrown back by an invisible force and slammed into the ground. It hits me, too, bursting out in all directions, and my shoes squeal against the floor just as a groan of pain escapes his lips.

"Hello?" Mother calls out, head whipping from side to side.

If I can just stay quiet enough, perhaps—

The click-clack of her heels grows suddenly louder as she stomps towards me. I scurry to the side, but Mother's not looking at me. She throws open the doors and yells for guards. Sparrow stares wildly around as though just as baffled as she is, but there's a plastic quality to his expression that tells me otherwise. After spending a month with him, I do not doubt that he expects me to notice and understand this. It's his sign to me that he knows I'm here somewhere. And this gives me the confidence to act.

I dart out into the open, and sunlight streams down from the large window into my eyes. I curse and clumsily stumble over to the throne. But not without making a series of stomps.

"What was that!?" Mother demands, whipping around to face Sparrow.

"What was what?" he asks innocently.

"I heard something," she replies, her eyes narrowing as she peers about.

"Don't worry. Happens to the best of us, y'know? *The voices.*" There's confidence, even cheek, in his voice, as though my sole presence relit the flame in his eyes. He stares boldly up into the Queen's face as he lies.

I curl up behind the throne, desperately trying to stay silent. Mother narrows her eyes, turning to the crowd of soldiers spilling into the throne room. "I want this hall swept clean. Do you understand me?"

"Yes, Your Majesty," they chorus, dividing into two groups and spreading out to cover the area of the floor under the balcony.

It will be a matter of seconds before they pan out right to the back of the hall, and I am found. I could attempt to slither under the throne, but who knows what would happen then?

My hands are empty, and I have nothing to throw. If I make a run for it, I'll surely be seen and identified before I can exit the room.

"Hey!" A remarkably strong woman is on me in seconds, her iron armour so cold I cry out as it rubs against my flesh. She has a long, dark fringe and almond-shaped eyes the colour of ice.

Her broad, powerful shoulders are pumped with muscle, and her grip on my wrist is too tight to pull away from, so I struggle momentarily, gasping as we wrestle. "Get- off- me!" I wheeze.

In true military fashion, she remains indifferent. "As a soldier of the Flai Realm's military force, I order you to identify yourself. State your name!"

"Get *off*!" I hiss, but then I stiffen with recognition.

Tsubasa drops me like a hot coal, spluttering. Her eyes are suddenly alive with concern. "Raven? I- what are you doing!? What did I tell you about sneaking around this place!?"

"I'm sorry! Please, just don't tell anyone. *Help me*!" I whisper as I crawl away.

My breath is ripped from my throat by material pressing into my windpipe as a ginger soldier grabs me by the scruff of my gown and holds his sword to my throat. "I have her!"

"What's going on over there?" another man roars.

The ginger smashes a boot into my skull, and I tumble out onto the tiled floor, my face in full view for all. "It's the princess!" he cries in a strangled voice, clearly terrified of getting in trouble.

The guards hastily back away from me, and I lay there like an idiot, unsure if I should climb to my feet or beg for mercy.

CHAPTER 39

Mother looks concerned; perhaps I can play for the sympathy angle? Deciding it is my best bet, I make sure to squeeze out every gasp and wheeze I can, clutching my arms where red marks have already formed.

"Where am I?" I say uncertainly.

"Y-you're in the throne room. Do you really not remember anything?" she asks, distrustful.

"I remember falling asleep and then... I don't know. Here I am. I thought... I thought we were going to have dinner and spend time together..." If I can convince her I'm still locked in a surreal haze, I may just be able to defend my spying on her.

I catch Sparrow watching me out of the corner of my eye, looking at me as if to say, "What the hell are you doing?"

I shake my head ever so slightly. He stares right back, eyes popping out of their sockets with disbelief. I manage a subtle shrug, glowering as if to say, "What d'you want me to do?" He only facepalms.

"My goodness, you must be terribly confused. Oh, I am so sorry..." Mother says. She seems genuinely upset, and yet her eyes are still as cold as ice.

"It's okay," I croak, "But what time is it? What's going on? What are all these guards doing here?"

"*Too much!*" Sparrow mouths in critique of my acting.

Annoyed, I clasp a hand to the red marks on my arm as if in pain, rearranging my fingers into a... friendly gesture.

"There is... a possible intruder," Mother explains.

I plaster an innocent frown across my face. "How so?"

She waves me away. "It's no longer an issue. A false alarm. Don't worry; you are safe here, and no intruder will breach these borders so long as I am alive. Even if they do, as you can see, we are very well prepared for extreme circumstances. Speaking of which, we have a very important conversation to have. Have I *mentioned* how lovely you look? Oh, that dress is stunning on you. I handpicked your wardrobe myself, you know? Please, do sit!" she smiles, gesturing to the couch near the entrance.

I hesitantly do as she says, and Mother comes to sit on the couch opposite me. Sparrow backs away into the shadows, but the Queen snaps her fingers, and the soldiers move so that two men are between each pillar, lining the perimeter of the room. They shove him back into the light, and I gulp.

Now we're truly trapped, Sparrow and I.

Strangely, the knot of discomfort and unease in my stomach doesn't grow. I suppose I'm only as caged as I was before. This entire kingdom is my cage.

"Is this… necessary?" I ask in a small voice.

"I only have your best interests at heart," Mother replies, draping one arm gracefully across the cushioned velvet. "Now, how are you feeling about this place? Settling in well?"

"Exited. Comfortable," I shrug vaguely.

"Much better than a forest floor, I hope."

"Yeah. I really like the… curtains," I nod, "Cream and violet… yey."

"It is quite a lovely combination," Mother agrees with disinterest, "You know, the people are very happy to have their princess."

"Well, that's kind."

"And I assume you are aware that word of your recent rescue mission has spread like wildfire?"

"Oh, yes?" I say with a strained smile, "How's that going?"

"Not good For the Moon King, but brilliant for us," she winks, draping herself comfortably across the leather. A maid enters the room and hurries across the floor to hand her a fizzing glass. "Champagne?" Mother offers me cheerfully.

"No, thank you."

She continues. "You see, thanks to you, Frost is not only now financially unstable, but almost all of its available military, police force, and emergency aid has been sent to the north coast to deal with the aftermath of the Berg's explosion. And because you and your friend wormed your way through the security so easily, the public has also begun to question just how well the Moon King can protect them."

"He never could, not without his army," I mutter, folding my hands uncomfortably on my thighs.

"Exactly! Ex-*actly*!" Mother says passionately, pleased with my comment. "What other angle does he have, though? Power, might, and strength are his entire image. He's not sexy, beautiful, ambitious, seductive, a celebrity, or an advocate for cultural minorities or the lower classes. He isn't charitable— or young," she adds purposefully, her eyes locking onto me.

"He's not the Sun Queen," I summarise.

She tips her glass in my direction, a smile playing on her lips. "No. No, he's not, is he? He's losing leverage over the people. Losing his footing on the ladder of society. Thanks to our spies, we intercepted information from three days ago— unpublished reports saying the election is wavering in the Sun Queen's favour. No doubt that remains true, but the results are due tomorrow, so we'll see for ourselves. Anyway, the outcome is predictable. Unfortunately, the Queen cannot rule much better than him. She's trying to fix a collapsed country broken into too many pieces, many of which were lost to disease and famine. Ra is weak, its people are widespread, and its trade is still recovering after the Fall. In short, Evrilore is at a point of significant weakness, which provides an excellent opportunity for us."

"Us?" I repeat uncertainly.

She leans forward in her chair, her eyes shining excitedly as she sets the glass down. "You and your country, I mean. This land and its people have been waiting for this day for a long time, Raven. The day we finally take it back. With you here, the last piece of the puzzle, they finally have a driving force. Someone to believe in. You blew up the Berg, rescued a fellow Flai, bonded with others of your kind instead of letting man tear you apart, and survived an attack last year with the lowest odds ever heard of."

"So... what are you saying? What do you mean, "take it back"?" I ask slowly. "You said... yesterday, you said "peace meeting"."

She chuckles. "Raven, there's no point stalling, so I'll be honest. Do you genuinely think we'll stay here forever while the Flai outside is trapped and ruthlessly murdered? Do you think we're going to peacefully protest? Do you think we're going to stay put while the shield keeping men out of this kingdom slowly dies? I had to tell you those things about peace treaties. I didn't want to shock you. Alas, kingdoms rise, and kingdoms fall. Frost, Ra, the Willow District... they've had their rule. Now it's our turn."

I swallow, my throat bobbing. "What- what do you mean?"

She leans forward in her seat, sweeping a stray strand of hair from my eyes. "It's time Flai claimed what is rightfully ours. Tell me, Raven... are you ready for war?"

CHAPTER 40

"War!?" I exclaim loudly.

"Raven... Propaganda? Peaceful protest? They are killing us. Murdering us brutally and indiscriminately. One day, there will simply be no one left. The shield will break, and their men will storm these hills. Every last bit of precious tradition, ancestry, and stories we've passed down through generations will be found and destroyed."

I take in deep, ragged breaths. "But surely it doesn't have to come to war? This is ridiculous! Flai don't fight. We survive! When you said revolution, I thought you meant defence, not attack. Not war."

Mother sighs, gazing at me with an expression bordering on pity. She reaches out and gently places a hand on my arm. "Listen, Raven. I'm sorry I lied to you. I just didn't know if you were ready for the shock. I know that this is all so sudden... but you aren't just here to live in peace and happiness. You're here to help your family do it, too. These people that surround us are family. This kingdom is family. Sometimes, you must do bad things for the right reasons. The world is a dark place, Raven, and everyone has to do what it takes from time to time to ensure the safety and freedom of others and themselves."

I stare at her, long and hard. "That's not true," I breathe, "You can't decide what's justified and what's not. You can't decide what I'm here to do. I'm a teenage girl. I- I want you to help me to, *I don't know*, put rollers in my hair and paint my nails. I want you to listen to me talk about stupid things that don't matter, like boys and how my body looks and mean girls."

"That is just the stereotypical female teenage experience portrayed in human media, Raven. You don't know what you want."

"Not this," I gasp, my lip wobbling. "I want anything but to be shoved into the life I've run from. War and violence and death. That's not... that isn't healthy. None of this is healthy! You aren't..." My eyes widen as I stare at her, tears forming in my eyes. "You just don't understand me at all, do you?"

Crushed, she sets down her glass and takes my hands in hers. "That isn't true. I do understand you. I bore you, and I carried you in my womb. You're so precious to me, Raven, even if we're just getting to know one another. I have always loved you from the day I first cradled you in my arms when you were too young to remember. Please understand that I'm not asking you to throw yourself into devastation. I'm asking you to help prevent more of it. The world is in ruins. Help me rebuild it. Help me create something new. I waited so long for you to be here so that we could do this together."

Maybe I would've agreed with her weeks ago, but I've travelled through many different places and seen many different things. The cheering, clapping, and twirling of Willow District citizens. The sense of community and family between complete strangers at Boots and Shackles, a ramshackle inn in the middle of nowhere.

"You're wrong. The world isn't in ruins. There are so many good people, people who've treated me as their equal despite not knowing me. The citizens of the other kingdoms are brainwashed monsters towards us, but underneath it, there's kindness. Evrilore isn't bad. It's just manipulated," I argue.

She delicately lifts her hands off me and reaches for the drink again, her expression of pain melting into impatience. She exhales with disapproval as her lips meet the rim of her glass, and she takes a graceful sip, her arm poised at exactly the correct angle, her back arched like a wildcat mid-leap. "Then where..." She draws closer to me so that I can smell the alcohol. "Is Bronwyn?"

I freeze, numbness spreading along my limbs like wildfire.

Satisfied, she returns to her position. "Go on," Mother prompts, taking an elongated, dramatic sigh. "If you have a good answer, say it. We both know where she really is—stolen by the effects of a system humans created. So that everyone is threatened all the time, so that the people in power stay there, and so that the people of this island are constantly reminded that it doesn't matter who you are or where you came from. They can always take anything away from you. You know that more than anyone. They took *Peter*..."

The slosh of water, the bursting of pipes as we waded along the Berg's corridors, enveloped by darkness.

"They took *Bronwyn*..." Mother sings.

The crack, crack, crack of bullets hitting a metal wall as it slides shut with three voices crying out in desperation behind it.

"They took *Spok*..."

"You'll protect him! YOU'LL PROTECT MY SON!"

Mother cocks her head to one side. I wish to reach up and wipe away the tear rolling down my cheek, but my arm is stone, bearing the weight of three innocent people whose suffering I caused.

"Oh, Raven... do you see, now? That's what they do. They take their taxes, they build their castles, they find out what means the most to you, and they use it against you so they'll always be the groundling."

"N-Not all humans are like that. Not all humans are selfish," I retort. "Some are willing to negotiate."

"And some shoot you before you can say "Flai"," she snaps coldly.

Silence crashes down between us like a curtain, and the number of things I am weighing up and considering all at once is suddenly unbearable, developing into a brief but awful headache.

Sparrow is watching us intensely. Every muscle in his face conveys pain, and suddenly, I remember that he witnessed every event Mother listed. He watched his mother be wrestled into custody and watched my brother plead to do what would ultimately kill him to save Bronwyn. And suddenly, we're exactly the same again, no matter what my mother says.

He's just him. Just *Sparrow*.

He carries the same experiences, memories, and scars that I do.

When my head has finally stopped screaming, and I gather the nerve to meet Mother's gaze, the calm, glassy queen of the Flai Realm has returned. "When you say war..." I ask slowly, "What exactly are you talking about? Do you have a plan?"

"Of course," she replies coolly, sitting back on the pillows. One of the castle staff hurries into the room with a tray and pours her a fresh glass of champagne before hurrying away. "I gathered and trained the strongest Flai that ever entered these walls, put together a thousand troops."

So that's why there are so few Flai in the village. They're all here somewhere, training to die. I should have realized before.

"Man may have their technology, but they lack bravery, and their lands are divided," Mother goes on, "When the time comes, the kingdoms will abandon one another. For example, the Willow District engages in regular trade with the Frost Kingdom, and they have a steady supply of food and resources. However, the majority of its population are farmers, and the military forces there are weak. Frost has a low number of able soldiers right now, and the remaining forces lack the morale to continue a fruitless fight to capture a single child. It is unlikely the King will spare any soldiers for Willows at all, and if they do, it is a gamble for the Moon King and an advantage for us."

"And... Ra? They have good warriors. There'd be insanely high casualties. We'd end so many lives..." I trail off, faces flashing before my eyes.

Half-dead families, cast away to the sweltering heat with no resources, no land to farm on. The ghost people of Ra who somehow found compassion in their hearts to understand people like me because their situation is no better.

Mother waves her glass airily about. "Ra's population is widespread and malnourished, and its citizens are bitter and unfriendly to people from other kingdoms. Therefore, quite simply, they will be unwilling to volunteer to save the lives of Willowfolk. Their army consists of a few strong, able-bodied men and a few dangerous women who are lethal with knives. But whilst they are skilled, courageous warriors, they cannot prevent the collapse of an entire kingdom. Once the news of an invasion gets out, the Sun Queen will prioritize her own safety, and it's unlikely she'll allow her tiny army to even cross the border. So, you see, protecting one another will never be Man's priority. And because neither Frost nor Ra will assist the Willow District, it will be an easy surrender without great loss of life," she adds.

I take a breath, processing this. "Alright, and what about

the others?"

"Ra will be tricky, but we can cause less suffering by simply storming the capital and taking the Queen captive. The country will go down with her —she's the heart and soul of the kingdom, practically the only thing keeping them alive — and Frost's troops will not reach the kingdom in time to stop us."

"Why would Frost care what happens to the Sun Queen?"

"Why would Frost care that the Queen wants to rule Evrilore? She hasn't the strength nor the resources to launch an attack on Frost and defeat the Frost Guard. Oh, no. It's more personal than that. Something is happening. We just don't know what," the Queen says gleefully, invested in the royals' drama.

I swallow. Hard. "And the Raes?"

"They are poor, Raven. Nearly all of them live in poverty except for a few wealthy individuals who have close friendships with the Queen. Children starve and die from disease every day. If anything, we are liberating them."

"But where will they go? What will happen to the ordinary people?" My voice turns to dust, and she continues as though she hadn't heard me.

"Frost is the heart of Evrilore and the kingdom that will be most challenging to overthrow. Fortunately, it does have a weakness. The Willow District provides seventy-three per cent of its food. With us in control of their crops, Frost's people will easily starve once emergency food supplies have run out, blame the King when he has no solution, and their country will begin to rot from the core. The kingdom will collapse in on itself."

"And *starve*," I say bluntly. "Children. Adults. Teachers. Doctors. They'll all die. And you'll let it happen?"

She takes another sip and peers at me over the rim of the

glass. "No war goes without casualties."

I consider this for a moment, then finally allow the one question that has been on my mind this entire time to escape my lips. "What part do I play in all this?"

She's growing in confidence now. "You're going to lead us into battle. You're going to be my little angel. Literally, as that's what we are... sort of. More than that. I want you to be the face of the movement. To represent us. You're going to be the name people cower in fear upon hearing."

"I'm a malnourished, ugly child. I can't fight. Why would anyone fear me?" I frown.

"Because you're the Chosen One," she says matter-of-factly.

"What? But I'm not the... I-I went to the gates!" I cry, disbelieving. "I'm not anything! Not a stupid princess, not the "Prophecy Child", not any of these fake positions you want me to—" I stop. "Oh."

Mother's lips curl into a smile. "It doesn't matter if you're the chosen one because we can *fake it*. People, being what they are, will be very easily fooled." Sweet as a golden glob of honey, her voice exits her painted, claret lips in a cloud of sugar. "Do you see, now? I can give you the power that instils fear. And after you have power, Raven... dream. When it's all over, you'll have everything. Your efforts will be rewarded with a shower of gifts, a throne, and a crown! And all you have to do..." she coos, using two fingers to walk up my back, "Is say please."

Please? I draw back, bewildered. Why on earth will saying "please" make any difference? She wants me to have that throne regardless...

While I'm searching for an answer, Sparrow catches my eyes from across the hall. Perhaps he is shaking his head, or maybe he is just drilling his pupils into mine, hoping I will receive a hidden message.

Whichever it is, I never see it because now Mother has moved in front of me, a smile creeping onto her lips. "So?" she encourages, "Can you do that for me, darling?"

And I find that, as I rise out of my seat and step forward onto the sparkling, sun-lit tiles, I can. Just one word, and I am a princess. I can shed the tiresome, frustrating girl I've hated my entire life. I could change my name and my appearance, bending my reflection into something remotely likeable. Just one word, and I can free my people, fight for my best friend, and liberate every other innocent eleven-year-old like him. I don't have to live this pathetic existence anymore.

Mother extends a hand to me. Her voice is very soft. "Stop *hiding,* Raven."

I look up at her with big, hopeful eyes.

"*Don't.*"

The word is barely audible, but the moment Sparrow speaks it, the entire atmosphere is shattered, and I'm plucked from my whimsical trance. This time, when I look at my mother, my thoughts change. Suddenly, I am questioning the whole ordeal.

Then I just know. As though a switch has been flipped, I realize that saying "please" does nothing but empower her. It forces me to be begging for that crown, asking for her permission to wear it. That one word puts her above me. It makes me a groundling.

"C'mon, Rave. You're smarter than that," Sparrow says.

"Silence," Mother spits at him. She appeals back to me. "Raven?"

Swallowing, I shake my head, deciding I cannot succumb to her mind games. I cannot become one of the thousands who will be bowing down at her feet and doing whatever she wishes.

"I'll never take that crown," I answer with newfound strength, carving each word out of defiance.

She attempts to pull me back down onto the couch, and her expression is almost... concerned. As though there is something wrong with me. "Raven... you do realize this is for your own good? It's for our people."

"No, it's for *your* people," I say coldly, wriggling out of her grip.

She rises to her feet, setting the glass aside. "You know, this is an opportunity that most young girls can only dream of. Why on earth would you..."

"You really don't get it," I say, horrified. "You genuinely think that because we've spent one day together, I'll destroy an entire species for you. A-And it's not desperation," I stammer, becoming more sure of myself by the second, "It's not even a desire to act quickly before it's too late. Y-You're just a psychopath with no capacity to understand feelings. It was never him. Never Sparrow. It was *you*!" I yell, jabbing a finger at her.

Mother freezes abruptly, and I follow her stare to the Boy in the Bird Mask, who quickly ducks his head to avoid her gaze. "Raven... I don't suppose you're under the influence of a certain..." She drums her fingers on my shoulders, speaking the words with disgust as though they're hairs on her tongue. "*Boy*?"

Now that the threat in her tone is aimed at him like a loaded gun, my spout of sudden confidence dissolves.

"H-He has nothing to do with this," I stammer.

She's becoming impatient, her kind and loving facade crumbling to reveal something darker underneath. Something deadly. "Hmm, I don't think so. It is in his nature, after all," she says casually, "I wouldn't be surprised if he is the problem. Hmm, yes... associating yourself with a human may have become unhealthy. And, just to think! All the time you've spent together, being taken advantage of. Oh, dear. Perhaps I'll have to…" She lowers her lips to my ear. "Arrange a little accident?"

My heart smashes into my ribcage. "T-That won't be necessary."

"So, you think. But, of course, being human, that's what he wants you to think."

Unable to contain myself, I tear away from her grip. Emerald eyes fixed on my mother, I speak calmly, but it is the kind of calm that contains thunder awaiting its storm. Lightning awaiting black clouds to strike from. The kind of calm that easily disappears as I grow increasingly furious.

"Do you think I'm stupid? Or are you just genuinely that deranged? You can drug me and manipulate me all you like, but I have *eyes,* Mother! I have *ears!* I can make judgments for myself, and I trust him. God, you are so… so… *stupid!*" I cry in exasperation. "We bleed the same red as they do. If you put a bullet through our hearts, we die. We're human, mother. We're human as much as he is, and he's Flai as much as we are. The only difference between us is fear, and you know why? Because people like *you* create it!" I cry.

"How *DARE* you suggest that we are anything like the filth that is Mankind!" she booms at me, her eyes aflame. "How dare you suggest me to be a liar? I am your *Mother!*"

"And *he's* my *friend,*" I say fiercely.

"Enemies of our enemies are not our friends. Do not be deceived, you imbecile, by how he works for us and not his brothers! He wishes for your death, like every other of his kind!"

"I am not an imbecile, and if anyone is, it's you! Standing in this hall as though you deserve it! Wearing that crown as if it's yours! Trying to have a castle and a monarchy? You're a joke!" I exclaim.

"Perhaps, but when you sit here in my place someday, you will realize the power that goes with it. I am just a woman in a chair, but this chair makes me a goddess."

Scowling, she strides past Sparrow and sinks into her throne, draping one arm over the side and glaring at me from atop it as though her position as a phoney queen can possibly strengthen her argument in the slightest. "This is the future, Raven. I am your future. I am your queen. Don't you see what I have done?"

Disgusted, I shake my head. "Flai are supposed to live with nature. As one community. Not with royals, queens, castles, and all these lies! What are you trying to prove? Who are you trying to impress? You sicken me."

"Watch your tongue, or I shall have it cut out! We are not blithering fairies anymore, prancing about in the "oh, so whimsical!" woods! We have evolved, and we have evolved BETTER THAN THEM! We are superior!" she screeches.

"No, *you've* evolved! We're still the same Flai we once were. Not everything is about you!"

"I have always done what it takes to stay alive," she snaps, "But now we cannot live in the shadows. We must rise. We are angels! Fallen from the sky! From a place of death itself, we were born into a world of darkness. Now, that darkness must be hunted down and destroyed until there is nothing left— and I will not stop. I'm going to lead Flai into a new age. An age where the technology of men and the power of Flai will be combined into one empire."

"We're not *DESIGNED* to be an *EMPIRE*!" I shoot back, "We're designed to live like we were living before the Fall!"

"And what a whole lot of good that got us into! Come on, you stupid girl! You blew up a prison! You killed innocent men to free two prisoners, one of whom didn't survive the next ten minutes! You gave your people hope. You stood up to the enemy! Now you are turning your back on a revolution that you started!?"

"I want peace, not a massacre."

"For God's sake, Raven! There is always war before there is peace! Rain comes before a rainbow! You are young, foolish, and ungrateful! Look at what I have built! Look at where I have put you! You are a princess by my verdict! And you WILL LEAD MY ARMY!" she finishes.

"NO!" The word is lifted off my tongue more easily than I expect, ringing out sharply and clearly through the hall. "I won't!"

And then the two of us are just standing there, as though standing on different continents, an ocean apart, with Sparrow and I on one side and her and her castle on the other.

I have to choose; it's her or humanity.

Silence falls. Silence in which every breath I take is as loud as thunder.

""No"?" Mother finally repeats, breaking the silence, frowning.

There is no love in her cold pupils, just logic and order. Maybe there never was love at all, and I just wanted to believe in my family so desperately. She seems unable to process my decision for a moment until finally, I think it sinks in because something shifts in her face. She slowly walks down the hall, then back up, heels making a sharp, rhythmic click as she paces.

She isn't very motherly, is she? I frown at this thought. The word "mother" seems to be poison on my tongue, a name that was never meant for her at all.

"Why, Raven," she says sweetly, still pacing. "Whatever do you mean by "no"? I just want to understand... I-I need to understand." An eerie calm has overcome her, one that makes my heart thump in the worst kind of way.

"I-I said no because I'm not leading your army," I say weakly.

Your army. Not ours. *Hers.*

The Queen reaches out to take my hand. "Why not?" she asks softly. I jerk away, disgusted, recoiling at the touch of the snake that stands before me.

I do not want to be close to this woman. I do not want to feel her comfort. Her stare, positively dripping with ice, seems to penetrate my soul as she awaits an answer. "Well?"

I take a nervous step backwards. "You want me to storm a Kingdom full of innocent people. To take the lives of children. That's not justice, that's evil. Pure, murderous evil."

"They've taken our children. Thousands of them. Millions. They need to know what they've done, Raven. They need to be educated," she says sweetly.

"Education," I say through gritted teeth, "Is not homicide. No matter what you say, I'm not going to do it. I'm not like you. I won't *be* you."

Not like you.

What does that even mean? *Like* her? But I *am* like her. I am Flai. *We* are Flai. Since when was there anything more than Man and Flai in this world?

"Sparrow," I say, turning to look at him. "In the Frost Wilderness, how'd those guards find us?"

He stares at me, confounded. "What do you mean?"

"Did you call for them?"

"No?" he replies, staring at me as though nothing could be more obvious.

"He's lying," Mother snaps, seething.

"What?" cries Sparrow. He narrows his eyes. "What did you tell her? Raven, what did she *say*?"

"You led me to the Willows border, where the possibility of us being found in that cart was astronomically high. The only reason we survived was that those guards were drunk. So why did you take us there?" I continue calmly, ignoring both of them.

"I told you about the letter from the Flai Realm at 'Shackles, didn't I? After exchanging more letters, your Mother told me she would give us a one-week window in which the guards would be lightly sedated, helping us to slip through."

"*Lies*!" Mother hisses. "Why didn't he tell you, if not?"

"BECAUSE YOU TOLD ME NOT TO! She said- she *said* not to tell you!" Sparrow protests.

"*Deception*!"

"I'm telling the truth, Raven!" he gasps, appealing to me.

"*Deceit*!" Mother cries.

"Can you stop shouting nouns at people!" I snap at her, raising my voice. "Both of you, shut up. I-I need to think. I can't *think*!" My words escalate into a scream.

My hands are hot. Red hot.

I sway where I stand, trying to weigh up both of their arguments and weed the lies from the truth. "I just need to- need to sit—" I grapple for the loveseat's arm, attempting to steady myself, and freeze. I look slowly up at Mother. "What've you done to me?" I gasp.

"Now, Raven, just… just calm down…" Mother says.

A memory flashes through my mind of fog swirling up all around me as my eyes flutter. But not fog. Gas. Sleeping gas. "Don't touch me. Don't come near me!" I rasp, backing away from her. "In my bedroom, I… What did you do?"

"Raven! I believe you are having a panic attack. Please, just take a breath, okay? I understand that the events of these past few days have been sudden, and the truth about Sparrow is disturbing. I understand my confessions were very much beyond what you could've expected. But right now, I need you to look at me. Look at your mother," she pleads. "See here, it'll be alright. It's that boy, that's all. You need time and space, and I haven't respected those needs. I'm sorry. Why don't you sit down?"

"I don't want to sit down."

"Sit, Raven. It'll help."

"No. *No*," I say in a small voice, shaking my head. My words emerge as miserable and terrified. "If I sit down, you'll just wake me up tomorrow, and it'll all start all over again. You'll still make me do it... lead your army and destroy humankind," I whimper, pushing breaths out of my tight lungs.

"I'll never force you to—"

"That's not really true, though, is it? You'll keep me here like a pet until I agree. Persuade me with food, water, and shelter. I can't leave, can I? *Let me leave*!" I stumble towards the door, and the guards stiffen as I approach them.

"Raven!" Mother says sharply. "Come on, now, please. This is ridiculous. I have been patient with you, but I am losing my composure. *This*... all of this!" She waves her hand at me in my fragile state. "This is all happening because of Sparrow. It's the shock. You need to snap out of this incoherent state of terror and recognize the men and women standing around you as your own and this boy as an outsider and a traitor. If you can't make that differentiation and acknowledge your duty to save your species from our oppressors, then maybe you need some persuasion to see who the villains are?" Mother offers, her lips thin.

She nods to a pair of guards, and they break free from the rest, seizing Sparrow before I have time to do anything or even register the shock of the situation.

"You will stand as a tall and proud Flai, you will be so much more than my daughter, and you *will* lead my army into war against the human race. And I'll watch you, beaming, and utterly everything will be right in the world. That's the way it's going to be. We're going to restore and rejuvenate, and with my love, nurture and support, you will forget this human and grow beyond the damage he's inflicted."

It's really difficult to breathe now. "N-No. Stop. Please just stop this."

She strides over to me and tilts my chin up with one hand. "Raven, I promise to you that if you cannot make these promises to me at four o'clock today —that's five minutes exactly— I *will* kill him. And I never go back on my promises," she says simply, in a tone which suggests she's trying to be clear and comforting. It comes across as utterly venomous. "He has fooled you, tricked you, and thwarted your views, and now he must face the consequences. Don't you see?"

I shake my head, denying reality. They can't kill Sparrow. They *can't.*

My insides writhing, I stumble towards him, but they drag him further back and push him to his knees.

"But," Mother adds quickly. The word hangs teasingly in the air, and I know she is enjoying torturing me. "I am not a cruel woman. I am willing to compromise because I understand your consideration for the innocent. So, if you... *behave*," she says, choosing her words carefully, "If you simply lead my army, act as my symbol, and do your duty... I will spare the next generation of human children as servants. Prisoners," she finishes.

"And you'll let him live?"

She throws her head back in laughter. "Goodness, no! We can't go around sparing everybody, now, can we? What I'm saying is: Humanity or Sparrow? That is my offer to you. If you truly wish to save the unsuspecting and sinless, you will kill him and stand by my side. Preach all you want about good and evil, about innocent humans. This isn't about them anymore. Let's put *your* moral compass to the test."

I look back up at her, then at Sparrow, over by the pillar, remembering my words from months before today.

What if there's more to it than that?

If there ever is, we can talk about it when it happens.

Once upon a time, there was Man, and there was Flai. Now, there is so much more. Now, there is something to fight for. Drawing in a breath, I stand my ground, saying nothing as my mind whirrs faster than light can stream through the window. I'm exhausted from doing what everyone else wants me to do.

Gritting my teeth and straining against the drumbeat of my heart, I close my eyes.

What do *I* want to do?

Even seeing me consider my options sends Sparrow into a state of distress. "Raven... no. PLEASE! Please agree to do it! Are you mad? You can't let my species die—" Sparrow begs from his place by the pillar. Before he can finish, the guards shove his head back to gag him.

I bolt forward in protest, but Sparrow manages to raise his head a little, face pleading as they pull him forward into the centre of the room, and he does not fight.

He is begging me to let him die, for not just my own sake but for his entire species'. Our eyes lock, and I know this is what my mother wants me to do. The chivalrous thing. The *right* thing.

But how can I possibly sacrifice him to save the world... when I'd sacrifice the world to save him?

It is too late to change my mind— I must act. The grandfather clock's hands tick closer and closer to the hour.

Precious time is slipping away.

If I do not defend him now, Sparrow will be killed. He's several feet closer to me, shoved onto his hands and knees directly in front of my helpless face. He remains still, bowing his head, and they bind his hands together with lengths of raw, frazzled rope that bite into his skin.

They tear off his mask, exposing his skin under the chandelier's bright sparkle. I think he tries to say something, perhaps, but the cloth pulled around his lips muffles it.

My heart pounds desperately against my ribcage as one of the guards stands over him, drawing a weapon from their hip, and finally, I manage a weak cry, my palms flaring to life. "NO!"

Mother easily catches me in a gust, pushing me back with a flick of her wrist. "Have you come to a decision?"

"Leave him!" I scream. "You monster!"

"Ah," Mother says softly. "So, then. Willows or Ra? Who's going first?"

"You can't! You can't kill entire kingdoms, and you can't force me to play this little game. These are real lives we're talking about! Find your HUMANITY!"

"I have none," she spits, rounding on me, "I'm an *angel*!"

The word reverberates through the room, growing quieter with every knock of my heart against my ribs. *Angel. Angel. Angel.*

"And yet you'll rot in hell before any human," I whisper.

A pause.

"I see," Mother says, and when she speaks, her tone is only a mirror of my resentment. "Then the monsters we call humans will die with him. Say goodbye to your pathetic little friend and his species. Oh, and before we kill him—" she turns to the guards, holding up a hand then to me, "Are you absolutely sure?"

She says the words so slowly and clearly, with such cruel, bent lips, that I know I will never be pardoned again. Too terrified to even answer, I stand in helpless silence. She turns dismissively away from me. "Guards, you know my orders."

"N-No! Leave him alone!" I gasp, struggling against invisible ropes of air, courtesy of my Mother's tricky hands.

The guards ignore me, and one man raises his sword over Sparrow's back. I shrink back, terrified of what I am about to witness. Even if I run, I will never reach him in time to free him. The only other option is to break free of my Mother's restraints and shield him, to take the blow myself.

No matter my decision, a child will die today, either he or I, and there is no way out, no loophole.

Finally, I turn to the Queen. She oversees the scene with a face of stone. "Mother, PLEASE!" I cry, "LEAVE HIM!"

Nothing. No one.

Except maybe...

I turn to Tsubasa at the back of the hall, her face swallowed in shadows. Her eyes are wide with horror, and her lips are pressed tightly together. She withdraws her writhing hands into her cloak and ducks her head, avoiding my pleading eyes.

"N-No! You have to help me! *Help me*, you *coward*!" I gasp.

Nothing.

Dragging my hands through my hair, I whirl back to the guard who holds the blade over Sparrow's head. "Please, stop!" I cry.

The sentry ignores me, raises his weapon, and plunges it down. The metal whistles as it slices cleanly through the air.

I thrust out my hand, my eyes wide, as if to reach for Sparrow, but there's no way and no time, and—

"*SPARROW!*" I scream.

My arm is out, frozen, in protest. It matters very little.

The blade falls anyway.

CHAPTER 41

The sword explodes into a million shards, blasting metal in every direction like a million teeth ready to sink into flesh.

I hold up two arms in a pathetic attempt at shielding my body from the fragments that come flying at my face, but it hardly matters. One hits my forehead, opening a gash between my eyebrows, and the other strikes my leg, burrowing itself deep inside me.

White-hot pain attacks every inch of my body, and someone is screaming. I have a vague idea it might be me. Suddenly, the room is spinning, people are running in all directions, and I feel sick at the sight of so much blood everywhere— not all of it is mine.

My leg is on fire as I try to extract the shard of metal with clumsy hands, and for a moment, my vision dims and blackens as I sway between the border of the real world and unconsciousness.

I try to walk, but my leg buckles and I fall to my knees, looking up with eyes blurred by tears and blood, searching for a boy with bound wrists. But everyone looks the same in this hall of horror: screaming, bleeding, or slumped onto the floor.

Amongst the chaos, I cannot see Sparrow anywhere.

I wipe a smear of hot, thick blood from my forehead, my

hands growing increasingly warm and tingly with panic, and I drag myself back to sit against a pillar, painting a violent crimson streak onto the floor.

"Sparrow," I call out weakly, and for a moment, I don't hear his reply over the moans of the injured.

Looking down at my palms, I remember how I thrust my hand in front of me. Did I do this? And how? I'm not an air Flai. I cannot manipulate gravity so that swords fall a hundred times slower before they are shattered into smithereens.

My mind wanders to Tsubasa. Is it possible...?

"Raven!" a voice gasps as a bloody hand falls on my own.

I look up, and it is *Sparrow!* His jeans are soaked with blood from crawling around on the floor, but he is here, and he is alive! "Raven, you have to get out of here! Escape before it's too late!"

I shake my head. "Look at me. I'm dying. I can't move."

"No, Raven. You don't understand. You have to. Or it's all over for you. I-I know your mother. And I've never seen... Rave, this is bad. I've never seen anger. Not like this. Not from anyone."

"I'm dying," I repeat blankly.

"You aren't."

"Yes, I am," I say, prodding my leg and inspecting my fingers. They come back glinting like a forbidden ruby.

"Fine. But if you're staying, I am too," he says firmly, and I see he has stolen a shiny black pistol from one of the guards.

"Do you know how to use that?" I mumble.

"Raven, I *taught* you how to... never mind. Wait here while I deal with your mother."

"No- Sparrow!" I beg weakly, knowing he is walking into the line of fire, into death's arms.

He turns back, his brown eyes shining. "This is the only way, Raven. The only way you can be safe. She'll never stop. If she wants you dead, she's after me too. We're partners. We're a team. So if she wants me, let her have me. I can take her."

"Y-you really can't," I say quietly, trying to sit up. "She's got powers, and you're just a human..."

It's all I can do not to black out, never mind watch him die at the hands of my mother. I must help him... there *must* be a way to help him...

He marches directly out into the centre of the hall. My head droops with fatigue and drowsiness, and my eyes settle on something unexpected: my foot.

I freeze.

Is it really that simple?

With shaking fingers, I slip off my shoe and reach inside to find a single star still glowing brightly. There's a hole in the sole where the rest slipped out, but for some reason, this one remained. A star that once fell from a night sky dusted with so many of its kind still up there. For some reason, it chose to fall that day, and it chose to stay with me now.

This one star is special, different from its brothers.

Because it's the last one I have left.

I could use it to heal myself or to ensure the safety of mankind in the future, but instead, I draw it close to my chest and whisper three easy words. "Please. *Save him.*"

I press the star to my lips, repeat the wish three times, and then I have done all I can for the Boy in the Bird Mask, and the star vanishes with the only hope I have left. I let my arm fall and blink away more blood. And then, raising my head once more, I take in the scene.

Mother is marching slowly towards Sparrow, her long dress now torn and crinkled, her wrists slick with blood where metal struck her. I understand exactly what Sparrow said now about her inhuman anger.

The composed, icily calm queen that towered over me earlier has vanished, and in her place, there is a beast. Eyes blazing with hatred, muscles that move and jerk with poisonous precision. Bruises already pepper her skin, and her hair is a wiry mess. Sparrow stands before her, waiting, his gun raised at her head, his fingers trembling on the trigger. He raises it, and she halts in front of him, demonstrating all the self-restraint she has left.

"I don't want to kill you," Sparrow warns shakily, "B-but I will."

The Queen is indifferent to his words, her eyes aflame with madness. *Maybe*, I think, *she was always mad*. It just took me too long to see it.

"I'll shoot you," Sparrow repeats.

"No, you won't," Mother says coldly.

"No, he won't," I whisper in agreement. My heart aches.

He *won't*.

Even if the queen holds a knife to my throat, he won't. Sparrow is not a murderer. He's too good, too kind, too gentle, and utterly incapable of a deed that requires so much hatred for the world and its people. He can't take a life, not even to save mine. Not when he belives that absolutely everyone is of higher value than himself. In his eyes, everyone's redeemable, reformable, and loveable.

Everyone but him, because he's the Boy in the Bird Mask who can't even pull a trigger; he'd rather it was his death than anyone else's.

 Mother moves a little closer to him, her fingers twitching as sparks fly between them. Sparrow hasn't noticed, but I have. Any Flai would.

"Of course," she sneers, wiping her wrists on her face and leaving behind a bloody smear, "Because you love her. And —

let me guess— you don't want to kill the only family she has left? How sweet. But you're going to kill me, anyway, because you're a human and a cheat and a filthy little rat. A pathetic excuse for a living creature with free will."

Sparrow's grip tightens on the gun as a bead of perspiration runs down his forehead.

Just do it. Do it, please! I silently scream, knowing she will get to him first if he does not.

"If you let us go... if you let me take Raven and give me your word that you'll leave her alone... I-I'll let you live," he stammers, and Mother stares straight at him.

"I do not need your permission to live, you fool," she hisses, easily bounding across the final foot of the floor between them.

Her feet sweep off the floor a little as she hovers between flight and running, and Mother extends her hands, fire swelling at the tips of her fingers into a giant orb.

Sparrow stumbles backwards, and I thrust out a desperate arm, casting a wind to force his fingers down on the trigger—

But instead of a gunshot ringing out through the hallway, sending the woman crashing to the floor, all I hear is a click.

Sparrow blinks, and I try again, the barrel aimed at Mother's heart. *Click. Click, click.*

"Out of bullets?" Mother whispers, eyes locked on her prey as she eyes him up from every angle.

Then she comes for him like a mad lion, rage taking over her body, nothing stopping her at last.

Except for me, of course. I push myself to my feet, ignoring the agony that sears through my body like a whiplash, and flux into my full Flai form. My hands flicker at first, then erupt in brilliantly green, roaring flames, and I rush forward, even on my damaged leg, to stand right between my mother and Sparrow. She stumbles to a halt, skidding across the marble, and I turn to Sparrow, mouthing, "Run!"

He shakes his head and instead draws a sword from an abandoned sheath on the floor, taking his place at my side like a king to his queen before riding into battle.

My mother raises her head, but I do not meet her cold eyes. I crouch low and press my hands onto the cold, hard tile, and this time, it is not fire, air, earth, or ice individually that pounds the world around me.

It is a storm of the elements rushing to my aid as I summon every scrap of magic in Evrilore into my bloodstream.

For the first time, I am completely, utterly in control. I am an angel, a fairy, a Flai through and through— and my power comes from the fact that I'm a Flai who learned to be human.

Chunks of the floor tear themselves apart as I send loops of air into the cracks in the tiles, tearing them off the ground. Windows smash as rivers from all over the island and strings of salty ocean unite at my command, the water spiralling up into a grand tower.

The tiles torn from the floor fly into the gravity-defying stream, creating a deadly tornado of debris that encases my mother, spinning rapidly around her.

Within, she retaliates with her talents, already beginning to emerge unscathed, but I'm still not finished.

A ring of fire and air shoots around the hall, sending any guards that are still conscious flying to safety and then cutting them off from the middle of the room with a wall of flames so that they cannot aid my mother in battle.

I uproot the earth beneath the castle's foundations, commanding rocky chunks of earth to rise like soldiers from a trench, and at last, when I am about to deliver the fatal blow, wings sprout from either side of Mother's shoulders, her feathers gloriously white and unscathed, and she slices through the remnants of my water spiral.

"THIS ENDS NOW!" she screeches, and, hanging so high in the air, with her wild, dark waves framing her two mad green eyes, it is startling how much she resembles me.

Our wings beat in perfect synchronisation, and our skin is an identical chalk white. We both look like monsters. We're terrifying, hellish things, with veins bulging against our chalk-white flesh and our eyes glowing.

But this is a Flai. It's just what I am.

That's okay.

I take a millisecond just to breathe it in, to be free. I am a monster, and I have never been allowed to be anything else. But now, I am not hiding. I'm wild.

I realise Sparrow is staring at me, and my face falls as I think, for a moment, that it is pure fear that shines in his eyes. But then I notice something else: Wonder.

I am beautiful. A monster, but a beautiful monster. In his eyes, I was always beautiful, and he doesn't care what I am because he's beautiful, too.

"Raven!" he yells abruptly, "Behind you!"

I whirl around, and Mother is almost gone. But I catch her out of the corner of my eye, diving rapidly out of my eyeline and suddenly blasting me with magenta flames from directly in front of me, her body sliding into an expert crouch.

I yelp and limp away, barely managing to dodge them, but quickly hurry to my feet. In doing so, the pain from my leg rebounds so intensely that standing feels impossible, but at this point, survival instincts can fend off the agony. *I'm dying*, I think again, stumbling like a drunken man.

I throw out one arm and shoot a burst of air into Mother's chest. The attack is unexpected, and she does her best to deflect it with one wing, but my magic is too powerful and sends her spiralling through the air, her balance disrupted.

Hurriedly, I swish a wrist, and my wall of flames parts. I seize Sparrow's hand, command a current of air under our feet, and send us both hurtling toward the throne room doors. Just as I reach for the doorknob, the Queen's spell reaches Sparrow, yanking him from my grasp and smashing him headfirst into the wall.

"SPARROW!" I yell.

My hands fly up, but he's gone from one position to another in a millisecond. I stare wildly about, my eyes scouring out the throne room for him, but Mother takes advantage of my panic. Roots shoot up out of the earth and bind my limbs to the floor, curling tight around my ankles.

"AARGH-*MMMPH*!" I scream as they slither over my face, blocking my view.

I desperately raise an arm, but the plants crush my hand into a fist, reeling me into the earth like a descending coffin.

As I fight against the plants' grip on me, they pull my wrists further down, threatening to break my arms.

"*Raven!*"

My head whips from side to side in search of the voice's source as I gasp for breath. But there's nothing except Sparrow flying through the air and my panicked cries as I scream his name, exhausting my supply of remaining oxygen. I wheeze in an attempt to cry for help, coughing and struggling.

Raven!

Not a voice, a—

A *thought.*

Sparrow passes into my narrow field of vision once more, and it's difficult to tell where the blood ends and he begins, his battered body leaking life onto the cracked marble. I can't even scream. Can't even raise a single pathetic finger to command the vines away from me.

Raven!

My eyes snap open, and the first thing I'm aware of is that I'm no longer gasping for breath, and my ribcage is empty. There's not even a mild suggestion that a heart once beat within my hollow chest. The second thing I notice is that although I can see my body, there's no source of light to illuminate my figure, and my brain can't process anything around me. Nothing is describable, let alone explainable. Colours I didn't know existed and shapes I've never seen before flit in and out of sight.

"Where am I?" I ask no one in particular.

Peter appears silently beside me, light and shadow melting off his body as he emerges from nothingness. "Raven," he says, cheerful as ever.

His voice is familiar and comforting, and I'm not shocked nor bewildered in the slightest. Suddenly, it's as if my time away from him was only temporary, and I knew I'd see him in the end. Knew it'd come to this.

Yet, I'm terrified at the ease of it all. Of my recognition, my acceptance, of the soft, hazy, cloud-like quality of his words, and the way they embrace me with such a welcome. It's not quite time yet. At least, I don't think so.

"Peter?" I ask tentatively.

He nods. "Don't be scared."

"I'm not scared," I lie.

"'S'alright. I was. When it happened to me." He casts his eyes sadly downwards.

"Oh... Oh, God... I'm not dead, am I?"

"No."

"Then where are we?"

Peter looks curiously around. "It changes all the time, but it looks a lot like heaven right now. You must be thinking about dying."

I shake my head, sorrowful. "This isn't heaven. I wish it could be— wish I could let you rest. But, no. You're inside my head."

He frowns. "What are *you* doing here? In your own head, I mean?"

"I'm not sure," I admit.

"Oh." He looks thoughtfully up, raising a hand to touch the air. "Huh. No particles."

I stumble backwards as his figure grows brighter and harder, more real by the second. "I don't think I'm okay," I whisper slowly.

Peter nods, then clasps his hands together and strolls a little way past me. "You should decide, y'know."

"Decide what?"

"To do," he says simply, his expression serious now.

"Oh."

He walks around me, his eyes narrowed as they move up and down my body, seeking... something. As his gaze lingers on my wrists, I realise that I can still feel the vines on me, cutting off my circulation.

"Can you burn the restraints?" Peter finally asks.

"That's... not what I thought you meant. When you said I should decide," I admit.

Peter laughs. "Don't be silly. It's not a question of *if* you're going to live. It's a question of *how*."

"Well, my hands are bound. What can I do?" I ask hopelessly.

"Bound by gold?" Peter enquires.

I freeze, the realisation dawning on me. "No."

"Then why can't you burn them?"

"Her magic's too strong."

"*She* isn't, though. She's just a person," Peter points out.

Raising my palms, I close my eyes, thinking. "I can't take away her magic," I mumble.

"There's only so much of it, Raven, that we brought into this world," my friend reminds me.

"I can persuade it?" I guess.

He shakes his head apologetically. "Magic's got no ethics."

"Then, what?" I ask, growing desperate. Anxious. I can almost feel again. Feel as my nerves work feverishly to connect to my brain, urging my heart to pump. Emotion's striving to reconnect, too, now. I know as Peter's eyes meet mine that we haven't got much longer. It's all waiting for me.

"Peter—" I begin.

"Of course! It's *will!*" He steps forward, confident, and places his hand calmly on my chest. "If you want to live, you have to breathe, okay? You have to will those plants away. Ready?"

"Wait—"

"*Breathe!*"

I double over, clutching my throat. My lungs are back, and they're clenched, tense with a lack of oxygen. I gasp with pain. "Peter, I can't go! Not yet! I-I need to ask you something."

"Well, hurry, then!"

"Just- just tell me this: Why aren't I upset to see you?"

"Raven, I've been in your dreams and on your hands ever since I died. Why should I suprise you now?"

"Because that wasn't real. I-I just felt terrible," I wail.

He smiles sadly up at me. "It *was* real. I never left you, not for a second. But now, you have to choose to go. You have to let *me* go, too."

"But I won't... I won't see you anymore?" I whisper, distraught.

He stares at me as though I'm being ridiculous. *"See me?* You can't see me, Raven. I'm not there, remember?"

❊ ❊ ❊

I sit up, gasping for breath, as the roots slide off me. Crawling to my feet, I throw my aching arms up, commanding the roots to rise with me as towers of greenery. My chests seems to clench with the effort, rising and falling rapidly. It takes tremendous strength to control them, though, as though I'm playing a mental game of tug-and-war with Mother.

She catches sight of me and gasps, but no words can escape her throat before I've caught Sparrow in a fresh current of air, slamming her backwards with my spare hand. She stumbles, but steadies herself as she slides into a pillar, slowing herself just enough not to crack her head open and keep a hand extended to Sparrow. For a moment, he simply hovers between us, his body limp, head bloody, as we battle for dominance over his figure.

My wings beat harder, faster, harder, faster, until they lift me off the ground. Before I can register the shock, I'm soaring upwards, and I can feel the ceiling brushing my scalp. With flailing limbs, I look back down at Mother. The vines writhing about my shoulders twitch as she summons them toward her, and I halt them with a swift wave of my hand. It's like swimming through glue, trying to push myself through the air as we both fight to absorb and channel the energy around us.

I gasp for breath and let out a strained cry, and my skin pales even further.

Mother slowly, mechanically turns her head. "If you help him, you will burn in hell," she gasps. "Anyone who helps Humans will! Now let *go!* What are you doing!?"

Our eyes lock, mine flooded with tears of pure fury. "An angel's duty," I spit. "Being *human.*"

With a roar that shakes the pillars of abandoned earth, water, and debris flowing below me, I twist around and dive straight into the path of her spell that's grasping Sparrow Sparrow.

My palms are searing with flame, and embers shoot down from my neck. My veins freeze to ice, my wings expand to twice their size, and finally, I overcome her spell. Sparrow falls into my waiting arms, his head dangling over my shoulder.

As a last resort, Mother fires a hot, bright, fizzing streak of flame at me— a bundle of matter transformed into a bullet. A bullet racing towards Sparrow and I.

I throw out an arm, and the enchantment is reflected onto its caster, hitting my mother straight in the heart. She gasps and flies backwards into the very wall upon which the grandfather clock stands, clutching her chest where she was struck.

Crashing into the shattered stained-glass window, a shard of jagged glass suddenly pierces her wing, causing her to shriek and revert to her human form.

I instinctively reach out for her, but my mother, my Queen, my nemesis... is gone.

Perhaps it is simply that she's the only family I have ever known, or maybe it's because I have no idea what my future holds without her, but one of the two sends me to my knees in despair, crashing back down onto the ground with a dull thud as my wings sink sadly back into my shoulders. I set Sparrow down numbly before me.

I am not beautiful anymore. I am just a monster. A murderer.

"Mother..." I find myself whispering, staring at my hands as my wings draw back into my shoulders.

What have I *done?*

CHAPTER 42

So this is it. This is the end of the story. I killed my mother.

But if you don't get up, Raven, she will not be the only one to die today.

Finally, my eyes land on Sparrow, slumped against a cracked pillar as blood trickles down his forehead, cutting rivers into his nose.

Reality opens its walls to enfold me, reciting the unchangeable facts: Once upon a time at an inn far away, I looked down at clean hands and saw blood, a foreshadow of yet another life slipping away and me being unable to prevent it. Now that blood is real, and my hands are stained with it, and he is dying.

I bolt forward, my leg screaming, and desperately grab his hand, touching his cheek, afraid to shake him awake in case I should worsen his injuries.

I call his name, but he doesn't respond, and panic grows in a tight knot in my chest. My fingers move to his wrist, but with so much blood, it's impossible to locate a pulse.

"No, no! Sparrow, stay with me!" I gasp, my voice fading into a whisper as the words escape my lips. "I can't lose you too…" And that's the truth. I can't.

Because if he is dead, I have completely isolated myself and killed the only three people I have ever loved. Peter, my mother… and now Sparrow.

"Please..." I manage shakily. "I couldn't save Peter, and I didn't save Spok... but I can still save you. I can if you would just wake up!"

His chest rises a little, and his lips part to take a faint breath.

Breath.

It's a petrifying thing, like a weed withering in the wind. Ready to be plucked, uprooted, and carried away. Carried to a new place and planted in a calm, new bed, into a new body, in a place where he is gone and I cannot reach him.

It's a lifeline, it's an indicator, a gravestone being written. How often it occurs and how much you take in determines your entire fate. Determines his.

"Raven," he mumbles at last.

"Sparrow! Are you okay?"

"Raven," he repeats, still not moving. Memories and swirls of colours mix in a dazed rainbow over his eyes, as they focus and un-focus. Here yet vacant. He frowns. "You changed your hair."

My vision clouds with tears. "Don't be an idiot. *Don't*, when you... When I... Sparrow, I don't know what to do. How do I help you? What do I *do*?" I'm asking him as much as anyone.

"It's shorter," he observes.

"*Sparrow!*" I beg.

"Home?" he asks suddenly, seizing my hand with desperation. "We're home?"

"Stop... stop it, now. C'mon, sit *up*. Please, you're scaring me," I whisper, avoiding the question. I don't want him to know that we've simply no home left.

"Home," Sparrow says again. "'Sall I can think about. 'Sall I'm good for, bringing people to the realm."

"I— *yes*, we're home, alright? But—"

"You're home... Good," he repeats quietly, then his grip on my fingers loosens, and he exhales, falling silent, slipping away more and more every second.

A single tear slips down my cheek as I stare at his almost motionless body, numbed by shock. "S-sparrow?"

Nothing.

"*Sparrow*!" I say, louder this time, a lump rising in my throat. Still, he lays there, almost lifeless, exhausted, and defeated, his head a bloody mess, and I very gradually lose my crawling position, my arms trembling, then giving way.

I collapse beside him, drained of the energy to do anything except curl up in a ball. "Y-You can't die, Sparrow... It wasn't supposed to be like this. This... this isn't the home I wanted," I whisper.

His fingers twitch, and then, with slow, robotic movements, he reaches for my hand— still alive. Barely. "Then..." Another shallow, shallow breath. "What home... did you want?" he says slowly.

I hush him, telling him to save the air in his lungs, but it's not as though it matters.

"No... tell me," he says.

"Sparrow, please. Don't talk, just... I'm going to go get help, alright?" I say, beginning to get up.

"No— Raven!" he grunts, tugging my wrist. "Stay."

His eyes are a mirror, reflecting a memory of myself at Boots and Shackles, imploring Sparrow not to leave me dripping wet and alone in my room. Begging him to stay by my side until the morning. I was fragile, terrified, and lonely.

And now it's Sparrow, not me, and he's spattering so much more than water onto the tiles, damaged and delicate like a cracked hourglass.

I pause, then lie back down.

"You weren't going to let me die all alone, were you?" he says, managing a weak grin.

"Sparrow," I say seriously, my pupils locking into his like a sniper's bullseye. "Don't *talk* like that."

"Okay. I'm sorry," he says quickly, fighting for attention with my overwhelming fear. "Rave... what home did you want?" he says again. "Answer that, and then..."

"Then you'll rest?" I plead.

"Then I'll rest," he nods.

"I thought... I thought I wanted this. I thought maybe I could be happy here. But I was stupid and blind and ungrateful, and... Oh, *Sparrow*..." I almost wail. "My Mother is nothing close to you. I don't want her, and I don't want any of this. I just want my friends back. I was happy before. I was happier with you."

"Me?" he repeats as though comparing it to the luxurious throne room.

But there is no luxurious throne room. There are only ruins, wreckage, and fake power. The only real thing I know of lies beside me, and he's fading away.

"Only you," I say.

The ghost of a smile appears on his lips, and then his eyes flutter shut, and he seems to exhale all the life he has left. And it seems that I could catch a thousand stars, and it would not matter.

Sparrow's going to die.

I slowly reach up to his face with a trembling hand and tilt his chin towards me. "Look at me. Please, just open your eyes and- and tell me what to do," I choke, "You always know what to do. There's always something. There has to be! Sparrow, I-I know you can hear me, come *on!*"

He opens his eyes, but they're gazing up, up, up. I have to bring my ear to his lips to catch his whisper. "I don't know this time, Raven." That's all he says. He doesn't know.

I reach for his hand, locking my fingers tightly between his weak, unmoving ones, and stifle a sob.

"Sorry," Sparrow murmurs. "About Japan."

"It's fine," I try to say, but the words are too shaky to be audible. I slide an arm under him, pulling him into my arms. "It's fine, it's fine, it's fine. You're *fine*."

Sparrow can't look at me. "I don't know," he repeats, a tear slipping down his cheek.

I duck my head, clenching my jaw together to stop myself from screaming. If I can only focus, if I can only stop time, stop my heart, stop everything... There's a way. There must be. My eyes blur with tears as I stare at the floor, my mind blank. Somehow, I lose track of time that doesn't seem worth counting. Minutes pass, maybe hours, and the scattered uncouncious and injured begin to stir, murmuring softly. Sparrow's head hangs back, his eyes still open, and I just gaze at his face, my heart wrenching. I can't scream, can't wait, sob, or yell. I can't do anything. Anything.

Anything. Please.

The scattered beams of light streaming through the shattered stained glass dim. The dust settles, and the blood dries, and eventually I begin to weep, my anguish and hopelessness surrendering to grief. My isolation is the loudest sound of all, the echoes of my every movement forming a wall around me. The silence that fills in the gaps between my breaths is deafening. Magic melts off my body and back into the earth as the soil pieces itself back together and Mother's vines retreat into the floor. I won't be needing my abilities for quite some time, I suppose. I've done more than enough damage today to last the world a lifetime.

Numb, exhausted, and weak, I roll onto my side to face away from Sparrow. But I can't escape anything more than the sight of him. There's still so much blood, and a dead brother, and a dead mother, and a dead—

A hand reaches slowly up the back of my neck, its fingernails brushing lightly against my skin, to feel my hair with mild interest, stroking through the styled chunks. "I was only going to say that it's pretty," Sparrow reasons weakly.

I burst into tears. "I hate you! Why aren't you dead?"

"Come on, don't cry. I'm okay. Everything's fine, Raven. I thought I was gonna die, too, you know."

Really, I knew. I wished upon a star, didn't I? I pleaded with the heavens for his life through a tiny glowing diamond in my palm. He was always bound to survive, and yet I had truly believed I'd lost him for a moment.

And it'd terrified me.

I shake my head, aching all over with grief, numbness, and relief. "Shut up. Just *shut up*, Sparrow. I thought you were DEAD!" I sob. And then I slap him, my wrist moving of its own accord. "THAT'S for scaring me! I thought I lost you!" I cry. Then I pull him into my arms, burying my head into his chest and wrapping my arms tightly around him. "And this," I say, "Is for being the best friend I've ever had."

He relaxes into my embrace, wincing slightly and slowly arranging his arms around me so as not to worsen his wounds. As I sob, the pain and distress in my stomach lessens, giving way to a feeling of absolute calm. Somehow I know that everything is going to be alright, now. I can still get my sister back, still be with Sparrow. The rubble and the blood and the many thrones looming over us seem insignificant obstacles when I'm in his arms.

"I think, Raven," he murmurs, "We just saved the world. Or, at least, humankind."

"I bloody well hope so, after everything."

Sparrow pauses, drawing away from me. "I was just thinking... Things aren't so bad, are they? After an explosion, death, armies, and fortresses... things turned out more or less alright."

I laugh, surveying the destruction surrounding us. "Can't say I'd do it again. I need a break, I think... Need to get away to somewhere."

He looks up at me, his eyes glittering with... something. "It's a big island," he says.

And that sparks another feeling, beyond the relief and the comfort. Something that I can't quite name.

But I suppose that's another story. A story that, someday, when all the answers are clear, I'll tell.

And until then, I'll be catching stars.

ACKNOWLEDGMENT

Thank you to my whole family for supporting thirteen-year-old me when she set out to write her first novel, and thank you for continuing to encourage me, now.

Special thanks to Mum for giving me hope and motivating me— you are the sole reason I didn't give up on this story, and it wouldn't exist without you.

Thank you to my English teacher, Mrs H, for developing me as a writer, to my supporters online, and to the authors who inspired me and continue to do so daily. I hope that someday I can inspire someone somewhere, too.

ABOUT THE AUTHOR

Evie Mae O'Kane is a young-adult fantasy author based in the UK who combines imagination and mystical creatures with real-life topics and relatable characters.

Printed in Great Britain
by Amazon